The Ecuador Effect

COLOMBIA • Pasto

Pacific Ocean

ECUADOR

Quito

Mt. Chimborazo • Ambato
6310 m ▲

Riobamba •

Guayaquil

Gulf of Guayaquil

Puerto Bolívar — Cuenca •
Jambelé — • El Tablón — • Girón
Peninsula — Machala — Santa Isabel
• Lluzhapa
Paraíso de Celén
Trapichillo • Chuquiribamba
Loja **PERU**

0   50   100
miles

• Namballe

Map by Charlotte Cobb

THE
ECUADOR
EFFECT

DAVID E. STUART

University of New Mexico Press
ALBUQUERQUE

YEAR   PRINTING
12 11 10 09 08 07   1 2 3 4 5 6 7

Library of Congress Cataloging-in-Publication Data

Stuart, David E.
  The Ecuador effect / David E. Stuart.
     p. cm.
  ISBN-13: 978-0-8263-4099-3 (alk. paper)
  1. Ecuador—Social conditions—20th century—Fiction.
I. Title.
  PS3619.T827E25 2007
  811'.6—dc22
                         2006031721

Book design and composition by Damien Shay
Body type is Utopia 10/14
Display is Azteca and Avant Garde

For Rory Gauthier... thanks for the ride.

CONTENTS

AUTHOR'S NOTE

A s an anthropologist I lived and worked in Ecuador many years ago. That experience provided the rough framework for this book. But the characters in this work are fictional, as are the events depicted in it. The place names, of course, are also used fictitiously.

Nonetheless, Ecuador was a distinctive, and mixed, social and economic reality. This novel, set in 1970, echoes the history of a country that has had twenty-two presidents in the last thirty-five years. The Ecuadorian government, according to the US State Department, still dramatically underreports its Indian population—obscuring the fact that they may be the majority population in many parts of the country. Two percent of the nation's elites still own more than 90 percent of its resources, according to a current CIA Web site. Mestizos still raid, and occasionally burn, Indian settlements to drive them away.

Ownership of land is still the great arbiter of social class in rural Ecuador.

DAVID E. STUART
Flying Star Café
Central Avenue/Route 66
Albuquerque, September 15, 2005

ACKNOWLEDGMENTS

First, I'd like to thank Anne Egger, poet and freelance editor, who has helped me make this book come to life. I also owe a debt to my prepublication readers, Cynthia Stuart (my wife), Kathy Linn, and Kijrstin Bauer. The passages in Quechua were edited by Bolivian-born Sara Vicuña Guengerich; the Spanish by David A. Briggs. Both are doctoral candidates and teach at the University of New Mexico.

Thanks also to the folks at UNM Press, Luther Wilson, Maya Allen-Gallegos, Damien Shay, and copyeditor Sarah Soliz, who design and publish wonderful books.

Finally, thanks to the Bernsteins—owners of Albuquerque's bustling Flying Star enterprises—who indulge me in writing my books at their Central Avenue location. Thanks also to their staff, who've found me tables and fixed my coffee through four book projects: Diane, Erika, Katie, Dominick, Paul, Mazen, Jadira, Josh, Nathan, Kayla, Mannie, John, Jessica, Englan, Lisa, Efraín, Nilka, and Leona.

CHAPTER ONE

HACIENDA ATALAYA, SOUTHERN ECUADOR
MAY 20, 1970

As flames rose into the night, an immense column of smoke and hot air suddenly burst upward and the Southern Cross rippled eerily in the crystalline Andean sky. Until Hacienda Atalaya's second story—packed with dried corn and firewood—caught fire and transformed into a raging inferno, I thought the guttering fire we'd surreptitiously started under one end of its columned gallery was doomed to fail.

Outlined on the ridge above us, the hacienda's great watchtower was the next to be consumed. I stared, fascinated, until a body teetered on its blazing parapet then, arms flailing, hurtled to the rocks below. I prayed that it was that bastard Veintimita, and not one of his servants.

As we belly-crawled down the slope to our horses, the impact of what we'd done twisted my stomach into a burning knot. Without a word, Efraín helped me mount first, then waved and nodded as he wheeled his horse and disappeared into the night. I never saw Efraín again. Never knew what became of him. My work in Ecuador was done and it was time to get the hell out.

CHAPTER TWO

GIRÓN, ECUADOR
MAY 21–22

It was hard to stay in the saddle with my shoulder in a cast. I moved slowly, my "borrowed" horse reluctantly picking its way along the precarious trail cut into the rim of the Rircay River gorge. I panicked several times, nearly certain that the roar of the river below masked the sound of Veintimita's armed *mayorales* (straw bosses) riding to intercept me.

About two miles from the hacienda, I turned the horse uphill, away from the main trail and on up the narrow path shown to Efraín and me by one of the hacienda's goatherds. It was the shortest, but roughest, route to the rutted dirt "highway" that wound its way out of the Santa Isabel district until it intersected the crossroad at the mountain town of Girón.

Twenty minutes later I topped the rocky crag and stopped to listen for horsemen on the goat trail below. At this distance, the sound of the rushing Rircay was deceptively muted. Apparently, no one followed.

Hacienda Atalaya still lit up the usually inky night sky. Blowing embers had started several additional small fires near the "big house." No time to linger; I spurred the horse across a grassy bowl beyond the summit and, as instructed, drew the gelding up to the small stone and pole corral next to a cold, desolate three-sided hut, which was seasonal home to neighboring Hacienda Los Faiques' shepherds. A "cousin" of Efraín had promised to retrieve my mount and have him back in Los Faiques' horse pen well before dawn.

I saw no one, but the hair on my neck bristled as I experienced that creepy feeling I get when I know I'm being watched. Dismounting was an ordeal, as broken up as I was, but I got it done, hitched the horse to the corral, pulled my poncho and satchel from behind the saddle, and braced to go the rest of the way on foot.

I had a tough three-mile walk to the Girón road ahead of me and it was already about two in the morning. Before walking away, I wedged a pack of smokes wrapped in a hundred-sucre note (US$5) into the stirrup for the nameless cousin who was risking his ass for Efraín and me. I didn't blame him for hiding in the dark.

If Veintimita's men got him, they'd torture my identity out of him easily. They were good at it and enjoyed it. When the Indian sharecroppers on his place got out of line, Veintimita's mayorales would get their attention finger-by-broken-finger, testicle-by-ruptured-testicle, and toe-by-severed-toe, if necessary. They particularly enjoyed slicing a quarter inch off the very tip of a guy's penis to start things off.

I could no longer see the glow from Hacienda Atalaya's house and tower, so moved on quickly, the heavy striped poncho covering my body cast and a mayoral's *chicote* (brass-mounted whip) looped over my shoulder. The "disguise" would work only from a distance.

At a quarter to five in the morning I reached the dirt track to Girón, lit a smoke, and hoped one of the big diesel *mixto* banana trucks from the coast would come along before full light. Those trucks were called "mixto" because they usually sported several rows of hard, narrow wooden benches between the cab and cargo bin. Cash fares to the next town made up a big portion of the drivers' incomes.

At 5:20 AM I got lucky. Waving a fifty-sucre bill from the side of the road drew a lumbering, canvas-covered produce truck from Machala to a rolling stop. By 9:00 AM I was back in Cuenca. News of La Atalaya's ruin probably reached the city about the time I stepped, redressed as a tourist, onto the old DC-3 that made the weekly afternoon flight to Quito.

Twenty hours after La Atalaya's storerooms caught fire I was on an Ecuatoriana flight out of the country. By the time my flight reached Bogotá, I'd had time to ponder just how I'd sunk into a cold rage and participated in torching the two-hundred-year-old hacienda without any thought whatsoever of the consequences. I chalked it up to what I called the "Ecuador Effect."

As the plane descended into Bogotá, I imagined installing a gigantic toilet chain on Ecuador, then pulling to flush it away. The thought calmed me.

Ecuador was populated by a small group of *hacendados*, "ranchers," doctors, lawyers, bankers, engineers, impresarios, and important merchants—gradations of the ruling class. Easy to recognize. Relatively tall and light skinned. Good teeth and nice clothes. Jeeps, Land Rovers, an occasional Mercedes...and always servants. Many of them. Deference to bloodlines was lavish among the elites, but respect for "lesser" humans was an alien concept.

Then there were the mestizo schoolteachers, nurses, shop clerks, small-business men, bakers, cobblers, and other skilled tradesmen. Generally shorter, darker, and with few, or no, servants, they were more numerous than the elites in towns and cities, spoke mainly Spanish, and prided themselves on their "Spanish" ancestry. Dignity mattered greatly to them, as it was fragile, therefore precious.

A much larger cadre of struggling mixed-bloods, variously called *cholos* (part Indians with the "conceit" to pretend and act like Spaniards), *chazos*, or mestizos, struggled to fit in and make a living—waiters, waitresses, seamstresses, bus conductors, counter clerks—they dominated the lower-echelon service industries.

Beneath them were the millions of Indians who farmed the land, were bought and sold with it, in spite of Ecuador's formal laws. Descendants of the Inca, or other regional pre-Columbian dynasties, they spoke mainly Quechua or Aymara. Some spoke Spanish. A few even had skills—but, as to value, they were considered by the ruling class about equal to a burro.

On a good day, the traditional Indian community was merely ignored by the outside world. On an average day, the farmhands envied the ubiquitous, underfed burros. On a shitty day—well, that's when the Ecuador Effect took over.

Then there were the rest—the Pacific coast blacks, first imported as slaves during colonial times, eked out a living as fishermen and laborers. The rare black mixed-bloods were still variously called mulattos, or *sambos*.

Me—I was just passing through, but perhaps I should begin at the beginning...

I made my living, such as it was, finding out stuff no one really wanted to know about, so it never paid much. I was a low-rent hired hand for big foundation boards I'd never met. They were, I'm told, well educated, refined, important, and *concerned* about "issues" they were apparently too fuckin' lazy, or frightened, to scope out for themselves. Well, I shouldn't be critical—it gave me a niche. And I got to see big chunks of the world.

My domain was "human rights." Yeah, I already knew it was an oxymoron as an occupation because it meant I was most always sent someplace where no one actually had any such rights. But as a single guy with two American passports, a British residency card, an education, a powerful aversion to nine-to-five workdays, and no real place to call home, it had its compensations.

Foundations were often interested in the sex trade. God bless 'em. I certainly didn't approve of white slavery, but I took some interesting gigs studying it. No complaints there. And my reports were flamboyant enough to get me more work, primarily by getting the kinkier foundation types off.

I'd made a real splash among the foundation folks in New York with a report about young Eastern European blondes kidnapped for shipment to Amsterdam. After they'd been "worked" there for a couple of years, some of the less desirable "units" had been reshipped to the States and Mexico, their final "use cycle" allegedly for anal high jinks and genuine snuff films. The foundation asked me to follow up. I shouldn't have—it all turned out to be true.

Hopes, dreams, a fresh, pretty face, and a European baccalaureate at seventeen. A weary, dull-eyed Reeperbahn whore at nineteen. A celluloid horror show at twenty-one—throat slashed while some huge misogynist stroked away and her warm blood splattered the 9 mm camera, the sex still only half over.

I gave my boss, Penrod, the details and footage I'd gotten in Mexico City, then begged off the sex gigs for a while. But Interpol got on the story with a vengeance and I temporarily became the reluctant *National Enquirer* idol of human rights stories. I showered often after that gig.

I'd floated around Mexico and Central America, too. You know, the evils of agribusiness. Eccentric elections. A body here and there. I also worked in the South when I started out. Blacks. Mid-sixties. Personally met Bull Conner. Lovely man. Lovely dogs. It might surprise you that, news reports notwithstanding, he was actually a sweetheart compared to his private backers. They were the real pricks. But at least they knew it was murder when their cracker gofers went out and lynched blacks. Even the Southern flowers of street-level crackerdom actually got frightened after they started killing the college kids from the North. Yeah, they might have been damn Yankees, some even "uppity Jewboys," but Jesus, they *were* white. Buried those, they did. Knew it was naughty.

Yet none of this prepared me for Ecuador. When I took the hacienda job, I was already nearing thirty, had been on the road for years and thought I'd seen everything. I thought I was clever. When my identical twin brother got killed in Cambodia, I appropriated his passport. Sometimes I was "Edward," other times me—JA (John Alexander).

I often succumbed to episodes of cynicism, but snuff films and a childhood spent shuttling between foster homes, orphanages, and reform school notwithstanding, I'd learned that the world was full of basically good people, the scene spoiled by a rotten few. Yet Ecuador was just the reverse—quite biblical, in a sense. Among the angry, violent masses were a few still uncorrupted in their souls. Who knew?

All this had been for five hundred dollars a month, and "expenses"... and just what kind of a final "report" was I supposed to send to New York this time—"Oops, I got pissed off at reality and torched some buildings. It was justified"?

In Bogotá, I wondered what the newspaper headlines in Cuenca had to say. The Veintimitas were powerful there. Hmm... not *that* curious after all; I took a stinky third-class bus to Barranquilla, then a freighter bound for Progresso, Yucatan. I had friends in Mexico City. Others in Sonora.

Meanwhile, on instinct, I had entered Ecuador as my twin, Ed. Possibly a good move. The husk of his Zippo-scorched passport went over the freighter's rail about eighteen hours out of Barranquilla. I sighed as his smiling face curled up and disappeared. He'd been my only living family. *Sorry, Eddy. I hate to see you go a second time.* Guess I was stuck with "JA." Perhaps it was even time to explore a new line of work.

It seemed like a long voyage. The food was bad—even the beans were greasy. And I kept seeing that body teetering on La Atalaya's parapet. Arms flailing in the night. Truth be told, I wasn't into violence and just then didn't like myself very much.

It had started off innocently enough...

CHAPTER THREE

MIDTOWN MANHATTAN

EARLY JANUARY 1970

"**E**cuador says it is turning over a new leaf on human rights. Breaking up some of the big haciendas. Land reform law passed in '64. Trying to bring traditional populations into a new world. Check it out for us, JA. The pay stinks, but no one will bitch if you pad expenses a little. There's nothing down there to spend money on, anyway, I'm told. What do you say, my good fellow?"

I hesitated. Penrod bribed me.

"Look, JA, I've got another fat job in the works, a follow-up to those Yablonski killings in southern Pennsylvania."

"Really? The United Mine Workers, the coal wars. Good, Penrod. Very good. I'll wait."

"Uh, look, JA, this one will tide you over till spring. You speak Spanish and went to college down there; be a good fellow and take this assignment."

"College was in Mexico, Penrod—not Ecuador."

"Whatever, JA—I *need* you to do this. Quick. Simple. Clean."

The Yalie grant writer I did the fieldwork for actually talked like he was in a movie, so I'd answered, "OK, old boy—six months. No more. Ticket and some travel in advance?"

"Yes, indeed, JA."

"Done."

"When will you start?"

"Two weeks—I've got a girl to see in Mexico first."

"Another 'fiancée,' JA?"

"Yep."

"Gonna settle down with this one, JA?"

"Yep."

"That will be a cold day in hell, if you don't mind my saying so."

"I don't mind, Penrod—hell is exothermic, anyway."

"Huh. Didn't quite catch that one, JA."

I grinned, pulling the door behind me as I stepped out into the hall. I often took assignments on a few weeks' notice and often worked cheap. So, how was I to know I'd just signed on for a cut-rate assignment in hell itself?

CHAPTER FOUR

QUITO, ECUADOR

JANUARY 31

The bus station in Quito was picturesque. Just off a narrow lane that wound through the capital, its open front offices were covered in grimy white plaster set off by bright orange trim and dirty orange roof tiles.

It looked like a stable, but, sure enough, the words "La Flota Panamericana" (the Pan-American Fleet) were neatly lettered in orange above its wide, ancient wooden counter. *Good grief—what a contrast to Pennsylvania Station tucked underneath Madison Square Garden.* Well, at least there was a heavyset guy at the counter. "I am looking for the overnight bus all the way south to Cuenca at the other end of the country. Am I in the right place, Señor?"

"Oh, *sí, meeester*! We have the finest service to the South. Very modern and comfortable. First class or third?"

"How much is third class, Señor?"

"One hundred twenty sucres, *meeester* (US$6)."

"And the first class?"

"One hundred sixty, *meeester* (US$8)."

"I'll take a first-class ticket. Up front. Behind the driver, if available."

"Good choice, *meeester*. That can be arranged for a surcharge of ten sucres (US$0.50)."

I laughed to myself, succumbing to a moment of cynicism. Out loud I said, "It's expensive being a foreigner, no?"

He glowered. "I don't understand your Spanish, *meeester*."

"I'll take one seat; when does the bus leave?"

"Forty minutes, *meeester*."

"Where do I wait for it?"

He motioned me out back—"The big blue one named El Azuayano." Not realizing that, like ships, Ecuadorian buses had names, I checked again.

"Did you say 'El Azuayano'?"

He rolled his eyes in derision and, in a careful schoolteacher's voice, educated me. "Yes, *meeester*, it's named for the southern province of Azuay. Cuenca is both the province's capital and the South's cultural hub." As he counted my money for the third time, I thanked him. But he merely waved me away. I gathered my duffel, sleeping bag, and knapsack, then pointed myself in the direction he had indicated.

I turned the corner of the low-slung station and stepped right into a major time warp. If I'd had any brains at all, I'd have simply retraced my route from the airport and gone back to Mexico right then. But, oh no, I wasn't the back-out-of-assignments type—not when there was something to prove to myself.

The bus yard in front of me was right out of an exotic movie set. The floor of the yard was actually Inca-period stonework and jutted out over a deep gorge that dropped two hundred feet straight down, a mere two feet beyond the last row of buses.

The "modern" buses were, in fact, tarted up American-style school buses painted in bright colors, each sporting the "La Flota Panamericana" script logo in a huge orange slash down each side.

Mine, the blue one, was at the head of the line. A neatly lettered wooden sign, "Expreso Cuenca," struck me as incongruous. I'd never before ridden on a school bus reasonably described as an express.

The bus yard was unnervingly chaotic, as if the trip to Cuenca were a madcap, spur-of-the-moment event. Lots of yelling and cursing accompanied the frenetic cargo-loading onto the huge handmade wooden roof racks. My big duffel and sleeping bag were grabbed by a wiry, middle-aged Indian fellow who stood about four foot eleven, wearing a cheap, soiled panama with black hatband, a striped woolen poncho, and no shoes.

An equally dark but taller "supervisor" in a dirty white shirt and threadbare black trousers, sporting both leather sandals and a beat-up "Panamericana" bill cap, snarled a constant stream of commands to the Indian as he loaded gear, fitting duffels, crates, and suitcases into a stable pile, to be covered by the bus's canvas tarp.

Nonplussed by the chaos, I stepped up into the bus and took my seat, stowing the sleeping bag and knapsack. A gent across the aisle had already taken his seat and was elaborately combing his hair when several grimy Indian boys popped in asking for "orders."

Obviously, I was a curiosity. They gaped. The gent completing his toilette looked at me, grinned, and made nice. "You must be a *meeester*, no?"

I hesitated, still not certain if this was a gender inquiry, or some coded cultural one. He elaborated. "Is English your native language?"

"Yes, it is."

"I thought so. You have the look. Here in Ecuador you are a *meeester*. You will find Ecuadorians—those who speak Spanish, of course—very *culto* (cultured, refined). These Indian boys are taking orders for supplies for the trip—water, sodas, *cigarros*, food. You will need supplies—it will be a long journey, no?"

Actually, it wasn't. Ecuador was a tiny country and Cuenca was less than three-hundred miles down the Pan-Am Highway. But I decided to humor him. "What do you suggest, Señor?"

"Do you smoke?"

"Yes—*sin filtro*."

"Muy bien." He turned and gave the kids some instructions in a rapid-fire patois of Quechua and nearly unintelligible Spanish.

They returned with a nylon net sack containing a roll of toilet paper, two immense glass bottles of 7 UP, several packs of cheap cigarettes, mangos, hard rolls, white goat cheese, a small paper bag of boiled, still-warm purple potatoes, and a cheesecloth sack the size of a quarter-pound coffee bag filled with an unidentifiable aromatic grain. Total cost was ninety sucs (about US$4.50).

I started to give the boys a hundred sucres in tens, but Mr. Culto leaned forward, reached for the money, and handed it to the boys, quickly palming a ten-sucre note and demanding that the older boy give me a sucre coin in change. I pretended not to notice—being underestimated was nearly always a tactical advantage.

Looking fucked, the bigger kid fished around and gave me a fifty-centavo coin. Then they disappeared to the side of another bus. My first lesson in Ecuadorian culture cost precisely US$4.95.

Soon enough, I learned that screwing one another was a national pastime, known as *aprovechando* (taking advantage of someone by virtue of guile and/or social/racial position). In Mexico and Central America you paid *mordidas* (bribes, literally "bites") to cops and public officials to get things done. In Ecuador you paid the "bite" for an ephemeral semblance of everyday cordial behavior from ordinary citizens. Biblical.

Five minutes later, the scene became even more surreal. First, the bus filled up quickly. Lots of pushing and shoving as folks tried to steal others' higher-priced seats. I was getting the picture.

Then, a skinny, dark-complected young man wearing sandals, tattered pants, and an ill-fitting black blazer clapped his hands for silence and made an announcement. "The jewel of our fleet, El Azuayano, is bound for Cuenca, with stops in Latacunga, Ambato, and Riobamba." He paused a moment for effect, then continued: "*Damas y caballeros*, I now present don Ignacio Cordoba, captain of our bus and a *veterano* of the Pan-American route." The crowd responded with polite applause. With a theatrical air, the driver stepped up into the front well, took a bow at the front of the bus, and adjusted his elaborate blue cape, adorned with eye-popping gold-braided epaulettes.

Meanwhile, another attendant opened a huge brass-mounted wooden case, extracted a japanned box that cradled the driver's own carved wooden Virgin, then

17

installed her, facing the highway, on a rack built into the base of the bus's windshield. Next, he hung a huge portable radio at the top of the windscreen.

The badges of rank properly displayed, *el chofer* took his seat, flipping the tail of his cape rather like Liberace readying for a concert.

By then, a portion of the Quito press corps had gathered. Flashbulbs in their big Speed Graphics popping in the ice-blue afternoon air, they recorded the exit of the jewel of the fleet, El Azuayano, from the bus yard.

As if it were an event to be recorded for the ages, the driver's assistant allowed a photographer on board for one last compelling shot of the mighty assembled for the first-class trip to Cuenca. *Where the hell are we really going?* I wondered.

The burly, caped chauffeur pulled out slowly, allowing the pressman to step off as the bus thumped into the cobbled lane. Some in the crowd behind us continued to wave their hats and handkerchiefs at loved ones onboard. For a shocking blue refitted school bus, it was a pretty damned majestic send-off.

I settled in, doubly glad I'd taken the seat behind the driver. The seats behind me were spaced for folks with very short thighbones. I was only five foot ten but I towered over nearly everyone I'd seen since arriving at the airport four hours earlier.

It was about four in the afternoon, the sky a sparkling, nearly transparent robin's-egg blue. Quito was about ninety-five hundred feet in elevation. Its air surprisingly smoggy, the oxygen was as thin and ephemeral as a silk scarf. I breathed deeply and lit one of the local smokes—La India brand. Once lit the dark, coarse tobacco smelled quite like Quito—dominant scents of sweat, spiced with undertones of barnyard waste. Whooh! The cigarette left me momentarily light-headed. Well, at these altitudes, my habit would be pretty cheap, I reckoned.

In five minutes we left behind the windowless rows of low, tile-roofed houses crowded along the lane and, according to a large green sign, turned onto the legendary Pan-American Highway I'd always wanted to see, so I leaned forward to gawk.

What a letdown. It turned out to be only a lumpy, narrow two-lane asphalt road with no berms.

Disappointed, I settled back into my seat and tried to get comfortable. We bounced along at about fifty miles per hour as an attendant adjusted the chauffeur's huge battery radio. A cadenced flute music backed by tom-tom, guitar, horn, and fiddle dominated nearly every tune. Some were slower. Others were based on a distinctive, interrupted syncopation. But all had a mournful, tinkling quality.

I closed my eyes to rest. It had been nearly forty hours since my Ecuatoriana prop-driven flight had cranked up and droned down the runway at Mexico City's huge airport. I'd finally gotten comfortable and started to drift off when the bus hit a series of potholes and began to gyrate like Little Egypt. Chickens, net bags full of fruit, and several kids all cascaded into the aisle. Behind me, someone unloaded on the chauffeur in a weird falsetto, "¡Puto incompetente! (Incompetent faggot!)" In response, the driver's assistant cranked up the radio's volume to drown out the abuse.

The Pan-Am's pavement had run out at kilometer thirty (nineteen miles) south of Quito, to be replaced by a rutted dirt and stone track. Anxious to go to sleep again, I asked Mr. Culto how long the patch of dirt lasted. "All the way to Cuenca," he said. He smirked at me and shrugged. I didn't know it then, but those first thirty minutes on asphalt were to prove the high point of my assignment.

My first Andean sunset was spectacular. A pale, diaphanous pink, the towering snowcapped peak of Mount Cotopaxi began to fill the bus's front window. For several fleeting moments as the sun disappeared, the mountain was so vivid I had the illusion that I could have reached out and caressed it. Then total darkness enveloped the bus with breathtaking speed. In the Andes' great interior valleys, the sun sets thousands of feet below you. Only the folks on the coast have long sunsets, then twilight.

About four kidney-punishing hours later, a cluster of faint lights came into focus through the bus's front window. The passengers began to stir. Mr. Culto eyed me and asked for a smoke. As I handed him one, he leaned across the aisle and briefed me again. "The lights you see ahead are from the small city of Ambato. Unlike Cuenca, it is a very provincial town. Backward. Mostly Indians and peasants, you know. There is nothing there to interest the tourist." I thanked him and checked out the scene through the bus's front window.

Ambato was nestled under the immense snowcapped north face of twenty-thousand-foot-high Mount Chimborazo's protective flank. "We make a short stop there, *meeester*. Food. Bathroom." I nodded, then turned away to concentrate on the view. The mountain was brilliantly outlined in the pale moonlight, its snows cascading down like a mantle of glittering diamonds. No wonder it was sacred to the Indians.

Ambato, Tungurahua Province, February 1, Early AM

Thirty minutes later we entered the town of Ambato, the Pan-American, as in Quito, lined by unbroken rows of eerily darkened houses. Dogs barked and muffled shouts bounced off the window next to me. Two or three minutes later we burst unexpectedly into a brightly lit town square. Strings of pulsing red and white twenty-watt bulbs announced the bus station. We stopped with a series of jerks and ominous metallic squeaks.

As an assistant swung open the school bus door, passengers rushed to beat one another, pushing, shouting, cussing, "*¡Pucha carajo!* (Freaking hell!)" Smelly and rude, at least their insults were colorful.

Once the crowd passed, I stepped down. An Indian woman who smelled like stale piss pushed forward as I exited, hawking something in a large basket, *"¡Llapingachos una llora, meeester!"* I had no idea what a "llapingacho" was, or what a tear (llora) might have to do with it. I shook my head and she shouted louder. Clearly, my decade of speaking basic Spanish hadn't prepared me for the local dialect. I pushed past her.

Palm out for a tip, one of the chauffeur's assistants guided me to the "men's room." It turned out to be a long, chest-high adobe wall just off the plaza. Guys were lined up, urinating on the wall, which, judging from the piss-eroded base, had only about two more years of life left in it before it toppled. Even in the frigid night air, the shallow latrine pit next to the wall stank of urine, vomit, and decaying excrement.

Just across the wall, families passed by highlighted by Ambato's flickering Honda generator–driven lights, apparently immune to the proceedings. A young woman stopped abruptly opposite me, asking if I'd like to fuck her for twenty sucres (US$1). I froze mid-piss. Several men nearby laughed. Another offered her ten sucres and the pair stepped away from the wall into deeper shadows nearby.

I relaxed again and finished up just as a commotion broke out fifteen yards away. More shouting and jostling ensued, a deep voice snarling that it was his turn to piss on the Indian.

"What the hell!" I shouted, but no one responded, so I zipped up and walked over to the commotion. Subsequent events confirmed that I'd have been far wiser to curb my curiosity.

A dark, sandaled Indian fellow, twentyish, lay against the base of the wall, covered in blood and groaning softly, his severed arm clutched to his chest by the remaining one. I gaped, then shouted, "Get this man a doctor... and quit pissing on him!" But no one stopped. Instead, one guy from the bus laughed uproariously. "It's market day, *meeester*, the *inditos* drink *trago* (cane whiskey) and cut each other with machetes. It is nothing. He will live or die as God dictates. Do not interfere, *meeester*."

"So why urinate on him?" I asked angrily. A deep voice answered. "Because we can, *meeester*. Our *puesto* (social station) permits it. Not your business." As if to emphasize their perks, one of the others quickly straddled the Indian and defecated right in his face; steam and the scent of fresh stool wafted into the cold night air. In a wheezy falsetto voice, the defecator filled me in, *"Ya...le regalé algo de comer. ¿Satisfecho, meeester?"*

He shouldn't have asked. I snarled, "Clean him off, you pig!" He giggled as several guys formed an impromptu wall between me and the latrine, forcing me to step back.

Still stunned, I fixed the voices in my mind—my first question about human rights had been answered unambivalently. I stood there for another minute, trying to push the scene—and the rage—out of my mind, until one of the driver's assistants grabbed me and pulled me away, whispering, "My boss has notified the authorities. It is time to go." His voice was tinged with desperation.

"Will anyone come?" I inquired. He shrugged, but kept tugging at me. Dazed, I let him guide me back to the bus.

The driver opened the door for me—the others still milling around and locked out. He put his fat finger to his lips, requesting silence, and handed me a shot of hot, sugared coffee from his own thermos. A peace offering. I nodded and he instructed the assistants to reboard the other passengers. Several of the men involved passed me, snickering.

The one with the falsetto voice who had taken a dump on the Indian was a stone-cold freak. He reminded me of one of my foster fathers, who'd eventually been taken away in cuffs.

Skinny and taller than average, the freak on the bus was never still. Never quiet. He jumped up from his seat every few minutes, jerking as he paced the aisle. His flailing arms and feet were never in sync as he moved about, staring at whomever caught his attention, invading their space or wheezing snide insults, usually at the Indians, then giggled uncontrollably. His eyes were another nightmare—always moving, jerking, twitching. He was the kind of guy who drove people to the other side of the street in stateside cities as he jerked and talked to himself, attempting to share his insanity with everyone who entered *his* space.

At one point, he stopped in the aisle right next to me, stared—if you can call it that—and giggled. I stared back, thinking, *Right through you, asshole!* but cut it short. It was impossible to look him in the eyes—they never stopped moving long enough to engage him.

Cutting my glance short was a mistake—he grinned and gyrated ten inches from my seat for about thirty seconds, then jerked away toward the back of the bus. Just as

I breathed a sigh of relief, he turned, eyes darting God only knew where, and giggled again. "I see you, *meeester!*" Convulsed by his own amusement, he coughed, wheezed, then settled into his aisle seat, eyes still randomly probing the crowd.

That's when a voice in my head broke in, *You blinked, dammit! You are in trouble here. Don't let your guard down with animals!* I panicked and lit a smoke to calm down. This damn voice had tormented me from time to time since I'd been a kid. It had first come to me when the foster father who'd beaten Eddy to a pulp got taken away in cuffs. When the bastard bailed out and came back to even the score, "the Voice" had simply taken up uninvited residence somewhere inside me.

The Voice was both a protector and a tormenter, urging caution, detachment—often giving me conflicting orders. *Be tough, JA. Don't let the bastards get near you. If they mess with Ed, take them down!* The Voice hadn't visited me in a year or two. Its return now was not a good sign. This assignment was going to be tough enough without it. I lit another smoke, shrunk into my seat, and tried to shut it out.

At the next stop, Riobamba, I stayed on the bus. The driver turned to me. "*Meeester*, I fear for your safety. The men involved in 'the ugliness' are mayorales from one of the haciendas south of Cuenca in the cantón of Santa Isabel."

"And why is that a worry?" I asked.

"They are very primitive. Very powerful, *meeester*."

I nodded. "Thanks for the warning. Would you like a cigarette?" He started to reach for one but, startled, turned quickly away from me as one of the mayorales pounded angrily on the door. We did not speak again. As the angries crowded past, one tried to take a furtive swipe at me, but I was too fast for him. Once past, the rest of the crowd pushed in, preventing the troublemakers from coming back for round two. The driver's tall, skinny assistant posted himself just behind my seat until we were out on the rutted highway again. For the moment, the scene was calm.

A few minutes later, I pulled out one of my maps, flipped on my lighter, and located Santa Isabel, two finger widths south of Cuenca. Nothing else nearby merited a place on the map. OK, then, at least I'd be able to wire Penrod from Cuenca and tell him I'd already selected a destination. As cold rain spattered the windshield, I curled up to sleep.

Sometime later, I awakened to a series of jolts, a weird falling sensation, and shouts. The bus driver, like the captain of a ship, shouted orders to his crew, then turned to the passengers. "Move to your right. Quickly!" His lanky assistant pulled me into the aisle as I sneaked a quick look out the window. Nothing out there but pitch-black emptiness.

The bus had slid on a muddy curve and was listing about thirty degrees; the left rear wheel hung out over a several-thousand-foot void.

All passengers on the left side of the bus, including me, were ordered out. The driver's younger Indian assistant shoved big wooden blocks under the three grounded wheels, then attached a rope to the rear axle. A dozen of us managed to pull the bus about eight inches closer to the road, but we couldn't get the wheel up.

An hour later, the older assistant materialized out of the mists with an ox team. It took the oxen another twenty minutes to get the bus back on the highway and moving again. We stopped in Riobamba a half hour later, where everyone had hot, sugared coffee, courtesy of the Pan-American line.

I was exhausted when we arrived in Cuenca late the next afternoon. Another press group lined up, flashbulbs popping. I got a cheap room in a nearby *pensión*, soaked in an old-fashioned tub, and ate rice topped with fried eggs, then slept for fourteen hours.

The next morning, my photo, along with others', including two of the mayorales who had abused the dying Indian, were spread across the social page of the Cuenca papers, which announced "yesterday's arrivals from the capital." I clipped the photos, thinking it might be important to remember those bastards when I ran into them again.

At the telegraph station I wired Penrod in Manhattan. "Arrived Cuenca. Destination Cantón Santa Isabel. The place is a time warp. No fresh leaves obvious. More trees to investigate. 'JA.'"

I hoped the code would get "Old Boy" to be discreet if he sent a wire back. Sometimes he got it, but not always. In his defense, one rarely finds someone being pissed on in central Manhattan as they clutch their severed arm, bleeding to death.

CHAPTER FIVE

CUENCA

EARLY FEBRUARY

After the marathon sleepfest, I did some exploring. Cuenca was beautiful in an eccentric sort of way. Nestled in its high basin at eighty-three hundred feet in elevation, a small rushing, wall-lined river running through it, its old center was graced by exquisite colonial architecture.

Folks on the street seemed to fall into three categories. The tall, mostly fair-skinned, Spanish-speaking folks in ordinary street dress, judging from the deference shown them, were at the top of the local food chain.

The darker-complected, more numerous, poorly dressed, Spanish-speaking mestizos nodded and stepped off the narrow stone-paved sidewalks to let the *ricos* pass. The local Indians did not speak much Spanish and, just like blacks in the South, made no eye contact with anyone higher up in the food chain. Nearly all were shoeless, wore smelly ponchos, and sported outrageous panama hats, brims upturned, just as manufactured. Everyone but the Indians stared at me.

Tired of feeling like a museum specimen, I moved off the wide boulevard and drifted into the old quarter near the river. By sheer luck, I passed a stationery store and stepped inside to buy field notebooks and a more detailed map of Azuay Province.

Wonder of wonders—a pleasant-faced, light-skinned woman behind the counter looked up and actually *smiled*. I returned the favor.

"*¡Buenas tardes, Señorita!* I need to buy notebooks and a large-scale map of Azuay. Do you have these items?"

"Of course, Señor. Let me show you . . . and it's 'Señora.'"

"Ah, I'd not have guessed that. No offense, I hope, Señora." She beamed and subconsciously touched her soft brown hair.

I wound up buying another map, some field logs, and ordering business cards—mandatory among the "professional classes" everywhere I'd been in Latin America. Taking note of her comment that "Everyone of consequence in the province has a Cuenca address," I left the address line on the order form open for the moment and asked her what part of town she recommended.

"The Avenida Solano district, Señor—it is a newer part of town across the bridge over the Río Tomebamba. Very cosmopolitan. A ten-minute walk. There are parks and the university nearby."

"Really? That sounds lovely. Do rentals appear in the local newspaper?"

"Why yes, Señor. Do you require a house for your family?"

"No, I'm not a family man. I am single and live alone. I would like to find a small apartment or a large sleeping room with private entrance and bath. Someplace quiet."

"¡*Verdad!* What a coincidence—I am a widow and have such a place available."

Damn! I shouldn't have mentioned the "single" bit! Next she'll ask what work I do.

"You are far too young to be a widow, Señora," I noted, furtively checking out her trim figure, nice eyes, and sensuous mouth.

"I see from your card that you are a folklorist, Señor. Are you a scholar?" I groaned privately.

"Yes. I will be doing research here for a few months."

She caught me looking and cocked her head, one hand on her slender hip, the other impulsively rearranging her wavy brown hair. "Shall I phone my daughter, Andalucía? She's ten, and will tell the maid to expect you in a quarter hour, Señor."

"That would be very kind. I'd love to have a look at your 'accommodations.'" She beamed then blushed, reaching for the phone. It had taken her a moment to grasp my subtle but classic "JA" double entendre in "accommodations."

Phone in hand, she nodded to me, waving me away on my errand. Two minutes later, courtesy of the provincial map I'd just bought, I crossed the picturesque stone bridge over the narrow Tomebamba.

The river's waters ran swiftly as it swirled through town, its eddies unnaturally foamy and redolent with the scent of laundry soap. Below me, dozens of female Indian servants chatted in Quechua while washing baskets of clothes, sudsing then slapping them rhythmically on the smooth boulders in the shallows. Later, I discovered that their labor was much cheaper, and more reliable, than a washing machine.

I lounged there on the bridge a few minutes, got my testosterone under control, and reminded myself that folks had tried to marry me off to Latinas with kids since I hit Mexico at age twenty. An American passport and a few lines of Spanish were all it took to start the process.

It was a different world across the river. Avenida Solano was a wide cobbled boulevard and the houses, unlike the old quarter behind me, were on large lots, set back from the street. Here and there cattle and goats wandered, browsing. The odd juxtaposition of upscale housing and impromptu grazing lots amused me.

The house-numbering system's rationale also escaped me, but roughly three long Manhattan blocks later, I stood outside number 2-25. Red tile roof, two stories, second-story balconies, and a cozy front garden. The house's terraced front entrance sported two doors. I was trying to figure out which to approach, when the one to the left swung open abruptly.

A severe, middle-aged Indian woman beckoned, "The *patrona* did not tell me you were a *meeester*."

"Why is that a problem, Señora?" I asked.

She never had the chance to answer—not that I actually wanted one. At that question, a child pushed past her from behind. "I am *Miss* Anda—your apartment is over there!" She ran to the other door fronting the terrace and flung it open. "Do you really speak English? Will you teach me? My real name is *Miss* María Andalucía Gonzáles. I'm ten. I do well in school and I like to travel. What is your name?"

Annoyed, I responded, *"¡Señor!"* But my put-down didn't penetrate.

The kid certainly wasn't bashful. Despite her annoying chatter, she had a remarkable appearance. Light skin with freckles, and her face was a woman's. Big eyes and a finely chiseled nose set off her narrow chin. She was, in fact, beautiful.

But her head was half-again larger than it should have been—the overall effect was of a composite person. The beautiful medieval face of a sensitive woman, grafted incongruously onto an impish kid's body. In fact, the hop-skip and chatter routines were the only kidlike things about her.

As I tried to process her, I thought of W. C. Field's response to kids and laughed—not that I felt compelled to kick her. Ironically, my laugh encouraged her, so she nudged me through the open door, bouncing in behind me, uninvited.

We entered a big room with a red-tiled floor and a large, high window to the north, opposite the door. About three hundred square feet in the main room, a large closet and bath (shower and toilet) took up the end adjoining the main house. A painted wooden bed, large table with three chairs, a chest, and two big leather reading chairs completed the scene.

It was perfect, except for the still-chattering kid behind me and the still-glowering maid out on the patio.

"Where are you from?"

"The States."

"Verdad . . . Miami?"

"Yes and no."

"Which is yes?"

"The States."

"Your Spanish is educated, but you don't talk much, do you?"

"Sometimes I do."

As I stepped outside to escape and checked out the cast-iron table and chairs on the terrace, Anda shadowed me and pulled at my sleeve. "You never told me your name."

"It's 'John Alexander,' Anda," I answered in English, hoping to at least temporarily confuse her. It slowed her not a bit. "Please address me with the English 'miss.' I prefer that. 'Juan Alejandro'—what an interesting name. When shall we begin English lessons?"

"We don't," I glared.

"Oh, please, John Alexander...just fifteen minutes a day. Mother has been trying to find me a tutor—someone British or American. PLEASE!"

"OK. Fifteen minutes. Tomorrow at one, *miss*?" I suggested.

"But I do not return from school until 3 PM."

I paused, thinking I was off the hook. She pleaded. *Hmm...Mom needs a tutor. Maybe I can bargain on the rent.*

"Three, then."

She squealed. "At the store, or here?"

"Your mom will let you know. Until tomorrow."

She was still jumping up and down, making squealing noises, as I opened the terrace gate and stepped out to the street again.

Anda's mother met me at the street door to her little store. "My daughter phoned. Something about English lessons tomorrow. You're not obligated. I hope she didn't pester you."

"Not at all," I lied. "She was just *precious*. I *love* children."

The woman beamed at me. Lying to her about her kid had been worth it. "I should have introduced myself properly. I am Livia Ana Gonzáles, the proprietor of this store.

Did you like the little apartment? It was once my husband's study. He taught at the university. Classics. My daughter gets her precociousness from him. Brilliant ... "

I interrupted. "I liked it quite a bit, but am not certain I can afford it."

She smiled. "Eight hundred sucres a month, good value. Perhaps a rebate for English lessons?"

Now I grinned. "I'd *love* to teach Anda English!" I said without thinking. Just forty bucks US? Penrod had allowed for a hundred. A good home base and a very attractive thirtyish mistress of the house. "With cleaning service weekly?" I asked.

"Of course!" I gave her two months' rent and we filled in the business card's address line. It read,

Sr. John Alexander, MA
Folclórista
Avenida Solano 2-25 Prta. Der.
Cuenca, Ecuador

She gave me receipts for the rent and the print order and asked when I'd be moving in. "Later this evening, after the rains. I have some research to do on the Cantón Santa Isabel. There are songs and folktales that interest me."

"Really? You should see Doctor Saldívar. He was a colleague of my late husband's and has a *finca* down there. I'll write a note of introduction. Very culto. He's at Cuenca University—five blocks back across the Tomebamba. Turn right at the Benigno Malo High School."

Twenty minutes later, introduction in hand, I sat in aging Saldívar's office. He was cordial, in a regal sort of way. A lushly attractive young secretary fluttered about, pouring tea and fussing over "El Doctór." He dismissed her with a wave of his hand.

Everything about him was surprising. He was tweedy, sported a shaggy gray mane, and puffed on a curved briar pipe. In his mid-sixties, he insisted on speaking English. It was impeccable, and the upper-class Scottish accent was spellbindingly authentic. "University of Edinburgh?" I asked. He beamed. "Yes. Doctorate in '36. I spent five years in residence. I take it you are familiar with my alma mater."

"Yes, Doctór. Master's in folklore '64, but not much time in residence—merely a reading degree." Nodding in approval, he pushed a cup of tea toward me. "And your interest in Cantón Santa Isabel, young man?"

"An old question—displaced Quechua speakers from Inca times...I seek songs and folktales with Inca-period origins. Santa Isabel drew my attention because of the village named Cañaribamba several miles away. Most scholars argue that the Cañari people are found only up here in the northern environment of the Cuenca district."

That sent him into "professor" mode. And the ensuing lecture proved extremely useful. I'd gotten a priceless rundown on the Santa Isabel district. Three of the larger haciendas came up several times—large Indian populations. They were Los Faiques (the Thorn Bushes), El Trapiche (the Cane Press), and La Atalaya (the Watchtower).

Saldívar warned me off investigations at the Watchtower. "Basically closed to outsiders," he said with an enigmatic shrug. *Well, well. Thank you, Professor Saldívar,* I congratulated myself. "Stay in touch," he puffed through the haze of his briar as I took leave of him.

I walked back from the university, headed for the cheap pensión near the bus station. In a district of narrow cobbled streets bordered by stingy elevated sidewalks, virtually all of the shops offered items of wood, brass, or leather. Apparently, some variation of medieval guild districts lingered in these parts.

It was nearly three in the afternoon and right on cue it started to rain. The little guidebook I'd bought in the States indicated that February was the wettest month in the highlands. They had not overstated the case. Instead of wispy blue skies, it had been leaden and somber for the entire day and a half I'd been in Cuenca.

It came down in sheets. Cold, driving rain. Five minutes later it became obvious why the stubby sidewalks were so high. The narrow cobbled street had turned into a temporary creek. Within six minutes I'd also discovered why the sidewalks were only wide enough for one person.

A frigid curtain of rainwater descended from the high, tiled roof lines above—which extended outward from the ancient building's walls just far enough to give one person safe passage on the narrow sidewalks. Apparently there was a logic to some things—even in Ecuador.

While gaping up at these watery cascades, I was abruptly elbowed off the sidewalk by two smirking, well-dressed Cuenca teenagers.

"¡*Malcriados!* (Spoiled brats!)" I shouted. That merely doubled them over in laughter. Before running off, the tall, blondish one cackled over his shoulder, "¡*Bienvenidos a Cuenca, meeester!*" I would have gone after them and explained that I'd already been "welcomed" to Ecuador, preferably as I held blondie's head under water, but I had a hard time maintaining a footing in the rushing water.

The water in the street was at least two feet deep. My oiled Wellingtons were only twelve inches to the bootstraps, and icy water poured in instantly.

While I contemplated catching the smarmy pricks from behind and returning the favor, an unexpectedly familiar voice intruded.

"*¡Mira al meeester, sus botas están fregadas con las aguas!* (Check out mister, his boots are screwed up from the water!) Heee, heee, heee, aack, rasp, wheeze."

In his wheezy falsetto, the guy who had shit in the Indian's face at Ambato was pointing at me from a nearby eight-foot-tall shop door, overcome with mirth. A pause ensued as his partner with the gravelly baritone voice jerked his buddy back inside and growled, "Shut up!"

I fixed on the shop doorway, its leather goods hanging inside, taking a mental picture of it, then struggled back to the far sidewalk, pretending no notice of the proceedings. *I'll get your freaky ass, yet,* I thought to myself.

Two blocks later, I ducked into a dry alleyway and emptied my boots. I reached for a smoke, but even my cigarettes had dissolved. Soaked and cold, I headed for the stationery shop as it was much closer than the pensión where I'd stored my gear.

Livia's smile faded as I crossed her threshold. "What happened to you?... You are soaked to the knees." I tried to grin but was shivering a bit too much to pull it off. "Got knocked off the sidewalk into a narrow street. The water was deep."

"I will never become completely accustomed to these people... no matter how long I live here."

"Huh? You are not from here?"

"No, I was raised in Popayán, Colombia. I came to the university here—I was an only child. My parents were already dead. I met Professor Gonzáles here. He was so gentle, distinguished. We married after I graduated. My daughter was born two years later, then Alfredo died suddenly when she was four.

"His brothers—her uncles—helped me open this little store, so I stayed."

"What did you study?"

"The classics—mostly Greek tragedy."

"There's irony in that, Señora."

"Are you making fun of me, Señor Alexander?"

"No! Not at all. I can relate. My father was a scholar but died—or disappeared—when I was a baby."

She steered me into the back room. "Get these clothes off...here's a blanket to wrap up in. I'll get you hot tea. We can hire a taxi and collect your belongings when the rain lets up a bit."

Her hand brushed my shoulder as she tucked me into the blanket. "And please call me 'Livia.'" Closing the stockroom door behind her, she blushed again as she withdrew. Well, we'd connected on the orphan thing, but I couldn't believe I'd blabbered about my father.

Clothes off and the thick local blanket around me, the shivering slowed. Cold and wet in the highlands was just as bad as cold and wet in Edinburgh had been. Straddling the equator didn't automatically deliver the climate I'd always imagined—dense equatorial forests, monkeys screeching in the trees, natives calling me "B'wana."

Instead, on this assignment, I had taken a detour straight into the twilight zone. I was rattled. And I wanted to hurt somebody. Not like me. I was usually both too cool and detached to get uncontrollably pissed off.

Livia knocked. "Ready for tea?"

"*Sí, listo.*"

She breezed in with a tray, handing me a huge glazed mug of milky tea laced with brown sugar and a sweet roll.

She was looking more girlish and less matronly by the minute. *Did the altitude here have the same effect as three drinks?* I wondered as she glided out, hips swaying, my soggy clothes in one hand.

After absorbing the tea, I drifted off to sleep, curled up in a corner of the room. I started, bolting upright, when she awakened me later.

"Señor, your clothes are cleaned, dry, and pressed." I must have looked surprised. She laughed, rich and throaty.

"How much do I owe you?"

"I already took it from the coins in your pocket—ten sucres. I hope you don't mind."

"Not at all—I am grateful. I did not realize I'd be so tired."

"The altitude. You need to eat soup for the first week. Don't drink much alcohol. The same with your cigarettes. It will take time to adapt…and don't cut yourself," she chided nervously, handing me the long French folding knife I carried everywhere. "This is a very intimidating knife for a folklorist."

"I should have used it on those brats in the street!"

She recoiled and studied me, her brow knitted. I needed to tone it down.

"Sorry. Actually, the knife was a gift from a friend in Paris. It is for cutting bread and cheese. On the back, the corkscrew is for opening wine bottles."

"But the blade…"

"The long blade is a customary French design—for bread. It's not a weapon." She nodded, obviously concerned, in spite of my explanation. It also happened to be the truth. *Has Ecuador made her cautious—or is it the orphan thing?* I wondered.

Still edgy, she wanted me gone. "Dress, it is only *lloviznando* now. We shall move your things to the apartment.

Dinner will be at eight. Anda is expecting you." A few uncomfortable minutes later, an ancient Plymouth pulled up in front of the store. The taxi's old-fashioned running boards surprised me. Inside, its damp wool upholstery smelled of mildew.

After retrieving my duffel bag, sleeping bag, and knapsack, we pulled up in front of the house on Solano, little Anda's huge head bobbing in the front window. I paid the taximan, carried the gear inside, and unpacked.

An hour later, Livia knocked at the door but didn't step in when I answered and held it open for her. "You will need supplies, Señor."

"His name is 'John Alexander'!" shouted Anda from the other doorway where the family maid had her under guard. Livia ignored her and completed her thought, "...matches, candles, kerosene, toilet items, a good blanket. A raincoat and umbrella."

"Kerosene?" I commented, incredulous, also ignoring Anda.

"Don't be fooled—when it isn't the wire, it's the rain. The lights go out often during the rainy season. Very inconvenient."

"You're kidding?"

"No," she smiled and shrugged. "People steal electric wire all the time. One must check the switches before dark." Absentmindedly, she stepped in and flipped the two switches by the door. "They seem to be working now."

She watched intently as I rummaged in the duffel. My throwing things into drawers must have triggered something. "Here," she motioned, "hand me your clothes." With that, she began arranging them neatly in the bureau, just like orphanage matrons had once done.

She indulged the same compulsion with the contents of my knapsack. Either she'd played this role for the late Alfredo—*lucky middle-aged fart*—or she was checking for other signs of danger. The knife had troubled her.

But the "organizing" ritual seemed to relax her and give her more confidence. "I am sorry about the knife comment..." Livia said eventually.

"Call me 'Alex'—all my close friends do."

"Thank you, Alex. Dinner at eight."

"See you then." She walked out. Nice view.

It was six-thirty. After the door closed behind her I rearranged my gear and made a list of items I'd need—batteries, BIC lighters, Kerex, TP, halozone tablets for water purification, candles, walking stick, etc.

That done, I cleaned up in tepid water from the black rooftop tank that fed the shower, changed clothes, then sat out front at the ornate cast-iron table, savoring an American cigarette from my only remaining pack of Lucky Strikes. The rucksack in the pensión had saved them from the spoiled pricks in the street.

On the third puff little "Miss" Anda materialized, staring silently, her eyes following each arc of the cigarette as if she were hypnotized. She said nothing, but watched until I finished and stubbed it out under my heel. At that move she darted away. Returning quickly with a dustpan and whisk broom in hand, she shoved them at me and nodded at the crushed butt. "You must clean it up—the scent will damage the flowers. They are fragile and no one has ever smoked here."

The colorful pansies scattered about in pots looked pretty hardy to me, but I grudgingly swept up the little pile to appease her, emptying the dustpan out in the street.

Anda flashed a huge smile, then grabbed the implements, turned, and disappeared into the main house, skipping as she went. I studied the map of Azuay Province and adjusted my compass for magnetic variation, one eye on an old guy on a ladder repairing an iron streetlight up the avenue. As I fiddled, the Indian maid appeared, as sour as before. "*¡A comer, meeester!*" No smile from her. Perhaps she did not like "*meeesters.*" Or she may merely have been wary of all strangers. That seemed a common reaction in these parts.

"*¡Gracias! Voy,*" I answered.

As I stood to follow her, the old guy out on the street carried his ladder to the next light and climbed to the top. He inserted his hand into the fixture and it lit up. The maid grunted, already at the door.

Still curious, I followed her into the main house. Inside, it was bright and cheerful, in spite of the leaden weather outside. Livia obviously went for color. There were cut flowers everywhere, and potted plants lined every window. Even the tablecloth was brightly flowered.

When Livia entered, she was, too. Wearing a splashy flowered shawl, her lovely brown hair done in a soft French roll, she looked radiant. "Good evening, Alex."

"Hello. Tell me about the lamplighting outside."

She laughed. "When they installed modern lights, they kept the lamplighter. He flips the switches."

I smiled and spoke softly—no hint of my ordinary brusqueness. "That's quaint...and thanks so much for the invitation. Permit me...?" I seated her, then pulled out a chair for myself. That's when Anda waltzed in. "Thank you, John Alexander. That is my chair." *Shit! Why's the kid here?* Glancing at the lovely Livia, I bit my tongue and adapted.

"What a nice surprise, miss." Livia flashed an amused grin. I think she detected the thinly veiled undertone of sarcasm in my voice. I pulled out the third chair, seated myself, and "Cook," still sullen, brought the soup.

Anda stared back and forth between Livia and me, silent for a change, but watching us like a hawk. The food passed. After soup came rice with vegetables, slices of succulent *lomo*, and braised potato. As the first forkful of pork was about to reach my mouth, Anda's silence ended. "We've never had a man to dinner before." *Well, good*, I thought, *no serious suitors*. But Livia was irritated.

"Of course we have, Andita—Professor Saldívar and your uncles."

"I suppose so, Mother, but it's not the same. They are not your lovers." I laughed, while her mother nearly had a seizure. Anda, undaunted, continued. "So, are you a single man as you claimed, John Alexander?" Her impeccable pronunciation of my name was remarkable. Her frankness, however, was irritating.

"Yes, I am not here neglecting a wife and children, if you must know."

"Thank you, Alex," Anda grinned. "I may call you 'Alex,' mayn't I?"

"I prefer not. 'John Alexander' will do nicely."

She twitched her nose, and thought a second. "Very well . . . then you *are* lovers. You have my blessing, but I do not approve of the smoking, John Alexander. Please reflect on that." As Livia turned from pink to purple and started to stand up, I put a palm out to calm her. "Let me, Livia." I gave it to the kid cold, but dignified.

"Anda, your mother and I are *not* lovers. We have only met today. We are merely acquaintances!"

"That will change soon enough," grinned Anda. *Damn!* She was unfazed. I stood and turned to Livia. "Perhaps I should leave the two of you alone to talk."

"Please, wait, Alex. I'll handle this." With that, Livia grabbed a startled Anda and dragged her into the kitchen.

I could hear most everything. "Have you been reading those French novels of your father's again? Answer me...I thought so—that material is too mature for you, and this time, your fantasies have embarrassed me. *No more* of this talk, young lady. Do not ruin our conversation. *¿Comprendes?* Now let us return to the table and behave with decorum. You owe Señor Alexander an apology."

They emerged, Livia exasperated. Anda, still startled, complied.

"Lo siento, John Alexander. Perdóneme, por favor."

"Apology accepted, miss. Now I shall seat your mother again and I'd like to hear more about her, Cuenca, and your family. OK?" The kid nodded and picked at her food.

Livia looked relieved but became more formal, giving her daughter no new avenue with which to pursue her fantasy. "I came to Cuenca for university when I was nineteen. Being with other students my age was marvelous and there were no nuns to contend with. I married, had Anda, and after my husband died, opened the shop, catering to the university clientele. I liked that ambience."

"Yes, university life is great. I miss it at times."

"What universities did you attend, Alex?"

"Several. I started college in the States, but later took a master's at Edinburgh."

"Oh, my! Such a coincidence that I sent you to Professor Saldívar. With him it's Edinburgh, Edinburgh, Edinburgh! He's so proud of it."

"Well, he ought to be. I am, too—it's a great school."

"Well, then, Alex, just where did you learn your Spanish?"

"In Mexico City—I lived there in my early twenties."

"Did you like it there?"

I shrugged. "I like Paris more." She let it go.

Then the conversation drifted to Cuenca, its great families, and the local museums. That gave me an opportunity. "Do you know anything about Santa Isabel, south of here? I intend to pursue folklore studies there."

Her reaction was odd. Fear flashed across her face and her voice was tense. "It's rural—I've never visited. I stick close to the university." She paused.

That's when Anda butted in again. "Cook is from that cantón. She said that is where they beat the Indians."

"Does Cook know that for a fact, Anda? Or is that merely a rumor?" I asked.

"*María* is *from* Cantón Santa Isabel! She once told Nestor she has witnessed it...and some years ago, they injured her little brother so that he could not be a father. That is when her family had to leave. The *patrón* of her hacienda was displeased with them and sent them away. Her little brother protested—that's when they hurt him."

"Was it a hacienda called Atalaya, by any chance? Professor Saldívar said it was closed to outsiders."

Livia snapped, irritated again. "Andita! Listening in on others' conversations, then fantasizing about people you do not know is unacceptable."

I wanted to ask more but, reading Livia's tension, let it drop and went on chatting casually with her while Anda sulked. No sense involving these folks in my assignment.

An hour later the maid saw me to the door. As I stepped outside, she followed. "*¿Meeester?*"

"Yes?"

"The child is not lying . . . such things did happen to my little brother."

She had already stepped back inside and locked the door before I could form a question. Clearly she understood Spanish fully—not just the "kitchen Spanish" that most Indian maids in Mexico claimed.

My Apartment, Cuenca, February 1970

The wooden slatted bed was hard, but I slept well in spite of it. When morning came, a hint of sunlight brightened the clouds. I dressed and walked back to the city's old commercial quarter, filling my pack with necessities.

By design, I passed the shop where Mr. Falsetto had giggled at me the day before. The store's walls held a huge array of wooden-handled whips made of expertly braided rawhide and similarly fashioned horse tack—bridles, lariats, headstalls—the works.

I purchased a heavy-handled mayoral's chicote like those carried on the Pan-American bus by the badasses from Santa Isabel. I also purchased a dense *palo de fierro* walking staff and asked them to mount a brass knob on the head and a short steel spike on the tip.

As they put the finishing touches on the stick, the manager asked me how I came to find his shop. I took a chance. "A fellow I met on the bus from the capital—high-pitched voice, giggles oddly—was carrying one of your whips. I admired it and he gave me approximate directions. I needed a whip for dogs—they appear to favor '*meeester* meat.'"

He laughed. "Good idea. The Indian dogs are like the Indians themselves—*brutos*. Your acquaintance is known as El Garrote—one of the mayorales on La Hacienda Atalaya, some miles south of here."

"Well—thanks for the whip and stick—very well done."
I gave him two hundred sucres for both items and departed.
I was on a lucky streak. In just twenty-four hours I'd found a
nice home base at cheap rent, an attractive widow who
blushed, and drawn a bull's-eye on Hacienda Atalaya.

Next, I purchased a dark red poncho, two heavy
wool blankets, and a wool felt hat that would stand up
to the rain. In the duffel, I had an oilskin shoulder cape
I'd acquired in Edinburgh years before. It kept the worst
of the rain off and worked well as an impromptu sleeping tarp.

Loaded down with my purchases, I hailed a cab and
went back to Avenida Solano. I unloaded my goodies and
rearranged my room. Bed away from door and big rear
window—at a forty-five-degree angle from the corner. A
large reading chair pulled near the bed, I could work with
my feet up. Guy style.

As I freshened up, someone rapped at the door. Anda.
Carrying a large ashtray. "Use it, *please*."

"OK, miss—I'll be careful with the cigarettes."

"You like flowers?"

"I tolerate them, miss."

She scowled. "We have an English lesson at 3 PM...
¿Correcto?"

"No, your mother said you were being punished."

"Please!" she grimaced, shifting rhythmically from one
foot to another. It was the perfect opportunity for a "come
to Jesus" conversation.

"*If* I give you a lesson today, will that be the end of your
comments about my relationship with your mother?" She
nodded, hopeful. "And no more bratty 'orders' like the ashtray?" She nodded again. "I'm not kidding, Anda!"

"I know."

"OK, I'll see you at three for twenty minutes only."

Anda bounced away. So I closed the door, pulled the curtain, and practiced some moves with my new stick. It needed a modest rebalancing, a bit of brass ground off the head should do it. I took it with me when I walked back downtown to get lunch.

I dropped the stick off at the maker's shop, asking him to slim the brass knob a bit, and ate lunch at an impromptu courtyard "restaurant" down the block. I marveled at a huge bowl of *locro de papa*—a potato soup that was served nearly everywhere. Full of cilantro, potato, spinach, spices, and goat cheese, it was superb with the crusty local bread.

I retrieved my walking stick—the owner, unlike earlier, now nervous and oddly reserved. Done, I headed back to Solano for Anda's lesson. She was waiting at my door as I came through the gate. "What's the *bastón* for, John Alexander?"

"I'll be doing field studies in the countryside—it's a walking stick."

"With a brass mounting?" The kid was acting like a miniature Hercules Poirot.

"It's not your business." She hung her head. I'd made my point, so answered, "But, I liked the look of it—old-fashioned, romantic. Like one sees in old British films." She began chattering—"So, can our lesson begin with a film?" I went for something dense to dull her ardor.

"Do you know *War and Peace*?"

"Yes, but I want something *American*—like *To Kill a Mockingbird*. What does the title mean, John Alexander? And the South—is it as much like Ecuador as it appears?" *Hmm*...the kid was a flat-out genius...and a surprisingly insightful sociologist. I wasn't going to outmaneuver her easily. Out of grudging respect I gave her long lessons over the next two days. Even those didn't wear her down. She absorbed English like a sponge, but her mother was still blushy and scarce after her daughter's "lovers" conversation. *More's the pity.*

Between lessons I read through copies of the *Revista de Antropología* published by the regional Casa de Cultura. Lots of local folklore to bone up on. I even took notes. Got to seem authentic, you know. Besides—it was interesting.

Anda, perhaps confusing "I tolerate" with "I want more," kept bringing me potted pansies as peace offerings. By Friday evening, resigned to the kid's eccentricities, half a dozen pots full of bright flowers graced my room. I'd located maps of Santa Isabel and busied myself marking the trails and haciendas on them. Among them was La Atalaya—its tower allegedly then already two hundred years old, perhaps even older. That was certainly possible—Cuenca had been founded in the late 1500s. The Spanish had been in these parts nearly four hundred years.

Suffering from my version of cabin fever and unable to corner Livia, I was restless to go downtown. So, I rushed Anda's Friday lesson. I needed both a good meal and a break from the kid. Professor Saldívar had recommended a restaurant named Día y Noche where they served a nice mixed grill and good Chilean wine to go with it.

I ditched my warm poncho, put on my only Harris tweed jacket and a tie, and went for dinner. Given all the starches—rice, boiled potatoes, and fried banana were usually served as one meal—I was ready for protein and wine to smooth its passage.

The restaurant, but one block from the plaza, was classy for Ecuador. A light-skinned, well-dressed clientele filled the place, some of them university men judging from several other baggy tweed jackets. I ordered the grill and a half bottle of Chilean *rioja*. Taking in the scene, I relaxed and enjoyed myself.

By 9 PM, I'd drawn out the dinner experience to the point of boredom, finished my wine, and, in a good mood, decided to stroll over to the plaza. As I stepped outside and turned the corner, I heard a creepy falsetto giggle behind me. As trained, I spun reflexively to the right. Everything went black.

CHAPTER SIX

CLÍNICA SANTA ANA, CUENCA

FEBRUARY 5–6

Sometime after, I remembered a flashing light, shouting, and the smell of antiseptic. But I couldn't get my eyes to open or awaken fully to find out exactly what was going on.

When I did finally wake up I was in a clinic—Saint Something-or-another, the nurse said. Standing over me were Professor Saldívar, Livia, and another gent I did not know. I opened my mouth to say hello, but barfed instead, then blacked out.

My next flash of reality yielded the sensation of numbing cold. No wonder—they had packed my head in ice. Trying to limit the brain swelling, I assumed. That's when I remembered that creepy, now familiar falsetto giggle, just before someone flipped my switch to "off."

Later in the day I came around and stayed awake. The nurse said I had a severe concussion and more than a dozen stitches to close the head wound. I'd been in and out for ten hours. Not good. The Voice wasn't content with the situation, either.

They kept applying ice to my head and feeding me broth. The next morning the doctor visited, doing the standard "follow my pocket light" routine. At noon they sent me home with Livia and the unknown gentleman who had been with her earlier when I'd puked.

Both of them helped me into my apartment and propped me up in bed. Anda was there, but timid. She looked as if she'd been crying. Livia's face was warm and tender. Emotionally confused, I settled for the silver lining, *Well, at least she's no longer avoiding me.*

The older man with Livia turned out to be one of Livia's brothers-in-law and Anda's uncle—Abelardo Gonzáles. "Did they steal anything from you—a passport, money?" he asked.

I took inventory in slow motion as Livia held up each item found in my pockets. "Nope," and shook my head no—a big mistake, given the stitches. I groaned involuntarily, my face constricted from the stabbing pain. When I was younger I could dissociate at will and withdraw into a dreamlike state—completely avoiding pain or distasteful situations. But that was then...I groaned again.

That rattled Anda. She clamped her hand over her mouth and fled the scene, sobbing as she ran off.

"I don't understand why they did not rob you," the uncle repeated.

"Nor I," I answered. No sense in revealing what I knew. Or why I was really in Ecuador. Abelardo interrupted my thoughts again, "You must be careful. It is not ordinary for someone of your *puesto* to be assaulted here in Cuenca."

I'm not buying that bullshit! screamed the Voice, outraged.

Me, I was too wasted to argue with either of them, but the fact remained that I'd already been pushed into the street by two well-dressed young men who could actually have been Abelardo's nephews, if he had any.

Señor Gonzáles left a few minutes later, ordering his driver to return and watch the terrace door through the night. That pleased Livia, who hovered over me.

She was gentle, still a bit frightened, but a warm presence. "Alex, this has panicked me. I am a bit flustered by it, so tell me what you need."

"A cool towel for my head, perhaps?" She brought one, cradling me as if I were a fragile child. Her touch was unexpected and mesmerizing—soft, gentle, and pregnant with suppressed sensuality. Her eyes studied me, then she wrinkled her brow. "The doctor said it was a miracle that you were not killed. Had the blow struck but thirty millimeters closer to the spine, you would have suffered a fatal brainstem injury."

I said nothing, so she caressed my cheek and pressed her lips gently to my forehead. As my pulse increased, so did the pain. Yet I did not wish her to stop. Her lips were warm, moist, soothing. Then she pursued her thought. "You really *were* lucky, no?"

What do you tell an innocent? An orphan who married a middle-aged professor, then undoubtedly nursed him in his dotage, left only with a remarkable child for comfort? I could have said, "They taught me this in a special school in Brussels. Eighty percent of attacks from the rear are made by right-handed men. Turn quickly to your right and you stand a decent chance of a huge knot behind the ear instead of a crushed brainstem. If it's a knife they carry it won't matter anyway..."

So, I merely smiled. "Luck was with me."

"I'm glad," she grinned. I fell asleep again, awaking in the night to find her curled up on the foot of the bed, snuggled in a blanket, her head cradled between my calves. Was she really there, or was my addled brain teasing me with a mirage? I reached out and felt a thin strand of her hair slip gently through my fingers. Yes, an innocent. And I'd known so few of them in my life.

I leaned forward, touched her soft, brown hair again, and sighed. I could get used to a woman like this. As I stroked her hair she murmured something inaudible. I leaned back and fell asleep.

By morning, she was gone, replaced by Anda, who had composed herself. "They hurt you but did not rob you, Mother said. You must be careful, John Alexander."

"Is that an order?"

"No, a hope...is a hope OK?"

"Sure—hopes are acceptable." She smiled.

"Can you walk?"

"I think so."

"Good. You smell of hospital. Shall I help you to the shower, then wait outside?" I nodded in assent. "Call if you need help."

"Is that an order, miss?"

"Sorry! *Please*, call me if you need help."

"You are a fast learner, Anda. I respect that."

"Really? I'm doing OK, then?" She held her breath, waiting for the response. I grinned.

"You are doing quite well. Now, please help me to the shower." She squeaked and steadied herself to balance me. The room spun several times, but we made it.

I cleaned up, shaved, changed, and powdered, taking stock of the damage. The freak's well-placed blow would have been fatal in most circumstances. That giggling as his club whizzed through the air showed a spooky, practiced confidence, even for a psychopath. The bastard must believe he can do *anything*. Anda was right, I did need to be careful.

Out of the shower, I decided I'd try my land legs. I put on my boots, grabbed the walking stick, and stepped outside, still shaky. "I'm coming, too, John Alexander. You will fall."

She had a point. "A short walk, then, Anda. What do you say?"

"If it's short, I think it might be all right."

The first few steps took me to the patio, where I paused to steady myself against the iron table. The midmorning air was fresh and moist. Storm clouds had begun to gather, but occasional shafts of sunlight highlighted several of the red tiled roofs. Grass, trees, large-balconied houses, and the iron streetlights that had to be switched on by hand all marched away down the avenue—a backdrop for the cattle and sheep grazing just a few hundred yards away.

For some reason the open fields attracted me. I pointed to them with my stick. "I need open space. Hospitals make me claustrophobic. Let's go...and why do they call you 'Anda' instead of 'Lucía' for a nickname?"

"I insisted on it. I am simply not a 'Lucía.' It does not fit my personality. But 'Anda' does rather nicely. When I grow up and publish my first book, it will be by

'Professor Anda L. Gonzáles Chuca.' It is *not* an advantage to be a female scholar in this society." On that note, we started walking.

Well, the kid certainly was a realist—at least on the surface of it. We stopped to rest in an open field nearby, my head throbbing too much to go on. Anda chattered on about Ecuador. Unconsciously I twirled the stick to test its balance. *Still a touch head-heavy. Hmm, gotta fix that,* I thought. Anda watched, but said nothing until we started walking again when the pain had eased.

"Is it balanced to your liking, John Alexander?"

"It's good, but not perfect."

"Nestor keeps *raspas* in the shed at home. Shall I bring one?"

"Sure."

"Can I watch?"

"OK. By the way, who is this 'Nestor'?"

"Nestor Chávez—my uncle Abelardo's driver and assistant. He likes me and *adores* Mother. But he's too old for her...and of another social class." *This puesto thing is certainly pervasive,* I thought, but said nothing; you don't dump on kids for the crazy worlds adults construct around them.

Back in the room I went to work on the brass head, gouging pie-shaped slices from it, leaving four raised humps. Those I filed into a rather nice Maltese cross. Anda grinned. "Thy rod and thy staff before thee, John Alexander?" I grinned back at her and tousled her hair.

I paid for my effusiveness. Immediately she began to wheedle for another short English lesson. We did Steinbeck's *Grapes of Wrath*—something meaty that fueled her obsession with social conditions. As she left, she informed me that her mother had asked to dine with me, alone. "Is she still angry over your 'mature' comments the other night?"

She sighed, nodding, then shrugged, slamming the door behind her. An hour later Livia came to the room, looking nervous. "Alex...could we, umm..." Then, turning red, "oh, add some flowers to your room, or something?"

"Oh," I said, sounding disappointed. "I was hoping you'd ask me to dine alone with you."

"Really? Oh, I'd like that...wait...did Anda say anything to you?" she frowned.

"Yes, but I was thrilled. You are an island of brightness and warmth in a cold, rainy season." The frown vanished. She fluffed her hair and smiled, her hands behind her like a schoolgirl.

"Shall we eat at the table here?"

"By all means."

It was a pleasant dinner. She bubbled and flicked her hair, making eyes at me. The creases in the corners of her mouth added depth to her face each time she smiled. At one point she leaned to me and touched my face. *Ooh— she smells of buttercups and fresh straw.* I inhaled the scent of her hair, touching it gently.

Dinner over, we snuggled by the miniature corner fireplace. Her face was radiant in the flickering light. She looked as if she were twenty-five. Still the orphaned college girl.

I didn't expect it when she kissed me hard, her tongue pressing between my lips. She moaned and sunk her tongue even deeper, making little gasping noises. After a few minutes she shuddered, gasped, and pulled away, looking both surprised and dreamy-eyed.

"I *must* go, Alex. I must. This is not...I don't...ah..."

"I know...Livia. I know..." She left, still nonplussed. Her hips swaying uncharacteristically, she looked back once, blushed again, then closed the door gently. My pulse raced and my head throbbed. *But worth it,* I told myself. For me, that was a first. I had just experienced a woman reaching orgasm from a kiss. God knows what would happen after an hour in bed. She might simply explode, her suppressed sensuality unleashed like a bomb.

I held on to that thought as I dressed for bed, feeling better. A touch of romance goes a long way to soothe the realities of a world spoiled by freaks who thrived on violence and chaos.

CHAPTER SEVEN

CUENCA
FEBRUARY 11–12

The next day I visited Saldívar, asking for an introduction to the owner of a "progressive" hacienda near
Santa Isabel—one where I could collect songs and tales
without perturbing the daily business.

"I recommend Señor Ramón Uribe, owner of Hacienda
Los Faiques, within walking distance of Santa Isabel. I'll
phone him if you like. A graduate of Michigan State; he
runs a pretty modern farm."

"I'd be grateful. Find out, if you can, what room and
board charges would prevail. My grant is a modest one."

"Of course—I'll leave a message at Livia's if I am
unable to arrange a meeting."

Later that evening a message came for me to meet
Señor Uribe at a coffee shop near the plaza. Finished stick
in hand, wearing tweed and tie again, I met him as planned.

Uribe was surprisingly young—not five years older than I. He spoke no English with me, indeed made no reference whatsoever to the States, but had no problem with "folklore studies." He wanted assurance that I was on a "research grant"—I showed him the general letter of introduction, in Spanish, from the internationally known New York foundation that fronted for Penrod.

"No problem, Señor. No charge for a small sleeping room—one the mayorales often use. It's rustic." I nodded. "Twenty sucres a day for the meals of local custom—rice, beans, locro—an egg or two each week. We grow our own fruit—banana, mangos, limes. Eat all you wish. Meat you will have to buy on market day."

"Any formalities?"

"No—come whenever it suits your research. I will let my *mayordomo*, Antonio, know of the arrangement. He will see to matters down there. Pay him or the second mayordomo, Efraín, twice monthly for the food."

"And the directions to the hacienda house, Señor Uribe?"

"Ask anywhere in the village—there is bus service three times weekly from Cuenca. Then about a mile and a half walk down from the village."

"Thanks so very much, muy culto." I beamed.

He took off. I appreciated the fact that he had called me "señor." I went down further into the old quarter and lunched al fresco, locro de papa again.

Afterward, I decided to visit Livia's shop and change the order for my business cards—the Avenida Solano address might prove an invitation to hurt Livia. Or even Andita. I didn't want them involved, if it could be avoided.

Livia was radiant, not flustered and confused as she had been after the kiss. "Hey! You look lovely, Livia."

"I *feel* lovely. It's a nice experience for me." She touched my shoulder gently and laughed. Apparently, the blushing was under control.

"Listen, Livia, I still don't know what that head bashing was about. It has troubled me that I was not robbed. I don't want complications for you. So, I want to change the address on my business cards. Is it too late?"

"No, I was just now pestering the printer. I can call again. Easy."

"Do. I am going to the post office to get a box."

"Impossible, Alex. There is a year-long waiting list. Besides, my brother-in-law is sending his driver to stay with us for a while. It will be all right."

"Perhaps I should move, then..."

"No! Please—not necessary," she blurted, her brow knitted, blushing again.

I put my palms up in surrender. "*Pués*, I have an idea—we will change the address to Hacienda Los Faiques, Santa Isabel."

That suited her. She phoned in the revised order. It was modest camouflage, but camouflage, nonetheless.

Then came the questions. "So you are going to Santa Isabel, Alex?" The tone in her voice betrayed the same edge as at dinner with Anda when I'd first asked about Santa Isabel.

"Yes, in about a week. I am still doing background research here."

"Will you be leaving us then, Alex?" A doubtful tone in her voice, it was the closest look to a pout I'd seen on her face.

"No, Livia—your apartment will be my home base. I'll spend a fortnight in Santa Isabel, then return here for four days. We'll see how that goes." Then, on a whim, I said,

"I'm going up to the university library now, but might I *invite* you to have dinner with me about eight thirty—a nice restaurant here in town?"

She glowed. "El Retiro, Alex—the food is good and I have seen couples dancing through the window as I passed. Do you dance?"

"Of course. I can't wait."

The last vestiges of her frown disappeared as she picked up the phone, looking girlish again.

Back in the bowels of the library I worked my way through dusty tomes, many of them handwritten journals, in the "local history" section. This forgotten section was a gold mine. Slow going, but the nuggets were worth it.

The first mention of La Atalaya's tower was in 1757:

> The great tower built on the ancient *tambo*
> (Inca way station) has been in the hands of the
> Veintimita family for some five generations.
> Before that it was the property of don Alejandro
> Crespo, whose eldest daughter, Juana, according
> to the family Bible, married Martín Veintimita of
> Yunguilla (the valley along the Río Rircay) in the
> year of our Lord 1721. The earliest of succeeding
> great houses next to the tower is said to have been
> founded in 1607, but there are no records of the
> time—the original church at Santa Isabel having
> burned about 1640 amid local unrest perpetrated
> by Quechua-speaking wild Indians of the district.

Well, that put things in context. The old, big-name, landowning families of the district were the Veintimitas, Crespos, Landívars, Corderos, and Malos. Professor Saldívar's family appeared much later, minor landholders, who used their farm of about one hundred hectares (about 225 acres) as mostly a finca—or family country retreat. The Uribes and Los Faiques weren't noted until the 1930s. Los Faiques was only about six hundred acres but "highly productive."

I had begged off Anda's lesson that day, and so stayed at the books until about 5 PM. I decided to hit the older church records in town to round things out before heading to Santa Isabel the following week, after my stitches were removed. They were already drawing uncomfortably as the healing progressed. On the upside, the constant throbbing had subsided.

I freshened up at Solano. I didn't see Livia or anyone else about, so I walked up to the Tomebamba bridge at eight, asking directions to El Retiro. I'd worn my twin brother's favorite tie—a cubist's red and black silk—for the occasion, since my usual navy-blue one had been soaked in blood the night I got bopped on the head. Ed had been into bright, splashy ties.

Livia was already seated when I walked in. The sweet thing didn't even know that a woman is expected to keep the man waiting in a state of nervous anticipation. Her hair in the French roll again, she radiated warmth and energy—such a contrast to the blunting of emotional affect and blank stares so common on the street.

We had the local version of paella. About 9 PM a surprisingly good trio struck up and several couples began to dance. The main course finished, I asked her to dance before the salads arrived.

Sighing and murmuring, she clung to me, enveloped by the gentle scent of flowers. We returned to our table, ate the salads rather too quickly, then like high school kids, hit the dance floor.

I pulled her in tight, slowly caressing her back, then eased my hand down lower. She shuddered, moaned in my ear, then started to emit heady volcanic tremors. Her scent had transformed from soft flowers to the primal aroma of a tigress in heat.

She panted in my ear, biting it hard, her eyes closed. Then she shuddered again, her long eyelashes fluttering spasmodically as her belly contracted against my belt. I felt her orgasm all the way from my ear to my knees. "Oh, God, Alex...I, uh, need to excuse myself!" She grabbed her purse and disappeared.

When she returned, she announced, "The house on Solano is empty tonight...Anda and the maid are at a sleepover with one of her cousins. Does that interest you?" *Nicely done for an innocent,* I thought to myself. My own pulse hovered around 160 in anticipation.

But after I paid the bill and began to wrap her shawl around her, I heard a familiar voice. Mr. Falsetto's burly, baritone-voiced partner was in the restaurant doorway. "Who is the woman with the *meeester* wearing the bright tie?" he asked the head waiter, handing him a banknote.

The waiter shook his head and shrugged. Baritone leaned in, asking another question that I couldn't hear.

Being hit on the head was one thing—but having the hottest date of the new year ruined was quite another. Pissed off, I tried to think the situation through, struggling with just how to handle the mayoral who straddled the door, blocking it, when in popped Nestor, Abelardo's driver. Nestor was balding, medium complected, had penetrating dark eyes, and was built like an NFL linebacker. Pushing past La Atalaya's finest, Nestor was a full two inches taller and tensed for trouble.

We'd obviously been surreptitiously chaperoned, but I was grateful. Nestor strode over to Livia, announcing, "Don Abelardo wishes to have coffee with you at his residence—the car is waiting."

Baritone had already vanished when, Livia between us, we ushered her into the car's backseat. Nestor pointedly held the front door for me. No time for second guessing, I stepped in quickly.

As we pulled away, I got one glimpse of Baritone through the car window. He was heading up the street toward the stone bridge that crossed the Tomebamba. Nestor saw me watching him and barked, "*¡Carajo!* He's going to don Abelardo's." That startled Livia, so Nestor turned abruptly in the other direction, stopped at Livia's stationery shop, got her key, went in, and made a phone call. We waited in the car. While he phoned, Livia pouted. She'd already forgotten about the mystery man and was fuming over her ruined plans for the evening.

"My brother-in-law should not be treating me like his daughter. I am no longer a convent girl to be watched." Thank goodness, she didn't quite get it.

Nestor came out, whisked Livia home to Solano, still protesting, and asked me pointedly, "Do you need your walking stick?" I nodded and retrieved it from my apartment while he waited. Nestor told Livia—still upset and refusing to close her front door—to go inside and *relax*. "Don Abelardo wants to talk to him. I'll return with him in an hour, no more," he promised. That quieted her.

We glided, headlights off, through the old quarter till we saw Mr. Baritone standing near the high alley wall behind don Abelardo's town house overlooking the river. Nestor stepped out, finger to his lips, pointing me toward the alley's far entrance. Then he slipped back behind the wheel and drove past, stopping ostentatiously just ten feet from Baritone. Nestor, humming a local *pasillo*, stepped out casually to face him.

The mayoral went for it. I crouched behind him, unseen, as he stepped forward to size up Nestor. As Baritone focused on Nestor, like a mongoose on a cobra, I drove the brass head of my stick right into his spine, just below his kidneys. He went down like a sack of rocks, his legs jerking convulsively from the spinal jolt.

Nestor stood over him a second and whistled. Two more burly "servants" materialized from the alley gate and unceremoniously dragged Baritone into the walled yard. They stayed there with him, then Nestor came back and escorted me through the front door.

"I want an explanation!" Uncle Abelardo demanded. I filled him in. "I saw them mistreat a wounded Indian in Ambato and asked them to leave him alone."

"And?"

"They ignored me. The driver said they were mayorales on a hacienda near Santa Isabel."

"Did you fight with them?"

"No, I protested briefly and they ignored me—nothing more."

"All this over that?"

"Apparently."

"Did the mayoral see you tonight?"

"At the restaurant, but not here. No."

"Wait...I have a phone call to make."

Dignified Uncle Abelardo proceeded to roast one of the Veintimita's asses on the phone—the word "culto" came up frequently—then demanded, "You must collect your trash from my yard and see to it that my sister-in-law and her friends are *never* bothered again!" Obviously, someone protested. Abelardo went regal. "Well, then, I shall put the matter to don Benigno if it cannot be settled *now*." Apparently, that got results.

I assumed the "don Benigno" to be the one that the high school was named after—Señor Benigno Malo, one of Cuenca's reigning grandees.

When Abelardo returned, he was far more gracious than I expected. "Our Livia made my older brother very happy. She likes you quite a lot and you give lessons to her daughter. Nestor will drive you home.

"By the way, you should know that one of Veintimita's sons wanted to date Livia when she was still a student in the university. She was not interested. When my brother died, he tried again. He showed ill grace when she refused his advances. This is clearly an old family matter. Please let us resolve it ourselves. Do not explain all this to Livia. I will phone her myself now, before you see her again."

I shook hands, thinking, *Ooh! You are as delusional as everyone else I've met lately.* I had pissed off La Atalaya's mayorales royally. My head hurt because it was personal. On the other hand, Abelardo's interpretation was mighty convenient. So, I dissembled. "Thank you, Señor—I had feared that what I witnessed in Ambato might have initiated this."

He smiled. "Veintimita's sons have hired some ruffians for mayorales. They are *often* troublesome. It reflects badly on their family."

I nodded, then was whisked away by Nestor. Livia was waiting, a bit distraught. "Abelardo phoned, explaining the Veintimita family connection to this matter. He underestimates the evil that several of them are capable of. *Please*, Alex, don't make the same mistake when you are in Santa Isabel." I shrugged.

She frowned, then gave me her own version of what don Abelardo had more circumspectly told me. "One of Veintimita's sons wanted me for his mistress after my husband died. He was furious when I refused. He actually slapped me." The fear in Livia's eyes was a startling contrast to her ordinary demeanor.

"I am surprised—and dismayed—that my refusal is still an issue. Fermín Veintimita had it all planned out—a small house purchased for me in Calle Rocafuerte, Anda to be sent to a convent in Peru...as if I would agree. That is what happened to me when my father died. My mother was forced to send me away when she remarried. She died at thirty-five, a late pregnancy gone wrong. I never saw her again after I was sent away." *We share more than she realizes,* I reflected as Livia unburdened herself.

"My husband was like a father to me. Gentle, kind, cheerful. I was reborn during our marriage. Some viewed it as eccentric—he was twice my age, not merely the ten years older of custom. But I was happy...and my Anda was a wonderful gift. He rocked her every night, telling her stories."

I wanted to comfort Livia. Erase the fear. But hesitated...and lost my chance.

"I need to rest now, Alex. Anda will return at breakfast. She's counting on her lesson tomorrow."

"I'll deliver it, Livia, don't worry."

Caressing my face gently, tears filled the corners of her eyes. "I had a lovely dinner, and the dancing was, was..."

"Delightful?" I suggested. She nodded, smiling. "Good night, then." *A damn shame,* I confided in myself. *Her words don't match her body language. She caresses me then turns and wrings her hands.*

I closed the door to Livia's house behind me and smoked on the terrace until Nestor reappeared, gliding stealthily along the terrace wall.

"Psst, Señor. *¿Hablamos?*"

"Sure—inside?" He nodded. Once inside the apartment, Nestor had questions.

"The mayoral claims you were stalking *him* and his *compañero.*"

"If that were the case, why is it that I am the one with stitches in the back of my head?" He shrugged and nodded at the logic. Made sense.

"He claims he and his companion inadvertently caught you in an affair with Señora Livia." As he waited for an answer, his stare penetrating, he held his breath...

"Nonsense. My *only* unchaperoned social contact with Livia was the dinner and dance *he* ruined by following us tonight. I am irritated at such accusations. Even if I were not a gentleman, the señora is a proper lady. She cannot be changed—she is decent, an innocent."

Apparently, that did it. He relaxed and nodded, agreeing with me. I guessed, then, that nearly every man with whom she was in regular contact idolized her.

Nestor left with a caution. "In Santa Isabel, stay far from the Hacienda Atalaya—Veintimita's sons manage the farms there. They are obsessed with their own power, and they're malcriados. Beware of them."

"Thanks, I will accept your advice." As I told Nestor what he wanted to hear, I was actually rejoicing. *Bingo! Between the mayorales and the story about Livia, this Veintimita character has just won the daily double for unwanted attention.* He strode to the door, but turned unexpectedly before exiting. "The blow you struck tonight was masterful—practiced. I am the only one who knows of it, and even now my memory fades. It should remain that way." I nodded in agreement.

"And you, Nestor, are not simply a loyal retainer to the Gonzáles family. At least, you do not act like one." His turn to shake his head and grin. "And we all thought the only genius in this house was little Andita..."

He was still chuckling as he crossed the terrace, catlike and self-confident. I wasn't. The only thing folks agreed on was that the Veintimitas down in Santa Isabel were the social equivalent of toxic shock syndrome.

CHAPTER EIGHT

CANTÓN SANTA ISABEL
FEBRUARY 16–18

The week passed quickly. More lessons with "Andy," as I had taken to calling her, a worried, withdrawn Livia, and a bit more research at the university, then I found myself packing for the early morning bus to the village of Santa Isabel.

The local bus service had come as a surprise—a first-class ticket (80 sucres/US$4) brought the bus right to your door—with curbside service for an extra dollar. Of course, the peons who had boarded at the bus yard and had paid a regular fare were obliged to sit it out for each first-class pickup. The puesto thing, you know.

I had asked for a pickup across the street, up by the empty field about two hundred yards from Livia's house. A touch of discretion seemed wise. But that didn't stop little Miss Andy from materializing to wave goodbye at 6:30 AM.

"Your daughter?" asked a well-dressed mestizo guy in the front seat behind the driver.

"God no. A student, actually, Señor—I teach English to help support my research activities."

He smiled. "What kind of research, *meeester*?"

"Folklore. Songs and oral traditions from the late Inca period." I smiled as I took the front seat next to the door. Leg room. Critical.

We bounced along the dirt Pan-American "Highway" south toward Santa Isabel until we reached a fork straddled by a small settlement. The left fork wound its way over the Tinajilla Pass at eleven thousand feet, then meandered on to the provincial capital of Loja. We took the right—no road signs, of course. If one didn't know the way, I assumed, one didn't belong in these parts.

I made trip notes on the little ring-binder pads I always kept in the flapped breast pocket of my tan field shirts. As we descended from Cuenca, the scenery took on a warmer, less somber tone—a few hardy palms and a profusion of flowers graced squat farmsteads along the road.

We jolted along, nearing the town of Girón, where the highway narrowed to one lane. Several of the curves snaked through ancient mountain cuts still supported by Inca-period stonework. At one, our driver lost the "beep first" contest that dominated Ecuadorian bus travel. At each narrow curve the loser had to back the bus to a wider spot, hugging the sheer rock face of the mountains, while the winner roared past—only inches from the losing bus's outer windows.

Sometimes the testosterone-sodden winners zipped by so exuberantly that they miscalculated by six critical inches, tumbling into a canyon below. That was a weekly occurrence in Ecuador and always made great newspaper copy. I actually preferred it when my bus lost—tucked fairly safely against the inside of the curve.

Of course, this being Ecuador, a pissed-off losing driver, his bus partly hidden around a curve, might park the nose close to the mountain, but leave the rear out a foot—nothing like forcing a competitor over the edge at the last horrifying moment. And the passengers...well, fuck 'em. This was about honor, testosterone, penis length. Machismo.

Our driver was pretty timid, God bless him, so we had only one heart-stopper on the trip. Just beyond Girón we swung wide around a curve to miss a broken-down mixto tucked against the mountain. As we floated past, just as had happened on the Pan-American Highway from Quito, the bus's outside rear tire slipped partway over the precipice's mushy edge. We lurched. Again, everyone but me automatically leaned to the inside, crossing themselves furiously and spitting on the floor. This time it actually worked. The bus righted itself and the rear wheel caught solid ground. Me—I just sat there like a dumb-ass and quietly aged six months.

Later, the bus stopped for ten minutes in the mountain town of Girón, where two- and three-story balconied, orange-tiled buildings crowded against the "highway." At one, several small tables were set out on a stone terrace nearly level with the bus's windows and only a foot from them.

The driver stepped up, inviting me to follow. "Good *tinto* (coffee) with goat milk, *meeester*. Try it—my aunt is the proprietor."

"Close call back there," I commented.

He grinned. "Then you *need* a coffee." I did. It was good . . . and cheap. And they assured me that they'd boiled the milk while preparing the coffee.

Most of the cattle, and many of the goats, carried TB in southern Ecuador. "If you think pulmonary TB is nasty, you should see what those local bovine varieties do to you when they attack bone marrow," a Manhattan specialist in tropical medicine had warned. That, of course, had followed other warnings about yellow fever, plague, dengue, malaria, and amoebas capable of going AWOL from one's intestines in order to burrow into your liver.

We reached Santa Isabel about 8:30 AM. It stood on a high, prominent ridge, orange tiled and looking for all the world like a medieval Italian village on a travel poster—until we got close. That's when the stunning wear and tear came into full focus.

Wooden stairways were missing steps. Shutters hung at crazy angles, and peeling plastered walls jumped out of the morning sun like pop-ups in a cheap amusement park's "Tunnel of Horrors." The political and religious "county seat" of the cantón, Santa Isabel might still have been grand in 1850. But by 1970 it looked like the "after" photo of bombed-out Montecassino in World War II.

Hoping for a tip, the bus driver played tour guide. "*Meeester*, the town becomes festive and vibrant on the two Sundays each month that are market days. That is when it's most delightful." I was obliged to take the bus driver's word for "vibrant," since at the moment of arrival, the only local folks in evidence were grimy, barefooted Indian boys lined up to carry the passengers' bags—the Andean equivalent of Africa's "porters."

That changed a bit as mayordomos brought their haciendas' ancient Land Rovers and Nissan Patrol Wagons alongside the bus to pick up a few of the local elites. I engaged one of the taller porters to carry my duffel after he assured me, "I know the footpath below leading to Los Faiques' big house, Patrón." The constant ass-kissing "Patrón" bit got old quickly.

We walked across the town's open, muddy plaza, its rather grand church looking quite out of place, and headed back down the road we'd just ascended in the bus. "You should have asked the driver to let you off at the old footpath to the house," the kid advised me.

"Do they stop where one requests?" I asked.

"Yes. If you are important." *Huh,* I noted, *puesto comes with a four-dollar bus ticket.*

A mile later we turned abruptly downhill, descending a steep footpath straight down the hill. The town, looking like a mirage on its hot, dusty ridge a mile away, shimmered above us. Below, we picked our way gingerly down into the valley called Yunguilla (meaning "little valley of humid lowlands" in Quechua/Spanish). In fact it was the valley of the narrow, roaring Río Rircay.

Fifteen minutes later an impressive expanse of orange-tiled roof came into view to the left. The path ended at the right end of a large, whitewashed, two-story, porched and colonnaded late colonial great house tucked into the mountainside.

In front, the house's quarter acre of flat, partly cobbled *plazuela* was bordered by a new outlying house being built yet farther to the right. A cluster of ramshackle equipment sheds partly obscured the view beyond the plazuela. The big house faced southeast toward a long-tilting bench of rich land above the rushing Rircay—just a narrow ribbon below us.

Mangos, bananas, corn, papayas, sugar cane, and crops I did not recognize were spread out below. Several tethered burros brayed at the far end of the plazuela, their panniers laden with mangos. Indian boys attended each burro, as a tallish, lighter-skinned fellow in black felt hat and high-topped rubber boots assembled them.

Surprised, the tall one turned to me, rushed over, and introduced himself. "I am Efraín—the *tractorista* and second mayordomo—you must be the *meeester* the patrón said would be a guest." He pulled off the floppy hat, holding it in both hands. His hands were big, gnarled, and calloused from hard work. His face was angular and determined. I answered, *"Señor Juan Alejandro a sus órdenes."*

He cracked a quick, fleeting grin. *"¡A lo contrario!* Shall I put off taking the burros up to the bus—mangos for the market in Cuenca?"

"Not at all. *¡Sigue, no más!* I'll wait and relax on the porch."

"Good…María will bring you something to drink. I'll be back in an hour; have the boy take your gear upstairs to the *balcón.*" Ill at ease, he turned back to the task at hand.

The burros filed out, still braying and straining under their loads as the Indian porter hustled my duffel up the stairs. He asked me for seven sucres, looking doubtful. So I countered, "Here—five." He nodded and I gave him the note. He looked pretty happy with his US$0.25.

A few minutes later a tallish, heavyset woman in Indian dress covered by a dirty apron mounted the stairs with a tray. She said nothing as she set it down next to me. "You must be María." *Were they all named María?* "I am Juan Alejandro."

She nodded, making no direct eye contact. "Tea, mangos, and water, *meeester.*"

"Thank you, María." I nodded as she withdrew with a backward curtsy, as if I were royalty. Thirsty, I checked out the water, but passed on the big clay mug, imagining that I could see amoebas in it doing their equivalent of a carefully choreographed Busby Berkeley aquatic dance routine. The idea of the runs didn't daunt me—I'd had them dozens of times on assignment—but liver damage was another thing altogether.

The steaming tea was delicious—spiked by a local mint and a flowery flavor I couldn't accurately identify, it was softened by cane sugar and boiled milk, still steaming in a second pot. A pot of tea, two mangos, and a smoke brought Efraín rushing back more quickly than I imagined.

"You have your tea. Good. Now to your room." He led me to a small upstairs room on the far left of the big house's roofed gallery. Looking nervous again, felt hat in hand, he explained, "The patrón and his family reserve the porch and rooms past the table where you sat for their exclusive use. We shall put a chair and small table out front here for you."

"I'd like that, Señor."

"Efraín, please. And how do you prefer to be addressed?"

"I prefer 'Señor Juan' or 'Juan Alejandro.'"

"'Señor Juan' is good, if that suits you."

"Sure. May I put my things in the room?"

"Yes—and here is a key. Lock your things up when you are gone. The *arrieros* come through here with their mule trains every eight or ten days as they have for centuries. They pay for water by custom, and are provisioned with fresh fruit and chickens, but they are not local. Some are, uh, *manioso*."

"Thanks for the warning. I'll need to go up to the village and purchase personal items later. Is there a store or *bodega* you recommend?"

"Yes, El Cantón, across from the church on the near corner—tell the proprietor you are a guest here. He will give his preferred price."

"Thanks, Efraín. Don't worry further about me, I'm pretty self-sufficient." He smiled and nodded at that but still looked nervous as he hustled off to the business of a working farm.

My "modest room" was actually about twelve feet square. A narrow, locally made, wooden-slatted single bed was tucked into one corner; a squat antique chest with two huge drawers stood next to it. A small table with chair, candle holder, and chamber pot underneath were the only other furnishings. A large plank shelf—a foot or so wide—ran along the wall opposite the bed. There were several candle stubs and a stack of old-fashioned wood matches on it.

I folded a blanket and my sleeping bag onto the bed to provide padding, rolled my rain cape into a makeshift pillow, and unloaded some of my gear. On the way out, I locked the door, as instructed, and headed back up to the village.

The climb was a workout—the hacienda itself was about forty-eight hundred feet in elevation. Santa Isabel nearly fifty-six hundred feet. A thousand feet in a mile and three-quarters wasn't for heavy smokers.

Once in town, I surveyed the scene. The church was fronted across the plaza by an unbroken facade of high-roofed, one-story buildings about 150 feet long. There were pungent mule and burro corrals behind this block. At the far end of the plaza a two-story, porched, orange-roofed building served as the cantón's "administrative center." It included a rustic "infirmary," two-person "police" station, and a courtroom with offices for the judge who, I was told, came along with the padre every other week on market days.

Located at the other end of the plaza were a "pharmacy," public scribe's office, and a general merchandise store, which closed the plaza's west end. I took a look in the church. Pretty impressive. The high altar protected by an ornate handmade iron gate was adorned with a surprising amount of silver for a district church. A few touches of gold in the rays, or *esplendor*, of saintly statues floating above the altar punctuated the impression of comparative opulence.

I wandered into the Bodega del Cantón—a general merchandise store, like those stateside grandparents now talk about wistfully from their childhoods. Tools, lanterns, matches, boxes of candles, cans of Kerex (for lanterns), wicks, nails, and sacks of rice, coffee, sugar, and tea cluttered every inch of available space.

I purchased a large green glass water bottle (about five gallons in capacity), cigarettes, candles, matches, toilet paper (in short supply), a small, used kerosene lantern, wicks, and a big bag of *machka*. This was the mystery grain I'd bought in Quito for the Pan-American bus. Delicious, the local variant was a dried, toasted preparation of quinoa, wheat, and barley. High in protein, it had a distinctive nutty flavor. Machka was an ancient food in the Andes—long predating the Inca period—and an all-purpose dry meal for the trail, or for thickening stews.

I also bought local raisins and sun-dried cherries to add to the machka and make my own trail mix. There was neither meat nor eggs for sale. "Come to market day this

Sunday for those," the proprietor consoled me with a shrug. As an afterthought, I bought a sack of tea and ten kilos of brown rice as gifts for the hacienda larder.

"Can I get help carrying my purchases?" I asked.

"No problem. Would the boy who helped you this morning do? He's good with the burros. His name is Cayé."

"Yes—I guess he'll do."

"Then engage him to run your chores for you—he is very reliable and honest, an altar boy at Mass. Los Faiques' patrón don Ramón even sends him with small quantities of cash for cigarettes or 7 UP." *Hmm. Cayé—honest and reliable—as opposed to what? I wondered. Is it customary to distinguish an Indian kid like this?*

I was about to ask when Cayé bustled in and the proprietor nodded at him. He tipped his hat to me in deference, then rushed out. He had a burro out front in minutes. I didn't have to load anything. "Twelve to fifteen sucres is appropriate, *meeester*—he pays us six sucres for the burro if the trip is less than two hours. That is equivalent to a day's wages for temporary farm labor—of course, that excludes the customary meal that such laborers receive."

"Thanks for the service and advice." I handed the proprietor 220 sucres, and he made small change.

"Your *yapa*, Señor?" he asked.

"Yapa? I do not know that word."

"In some places it is called the *vendida*" (a bonus to close the sale—a baker's dozen).

I paused. He smiled. "It is customary for *regular* customers. You like dried fruit. Here, I have some *cirgüela*. Very nice." He handed me about six ounces of prunes in a small paper sack.

Cayé and I headed down the hill again. "Cayé, can you make a regular trip for me twice a month to market on Sundays, and twice a month midweek for smaller purchases?"

"Of course, Patrón. I shall be as discreet as a priest in the confessional." Actually, I hoped for better, but simply said, "Good. Let's move on." He was bubbly—"My full name is Cayetano Palma Hachundilla. I am an Indian— but not un bruto. I am civilized. I am Catholic and my uncle can *read*." *Jesus. Even the Indians have to make excuses for themselves,* I goggled. Penrod would have arched one of his patrician eyebrows at this. So, I reassured the kid.

"Impressive. But you'll find that I like Indian people. I have come to collect traditional songs and stories."

"Really? And you are a scholar?"

"Yes, but I am still young and not yet established. I am struggling to make a place for myself."

"I understand that...and I can help. I know all the Indians here in the valley of Yunguilla—even the brutos."

Cayé was about twelve or thirteen years old. Lively, intelligent, and wild to get his hands on "strong wages" of fifty sucres a *month*—US$2.50. Tall and wiry, he had shaggy black hair; wore a black poncho, sandals, and baggy cotton pants; and had an angular face dominated by a prominent nose.

Down at the hacienda we took a few minutes to unload the purchases and work out the monthly calendar. I wanted to spend more time around Livia and Andy, so I modified my original plan. I'd work eighteen to twenty days monthly in Santa Isabel and spend ten to twelve days a month in Cuenca. Most market weekends would be spent in Santa Isabel.

This plan would force a shifting schedule. Hard to track in case anyone remained too interested. Even better, Cayé had indicated that the early-morning mixtos from the coast would stop for a waving hat and twenty-sucre note if the local bus schedule didn't meet my needs. The kid had already earned his month's wages, as far as I was concerned.

Now to settle in. Do the traditional census and identify just who might be willing to have me record songs, stories, perhaps even drink a trago or two with me…and tell me what I *really* had come to find out.

Dinner—a mound of rice, potatoes, and fried banana— was served about 7 PM at a table under the big house's cobblestoned ground-floor colonnade. The lower level included tack rooms, a bodega, the hacienda's "office," where money was counted and records kept, and the indoor/outdoor kitchen.

There should have been a number of people at the table with me, but I was the only guest. Alone at the table, I tried not to notice María, Efraín, and a short, older guy in a frayed straw hat whom I hadn't yet met, all intently watching me eat from a respectful distance. If puesto also meant eating alone, it made no bloody sense to me. I nodded to Efraín. "Care to join me?"

"Thank you. Thank you, Señor Juan. Very culto. But it is not permitted—only the patrón, his family, and guests eat at this table. Do you require anything else?"

"No, thanks." *Hmm—he's still formal and nervous.* I assumed Efraín wasn't accustomed to *meeesters.* Later, I was to discover that he was, by nature, nervous—and never more so than when he was forced to speak. Efraín was the kind of man who "spoke" in grunts, jerking thumbs, and nods. Words seemed to make him uncomfortable.

After dinner virtually everyone disappeared, even María. I had the big house to myself, except for Efraín, who slept on a cot in the office below, an ancient Damascus-barreled, black-powder shotgun propped next to his bed. I gave him an American cigarette before going upstairs to write.

He took it, looking surprised, but did not speak. Instead, he smiled, nodded, and touched the brim of his hat in gratitude, then grunted and withdrew to his room. A few minutes later I caught the harsh scent of his sulfured match. Then the distinctive, creamy aroma of the Virginia tobacco wafted up to my table on the balcony above him.

As dusk fell, even the burros quit braying and settled down. I hung my battered Kerex lantern in my window and went down to the small, tiled aqueduct that carried a steady trickle of water from a spring on the hill behind the house. Using a coffee filter, I filled my green five-gallon jar, hoping that the larger, nastier critters living in it wouldn't make it through the filter. I dumped in three halozone tablets for good measure, corked it, and headed up to my room.

As I passed along the lower gallery, Efraín popped out of his doorway and surprised me. "That is a task not appropriate for someone of your station, Señor Juan. You should have asked me or María to do it for you."

"Well, Efraín—I am accustomed to such chores. A man of my means does not have servants in the States."

He paused, his turn to look surprised. "Then you should have Cayé do that for you as part of your arrangements. More appropriate to local custom."

"Thanks. I'll arrange that when I see him again." He nodded.

This puesto thing is a major pain in the ass, I thought to myself as I hustled the big green jar up to my room and put it on top of the ancient chifforobe next to the bed. I took the lantern out to the porch and wrote in my journals, ate a mango, then went to bed.

I didn't sleep well. Constant scuttling noises came from the high ceiling above me, frequently waking me up. About 3 AM, I switched on the flashlight when the same noises moved to the heavy plank floor across from me. *Lord love a duck!* A freaking rat the size of a small cat was gnawing at my backpack. I banged the brass head of the walking stick sharply on the floor. That sent the ominous gray bastard scuttling back into a wall.

I relit the Kerex lantern and got all the dried fruit and machka up off the floor, wrapping it in a small plastic tarp. Completely awake, I went out to the porch, pulled the table to the rail, and got a wonderful view of a clear, starlit Andean sky. I finally spotted the fabled Southern Cross after a careful search through my binoculars—it isn't very impressive—and enjoyed the sensation of seeing new things in the night's solitude. Finally tired after watching the stars glide past the timbered eaves of the porch, I slept late, till a banging at my door wakened me.

It was broad daylight—8:30 AM. Cayé was at the door. "Do you have additional errands?"

"I need a rattrap and a hanging wire basket from El Cantón...and several large bottles of 7 UP." He advised me that he'd see to my water bottle twice a week and other chores when I was in residence. I nodded.

Cayé trotted off up the hill to Santa Isabel. I hollered after him, "I need to give you money!" He waved me off, shouting, *"¡Firma!"* and disappeared. About forty-five minutes later, he returned with a big wire basket and *the* biggest, nastiest-looking rattrap I'd ever seen.

Locally made, it was fitted with serrated iron jaws like a small muskrat trap *and* a lever with a four-inch spike attached to a stiff wire above the jaws. Cayé hung the basket, then went to set the trap where he'd found a fist-sized hole in the wall hidden behind the big chifforobe.

He baited it with a cherry while I stood on the jaws to hold them open. "This is one helluva rattrap, Cayé."

He laughed. "The loft above us is filled with dried corn and firewood for the kitchen. The rats are very big here, Patrón. When there is no corn, they sometimes bite off a baby's fingers at night. Very ugly. I will tend your trap, but I want the rats as payment. The big ones make a fine meal." Before leaving, he handed me a bill to sign and trotted back to the store with it.

I was becoming more humble by the hour. *But how much of Cayé's "rats are good eating" tale is true? I wondered. Is his story local effect for his greenhorn "patron's" benefit? Or, perhaps just a way to get yet stronger wages out of me? Well, I'll find out soon enough...*

María brought bread, a mango, a banana, and tinto with *leche* for breakfast. After I stood and motioned for him to sit, Efraín, looking uncomfortable, joined me at "my" balcony table. María stared at him disapprovingly. Pushing a mug of coffee to him, I told him I needed to do a census of the district and interview folks on the hacienda. He nodded. Looking nervous and thumbing the brim of his hat, he filled me in. "Manuel, a mayoral, will assist you in introductions. Our patrón asked us to help you as much as possible."

When I tried to engage Efraín in further conversation, he fidgeted like a kid trapped between his elders in a church pew. To resolve the situation, he offered to go fetch Manuel. "Manuel knows things... can answer questions." I nodded and Efraín jumped out of his chair like a jackrabbit, his rubber boots squeaking as he trotted off.

Fifteen minutes later, Efraín returned with Manuel, the straw hat–wearing man I'd seen from a distance at dinner. At first glance, he appeared to be about sixty years old, but he was probably younger. In the developing world, laborers age quickly. Weathered, his teeth half gone, he was as short as I'd assumed and wore rubber galoshes, the frayed straw hat, and a tattered European shirt. A mestizo from his lighter skin and European features, he was bright, had been raised in the valley, and knew lots of history. Manuel was a talker.

"I don't want a 'wage' for my assistance, but occasional gifts—a can of Kerex, smokes, that sort of thing—would please me greatly." He had a calm, outgoing personality, and others—even his boss, Efraín—showed him respect. *His age?* I wondered.

The basic census I needed was time consuming, but necessary. I'd done the same many times, in many places. Through the census, one identified unfiltered reality and found the natural "talkers." They were the pay dirt. At least the "research expenses" weren't going to light up Penrod in Manhattan. If I spent fifty dollars a month, it would be a stretch.

After an afternoon spent talking to Manuel and taking notes, I turned in early, ignoring the scuttling noises in the rafters above me.

And, just as Cayé had predicted, the rattrap would both work—and waken me. About 2 AM it slammed shut on a three- to four-pound rat. Startled, I flipped on my flashlight—the ferocious gray bastard's red eyes glowing in rage, it squealed and struggled to pull the jaws upward, knocking over one of my boots…then managed to crawl partway inside. That triggered the spike from above.

"Goddammit! I have a dead rat stuck in the top of one blood-soaked boot, and I need to pee," I whined out loud as I maneuvered past the carnage in bare feet and pissed over the balcony.

I considered the rattrap a technological allegory for the medieval pall that still smothered southern Ecuador. When I got up the next morning, I extracted the dead rat from my boot and hung it on a peg by my door. I leaned over the rail and shouted down at María. "Is breakfast ready?"

"Yes, *meeester*, but I am too busy today to bring breakfast upstairs again." So, I went downstairs for the coffee and fruit. Manuel waited at a respectful distance while I ate. María smirked. *Hmm—a second mayordomo can sit at my upstairs table, but she won't let a lowly mayoral do it.* When I finished, Manuel and I started the basic survey of the hacienda's Indian population.

CHAPTER NINE

LOS FAIQUES—
THE INDIAN
SETTLEMENTS
FEBRUARY 18–20

It proved harder than I imagined to get people to talk to me. A number of the "sharecroppers" worried that I was an outside agent for the hacienda owner, trying to identify the disloyal. Fear of being sent away was a huge issue. Land was generally unobtainable, except through *huasipungos* (house and garden plots "loaned" by landowners). Being ejected from a hacienda doomed poor Indian farmers to starvation.

Others thought I was from the government. Everyone had heard that the folks in Quito had invited young *meeesters* at huge salaries to implement new government farm policy. It took me a while to comprehend that this was how they viewed the Peace Corps volunteers.

I found the "huge salaries" ironic—at just one hundred dollars per month—and said so in one of the low, ancient Quechua huts I visited. "So, how much are they paid, *meeester*?"

"One hundred dollars per month," I'd answered.

"How much is that in sucres?"

"Two thousand sucres."

"*¡Pucha carajo! ¡Ya!* A strong wage for a farm laborer is two hundred sucres a month, plus a daily meal. A schoolteacher makes sixteen hundred sucres—and everyone knows *they* are rich. They live in houses with *electricity*, have radios. Their children can see the doctor... and the whole family wears *shoes*. Even the mayordomo of the grandest hacienda only makes eighteen hundred sucres, *meeester*."

So, it cost many more packs of cigarettes, liter cans of Kerex, and small bags of machka than I'd imagined to get interviews. Some locals even turned their starving dogs loose on me, if I was alone. But the chicote slung over my shoulder stopped that in short order as word spread that the *meeester* knew how to put a welt on a dog's snout if it attacked.

Others merely barred their doors and refused to answer Manuel's knocks. But some succumbed to the Kerex and smokes. Most houses were long, low, thick-walled rectangles of rough quarried stone, or adobe block, covered by sapling and thatched palm frond, or cane and palm, roofs.

In one, owned by the Lloque family, whose two sons, Marco and Antonio, were friends of Efraín's, the squat, dark house stank unbelievably and had hard-packed dirt floors. A family of about ten, their living area measured about six or seven hundred square feet. There was no electricity. No running water. And no toilet or latrine to soften the daily reality of infants and the aged incontinent. That house was the olfactory equivalent of the fastidious Penrod's most primal nightmare.

Wooden-slatted beds piled with soiled sheepskins and blankets stood in rows opposite the low, heavy doors. The only possible interior light came through a two-foot-square window at the kitchen end. But every time I visited, it was shuttered, as glass was simply too costly for the field hands.

It, like most such houses, had a traditional stone hearth. A choking twig and dung fire smoldered. Nearly everyone coughed continually. In spite of these surroundings, the Lloques were gracious, upbeat, and sociable when I visited.

In other more "modern" houses, small, locally made, boxlike iron "shepherd's stoves" belched smoke. The stovepipes in these often set thatched roofs afire as the continual heat dried pole-like roof supports into low-grade charcoal.

For that reason, most houses with stoves also had tile or beam and mud roofs neatly dividing the population into poor and poorest. Thatch and open hearth identified field hands. In contrast, a glass window and stovepipe were a sure sign that the household was headed by a mayoral, mayordomo, or equipment operator.

The Indians themselves were generally quite short— four foot ten to five foot two—and wiry. Most had flat feet, deeply calloused from their countless miles of walking barefoot on stony paths. Many were physically deformed—bent over, limping, or favoring bad arms that had not been set properly when broken. And, as Cayé had indicated, there were a number of adults missing parts of digits. *Holy smokes—have some of these really been bitten off by rats?* I wondered.

My answer came on the third day of census, just before I was scheduled to head uphill to Santa Isabel and catch the Friday afternoon bus back to Cuenca.

Manuel and I had gone down to a settlement of small houses near Los Faiques' cane fields. At one, we entered, made our gift of a liter of Kerex and a wick, then sat on a homemade wooden bench to talk to a godson of Manuel's. He was known simply as Tomás Chico, the thirtyish man of the house.

A few minutes into our conversation in broken Spanish, a woman emerged from the shadows carrying a baby. The woman began crying, disconsolately, "*Patrones, mi huahuita perdió tres dedos anteanoche. ¡Los ratones!* (Sirs, my baby girl lost three fingers night before last—the rats!)" Her baby's clothes were covered in dried blood. She moved to the doorway for light and held up a miniature hand to make her point—three tiny fingers were gone—grotesque, blackened stumps still oozing serum.

"My baby needs a doctor. For the saints' love, give us sucres to take her to the doctor," the woman sniffled. "Tomás's wife," whispered Manuel. "Unfortunate, but you do not need to respond, Señor Juan."

As I stared at the baby's fingers, my twin, aged six, popped into focus. A foster dad had burned little Eddy's fingers with a cigar lighter to "discipline him." Eddy looked at me, helpless. "Will I lose my fingers, John?" he'd sobbed in agony.

Tomás Chico, embarrassed, said something to her in Quechua, turned, and began to apologize to us in cryptic Spanish. I stopped him, palm up. "Señor, let me take her to the clinic in Cuenca with the child when the bus descends. If you approve, please have them ready by the side of the road."

"Are you certain?" Tomás asked. Manuel butted in, "You are accepting a huge obligation, Señor Juan." I paused. "I'm certain. Have her ready." Tomás nodded in approval as his stunned wife tried to kiss my hand without dropping her child. I left quickly. *Chump!* the Voice chastised me as I teared up walking alone to the big house. Intellectually, I knew that going soft meant trouble, but I hadn't been able to help it.

Cayé was already there waiting to help me carry my duffel on the long climb up to the bus. I pretended everything was normal, but he must have sensed something of my mood and omitted his usual constant chatter. I tipped him at the side of the road.

Aboard the bus, I settled in behind the driver and focused on practicalities. "Capitán, can you pick me up at the footpath to Los Faiques every other Thursday morning?"

"Of course, *meeester*; there is only a ten-sucre surcharge."

As we ground down the steep, muddy grade leading north from the village, I saw a small roadside group huddled at the mouth of Los Faiques' footpath. Efraín, Manuel, Tomás Chico, his woman, and baby at her breast all waited, along with an older Indian man I'd not met.

The driver opened the door and I stepped out to assist, but Manuel pushed forward and did the honors, while Efraín pulled me aside. "Not a word to the patrón, *please*. Nor to others. It is not customary for people of your puesto to concern themselves with the affairs of the *partidarios*" (formally, "sharecroppers," in reality, a euphemism for peasants who were bought and sold with the land).

"Muy bien—comprendo." Now it was Tomás Chico's turn to kneel and kiss my hand. *Christ!* I had an instant case of the cultural creeps. I wasn't the pope—I pulled my hand away. Having my hand kissed by a kneeling suppliant violated every American social instinct. I turned and stepped up into the bus, attempting to use visions of spring in Central Park to blot out the reality in front of me. I imagined brilliant yellow daffodils and bright crocuses peeking out from around the huge boulders above the pond at the park's lower entrance in Manhattan.

As I took my seat, I looked around for Tomás's wife—she was seated in the rear with the child. Manuel stuck his head in and whispered in my ear, "Señor Juan, it is important that you not acknowledge her on the bus. People will talk...make demands of you and *our patrón.* You must understand." I hadn't thought about the ripple effect. I nodded.

When the bus descended into Girón for its stop, I leaped out and ordered my tinto and steamed goat milk, handing the waitress a big clay mug of my own. "Coffee to go." And in a clean mug. Several passengers on the bus marveled at the *meeester*'s inventiveness. Any change from local custom, however infinitesimal, was big news in hell's waiting rooms.

Ten minutes after Girón, the bus pulled to an unexpected stop for an Ecuadorian jeep and half a dozen heavily armed soldiers. "Contraband check," whispered the driver over his shoulder. *"¡Pucha carajo!"* muttered someone behind me.

"How inconvenient," I answered the driver.

The driver exited to talk to a guy with polished jackboots who looked like he was in charge. I lit a smoke and relaxed. The driver's consultation did no good. Not a minute later, the bus's back door slammed open with a crash and three troopers charged in, frantically rummaging through the bags of every poncho wearer on the bus.

The soldiers were dark-skinned mestizos. Finding nothing in the rear of the bus, they started pushing the Indian men around. One young guy in dark hat and indigo poncho didn't shuffle fast enough for a tall corporal, who sank the butt of his rifle into the guy's crotch. Next, he and another soldier moved into the row where Tomás Chico's woman shielded her baby. Eddy looked at me with sad eyes. That did it. Ignoring Manuel's instructions, I stood up and moved toward the rear. "*¡Alto!* Corporal. Do not bother my *criada* and her baby!"

Amazed, the tall one stepped back and stared, incredulous. As he realized I was only a *meeester*, he tensed, ready to spring. I choked up on my walking stick and moved a step closer—balanced to nail the bastard in the throat. "No offense meant, Señor," came a smooth, oily voice from behind me. "Good," I replied, "then your men don't need rifles to check my bags under the front seat."

"We're done," came the silky reply. "*¡Desemboquen, muchachos!* (March out, boys!)" I turned. The captain nodded. I gave him a forced smile and offered him a cigarette. Not fooled, he declined, but stepped down from the bus anyway and again positioned himself regally on the tatty Jeep's front seat, nonchalantly waving his group forward.

The Indians in the rear were still gathering up their ransacked belongings as the driver hurriedly pulled the bus away before the captain could change his mind—or lost control of his frustrated mestizo troopers.

The rest of the trip was peaceful. Indeed, eerily quiet. In Cuenca, I stepped down, the other riders still whispering among themselves, collected my gear, and exited the bus yard, looking for Tomás's woman. She stood at curb-side, impassive, babe in arms. I stepped up to her and nearly fainted—I'd never gotten a close look at her in the dark house. She was *young*. But in the dark house at a few feet's distance it had been impossible to see that.

Her name was Araceli. "How old are you?" I asked. "Twenty, Patrón." She looked twice that age.

"*¿Recién casada?*" I inquired. She looked confused. "No . . . I have been Tomás's woman since I was fourteen."

"Oh, somehow I thought this might be your first child."

"No, she is my third, Patrón, but the others died. I so badly want her to live." *Take a deep breath,* I told myself, *two-thirds of the world lives with this shit every day.*

I hailed a cab, took Araceli to the large Santa Inés clinic across the Tomebamba, registered her, and gave the clerk a one-thousand-sucres advance on the bill. "Have the doctors see her. Clean the kid's stumps. Watch them for a day or two, longer if necessary, and discharge her with a generous supply of penicillin," I explained, handing her my business card. "Phone me if there are complications."

Araceli looked dazed and a bit terrified as they led her to the rear.

She stopped and turned to me, a pleading look in her eyes. "I've never been in a hospital, Señor. Will they permit me to go back to Tomás one day? How long must I work for them before I am free to go?"

"You will owe them nothing. They will send you home in a few days." She forced a half smile, but obviously couldn't quite believe me. "What must I do to repay you, Señor?"

"Nothing, Señora." The ward door opened, and the clerk nudged her through, still looking incredulous.

I stepped out into the street, gulped fresh air, and tried to squeeze the child's blackened stumps out of my brain. *Don't go soft, idiot,* the Voice scolded me. With the exception of my twin brother, my whole life was based on looking out for numero uno. That strategy had worked so far. No sense in fucking it up now.

But the truth was that my first weeks in Ecuador, and at Los Faiques, were both an eye-opener and an initiation into daily realities that were rawer than anything else I'd experienced.

The country had a remarkable way of getting past one's defenses, embedding itself under the skin like a blood-sucking tick. The resulting malady seemed to either make people mean and calculating or grind them down into nothingness. So far, Ecuador offered no compromises.

CHAPTER TEN

CUENCA

FEBRUARY 20

As I walked over to Avenida Solano, duffel over my shoulder, all I wanted were the luxury of a shower—and Livia. No Livia at home, I headed straight for the bathroom.

Towels, soap, running water. Giddy, I sang to myself, trying to forget the scenes of my first week in the valley of Yunguilla—instead picturing Livia...well, parts of her, I admit.

All fresh and smelling of soap instead of the fetid bacterial smell that consumed the peasants in Santa Isabel, I bought flowers at a streetside stand just across the Tomebamba and went to the stationery shop.

But when I stepped in and wiggled the flowers coyly, she looked up, her eyes wide and vacant. Then shook her head. "I expected you next Wednesday. Not today...Alex...there have been some changes."

99

"*¿Qué clase de cambios, Livia?*"

"Pués, I am no longer in residence at Solano. Andita and I are now living with my brother-in-law."

"Is this temporary?" She shook her head, no, and cried.

"What happened? Another attack?" I blurted out.

She stopped cold and stared, tears running down along her nose. "I am no longer permitted to see you. Nor is Anda, who is very disturbed by all this. She wants to continue her lessons."

"And you, Livia? Do you also want to see me?"

"I don't know what to think, Alex. Mostly, I'm feeling trapped. Just two days after you left, my brothers-in-law conferred with don Ben..." I stopped her. "*¿Malo?*"

She nodded, shrugging. "Fermín Veintimita protested Abelardo's decision to let me live my own life. The reigning 'council' of old men met and decided that it was an insult for me to reject a Veintimita—especially for a foreigner."

"In other words, if Veintimita can't have you, no one else can, either."

"Yes, especially a, uh..."

"*¿Meeester?*" I suggested. She nodded and shrugged again. "Do you own this store, Livia?"

"No."

"Do you have title to your house?"

"No—it is Gonzáles family property."

"I see... they leave a widow few choices, don't they?"

"Yes, I am now also like family property. Just as was my mother. Yet Abelardo is decent, like my husband. This bothers him deeply. At the moment, he is as trapped as I am."

"Want me to talk to him, Livia?"

"I don't know. I don't know anything just now..." Her composure used up, she went into weep mode, her deep, racking sobs full of anguish. Five fiancées in less than a decade and I still didn't know how to deal with it, so I panicked.

"Stop crying, Livia! I need you to answer *one* question for me." At least I'd gained her attention for a moment. She stared at me, so I asked, "What do *you* want?"

She stopped crying, but took a long time to answer... "Anda. A new life. You—maybe. Or, perhaps the way things were before you came... all so impossible... oh, Lord, how did I wind up like my mother—unable to give my child what she wants."

Blowing her nose, she went on, "And Anda wants the three of us together. For me to have the lover of my choice; she, the father she needs; you, the family you never really had. Something to keep you from drifting from country to country. World to world."

"Well, little Andy, as usual, is certainly clear on her plan for us all," I commented icily. Livia stared at me again. Perhaps reading my thoughts about "family," she panicked.

"You'd better go, Alex, before someone sees you here. But do talk to Abelardo, that is, if you really wish to."

I spent a long evening on the terrace at Solano. An even longer night processing the situation... and my own feelings. They had nearly always been a mystery to me. I was an outstanding observer of the world around me, yet only dimly aware of my own internal emotions.

No longer feeling so self-contained, I did not sleep well. The loss of my veneer was becoming profound, like an insidious reaction created by the sensation of falling into a world where puesto was everything and "free will" meant nothing. "I pissed on the Indian because my puesto permits it, *meeester*. Do not interfere..."

Well, for once I intended to do precisely that—enter the world around me. And interfere till people pissed on themselves, not on just another nameless unfortunate. *Shit,* I thought as I finally drifted into sleep, *I am becoming just like these bastards.*

Cuenca, February 21

When I visited him the next day, Abelardo was one very unhappy man. The Veintimitas had pulled rank on him. His sister-in-law wasn't speaking. His precocious little niece, on the other hand, wouldn't shut up and give him a break. Even his own wife and kids were on his ass over Livia's "house arrest."

I almost felt sorry for him. The poor fart had puesto troubles, women troubles, and ego troubles. Hell, he even had "male" troubles. His family were big investors in one of the Malo family's enterprises. At the moment, old don Benigno had an iron-gripped ball-lock on the entire Gonzáles clan. Abelardo was as helpless as the rest of us.

We talked in the library, a white-jacketed manservant standing by in case our hot tea needed freshening. Yep. I bet it was hard to face giving up a lifestyle like that, especially when it had probably taken several centuries and lots of ugly compromises to establish it. It struck me that the line between realists and cynics simply might not exist in Ecuador—a place where facing reality itself required one to be a cynic.

Abelardo wanted to know my intentions with regard to Livia. I thought for several minutes then, consciously rejecting the cynical, I leveled with him. "I don't yet know. I have a girlfriend in Mexico—a butterfly, rather like all the others I've dated. Livia is so different. A woman, yet an innocent...it's hard to explain...it, it...makes me want to do both the right thing and to possess her as any man would wish."

"Actually, Señor Alexander, it is easy for me to comprehend this and to appreciate that you actually understand Livia. Yet, I am at a loss in this matter. The Malos... well..."

"I also understand, Señor Gonzáles. For the moment, patience seems to be in order."

"PATIENCE! How dare you say such a thing, John Alexander," an outraged Andy shouted at us from the doorway. She'd snuck in behind the manservant, who looked as if he was about to suffer a heart attack. Abelardo silenced her—"To your room, young lady. *Now.*"

"If you will do nothing, Uncle, then *I* will talk to don Benigno. *I* am not afraid of him."

That pretty much wore out the frayed ends of Abelardo's sufferance. He grabbed Andy with a jerk, palm open, and was about to slap her on the butt when his wife came in, hissed, and pulled the kid away before Abelardo could spank her. In parting, she gave Abelardo the look that nearly all men fear. One that actually keeps some men, me among them, bachelors.

I wasn't all that afraid of Veintimita's mayorales, or even death. But a righteously pissed-off woman—orphanage director, social worker, Latin teacher, or lover—was altogether another matter. That Abelardo shared my fear was obvious. I saved him. "Whooh... her look unnerved me."

He grinned. "She's *very* good at it. You should see her when she's really angry."

"No, thanks, don Abelardo, I'm not that tough. I'd better be going. Can we talk again in a week or so?"

"Certainly. It is an untenable situation. I have even discussed it with my half brother, Nestor." *Aha,* I thought.

I did figure him for some sort of relative. I took my leave, walking along the Tomebamba, watching kids play and the Indian servant women rhythmically beating their rich patrones' clothes on the smooth rocks below. Incongruous.

Frustrated, I returned to Solano. The electricity malfunctioning, I lit candles to brighten the room as late afternoon storm clouds gathered. Soon everything in sight would be cold, gray, and soaked again.

An hour later, it was pouring outside, so I started a fire in the small corner fireplace, pulled up a leather chair, and drank some cheap, high-octane Peruvian *pisco*. It didn't help.

About eight that evening, someone entered the main house. I hoped that it might be Livia, but after rummaging around for a few minutes, whoever it was came to my door, knocking heavily. Definitely not Livia. I grabbed my stick and cracked open the door. It was Nestor—looking panicked.

"Have you seen Andita? She's missing. Livia thought she might be here."

"No, I'd have made her call Livia if I'd seen her. Did you try the maid's quarters out back?"

"Yes—no one has been there." As we stood there, Livia's phone began to ring. It didn't stop, so Nestor went back inside to check, then shouted, "She's been found!" He locked up quickly and stopped briefly at my door. "She's OK—I must go now."

"Do you need company?"

"No—it's family business. Besides, you are nearly drunk. You smell of pisco." *He has a point,* I conceded to myself as the car door slammed and the vintage straight-eight Pontiac rumbled away. I threw more wood on the fire and apparently finished off the pisco.

It was midmorning when I came around. My head throbbed even more intensely than the night I'd gotten it bashed. Worse yet, I'd barfed all over myself and smelled to high heaven. In order to move I had to first untangle myself from an overturned chair. "Nice work, JA," I said out loud.

It took quite some time for me to pull myself together, reshower, bag my stinking clothes, find clean ones, and mop up the tile floor. I heated canned soup on my hot plate, dressed, and decided to walk over to the stationery store.

When I got there the place was locked up. Same story at Abelardo's—no one there but a groundskeeper, who had absolutely nothing to say about anything. *Well, it's Ecuador,* I reasoned. *There is no sense to be made of it.* Disgusted with myself, life, women, cut-rate assignments, kids, dogs, and anything to do with puesto or patrones, I set out walking.

At the southern edge of town, beyond the Solano district, the rough pavement turned to dirt. The sodden roadway turned into mud the consistency of wet concrete, and it began to rain again. The cold, driving rain generated puffs of steam that rose from the highway, warmed by flashes of morning sun.

An hour or more into my walk, the road turned into a long, grinding uphill grade pointing out of the Cuenca basin. I followed, my poncho heavy and soaked despite the oiled rain cape. A steady stream of water poured down from the brim of my felt hat.

My misery and disgust began to subside, replaced by a numbing resignation. I talked to myself off and on, carrying on two-part arguments with don Benigno, Livia, and whichever Veintimita was responsible for the current state of affairs.

The road flattened out at about nine thousand feet in elevation and I was in the sticks. Indian laborers in their district ponchos trudged along, huge loads of pottery, firewood, or corn suspended from hemp nets, supported by forehead tumplines.

I was still muttering to myself when one group passed me, close by. Three sets of ropy jaw muscles protruded from beneath battered bowler hats, working away furiously to masticate the coca leaves many Indians chewed to soften the cold, hunger, and pain of endless toil, and here I was in a funk over a dozen stitches and a ruined date.

Relaxing a bit, I tried to enjoy the scent of the rain and the misty vistas of ancient stone-walled farm plots lined by tall, spindly rows of eucalyptus. Then it started raining harder again, right on cue—as if Ecuador was itself a sentient being determined to squash any hint of inner peace that intruded on its existential version of misery. *There will be no free will*, the sheets of rain seemed to murmur.

Lost in that odd little fantasy discourse, I didn't notice a car shadowing me until the horn tooted and a rear window rolled down. Instinctively, I tightened my grip on the walking stick as the black Mercedes pulled alongside. *A black Mercedes, here? Now what!* I thought.

But instead of a scene from *The Godfather*, an older gent in the rear seat motioned me over in a beautiful upper-class British accent. "I'd like to meet you, young man. I'm Benigno Malo. May we talk a moment?"

"Certainly, sir. I'm honored," I heard myself say, then thought, *Jesus! Now I'm kissing ass like everyone else around here.*

I leaned to the window, resting my elbows on the door-sill. Don Benigno was seated serenely, but regally erect, alone in the backseat of his town car, his black briar-handled brolly rolled tightly, supporting him like a cane.

He got right to the point. "University of Edinburgh, they say." I nodded. He went on. "Ecuador needs new blood. Bright young men to add a progressive tone. Young men who can fit in, but see possibilities, where we only see the dictates of tradition. Are you such a young man...?" Instinctively, I answered in the formal Spanish I'd once used to address my professors in Mexico City.

"I am not certain, sir. I am still sorting out my life's goals."

"Would one of them be a good woman?"

"I had thought so until the last few days, but there have been obstacles."

"So I heard. At least, that is the view of a rather remarkable child I met recently. That child thinks highly of you...do not disappoint her." *Hmm, the kid looks up to me. Why does that make her my problem?* I grumbled to myself. He paused again, then ever so courteously noted, "The poncho and Indian hat do not become you, young man."

He tapped the floor with his brolly, resplendent in a magnificently tailored British suit. In response, the car pulled away gently, so as not to spray me with mud.

Whooh! A Mercedes town car materializes out of nowhere, on a muddy road to nowhere, and a guy in impeccable Oxford English holds forth, recruiting for the local intellectual pool—well, more accurately, the local gene pool—then disappears. He even seemed sincere. Perhaps that was what made him a grandee in these parts.

On the other hand, he wasn't so sincere that he actually wanted my scruffy, rain-soaked ass soiling the spotless leather rear seat of his town car.

It sounded as if little Andy had made good on her threat to go to Cuenca's leading citizen. So, the kid might not have been missing at all but, just like me, "on assignment." Remarkable. Was the kid the only person left in Ecuador exercising free will? I kept walking.

An hour later, the rain let up and a huge mixto heading toward Cuenca labored up the grade below. I walked to the other side of the road, my hat waving. As he stopped I passed a twenty-sucre note up and climbed to a wooden bench just under the edge of the truck's dripping canvas tarp.

Back at Solano I collected my gear and arranged for an early pickup on the morning bus to Santa Isabel. Nestor came by briefly to check the house. He didn't knock, and I didn't go out. If no one was going to update me, I certainly wasn't going to ask. "Free will" was the issue. I'd already compromised it enough. On the other hand, Andy hadn't. That impressed me.

In the morning, the bus tooted and I carried my gear out. Love interests aside, it was back to my cut-rate assignment—my penance for failing the free-will test by not pulling up stakes and walking away from Penrod's "Please do this one for me, JA."

CHAPTER ELEVEN

HACIENDA
LOS FAIQUES
FEBRUARY 23–28

I was in a sulk all the way to Santa Isabel. Why had Livia not contacted me? And why did I care? At least the bus stopped at Los Faiques' footpath, saving me a half-hour walk from town.

Back at the big house, I stowed my gear, curious at the layer of dust and gritty, brown-speckled material that had blanketed everything in my room.

When Efraín came up I asked him about it. "The patrón arrives Friday. We have been preparing for his arrival—working in the loft and cleaning up the kitchen area. It is only dust and fragments of corn husk on your bed."

"Can I borrow a broom?"

"Yes, but it is customary to delegate such work. I will arrange it...and not a word to the patrón about the *indita* and the baby, OK?"

"Fine—and how are they?"

"They arrived yesterday in a mixto. The child will live. Chico's woman is very grateful. It will be she who sweeps your room and does such chores."

"I don't want repayment, Efraín."

"I know. But they wish to show you that they are honorable *gente* and not *indios brutos aprovechándole* (wild Indians taking advantage of you)."

"Then send her to clean my room."

Cayé appeared, having heard I'd arrived. I sent him for supplies and went below for tea, fruit, and a handful of my own trail mix.

Araceli cleaned my room while I enjoyed my tea. She passed my table as I finished breakfast and made additions to my field notes. She said nothing but curtsied quickly and smiled openly as she walked past. I looked away, uncomfortable at the curtsy.

I'd boned up on Ecuador at the New York City public library before my trip. Indians had been "paying" whites with labor for more than four centuries. The *mita* it was once called—the obligatory four long days of weekly work demanded in payment for the right to farm tiny garden plots on the lands of the great hacendados. Of course, before these hacendados arrived, it had been the Indians' land anyway, and the Incas had demanded the same from them. So nothing had really changed except the destruction of traditional religion and expanded labor burdens imposed by colonial Spanish overlords.

By the time I left the table, the usual crowd of onlookers were beginning to drift away. Every time I wrote, either in the breakfast area or on the gallery above, both Indian kids and adults gathered silently to watch every pen stroke. The miracles of writing and reading made one powerful.

Few Indians in the Yunguilla district were able to do either, and the crowd had become bolder with familiarity. At first they positioned themselves at a distance of twenty feet, then ten feet or so. By this second trip to Los Faiques they were just three feet from me and inching closer to watch the proceedings over my shoulder.

"Can you write in Quechua?" asked Feliciana, a giggling teenage niece of Efraín's who spoke decent Spanish.

"No, I only know a few words of your language. But I can write in Spanish, English, and French."

"Imagine," said her more reserved twin sister, Ofélia. But the less timid Feliciana was still curious. "What is this 'French,' Señor Juan?"

"It is the language of the country of France. In Europe—east across another ocean."

"Have you actually seen this place?"

"Yes, Señorita, I have friends there. It's lovely. Paris, its capital, has many huge parks and wide boulevards."

"And the poor people?"

"There are few poor. It's not like Ecuador. There are no haciendas as you know them."

The twins gaped. Everyone on the hacienda liked these girls—they were bubbly, fair complected, and adorable. When they visited their boyfriends—the Lloque brothers—there was always music and laughter.

Then one of the adult men made a suggestion. "We would give you songs and traditional stories, *meeester*, if you taught our children of the world and wrote an important letter now and again for someone in need."

JA—smart-ass turned country scribe? I had begun to decline politely when loquacious Manuel caught my eye from behind the crowd, nodding his head, yes, animatedly. Manuel had accompanied me on all my census forays and folks looked up to him. So I switched midsentence and accepted.

Just as quickly, my job got much easier. That afternoon, I explained "France" to about twenty Indians, mostly kids, including Feliciana and Ofélia, then got invited into house after house to set up interviews. No more dogs, no more Kerex, but cigarettes for the adults and candy for the kids still much appreciated.

Later, down at the Lloque family's house, I was formally introduced to Ofélia and Feliciana. As always, the Lloques were cordial. Marco and Antonio were about eighteen and clearly besotted with the twins who had been born and raised at La Atalaya.

It turned out that the Lloque brothers' courtships of Efraín's twin nieces had reached a crucial stage, and talk of engagements was in the air. The aura of young love cleansed and brightened the usually oppressive farmhouse.

Tired, I went to bed early and slept well until the familiar overhead thumping wakened me. The room smelled funny and my face was spattered with some kind of rancid goo. I lit the lantern, instantly wishing I hadn't.

The ceiling was leaking thick, viscous drops of black, smelly liquid and two immense rats on the floor near the chifforobe twitched and jerked in slow circles, vomiting the very same goo that was falling in thick gobs from the caned ceiling twelve feet overhead. It was like a scene right out of Dante's *Inferno*.

Rats shrieked and fought in the ceiling above me. Spasmodic thumps echoed for the rest of the night. I pulled my bedroll out to the porch, washed my face with water from the green bottle, then spent the remainder of the night on the chilly gallery, avoiding the horror inside.

Efraín tapped me on the shoulder about 6 AM. "What's wrong?"

"It's raining rat vomit and black liquid in my room. What the hell is the black stuff and what caused it?"

He looked inside, making odd, grossed-out noises and shaking his head. "The liquid is rat blood. I didn't know it would be so bad. The men put 1080 rat poison in the loft. They may have used too much." *No shit,* I thought, but merely nodded. "Ten-eighty" rat poison had long been outlawed in the States—far too toxic for everything in the food chain, including dogs, kids, and pregnant women.

Efraín took off to the Indian settlement below the lip of the hill, returning with half a dozen women to scrub everything and throw any dead, or dying, rats into a big flour sack. My room was to get the workout as well. The next hour was spent securing valuables from the patrón's quarters down in the hacienda office.

I got one look at the main bedroom when I helped Efraín lug a heavy antique chest full of "valuables" down the staircase to the office. It was a big room, about eighteen or twenty feet deep and more than twenty feet wide. Nicely furnished with late colonial antiques, the rough plank floor had been covered with several magnificent hand-tied wool carpets made in the Ambato and Riobamba areas nearly two hundred miles to the north. They were as well made as midgrade Persians, only thicker, and in rich shades of gray, umber, and chestnut.

When we got the patrón's heavy chest downstairs and paused to catch our breath, I noticed that there were monstrous dead rats lying all over the plazuela. Efraín panicked as several of the nearby Indian women scooped them up in their picturesque, but smelly, multilayered *pollera* skirts.

"Don't take the patrón's rats!" shouted Efraín. But to no avail. The women scooped them into their billowing skirts and ran off.

"*¡Pucha carajo!*" he growled. "We are going to have sick workers all over the place, and the patrón is due in but one day." Two of the youngest, apprenticed, one-day-to-become "mayorales" were dispatched immediately to retrieve as many rats as possible. "The stupid Indians will roast them for meat, then the poison will give everyone bloody cramps. *¡Puchaaa, carajote!*"

The situation called for desperate measures. You couldn't have the patrón show up with his labor force all indisposed by bloody runs. Several boys were recruited to collect piles of small rocks and use their woven slings to bean anyone stealing rats from the plazuela. The kids were deadly with those modest two-foot-long braided–yucca fiber slings. Whoosh, whoosh, whoosh, wham, plunk! Several volleys were all it took.

The amount of shouting, arm waving, and cursing was spectacular: "*¡Indio bruto, lárgate!* (Shove off, you savage!)*"; "*¡Cholo malcriado!* (Rotten, spoiled mestizo wannabe!)*"; "*¡Bestia rapaz!* (You thieving female animal!)*"

Ironically, this fracas seemed to lower tensions after an hour or so. Manuel and Efraín broke out a liter of cheap trago, inviting the combatants to have a drink on the far side of the plazuela. Several of the Indian men pulled out their pan flutes. Another brought his small guitar, a third, his homemade fiddle.

Some of the patrón's dried corn was passed out as a peace offering to replace the rats, and Manuel gave a sucre coin to everyone above the age of ten who helped clean up. María added potatoes to a huge pot of beans that had been cooking all morning and started to boil yellow rice.

Someone yelled, "Hey, *meeester*—give us fifty sucres for the fiesta of San Ysidro and we'll play traditional songs for you." I glanced at Efraín—he nodded, but touched his elbow—local sign language for "too much, cut the price." I gave them thirty sucres and the band grew to five men.

I raced up to my room and grabbed my battery-powered tape recorder. It was the first time I ever heard lovely traditional tunes like "Antonio Mocho" (Crippled Anthony), "Leña Verde" (Green Firewood), and "Si Tuviera una Pluma" (If I Had a Pen; that is, if I knew how to write).

An hour and a half later, the cane whiskey was gone, the beans and rice eaten, and the house and grounds surprisingly clean. It would take the last of the tougher rats yet another day or so to expire, twitching and vomiting thick, putrid blood, but the worst of the crisis had passed.

Nervous tensions rose again the next morning by eight as the heads of household in the surrounding settlements gathered on the edges of the big house's plazuela to await the patrón—don Ramón Uribe. Their expectation was heightened by the rumor that his wife and a son would be with him. It was still the social season in Cuenca, so there were virtually no hacendados' wives or daughters in the valley. The families came in the drier months of mid-May to early September—probably a centuries-old response to endemic malaria in subtropical niches like Yunguilla. Even I knew enough to take the new drug, Arelin, to prevent it.

The morning hours passed, the men waiting with passive resignation. It was almost noon before a big, old Land Rover came grinding over the dirt track above the footpath. The vehicle wheeled around the plazuela in a cloud of smoke and pulled to a stop in front of the hacienda's office door.

Out stepped don Ramón, followed by his senior mayordomo, Antonio—Manuel and Efraín's boss—from behind the wheel. Uribe ritually embraced each of his mayordomos in turn, then his two young mayorales. No family in sight and nothing murmured of it, he turned to his sharecroppers, who were lined up from the most senior to most junior in a reasonable facsimile of "at attention."

Uribe was expansive. "*¡Buenos días, muchachos!* The cane harvest needs to be speeded up before prices drop. My mayorales will direct you. We also need to add more papayas when the rains end. Thank you." The group made compliant noises. Some nodded.

Flanked by his mayordomo and mayorales, don Ramón then received each man individually. The ritual was quick and methodic. Each stepped forward quickly, stooped, and kissed the back of their hacendado's extended hand. That he wore a Michigan State class ring on that hand substantially enhanced the surrealism. All I could think of was the pope's ring.

After the kiss, Antonio, the mayordomo, handed each man either his month's wages or a slip acknowledging his additional debt to the owner for seed or necessities. The wage earners and debtors were about equal in the crowd of fifty-odd men. That likely meant that 300 to 350 total occupants, or about sixty households, lived on Los Faiques' deeded land. Most of the "family plots" awarded by the owner had to have been tiny.

The few plots I'd already paced off ranged in size from a quarter to half an acre. That was enough to feed two or three people at most, but most households averaged five to six individuals.

On the other hand, no one seemed to be afraid of Señor Uribe. Dressed in madras shirt, pressed khakis, and polished Wellingtons, he was handsome, educated, about five foot eight, and had a pleasant, if businesslike, air about him. And his mayorales, based on my own experience, were decent men.

The ritual over, the assembled disbanded and went back to work. Efraín and Manuel stood by with María after the table was set. Uribe and I lunched with Antonio, the mayordomo. They were pleasant but formal. Uribe was gracious. "How go your *investigaciones*?"

"Quite well. I've visited some of the households, asking questions about ancestry and folktales."

"Have my people cooperated?"

"Mostly. Some are shy around a stranger like me, which is pretty ordinary, so I've focused on performances."

"*Performances*? I don't follow."

"Of course, Señor Uribe...I should have explained. In the evenings María occasionally serves beans and rice to a small group of musicians. I provide the beans, rice, and cigarettes. I set up my tape recorder. People are more open in song and as a group. Less shy. It's enjoyable."

"Oh, that sounds interesting. Has it been successful?"

"Yes. I've collected some local songs, taped a number of regional ones, and have begun to interview the long-term Indian families about any oral traditions relating to the Inca. I am still learning key words in Quechua that might trigger my interest."

"Interesting, Señor Alexander," Uribe interrupted, "and what might some of those key words be?" *At least he didn't use the "meeester,"* I thought.

"Things like 'tambo,' 'Inga-anything,' like 'Ingapirca' (Inca walls) . . . all the words like that."

"Old Manuel speaks some Quechua. I'll ask him to help you." Uribe waved expansively in Manuel's direction.

"Thanks. He's been very helpful—introducing me to some of the indigenous families here." Manuel beamed, but kept his distance.

"Good. And are you learning much about the hacienda business?"

Sounding flustered, I answered, "Well, I am embarrassed to say so, but not much. I have been busy with the songs and fragments of old stories. I hope that is all right." As I suspected, that proved to be the right answer. He and Antonio relaxed instantly.

"Oh, quite all right. Professor Saldívar told me that such a folklore study would, quite likely, be published by the Casa de Cultura in Cuenca."

"Really, Señor Uribe. That is exciting."

"Call me Ramón. May I call you Juan?"

"Of course, Ramón. Delighted." *My lips are chapped from this bullshit, but it just might work,* I consoled myself.

And it did. He and Antonio beamed at one another. I settled for beaming inwardly.

"Good, Juan—can you play cards with us tonight? Some of my colleagues—other hacendados—are coming over. It will give you a chance to meet them. Do you know how to play draw poker?"

"Not well, but I'd enjoy the diversion."

"Good. That's settled—at nine this evening, then. Now to farm business."

They left, and I took off to the settlement below to conduct interviews. I stuck strictly to questions about songs and legends, figuring that every hacendado had a couple of stoolies in his flock, as had been the case in southern Mexico. I was particularly cautious in houses where the garden plots were larger than average or where folks seemed suspiciously well-off. "Well-off" meant meat, cigarettes, shoes, or newish clothing. There were several possible spies who asked me furtive questions.

But most were ordinary wretches living in their dark, fetid houses, squealing guinea pigs constantly underfoot. Those houses were hard to stomach. Besides, one could not actually see who might be in the shadows. So, I dragged the menfolk outside whenever possible...and some of the traditional tales they told me were interesting. The colonial Spanish conquest may have ended the Inca as a political entity but had never extinguished many of its daily cultural realities.

The hacendados, according to María, were off eating dinner somewhere. About 9:15, Uribe's Land Rover returned. Others followed over the next half hour. The poker party was set up in the hacienda's office.

I got introduced around. Several Crespos, a younger Saldívar, the village pharmacist, a "by marriage" member of the Malo dynasty, and, at last, Fermín Veintimita, who glared petulantly when greeting me. *"¡Mucho gusto, meeester!"* The others had used the courtesy of "señor"—reserved in those parts for humans, specifically whites, and those from whom one sought favor.

119

Veintimita surprised me. He was short, thick, about forty, balding, and had about a three-day stubble of unshaved beard. He needed a bath and his weak little piggy eyes didn't add much, either. He blinked incessantly and had a hard time reading the cards.

The game itself went well. I lost, which pleased everyone, and there were snacks—lots of them. *Cuy* (guinea pig) on roasting sticks, popcorn, the goat cheese and potato llapingachos, crackers, and cheese. Plus lots of booze. Mostly cheap brandy. Veintimita glared at me all evening, raising "the *meeester*'s" bets defiantly, his hand shaking each time he raised.

It took me only an hour to figure out that the hand shaking wasn't merely about anger and nerves. It was clearly also about blood-alcohol levels. Fermín, with his stubborn little pig face, was an angry, but hopeless, boozer. No wonder he revolted Livia.

I quit the party about 1 AM, leaving the others to drink and talk. Uribe was scheduled to be off somewhere on Saturday and I had real interviews to start in the early AM. As I mounted the stairs I heard a familiar keening falsetto giggle from one of the Land Rovers at the side of the plazuela. The Voice was already on full alert, warning me to watch my back, before the prick even spoke.

"*Meeester*—I see you. Sleep lightly, *meeester*. Hee, hee, hee." Then, Baritone laughed. "Bedtime, *meeester*." Apparently, Veintimita traveled with a pack.

Showing no outward sign of hearing them, I faked drunk, pulling myself carefully up the stairs and along the rail. "Hee, hee, hee, aack. *¡El meeester está borracho!* Hee, hee, hee."

I staggered inside, closing the door behind me. Then got to work, quickly setting the rattrap by the door and rolling blankets to make it look like I was in bed. I extinguished the lantern and withdrew to the utter dark of the empty far corner—walking stick in one hand, my French knife in the other.

The party below was, if anything, still cranking up. Loud laughter and the clink of bottlenecks on glass drifted up from below. With luck, one of the mayorales wouldn't be able to resist staging an "accident." I imagined the explanation. "*Meeester* was drunk and fell over the rail, hitting his head. We both saw him fall, Patrón."

Thirty minutes into my wait, I needed to pee and was about to give up when the door opened a crack, the light from below illuminating a small vertical strip of wall just three feet from my right shoulder. I tightened my grip on the stick.

It was Falsetto. Damn, I'd heard nothing. No boot steps, not even a scrape on the planked gallery. Perhaps he was better at this than I had reckoned. He paused, then stepped forward quickly, his brass club poised to brain my blankets.

I heard a creepy, high-pitched "Hee, hee, hee . . ." interrupted by a sharp *clang! snap!* then a falsetto scream, "Yaaah!" Instinctively, he jerked his foot upward, trying to get away. When the spike came down, he jumped two feet straight up, driving it in even deeper, and started crying like a baby.

El Garrote backed out to the porch railing, crying, *"¡Mamá!"* No wonder. The prick had taken off his boots to come up the stairs.

The Rover door below opened with a clang and Baritone started up the stairs just as his buddy went over the railing backward, my rattrap still attached, blubbering like a baby. I heard a sickening thud when he hit the cobbles. For one moment, it was very quiet. The laughter below ceased abruptly and the office door popped open. *"¡Qué carajo!"* someone shouted. I dropped the old-fashioned latch on my door, stripped off my clothes, and hopped into bed to pretend I'd been asleep.

Baritone's voice answered, "The *meeester* did something to Garrote. I *saw* him." Silence, then, "*¡Pucha carajo!* It's one of my rattraps from El Cantón," came Uribe's voice, clearly pissed off. "Has this skinny cholo bastard been stealing from me *again*? Serves him right."

Baritone interjected, but that just made Uribe angrier. "It's *not* the *meeester*—he's just an academic sissy who wants desperately to become a professor someday. Veintimita—ask your man to drive this SOB up to the 'clinic' in Santa Isabel...or to Cuenca. Your mayorales are troubled children—get them out of here."

I imagined Veintimita's little pig eyes spinning in their sockets as he ordered Baritone to get El Garrote into the Rover. He left with them, in a drunken huff from the sound of things.

I should have been thrilled. Stepping into the trap in stockinged feet had been at least a hundred-to-one shot. But Garrote's baby screams and crying for his mama only made me sick. And none of the hacendados had even asked if he was alive.

They went back to drinking, laughing, and poker, ragging loudly on what a "douche" Veintimita was and speculating on why his old man put up with the sons.

I tried to sleep, but Ecuador dominated my dreams... "Because we can, *meeester*. Our puesto permits it."

Worse yet, I'd laid the rattrap just like a sneaky kid myself. The moral line that divided Garrote and me had narrowed considerably since the night I'd arrived in Ecuador.

I had the morning tea and fruit to myself. Everyone was apparently sleeping it off, the other hacendados' vehicles still parked in the plazuela. Cayé came about 7:30 AM to get money for the early Sunday market-day purchase of eggs and meat.

"I want six eggs and two pieces of flank steak—about a third of a kilo should do."

"So many eggs, Patrón? It is hard to buy that many at once."

"Do your best, Cayé. Bring the purchases early, as I am going to spend most of the day observing the market activities."

He smiled, collected his second two weeks' wages, plus cash for purchases, and disappeared. I walked down to the settlement with Manuel, who said casually, "Efraín likes you a lot. 'Someone' mysteriously took a rattrap from the patrón's quarters last night. I thought that this news might intrigue you."

I smiled. "Efraín and you are gente—always doing wise things. Resolving mysteries. Many things you do intrigue me."

"Well then, Señor Juan, let's go see Tomás Chico and his woman—a quick visit. Five minutes, no more. It's important."

"Muy bien, Manuel, if it matters."

Tomás Chico was waiting for us, holding a jiggling gunnysack. Manuel stepped away, granting us privacy. Tomás had a story for me: "Patrón, my señora was doing her mita in don Ramón's kitchen last night. She heard and saw certain 'events.' When the mayoral fell, she realized that you, ah... 'lost' the rattrap Cayé bought for you. *Ahora está allá la trampa* (the trap is there again) in your room. I thought you should know this."

"That was *very* thoughtful of her." I grinned, jubilant. "I despise rats!" He laughed and continued, "Quite a large, nasty one was caught last night in the patrón's quarters, it is said. This particular rat is widely hated and feared. Very crazy. Very destructive. Be careful of it and its friends, Señor Juan!"

"I'll be careful." I chuckled. Tomás smiled.

"The *runa* (Quechua-speaking Indians) here in the valley are all intermarried. My wife's sister is married to a farmer at La Atalaya. The runa are grateful." Then, he handed me the gunnysack. "A gift—the two fattest cuy from my kitchen, Patrón."

"I couldn't, Tomás. Besides, I don't cook. I have no woman to care for me." Manuel, overhearing, stepped in. "I will ask María to prepare them for you at the big house."

"You must, Patrón. My wife insists...and she asks the great honor of a dance with you at the fiesta of San Ysidro in two weeks. Our baby is doing well, thanks to you."

I took the cuy, handing the sack to Manuel, shook Tomás Chico's hand, and told him we were even-Steven. He waved as we walked away. Manuel became effusive.

"This has all worked out well. The 'rat' will live. *It* is being tended to at a clinic in Cuenca, but Veintimita was humiliated, so he has recently discharged the rat. Only the big mayoral with the voice like a *tambor* (native drum) remains."

"You are a fountain of information, Manuel. Only *one* mayoral short, eh?"

"One cannot have everything. Deliverance comes in many small steps, Señor Juan."

Manuel—a mixed-blood, minor factotum on a banana and cane farm in the middle of nowhere—was a philosopher. In a country where reticence and guile were art forms, Manuel, loquacious and open, was, like Andy, living proof that some were above the Ecuador Effect.

Everywhere I went that Saturday, the Indian menfolk nodded and doffed their hats. On the way back to the big house at the end of the day, I asked Manuel, "Are there *any* secrets in these parts?"

"No, Señor Juan. None."

CHAPTER TWELVE

MARKET DAY— SANTA ISABEL

MARCH 1

O n Sunday morning I had two fried eggs and flame-toasted bread with my tea and fruit. No one from the local constabulary had come to inquire about the rattrap incident and Cayé was anxious to take me up to market.

When we topped the hill and turned the corner into the plaza, it was a remarkable scene. Tents and market stalls had been set up everywhere. Big, brightly painted mixtos laden with fruit, cloth, and manufactured goods were lined up along the side streets and midmorning Mass had drawn an overflow crowd. I don't know if "vibrant" was the right adjective, but "crowded" certainly worked.

So did "aromatic." As in any highland Ecuadorian crowd, I simply could not escape the heavy scents of sweat, urine, and other body odors that enveloped the plaza. Think of fourteenth-century Europe when everyone bought new clothes once a year and personal hygiene was an exotic concept. Add the bright Ecuadorian sun, some rotting fruits, a bit of tainted meat roasting over open fires, and a touch of vomit, and there you have market day.

Cayé served at the 2 PM Mass, so he gave me a hurried tour. The crowd was colorful. Deep maroon, black, tan, and wondrously striped district ponchos all collided, a whirl of colors topped off by the white straw and black or green felt hats that marked different highland districts.

Their off-white ponchos and pearly *toquilla* (palm) panama hats identified those from the Pasajé and Machala districts. Jaunty sulfuric white straw hats with black bands and fuchsia or indigo ponchos identified women from Cañar and the Indian settlements surrounding Cuenca.

After Cayé left for the church I wandered down to the cantón's administrative building. Sure enough, a row of Jeeps and Land Rovers were lined up out front, the offices staffed with professionals who had come in from Cuenca—a doctor, several nurses, a public health officer, a surveyor, a notary, and the magistrate.

Everything and everyone "official" had descended upon Santa Isabel for the day, recording marriages, land sales, debts, and settling land disputes, surveys, even minor court cases.

Through the tall, iron-barred window, I could see someone wearing a poncho sentenced to "two weeks' labor for the cantón" on a drunk and disorderly charge. Gaunt and trembling, he protested, "My babies will starve if I cannot work!"

"You should have thought of them before you spent your wages on trago," snapped the magistrate.

"Please, Patrón. Let me pay a fine. I must work!"

"Fortunately, I am not your patrón. In fact, he has my sympathies. *You* are responsible for your own misfortune. This case is closed. *Next...*" The bailiff dragged the Indian away, still pleading.

Several minutes later, a light-skinned, disreputable-looking mestizo in European dress was fined a comparatively modest fifty sucres cash for the very same infraction. His attorney protested and the fine was reduced to forty without comment. As for the last four hundred years, Indians paid in undervalued labor; others paid in silver.

Yet, at the Civil Registry I was surprised to discover that Indians paid less than whites to register a birth or marriage. "Why is this so?" I asked one well-dressed, light-skinned onlooker.

"It encourages the brutos to marry like more civilized people, *meeester*. Still, most of them do not. Two-thirds of them are bastards—a black mark on Ecuador's Catholic faith." I thanked him for the explanation, rolling my eyes as I walked away. Ecuador's "new leaf" of social change was still not obvious to me.

A large group of Indians had gathered near the burro stables at one corner of the plaza. At the opposite corner, the mestizos and cholos gathered. Meanwhile, the mighty—very light-skinned elites—stuck close to the church and administrative offices.

I headed toward the Indians and the music that had struck up. Dozens, already half drunk on trago, twirled, or staggered, to the beat of the music.

At the Indians' corner of the plaza, I had just begun to melt into the crowd when, suddenly, it parted, leaving me alone. I was white and, by custom, Indians made way for white guys. So I backed out of their colorful mayhem and, lighting a smoke, lounged against the pharmacy's wall nearby. The crowd quickly closed up again, returning to its own internal rhythm.

Absorbed in the exotic scene, I jumped and damn near had a coronary when someone tapped me on the shoulder, thinking it was Baritone. It was Nestor, and he read me accurately.

"The mayorales are in Cuenca, Señor. One of them suffered an unfortunate accident."

"I heard, Nestor. I was asleep and missed out on the fun." He looked bemused. I continued, "And what are *you* doing here? Has Livia come with you?"

"No, she is still in Cuenca, and still both angry at everyone and frightened, but Anda is here with me and wants to talk to you."

"Andy? Where?"

"I have the car one street away. Will you talk to her? She is afraid to approach you herself."

"I'll follow you."

Elbowing our way through the crowd of Indians was tough work. Passing through the cluster of cholos and mestizos at the far corner of the plaza was even tougher. Several of the macho pricks delivered jolting shoulder blocks as I passed, then turned quickly to pretend nothing had happened.

Nestor noticed. A moment later, one tallish, dandified, light-skinned fellow braced to shoulder me when I passed. Focused on me, he didn't notice Nestor's foot out to trip him as he surged forward. He still had a smug grin when his face hit the plaza's hard-packed dirt. I complemented Nestor. *"¡Bien hecho!"* He laughed. "My pleasure."

When we reached the car, Andy was, for the first time, tentative. She stood by the rear door, staring at her feet. "John Alexander, I am sorry that I was so rude to you. I asked Nestor to bring me today, hoping we'd find you. Mother is not behaving well—she is so frightened, even paranoid, that she simply cannot think. She does not even eat."

"I don't believe I can help much with that, Andy. I don't think your mother wants me around her."

Andy was quiet for a moment, then incisive. "She doesn't know what she wants just now. It is the fear. In my father's psychology text, it describes 'regression.' I think mother is regressing."

"Andy, you *aren't* a psychologist..."

"Well, no, John Alexander, but regression is certainly a possibility. And I have decided to *become* a psychologist. I need your help. We are going to start mother's therapy by taking her to the beach near Machala next weekend. Will you join us?"

"Does your mother want to see me?"

"I don't know. But *I* want you to see her. You made her sooo happy till all this confusion began. Please."

"I'm not sure. What about the, ah...Veintimita family 'complications'?"

Nestor coughed. We both turned to him. "Don Abelardo agrees with Anda. A vacation is in order. He was recently visited by don Benigno, in person. The prior complications have been resolved. Don Benigno's change of heart is still a mystery, but it is so." I said nothing about having met Malo on the Cuenca highway.

Andy chose the same path and maintained an innocent, detached air. She really was precocious...smart enough not to brag.

But Andy still intended to have her way. "Well, then. We shall go to Machala on Thursday. You will be there at the Hotel Las Playitas near the waterfront at Puerto Bolívar, just north of town. Can you arrive Wednesday night? It must appear to mother as a remarkable coincidence."

"Do you have any other 'instructions' for me, miss?"

"No, John Alexander. I didn't mean to sound as if I were ordering you, but it *is* a good plan."

Nestor agreed. "We can bring you back from Machala the following Monday evening and drop you off here in Santa Isabel wherever you think best. What do you say?"

Andy butted in. "Nestor will be with us..." she paused, then leaned to me and whispered, "He has a *pistol. Please*, John Alexander."

I knew it was dumb the moment I agreed, so I cautioned Andy, "But I'm not about to stay in Machala if Livia protests." She nodded. Then Nestor urged her back into the car. He explained, "*We* have been 'cleaning the house' on Solano in preparation for Livia's return. I'll be living out back in the servant's quarters. It's time to go before we are missed."

The dark green Pontiac's vintage straight eight coughed once, then rumbled to life. Its carefully polished chrome glistened in the bright afternoon sun as it pulled away.

Andy and Nestor gone, I wandered back to the plaza. It was nearing four, and the lines at the cantón's administrative offices were dwindling. Land Rover drivers lined up, wiping down their vehicles and waiting for the big shots' return to Cuenca.

I lit a smoke, lounged at the corner of the churchyard, and waited. At about 4:25 PM the ruling class's representatives came out to depart. Cuenca was only about sixty miles away, but a rainy season's muddy two-hour drive on the treacherous, winding Girón highway.

The line of Jeeps and Land Rovers prepared to depart as a caravan. Desperate, one supplicant in tattered European dress pounded frantically on the magistrate's Land Rover windows, imploring the judge to hear his case.

"I can't wait two weeks! The land is mine. You cannot allow it to be sold to the Veintimita family."

"Stop! Go away or I shall move your case forward another month."

"No. It's wrong. I have *papers*."

"Then stuff them up your smelly peasant ass!" shouted the fat, pasty-white, Spanish-imported padre who was trapped inside with the magistrate. Panicky, the magistrate and padre tooted the horn and screamed to the drivers ahead. That brought two burly driver's assistants to the rear of the line to push the crowd back.

The fellow's shrieking wife and several other supporters kept pounding and refused to budge. When pushing didn't work, a mayoral's whip finished the job. The poor guy's wife got the worst of it. The whip ripped her face to shreds and she fell. The padre made an obscene gesture to her stunned husband as the Rover pulled away.

The final vestiges of "civilization" vanished in little clouds of oily exhaust as the last Land Rover in line pulled out of the plaza. At almost the same moment, a ripple of angst emanated from the once large crowd of mestizos and cholo wannabes who simply blew away as quietly as a puff of smoke.

Most of the food stalls and tents were struck hastily, and other trucks and Land Rovers followed the elites, but ten minutes behind their caravan. Santa Isabel market day was over.

By five, the plaza belonged to the beasts—dogs, cats, burros, mules, sheep, goats, broken-down draft horses, the Indians, and me...a *meeester* of no identifiable phylum.

The mass of Indians by the corrals grew larger as Indian vendors joined it. Several bands from different districts separated into competing crowds. Several hundred black ponchos gathered around one trio. Maroons circled another. The striped ones crowded a third.

Trago flowed like water. The cane whiskey, about 180 proof, was as raw as diesel fuel. So it was cut half-and-half with boiling water, heavily sugared. That combination transported the drink quickly to the small intestine where it was absorbed almost instantly. The only way on earth to have raised the alcohol content of one's bloodstream more rapidly would be to inject it into a vein.

The effect of the trago on the tired, dehydrated, malnourished crowd was startling. By six, dozens staggered about, reeling from side to side, shouting insults at no one in particular. Most were hard to decipher, but one in Spanish really got my attention. "¡*Mestizo jodido!* Shame! Shame! Shame! How dare you *demand* my daughter as your mistress...she is only twelve years old." Every few minutes, fistfights erupted, then faded away in one part of the crowd till all hell broke out in another.

A half-dozen Indian men scattered through the crowd shouted at thin air, gesticulating wildly, as circles of onlookers surrounded them—quite like boys watching a schoolyard fight.

One of those men was near me at the corner of the pharmacy. Just five feet tall, wearing tattered clothing, smelly and as skinny as a rail, he was actually acting out two parts—the deep, Spanish-accented voice of a mayoral and the higher-pitched voice of a supplicant Indian male.

I couldn't catch all of the Indian's part because some of it was in Quechua. But the Spanish part was clear enough. "Indio bruto, you are nothing...a beast. You are slower than a burro, dumber than the sheep. How dare you question my count of your produce. I am *the* mayoral here at La Atalaya. I *am* your lord and master. Show me the respect due my puesto—now, kneel."

Cayé had come up behind me as I watched. "He is speaking of the big one—El Garrote's partner—who accused you at Los Faiques, Patrón."

"So I gathered, Cayé. Is this kind of display common?"

"Yes, the brutos get drunk, sometimes even the civilized Indians, and unburden themselves of their indignities. It is time for you to go, Patrón." The tone of his voice was worried, but I wanted to see more. "I'll stay for just another hour." He shrugged and sat down beside me.

Twenty minutes later, a machete fight broke out next to the sheep pens. Screams, curses, *"¡Indio bruto!"* *"¡Bestia fregada!* (Screwed animal!)"￼ Then an ominous groan. The crowd moved away, ignoring the carnage. A wailing woman in straw panama knelt and clutched at her son, about twenty, who lay in the dirt, his neck slashed through the jugular.

As the boy died, the "winner" shuffled away, bleeding profusely and groaning, his left hand nearly sliced off above the wrist. I handed a gaping Indian kid several sucres to summon the cops from the constabulary across the plaza. He took off, but before anyone came, Cayé dragged me off.

"Do not get involved, Patrón."

"Why not, Cayé?

"You are *white*. The mob will stone you. They are not afraid of *meeesters*—a *meeester* has neither land to give, nor land to take away. I already asked the sacristan of the church to summon the authorities. We must go, *now*."

Several of Cayé's family members rushed to join him, shouldering me off the plaza. As I walked downhill to the hacienda, surrounded by a small cluster of Cayé's relatives, I asked Cayé's uncle, the Reader, why they were so worried for my safety. At least he was honest, his trago-laced answer to the point. "You are Cayé's patrón. He *needs* you."

I didn't sleep well. The Voice troubled me and when I dozed, ugly scenes raced around in my brain. The Angel of Death wearing a striped poncho, a wailing mother, several hands dripping blood, and thick, gory rat vomit all blasted away at my subconscious.

CHAPTER THIRTEEN

LOS FAIQUES
MARCH 2–4

It was a slow week at Los Faiques. Uribe returned to Cuenca awaiting the birth of a child, and I awaited the Wednesday bus to Machala, anticipating my long weekend with Livia.

On Monday morning, ignoring María's displeasure, Efraín and Manuel joined me for breakfast. Unusual—and they were grim faced. Something was wrong. Efraín's felt hat twirled like a top. "I have family news, Señor Juan, I...uh..." He went silent. Manuel interceded. "His twin nieces, Ofélia and Feliciana Chaski, were betrothed yesterday to the two Lloque brothers. They are to be married in the church at Santa Isabel in four weeks."

I smiled. The girls' last name had fascinated me. "Chaski" was the name Inca dynasties used to identify their official runners—those who relayed messages along the empire's highways. "The banns...ah...were posted yesterday on Santa Isabel's church door," stuttered Efraín.

In stark contrast to Uncle Efraín, the girls were bubbly and talkative, asking me endless questions about Miami—Ecuador's best-known American city. They were very cute, light-skinned cholas but appeared to be only fourteen or fifteen.

Feliciana was the more outgoing. Every time she smiled at me, her huge, lively eyes almost made me forget that her lips were full, lush and inviting, like a woman's.

"How old are the girls, Efraín?"

"Sixteen...women. Ready to marry, but there are issues to be resolved."

"What issues?"

"My family needs to pay Hacienda Atalaya's patrón to forego his *señorial*."

"Señorial? I've not heard that word in years. It once referred to a lord's feudal right."

"You are correct, Señor Juan. Veintimita has the right to sleep with the girls born on his land before their wedding night." He paused for a response but got none—I was too busy processing this mentally. The processing wasn't smooth. Little Eddy whimpered, "John, why did he do *that* to me. It hurts! Do we have to stay here, John?" That stepdad beat the snot out of me for reporting the sexual abuse. In the end, though, I'd paid him back. Royally...and been sent to reform school because of it.

"Are you all right, Señor Juan?" he repeated as he shook my shoulder.

"No, Efraín, I am not. This is barbaric. It's *unacceptable*." For the first time in two weeks, I'd said exactly what I thought.

"I am gratified at your reaction. The Veintimita brothers are *the* last hacendados in Azuay to insist on this right. I hear it is still common to the south in Loja, but not here," Manuel fleshed out the dilemma.

"The worst of it, Señor Juan, is that don Fermín is actually their uncle by blood. His oldest brother, Jesús, demanded that right of the girls' mother when she became engaged seventeen years ago. The twins were a product of his señorial. My sister and her husband raised them as if they were their own, indeed they think of the girls as their own. But, you see, we simply cannot let this happen."

By the time he finished the sentence I was already standing over him, shaking. I would say I felt true outrage, but buttoned-down JA simply didn't get outraged. Too detached. Too cool. I merely needed to "compose myself."

"Even worse, Señor Juan, he has set the price at five thousand sucres each to release the girls from their obligation."

That was five hundred dollars for the pair—two years' wages for a low-caste mestiza shop clerk. Five years' wages for an ordinary Indian field hand.

"Can you help us, Señor Juan? We have no way to raise such a great sum of money. Our whole family can raise perhaps half that... and he wants *both* girls at once. They will never be able to look at one another afterward." Efraín looked sick. I was about to disengage and say no when little Eddy's face came into focus again. Eddy frowned at me, so I reconsidered.

"Has he really the power to do this, Efraín?"

"Yes. No one—whether magistrate or another hacendado—will interfere. They may not approve, but they will not prevent it."

"And the padre...?"

"His mistress is the daughter of one of Veintimita's mayorales. She is barely fifteen. He will say nothing."

Livia had been right—I *had* underestimated the Veintimitas' capacity for evil.

Efraín waited while I paced, conflicted, and thought about it. Finally, I turned to him. "What is the deadline for the payment?"

"Forty-eight hours before the wedding."

"I'll come up with half the money, in cash, *if* your family and friends match that. I'll have the money to you at the end of next week. Start raising yours...and *no* mention of my name to anyone, or I'll withdraw my support. I don't need more trouble from the Veintimitas." Efraín and Manuel exchanged glances but did not make eye contact with me. "*No!* You may *not* refer to me in *any* way. Others could be hurt. I won't have it."

Reluctantly, they nodded in assent. I stomped off to my room to calm down and think. *I owe them the money*, I reasoned. If it wasn't for me, neither Efraín nor Livia would have come to grief. Veintimita is one of those sociopathic little rats who fears and despises those he cannot control. Abelardo's "family issues" or no, I was the precipitating factor in all of this. My objection to his mayorales in Ambato must have set the ball of hostility rolling.

Well, JA, I told myself, *you've really hurt a lot of people this time, you clueless, naive SOB*. Eddy gave me a sad smile. "It's OK, John—you are a good brother. I love you." I vomited.

I cleaned up, composed myself, and lit a smoke. I was in control again by the time I flicked the butt of my cigarette over the gallery railing, gathered my gear, and met Manuel below. We had more interviews to do.

An hour later, I was halfway through an interview when Manuel excused himself, announcing that he had "patients" to attend to at the big house. *Patients? Hmm*...In any case, I no longer needed a constant chaperone, so was relieved. As a veteran of this human rights business I understood that freedom of speech is "inversely proportional to the number of listeners." Cut the number of listeners in half and you triple uncensored verbal output.

The interviews kept my mind off both Eddy and the Chaski sisters. And, by the end of the day, I had some juicy stuff for Penrod and his foundation benefactors. Names, dates, injuries, and perps. Most of the mayhem in Yunguilla came from the Veintimita brothers, several of their male in-laws, and their collective mayorales. As a group, they were one huge festering boil on the ass of Progress.

Time to lance it, I thought as I made the long uphill walk back to the big house, the Rircay roaring behind me. Down in the valley that damn river was so loud, one simply could not hear the region's exotic songbirds. Water is usually soothing, but the Rircay was angry and turbulent.

Did the anger and chaos of Ecuadorian society get absorbed by nature? Or was it the other way around?

As I neared the hacienda's plazuela, I spotted a small group of Indian men sitting around a central figure. Still too far away to see, I picked up the pace, curious.

When I reached the cobblestones in front of the big house, Manuel was in preparation for a "surgery" on one of his patients—a gaunt-eyed, hollow-cheeked Indian fellow, about thirty, was sitting on his haunches while Manuel slowly rubbed Kerex on a prominent bulging blister near his belly button.

The blister appeared to expand as Manuel continued to apply more kerosene. I thought it might just be a traditional *curandero* stunt to exorcize a foreign object from the patient's body, but Manuel proved me wrong.

Manuel carefully massaged the blister in slow, narrowing circles till it stuck out like an immense pustule. Cayé was assisting him, holding a thin, peeled stick over a small bowl of white goo, a topless Kerex lantern lit nearby. A moment later, Manuel paused. "*¡Ya! Necesito la navaja.* (Done! I need the razor.)"

Cayé passed its blade through the open flame, handed Manuel the razor, and twirled the stick into the white, sticky goo. Curious, I leaned to Cayé and sniffed. "Cactus juice, Cayé?" He nodded, smiling. One tiny flick of the razor opened the pustule and something stringy oozed out.

Manuel took the stick, probing the ropy, white mass, then began to wind carefully. Over the next ten minutes an immense tapewormlike creature emerged—stuck to the gluelike cactus juice on the stick.

The winding continued for another ten delicate minutes, Cayé applying a bit more Kerex around the diminishing pustule's margins. Finally, a flat "head," one dark spot marking its attaching hooks, emerged and about three feet of parasitic annelid had been removed.

Manuel nodded and the little crowd applauded. But Manuel was not done. He administered a powerful herbal tea as a purgative, explaining, "When these creatures go to reproduce, they move to the surface. If they are not removed then, the cycle of infestation will triple or quadruple and the afflicted will expire. The purgative will clean out any little ones still in his *tripas*."

Manuel relaxed and stretched, while Cayé inserted the worm into the nearly empty Kerex can. "Use Kerex on his stool, Cayé—and take him away from where others make their toilet. The stool must be smothered in Kerex."

Cayé and the patient departed. Done for the day, Manuel relaxed, lit a smoke, and María brought him tea. "I'm impressed, Manuel. How did you learn all that?"

He grinned. "When I was young, Señor Juan, I apprenticed as an attendant to the old veterinarian who once worked in the village. I learned much...and my aunt was a bonesetter. I enjoy this work. It gives my life meaning, dignity, and, of course, it provides a modest income."

I ate dinner, sat alone on the gallery, and organized the day's interview notes. *Why is it that Eddy's face comes back to me here in Ecuador, but not in Manhattan?* I wondered. Later, I smoked, feet up on the gallery railing, and watched the stars whirl slowly around the Southern Cross.

Fermín Veintimita was auctioning the virginity of two sixteen-year-old girls back to their family. His right of puesto. And, whether I liked it or not, I was involved in both ends of Veintimita's toxicity. Both in the cause...and in its effects.

I muttered to myself, *But the worm turns, Veintimita, it always turns.*

CHAPTER FOURTEEN

MACHALA
MARCH 4–9

On Wednesday at 10 AM I stepped into an old repainted school bus bound for Machala. A few miles south of Santa Isabel we entered a "dead zone"— rocky, barren mountainsides where no living thing, plant or animal, was visible. The landscape's ominous shades of dull brown and gray made it look as if it were nearing the end of its life, like a fading scene from a nineteenth-century tintype.

The Quechua speakers in the valley had told me of it: "haunted," "the devil's living room," "purgatory," "*wañuskay ahko pampa*" (desert of the dead). It was spooky. Farther on, tall cactuses appeared, breaking the eerie mood. As we continued to descend from the highlands, the air cleared. It was sunny. Hot. Humid. And green.

I stripped off a layer of clothing and unbuttoned my shirt. There were flowers everywhere. Ponchos and felt hats with exotically upturned brims were replaced by short-sleeved shirts, pants, and cheap wide-brimmed straw hats. We were in mestizo country.

The bus stopped briefly in Pasajé. I peed behind another wall and marveled at young women in skimpy tops and pedal pushers. Chicken, rather than cuy, was the meat of choice in several nearby bus-side stands.

I should have paid more attention to Pasajé itself but was already daydreaming about walking on a beach with Livia. If I could off-load Andy onto Nestor, I might even get laid.

By two in the afternoon, we had pulled into Machala's plaza. Big church, long colonial buildings with iron-barred windows, palm trees and flowers everywhere. The temperature was about ninety degrees. Humidity about the same.

From Machala, a local bus served the waterside settlement of Puerto Bolívar still several miles away. It was amazing to be at sea level again. Compared to the sierra, the air was heavy and moist. At first it was a systemic shock—like breathing a brick.

The Hotel Las Playitas at Bolívar was a whitewashed compound twenty yards from the water. Dense trees shaded its courtyard, and flowers, many new to me, were everywhere—cascading over balconies, climbing walls, brightening the roof, and smothering the bases of palms fronting the bay.

But the hotel's hopeful name was misleading. The "beach" in front was disappointingly narrow and muddy—a big letdown. Puerto Bolívar turned out to be exactly what the name implied, a working port. Sand was scarce.

To reach a real sand beach, one had to take a local ferry to the settlement of Jambelí—on a nearby low-lying tidal peninsula.

My room (by request) faced north—shade. I dropped off my duffel and walked the gravelly lane, hunting for a bathing suit. Hey—even ever-hopeful JA didn't carry such gear "on assignment." In Ecuador, "sexy," like protein, was hard to come by, and I really wanted to sun on the beach with Livia.

I found a little tourist shop about three-quarters of a mile away and bought a baggy pair of big polyester trunks and a bottle of sunscreen. If a stand-up slow dance with Livia turned her into a tigress, what the hell would a palm-ful of suntan oil do? I wasn't certain, but it merited further research.

The hotel lobby was brightly tiled. Fans suspended from the high ceiling turned slowly. There were colorful ceramic pots of flowers everywhere. Polished hardwood and leather takedown chairs, the kind called *equipales* in Mexico, filled the public areas.

I bought a copy of *El Telégrafo*, Guayaquil's premier newspaper, an ice-cold beer, and lounged under a fan, clad in bathing trunks, sandals, and a polo shirt. I saw no Indian servants at all. Poor mestizos served as the waiters. Blacks made up the rest of the immediate, unnamed "help." Guests called for service by gender: "Here, *boy*, I need a meal," or, "*Muchacha*, bring me a cold beer."

I strolled to the hotel's terraced, open-air restaurant and ordered dinner—grilled shrimp, seafood chowder, rice, and a fruit compote of mango, banana, orange, and papaya. I was amazed at what I could buy on the coast. After dinner, I walked along the narrow strand, enjoying a real sunset, then lounged in a hammock slung between two palm trees, listening to the tide lap under the nearest pier.

As I swung in the hammock, a lush Afro-Ecuatoriana waitress, tray in hand, asked, "Do you want anything from the bar?"

"You will do nicely," I said. Ah, the old JA was reemerging. Food, oxygen, and female legs were all restorative, but she saw no humor in it at all and stalked off muttering something about "*meeesteres fregados.*" Not that her response dulled my testosterone rush enough to dissuade me from ogling her as she walked away.

Ecuadorian women simply could not tell the difference between flirting and a hard-nosed proposition. Or perhaps flirting was simply unknown in these parts…a lost art, replaced by something subtle like, "Here are a hundred sucs—get down on your knees for me, baby. My puesto permits it." Hell, I didn't know. In any case, it was obvious that experimental approaches were simply not productive. *So just how does the population here double every twelve to fourteen years?* I wondered.

Two hours later, as I sagged in the hammock, snoozing under the evening stars, she returned. "I'm back. I want five hundred sucres for the night. *No kissing.* But anything else is OK."

"The whole night?"

"Yes—but no kissing."

"No, thanks," I retorted. "I don't sleep with women I can't kiss."

"Really?" Her jaw dropped.

Handing her a twenty-sucre tip, I confirmed, "Sí—really."

She sauntered off, irritated again. Several "fregados" floated back to me on the evening breeze…

The next morning I went into town to check it out. I purchased a bright, flowered sarong for Livia and, feeling guilty about being hard on her, a book about seashells for Andy. Then it was time for lunch at the hotel.

I was two sips into my cold beer, and feeling quite relaxed, when an arm arched over my shoulder and grabbed the bottle. I jumped out of the chair in one quick move, panting. "Yes, Alex, that's the way I, too, have felt lately. Not pleasant, is it?"

"No, Livia. It isn't." She looked tense, but lovely, in spite of a cluster of tiny new worry lines at each corner of her mouth.

"Anda set this up, didn't she...and don't *lie* to me." Livia had a hard-nosed streak after all.

"Andy's right, Livia—you have become both angry and afraid. That saddens me. She loves you...and I'm tempted to do the same."

Livia blinked rapidly a half-dozen times—body language that rarely misreports the blinker's true emotion—anger. She walked away without a word, crossing the lobby, her arms folded tightly under her breasts—female body language that makes every male on earth over the age of ten wary.

Well, at least our vacation has been brief and uncomplicated, I told myself. Then I went back to my beer, closed my eyes, and again raised the chilled bottle to my lips. "At least drink it from a glass, dammit...and just what do you mean comparing *your* emotions to Anda's?"

"Nice to see you again, Livia...and sooo soon."

"You sarcastic bas..."

"STOP it! Both of you," snapped Andy. "The two of you need to grow up. I came for a vacation. If you don't wish to see each other, it is your own little tragedy, but do not drag me into it." Then, without a hiccup: "John Alexander, please seat me; I'm hungry and want to order lunch."

"Don't be harsh, Andy...it's not necessary." She stared, studying me carefully. As a peace offering, I pulled out the chair for her. She looked regal. Her oversized head erect, she was totally calm. In control. Livia snorted, then stomped off again. I started to rise and go after her, but Andy reached for my wrist, her brow wrinkled. "Let her go...and do not react to her anger as you just did. You cannot extinguish her childish behavior that way. You know better, John Alexander. I know that you do."

"Your psychology text again."

"Yes," she nodded, "and it was your undergraduate degree at Wesleyan."

"How did you know that?" I asked, incredulous.

"Don Benigno came to the house and talked to Uncle Abelardo. He paid a detective agency in Miami to investigate you...I listened."

"Whoa! Why?"

"I *always* listen."

"No, Andy—not you—why did Malo hire a detective to check on *me*?"

"I'm not certain. It sounded as if he thought you were CIA or something like that—an American agent."

"Did he find anything to interest him?"

"An orphan with only a twin brother who earned a university degree in the States at age twenty. Then another in Mexico City, anthropology, at age twenty-two. A master's in folklore earned at Edinburgh by the age of twenty-three and an invitation to write the doctoral thesis without additional coursework. He was impressed—especially when he found out who your father was." The folks in Miami had certainly dug deep.

"I was just a child when my father died, Andy."

"I know. And I know precisely how it feels. I'm sorry." That hit home. The waiter, towel over arm, well...waited, while she recited my curriculum vitae from the overheard conversation at Abelardo's. She switched gears again and ordered, then settled back in her chair. "I'd like my lesson after dinner. Can we, John Alexander?" I nodded. She let me eat in peace.

The lesson went well until she started prying into my background again. "What did you do for money that enabled you to go to college, John Alexander?"

I shrugged. "A bit of this. A bit of that." She wasn't buying. "OK—not that it's any of your business, Andy, but I borrowed some money from the American government...and I played pool."

"Pool? What is 'pool'—something to swim in?"

"No, Andy—pool—with balls, as in *billares*, but with pockets."

"Oh, a billiard *table*...for money, wagers?"

"For money."

"That's eccentric, John Alexander. Quite eccentric for a scholar. Where did you play?"

"New York, Chicago, Pittsburgh, Philadelphia, Virginia Beach."

"Tell me of these places."

"That will have to be another lesson, Andy. Right now I'm going to take a nap. Perhaps Livia will calm down and spend some time with me."

"She cares for you, John Alexander. But she has changed. It troubles me. I do not fully understand it."

"Nor I, Andy." As I got up to go, Andy, suddenly more formal, asked me when she'd see me again. Grateful for a bit of distance, I said, "Don't know, miss, but I'm planning on dinner at the restaurant about eight thirty... and I have a small gift for you."

"Really, what is it?"

"*It* is *wrapped*, Andy. That's what *it* is. Wrapped." She laughed as I headed to my room.

I tried to nap, still wondering why Livia's emotional reactions were so dramatic. I was nearly certain that the Veintimitas' mayorales were motivated primarily by the Ambato incident, and not just by Livia's rejection of Fermín, the Veintimita clan's very own "Piggy." But why? And why do it when I was with Livia? *Was* there more to this than I realized?

I'd only been asleep for about thirty minutes when I was awakened by a persistent tapping at the door. Livia, perhaps? So, I got up. It was only a very edgy Nestor. He wanted to talk, privately.

He thought he'd seen the big mayoral, Baritone, standing at an open-air restaurant about one hundred yards from the hotel.

"Is that possible? How would they know where we are?"

"You must have been watched when you took the bus, then the Pontiac passed the same way a day later—there is only the one road. A few sucres would gain such information."

"When did you see him, Nestor?"

"About fifteen minutes ago. But I'm not certain." I reached for the compact 8 x 30 Nikon binoculars I'd brought for the trip out to the beach. "Let's check. I'll follow."

One by one we eased onto the veranda, using the palms as partial cover until we faced the spot Nestor indicated. I scanned the little restaurant and surrounding area. Seeing no one remotely like the mayoral I handed the Nikons to Nestor. He glassed the area, shaking his head in frustration.

"Perhaps I am merely seeing things not actually there. The tension..."

He was cut off midsentence by Baritone's jeering voice. "I'm here—right behind you pathetic turds!"

Shit! Double shit! I turned warily, my heart pounding like a caged animal's.

"You still do not understand, *meeester.* You are but an irritating, pale turd who continues to interfere with don Fermín's property. Livia is *his.* Since you have soiled her, don Fermín has given her to Garrote and me to share. She is *ours* now."

I laughed—this was quickly turning into something approaching a bad Charlie Chan movie—amusing, but not believable. Baritone actually looked hurt. He shouldn't have indulged himself—as he blinked at me, Nestor hit him like a freight train.

Baritone went down, Nestor pummeling the bejeebers out of him. But Baritone was unfamiliar with the concept of a fair fight. He stealthily pulled a knife from his boot as Nestor hammered away, lost in the moment.

Not that it actually gave Baritone much of an advantage. It took him far longer than it should have to realize that I was standing on his bicep, the knife basically useless. He tried to stab me in the calf, so I brought the other foot down on the curled fingers of his knife hand and shifted my weight. It sounded as if I was crushing peanuts.

Nestor continued to beat the stuffing out of him until he tired. Then he paused. "Had enough?"

"She's mine now," murmured Baritone. "You *can't* stop it..."

Another serious mistake. Nestor lost it completely, passionately declaring his love for Livia as he ball-kicked Baritone back into prepuberty. "I *love* her!" Kick. "I *want* her!" Thump. "She is a saint." Whack. "She cannot be *owned*—a saint, a Madonna..."

The animated crowd around us had grown—nothing like a good fight to brighten up an Ecuadorian afternoon. Finally, I pulled Nestor off of him—we were only a few blows away from the situation turning into homicide.

The hotel manager was having a fit. So I lied. "This man tried to steal money from us at knifepoint. Our driver stopped him." This time the authorities did come.

Baritone, still unable to speak for himself, was dragged away and thrown into the back of an old Nissan pickup labeled "Policía," all shackled in nineteenth-century irons. He gurgled loudly when they slammed his legs together to clamp on the leg irons.

Nestor was sheepish. I bought him a beer and squeezed his shoulder, avoiding eye contact, then headed back to my room.

Andy intercepted me at the lobby entrance. "I saw some of the fight, John Alexander. I don't think Mother should be told of it... it's, it's... troubling."

"I'm not sure I agree with you, Andy. Your mom has a right to know since it is *she* they imagine they own. Did you hear *that* part?"

She nodded slowly, biting her lower lip. This couldn't be easy for a kid whose life had been sheltered. "Andy, I'm going to go relax a bit in my room—I need to think."

"Me, too," she whispered, shaking.

I lay on the bed, lit a smoke, and talked to myself, working it through. *Veintimita's ugly little world certainly is twisted. Yet logical in a screwed-up way...* He'd been the first to "ask" Livia when she was still in college. He'd actually lowered himself to do the asking—fully expecting that his wish, as with most others in his life, would be granted quickly and easily, his right of puesto.

But Livia hadn't become his for the asking. He'd been spurned by an orphaned college girl who *should* have been both grateful and dependent enough to overlook his defects. After all, he was a Veintimita. This was compounded by the fact that Livia then chose an old man to marry. And she *should've* been even more grateful, and much more dependent, once she became a widow.

It must have driven him genuinely crazy to be rejected yet again... for no one at all. Then along comes this *meeester*, a nobody. So Veintimita convinced himself he actually "owned" her and could make a gift of her to his mayorales. The psychology of it was so "Ecuador"—so fucked up, and so wondrously pathological.

But now what to do? These psychos weren't going to give up easily. And Baritone would probably be rescued from the law by Veintimita, some sucres quickly changing hands in the process. The sick little prick obviously needed guys like Garrote and Baritone around him for validation of his delusions... and, as for me, I had obviously walked into Act Three of this twisted little morality play as naively as any schoolboy.

Livia still sulking in her hotel room, I had dinner at 8:30 with Andy and Nestor. Already aware that Andy had seen a portion of the afternoon's fracas, Nestor apologized for his excesses. Andy gently accepted his apology. "It is understandable, given the surrealism of the situation." Well, that was concise. Then she asked the most pertinent questions, "How long will he remain in jail?" followed by, "And what must be done next?" She sounded just like me when I was fifteen and Eddy had been busted for possession.

Nestor, one hand badly swollen, looked sheepish again and admitted he wasn't certain of either. I shrugged. Andy, looking disgusted, announced that she was going to get her mother.

Nestor fidgeted aimlessly, pushing food around his plate. He still couldn't make eye contact. Normal. Guys aren't good at this sort of thing. Dealing with a thug is simple and straightforward. Communicating feelings isn't.

After two more sips of beer Nestor headed out to the lobby's phone booth to contact Abelardo in Cuenca. "Good idea," I commented. Andy returned about five minutes later, exasperated.

"If you wish to see Mother, you must go ask her to her face. She wants to be 'invited.'"

"Perhaps begged?" I commented dryly.

"That, too, John Alexander—it seems quite childish to me." Actually, it wasn't. I'd learned long ago that if you don't tell it to a woman's face, it just isn't "real."

I said nothing to Andy as I got up and prepared to grovel but made a mental note to explain adult male and female communication to her one day. Women's Rule: "Tell it to my face, Jack." Men's Rule: "Tell it to my best friend if you really mean it." No sense in driving the kid nuts with the illogic of all this now. She wouldn't get it, anyway, till her hormones kicked in a few years down the road.

I knocked loudly on Livia's door. "Yes, who is it?" As if she didn't know. *Oh, well, it's part of the mating ritual,* I reasoned. I paused to process...

"It's Alex, Livia—I've come to ask you to dine with us. I'm sorry that things became so unexpectedly complicated.

I'd like to see you and spend time with you. Perhaps we can sort out some of this and enjoy a day or two."

"Perhaps, Alex...and did you enjoy the fight? The maids are all chattering about it. They never before saw a '*meeester*' casually crush a man's hand and calmly continue to smoke at the same time."

"Don't be nasty, Livia, that mayoral was going to *stab* Nestor, who was protecting you and had just finished publicly declaring his love for you."

The front door swung open. "Say that again."

"No, it's not a joke—Nestor loves you. The mayoral told us that Fermín had *given* you as a gift to him and another mayoral. He came to collect. Nestor objected— passionately."

Oddly, Livia became calm. "You aren't kidding, are you?" I looked her square in the eye and slowly shook my head no.

"Well, it's like Fermín Veintimita. He is sordid and evil. His idea of sex and romance is twisted. With him it's *degenerado*, power, control, and desperation." She sounded far too definite to be reacting from mere speculation. *Uh oh,* the Voice shouted at me, *Don't go there. Don't ask her a single thing about this. DON'T REACT!* My gut was churning and I was now nearly as pissed as Nestor, but I forced the imitation of a smile. "Join us?"

"Give me twenty minutes." Well, at least she'd given me a half smile.

Back at the table, Nestor and Andy were getting ready to order. I asked them to wait till Livia arrived. "Really?" beamed Andy. "Yes, we are going to eat, ah, uh...together. Now, here is a gift for you. Take it to the lobby and enjoy it for ten minutes. Nestor and I need some privacy."

Andy's eyes moved back and forth between us several times, then in classic Andy style, she admonished us. "OK. But *no* fighting over my mother. She has a right to decide for herself. Thanks for the book, John Alexander."

"Andy, you haven't even opened it. How do you know what it is?"

"It is logical, John Alexander—a gift shaped like a book, and given by a scholar, *is* a book." She ran off to open it.

Nestor turned his chair and leaned back into it. Guy business. Important. No eye contact allowed. I started. "Our little genius is correct. It's for Livia to decide. I've already told her of your feelings in explaining the fight. She didn't laugh. Frankly, I wish she had. She might be the perfect woman for me. But I'm not certain that I'm the perfect man for her."

Nestor exhaled slowly, nodded, and leaned forward. "Well, then let me buy you a beer. I insist. What will you have?"

"Anything you choose as long as it is ice-cold." Andy shouted to us from about thirty feet away. "Can I come back now?" Nestor answered her quickly, "Of course, miss."

"I like my book, John Alexander. Can we have a lesson on the names of shells in English? Perhaps we can take the boat tomorrow to Jambelí—there's a wide, sandy beach there."

"Sure, Andy—why not go ask your mom and bring her to dinner." She bounced off as a desk-man came to the table. "Phone call from Cuenca, señores."

"Both of us?" asked Nestor. He nodded. Nestor's phone call to Cuenca had produced immediate results.

Don Abelardo had corralled don Benigno. The grandee wanted first-person confirmation of Veintimita's alleged gift of Livia to his mayorales. He was actually on the phone; Nestor gave it to Malo—short and sweet. I was next on the phone. A voice that sounded like Malo's was still snarling at someone in the room with him.

"Your son, Fermín, has done it now—*given*, GIVEN— Livia Chuca, *viuda* de Gonzáles, to two of his cholo mayorales. *¡Cholos!*" Malo's voice ended on a surprisingly high-pitched emphasis on the word "cholos." I coughed to let him know I was on the line.

But no one was listening. Instead, Malo merely finished issuing his directive. "Undo this for all time and send a formal letter of apology. TONIGHT! If you cannot control your son, buy him land in Loja—or Bolivia—and send him away." The phone slammed back into its cradle. I winced.

Nestor looked edgy. He tilted his head, waiting for a report.

"He was dumping on someone in the room. Had to have been Fermín Veintimita's father."

"Well, what did he actually say to the father?" As I repeated it to him, word for word, Nestor slowly shook his head, a faraway look in his eyes. A moment later, Nestor focused on the here and now, sighing deeply. "Don Fermín will find a way to strike back, I fear."

Both Livia and Andy were already seated at the table, watching us as we returned. As we crossed the lobby, Nestor whispered, "The phone conversation was private." I nodded in agreement.

Livia was surprisingly upbeat. Knowing what was going on, however twisted, was far easier on her nerves than the horrors of the unknown. Besides, she obviously understood Fermín's capacity for evil in a far more tangible way than I'd imagined. We ordered.

The grilled shrimp, rice, and vegetables arrived on huge platters. Sumptuous, and Livia liked her sarong. "Perfect for the beach at Jambelí tomorrow. Shall we take the morning boat about ten? Good. That's settled. Now Anda, darling, it's time for bed."

Nestor announced that he was tired and needed to ice his hand again. Livia smiled. "Thank you, Nestor. Would you have breakfast with me tomorrow—early? I want to get your personal view of these recent incidents."

Nestor's eyelids fluttered. So did one corner of his mouth. He damn near grinned. "Good night, all. Till breakfast, Señora." Alone, I asked Livia, "Why do you seem so much calmer?"

"It is a relief to know that he has decided to 'give' me away. Besides—it is too outrageous, even for Ecuador. It is him, personally, whom I most fear. The others are merely dangerous and disgusting." *Odd that she fears Veintimita himself, but not the mayorales.* I puzzled it out. *Is this just another version of the puesto thing?* Then it hit me; the mayorales are *only* cholos—they could render physical damage, but not social destruction. They could kill or rape, but they couldn't take away the privileges enjoyed by a person of higher caste.

Livia tapped me on the shoulder. "Dance with me again, Alex…and hold me tight. I need to feel safe." While I'd been pondering, the hotel's after-dinner trio had begun playing dance tunes. I pulled the chair out for her.

She was stiff and formal when I first wrapped my arm around her waist and pulled her to me. It took her several dances and several glasses of crisp Chilean wine before she melted into full snuggle mode. Once there, she was in heaven again, biting and shuddering, "Your room. *Now*, Alex."

I lifted her into my arms and carried her straight off the dance floor. The Afro-Ecuatoriana bar waitress made a wiseass comment as I swept Livia past her into the hallway. I answered, "She kisses," and kept going. "What?" asked Livia.

"Nothing, *chula*."

"I'd no idea you were so strong," Livia murmured as I paused at my door, fumbling with the key.

"It's a talent," I wisecracked. "Being underestimated is of great value in life."

"And in bed?"

"Of even greater value." She nibbled my ear in response as I struggled to get the door open. Finally, I managed to get inside and put her down. "Got to close the door, Livia..." Standing, arms outstretched, she pulled me to her, blouse already unbuttoned, and went back to nibbling at me. I responded with some nibbling of my own—she even *tasted* like buttercups. Question answered, she exploded, "Oooh! Umm, where's my purse, Alex? I, umm, need my purse."

"Don't know, Livia—did you bring it to dinner?"

"Oh, my God. It's in the room with Anda. I can't, uh, oooh, I *can't*, umm, go get it like this. Oooh. Don't stop. Please."

Frankly, it was the best unconsummated sex, in the ordinary male definition of it, that I'd ever had. Not that I was all that fulfilled by it, mind you. She, however, was doing just fine without her purse. *This is cosmic,* I told myself. *Possibly* the *woman for me and fate itself doesn't want to hear it.* I sighed. Actually getting laid, like eggs perched atop my rice, was obviously too much to ask of Ecuador.

She dressed, fluffing her hair. "See you after breakfast, Alex. I'll make it up to you tomorrow night."

"Sure, thanks, Livia. Good night." Before she walked out she gave me another deep squeeze and nibbled at my earlobe again. Not content with that, she probed my ear with the tip of her tongue. Damn. Did she have any idea how much worse that made it? If she did, perhaps I shouldn't have been so hard on Veintimita. No telling what she might have done—or not done—to drive him around the curve.

I dressed, went back out to the bar, and ordered an immense pisco sour. My Afro-Ecuatoriana admirer read the situation accurately and provided some cultural commentary. "Was the sex you didn't get good, Señor?" I glared. "But, then, I imagine the kissing made up for the rest." When she left she blew me a kiss over her shoulder.

I finished the pisco. She noticed and sauntered back, puckering her full lips for effect. "Would you like another pisco, Señor... or perhaps something less bitter—perhaps something flavored with *panocha* (brown sugar)?" She left, her hips swaying sensually. I sighed.

The second pisco eased the ache in my groin considerably. It also left me with a nagging headache when I awakened in the morning.

Though it wasn't my original plan, I settled for breakfast on the terrace with Andy while Livia dined inside with Nestor. It wasn't all bad, as Andy proved a distraction to my funk.

"Don't worry, John Alexander; she cares for you."

"I'm not concerned with that, Andy."

"Yes you are; your brow is all knotted up." I started to go defensive, just as she handed me a note.

"What's this, miss?"

"It's a wish. Open it." It read, "I like it when you call me 'Andy.' I now prefer to be 'Andy,' to you." I smiled at her. She patted my hand. I was rescued from further conversation by the police sergeant from Machala who came to take my statement. "The jailed one's patrón has posted bail, but he can't be freed till Monday. No magistrate to handle the process on weekends," he told us.

Andy got it immediately. "Well, we get another day of peace and quiet. Now we can go to the beach today without fear of being attacked again, John Alexander."

"Yep, let's get ready to go."

We collected Nestor and Livia and drove to the ferry dock. The "ferry" to Jambelí was an open twenty-two-foot launch. It was hot and humid but pleasant once we got moving. It took about forty minutes to circle the north end of the low-lying Jambelí Peninsula—an island at high tide, I gathered from my map.

Livia was distant and detached. Nestor quiet. Andy watched. I smoked and checked out the shoreline with the Nikons.

The shoreline was low and swampy in spots. Lots of mangroves. But just south of the fishing settlement of Jambelí itself a wide beach strand came into view. We had four hours till the boat returned for us.

Several palm-thatched lean-tos were available for rent, and several vendors from the fishing village nearby offered cheap fruit and very expensive air-temperature sodas. Nestor and Livia went off for a walk by themselves, Andy eyeing them uneasily. Once they were out of sight, she squeezed her eyes shut, buried her head, and cried.

"Are you OK, Andy?"

"I suppose so, but I picked *you* for mother's lover. Now, I'm frightened. It is all so confusing."

I shrugged and sighed. She took it as a cue to pry further. "Are you hurt, too, John Alexander?" I broke eye contact and shrugged again. "Disappointed, then?"

"I don't want to talk about it, Andy, but thanks for picking me. As *you* said, your mother gets to choose. Who knows, she may choose neither of us. Want to collect shells and forget about 'confusion' for a while?"

"I'd like that, and thanks for not freaking out when I cried. I try to be strong..." I butted in again, "You are strong. But let's forget all of it for now."

"OK," she smiled, "but can *you* really forget everything—you brought your staff with you."

"I can forget. Let's go get shells. I want the Latin and English name of each one we find." That worked. She had no problems with the "assignment" whatsoever. Her English pronunciation was uncanny once she'd heard me say a shell's name.

Every time she found a shell from the book she'd examine it closely, her eyes wide—intent on knowing it completely. As she processed each specimen, I imagined her huge head enlarging perceptibly to make room for the new information.

Several hours later, mosquito bitten and hot, we trudged back to the lean-to, loaded with two burlap sacks of shells. Livia and Nestor were already there, the hotel's prepared lunch neatly spread out. We ate, and I watched birds with the Nikons, giving Andy a chance to teach me their names in Spanish. Livia yielded up no emotional clues as we ate, and Nestor still seemed sheepish. Andy studied them again, while I hid behind the Nikons and watched ships at sea.

At last, the boat picked us up, then made a stop at the settlement of Jambelí, where a group of locals climbed on board with sacks of salted fish, shell necklaces, and palm-frond fans. Sunday was market day in Machala. Some vendors intended to get there early. On the boat, Livia sat next to me. I didn't react much. She had become like a hot stove to a three-year-old—stretch to reach it and get burned.

After getting no reaction from me for about twenty minutes, she surprised me. "Dinner at nine? Some dancing and...?" I nodded yes. *It's your last chance,* I promised myself.

The boat docked at Bolívar where Nestor had parked the green Pontiac near the old stone pier. Nestor was wary as we approached it. Two men leaned against the far side of the car in its shade. We couldn't get a good view through the roof. I tightened my grip on the staff as Nestor reached instinctively for his waistband. Livia froze and the worry lines around her mouth went three-dimensional. She grabbed Andy, pulling her back.

I went left, Nestor right. He'd already drawn the old .38 Colt when Manuel called out to me. "Señor Juan. Efraín and I have come to ask your help. There is trouble in Yunguilla." Efraín, grim faced, gave us the news: "Don Fermín sent his mayordomo and three young mayorales to get the twins early this morning. They have been taken to La Atalaya."

Relieved but curious, Nestor quietly tucked the pistol away. "What twins? *¿Qué pasa?*"

"My twin nieces—they are sixteen. To be married in less than a month. He has snatched them away to claim his señorial."

As Nestor processed this, Livia called out, "Everything OK?" Nestor replied, "No, the snake has struck."

I explained it to Livia and Nestor, who agreed to take the three of us into Machala. Livia whined, "Must you go, Alex?"

"Would you want to be sixteen and in Fermín's grasp?"

She shuddered. "Am I partly responsible for this, Alex? Is it because of the business with me?"

"It's all connected, Livia. But it's not about us—it's all about him. The whole world revolves around him. If others do not cooperate, he punishes them. He wasn't able to punish you this time, so someone else must pay. Next year it will be another set of characters who've displeased him. And the year after that, yet another."

"Go, then. But be careful." Andy, stone silent, went glassy-eyed again. And once more, a date with Livia had entered the realm of "if only."

An hour later I had checked out of the hotel and was waiting with Manuel and Efraín at the bus station in Machala. Veintimita was seriously grating on my nerves. I'd have been laid twice over, perhaps even married to Livia by now, if the errant little psycho weren't so out of control.

CHAPTER FIFTEEN

TOWER AT
LA ATALAYA
MARCH 8–14

E fraín and I took the bus all the way into Cuenca, pass-ing Santa Isabel, where Manuel got off—his jobs were to raise money in the settlements and to pretend normalcy.

I went straight to the bank in Cuenca on Monday morning and Efraín went to Uribe to beg for a loan. After withdrawing most of my cash, I went to the central post office on Avenue Gran Colombia and encountered long lines. Mailing a letter was no small chore. The envelopes were weighed in one line, stamps issued in another, then hand-stamped in a third one. Claiming mail required a fourth stop.

I settled into the rear of that line, hoping Penrod had sent wages. At least half the people in the big, marbled waiting room turned to gape at me. Nearly six inches taller than the average member of the crowd, fair complected, and still dressed exotically from the Machala beach sojourn, I stuck out like a sore thumb. The tie-wearing head clerk noticed me, too, and waved animatedly for me to come to the front of the line. I pointed to my chest to make sure.

"Yes, Señor—you—the tall one. Step up." *What now?* I thought, wary now of nearly everyone. But he insisted, so I stepped out of line and went to the counter. "Is there a problem, Señor?"

"Not at all. Europeans receive preferred service. How may I assist you?"

Miraculously, my transactions were efficient and required only *one* line. The only sour note came when I showed my US passport to claim the registered letter from Penrod. He frowned. *Meeesters* didn't meet his definition of "European." He sneered and turned away as he handed back the passport. As I walked away, the peons still waiting in line grumbled and stared.

Efraín was already at Solano when I arrived. I asked about the post office, "Why so different this time, Efraín?"

"Were you wearing a poncho and chicote the last time you went, Señor Juan?"

I thought for a moment, then nodded. "Yes."

"¡Ya!" offered Efraín. *So simple,* I thought, *act white—go to head of line. Act cholo or Indian—wait in the rear.*

Livia, Andy, and Nestor returned to the house on Solano about the time Efraín and I were ready to leave for Santa Isabel. "Alex, why are you still here? Are the girls free?" Livia asked, shivering.

"He wanted five thousand sucres for each girl to forego the señorial. We needed money."

"WHAT? Money for the virginity of two teenagers?" Efraín nodded. I shrugged. "Do you have enough?" she asked us.

"Almost—we are short about fifteen hundred sucres." Without a word, she went inside and returned with a fistful of banknotes.

"Here. A small gift—take it and go quickly."

Andy watched us till we started to leave, then stepped forward quickly, whispering in my ear, "It will be *me* someday if he is not stopped, won't it?" I'd never before heard such panic in her voice.

"Don't worry. We won't let that happen, Andy."

"Destroy him if you have the opportunity, John Alexander—Mother cannot live like this, nor can I." I raised my eyebrows and looked into her eyes. "So I have your permission to employ harsh tactics?"

"Yes. I have been thinking of Niccolò Machiavelli's *The Prince*, John Alexander." At that moment, it was very hard to believe this kid was barely eleven. As we walked away, Efraín grunted, "*¿Qué?*"

"Something I call the Ecuador Effect." He nodded as usual but did not ask for clarification, which surprised me. Just Efraín, being himself? Deference to *el meeester*? Or did he actually get it? Efraín, the grunter, gave me no clue.

Out on the highway, without further conversation, we flagged a mixto headed to Pasajé, paid up, and rode atop a full load of sharp, lumpy stuff buried under the rig's tarpaulin. Efraín got out at the footpath to the hacienda. I moved to jump down with him, but he motioned me on. "Stop this side of Tablón." Well, at least I'd got a full sentence from him.

So I sat again and rode on through town to a quiet, barren stretch of road about ten kilometers southwest of

Santa Isabel. There, I lit a smoke and flagged the next mixto laboring up the long grade from Pasajé. I jumped off near the plaza and headed into El Cantón to stock up on cigarettes, matches, and fixings for more trail mix.

The proprietor's ordinarily surly son, Noah, was unusually effusive. "Well, Señor, you have come by mixto from Machala, have you?"

"Yes, I was late for the bus."

"Ah, well, then...and did you enjoy yourself in Machala?"

"Actually, I took a bus south at Pasajé (*bullshit*) and went to Peru—I have a friend in Tumbes (*true*) who is in the Cuerpo de Paz."

"Ah, I see...and what did you do in Tumbes?"

"Went with my friend to an ancient village near San Pedro de los Incas to record traditional songs for comparison to those I've been recording here. Very exciting."

His dad came over and Noah the Rat shut up. I paid half of my outstanding bill, promising to settle it after my next trip to the bank in Cuenca. Done, I shouldered my gear and purchases, passing the burro corral on my way toward Los Faiques. No Cayé, and they hadn't offered to summon him. Interesting.

The road was steep and slippery, so I had to readjust the load. As I did, I got one glimpse of Noah the Rat watching me intently from behind his father's store. *We all report to someone*, I told myself and decided to be even more cautious than usual about what I told Cayé when I saw him again. Any innocent comment might make its way to the enemy camp through the Rat.

Cayé found me by the time I'd started down the Rover track to the big house. He was nonplussed at why they hadn't called him for me. "Noah has seemed odd lately,

Patrón...here, let me take part of this load...truly, I did not know you were here."

I patted him on the shoulder. "Thanks, Cayé—you attend me well." He grinned and grunted as he shouldered a huge bundle of supplies. I was grateful. It was tough walking in the sticky Andean goo that passed for road surface.

Down at the big house, I dumped my gear, and Manuel popped out of nowhere. "Efraín is at the trapiche and needs some mechanical advice. Why not join us?" I'd have taken this as a casual invitation if not for the fact that Manuel had attached himself to my elbow, nudging me along.

"Well, well. Have we a council meeting?" I teased as we walked in under the trapiche's shed roof. A couple of the old men nodded. Everyone was first sworn to silence, a tattered copy of the free-to-peasants Gideon's Bible passing from palm to palm. Then came the briefing.

A cholo, judging from his beard (which full-blooded Indians rarely could grow), an old guy named Ezekiel, updated us. "The twins, Ofélia and Feliciana, appear not to have been 'ruined' yet but are frightened and have carried on so much that they have been ordered from the big house to the old tower."

"I already know this from Efraín," I interjected impatiently. Everyone scowled. So I shut up.

"El Garrote is their jailer," he continued. I butted in. "Garrote...he was fired."

"Well, *meeester*, he is back." The old boy sounded irritated. "He limps now, dragging one foot, but has returned. Also, the big one was brought back from jail in Machala with our mayordomo about two hours ago...they, ah, have no love for you, *meeester*."

Efraín interrupted, "Then we shall deliver the money quickly. Before serious damage is done. We have ten thousand sucres"—the crowd of about a dozen gasped—"and I need two witnesses to accompany me."

"*El meeester* and one of us?" whined a middle-aged gent with tattered poncho and a racking cough.

"No—two of *you*. Señor Juan cannot join us. Not in the girls' best interests." To his credit, the church's aging sacristan stood and volunteered.

"I am old and my wife is gone. I will go." At that, the old boy with the beard also stood, but Efraín refused him. "Ezekiel, you are their grandfather, but we need you and your wife to get us information. You are brave and honorable, but I cannot accept." Ezekiel sat down again, hanging his head. The grandfather... and I'd interrupted him in front of everyone.

"I'm sorry for the interruption, *hatun tayta* (grandfather). I did not know you were the twins' grandfather." He nodded and waved it off.

Then, one of Efraín's cousins, who lived on the Landívar farm, volunteered. A dark-skinned, sharp-looking fellow in his thirties, wearing a striped short-sleeved shirt and old dungarees, he had the air of an angry warrior. "*¡Pucha carajo! ¡Vámonos!* My patrón is culto. I may not lose my farm plot over this. My risk is small." Efraín grunted. "Done."

Efraín "borrowed" one of his patron's mules for the aged sacristan. They departed, the rest of us agreeing to wait at the trapiche.

Nearly two hours later, they returned, looking defeated. Efraín had a huge, swollen welt over his cheekbone. "We delivered the money. Veintimita himself came out and accepted it—telling us it was but half the payment. He has doubled the girls' price again."

"I protested, as did Efraín," cut in the sacristan, outraged, "but don Fermín merely laughed and ordered Garrote, the giggler, to cane us for our insolence. Efraín protested further, calling on La Atalaya's patrón to keep his word as a gentleman. But Garrote was already swinging his club and knocked Efraín down."

The thirtyish cousin interrupted, "Veintimita went wild when Efraín called on him to honor his word. He grabbed the big mayoral's chicote and ordered us to kneel and be whipped."

"What exactly did he say?" I interrupted. The sacristan did not hesitate to reply, "'I am your master. I grant land. Life. Make jobs for you animals. How dare you question my word, you lying peasants. For your insult, I shall claim my señorial this evening and invite the other hacendados to share the girls with me.'"

The sacristan continued, "I yelled at him, 'But, they are paid for—twice over. You violated your original bargain— you have been paid before witnesses.' Veintimita became even more enraged, shouting, 'I have not been paid, bruto—and there are no *witnesses*. Field animals cannot be witnesses. My mayorales simply accepted a *fine* from you animals as a remedy for your insults. The girls are *mine*. I shall enjoy them as I please. Go—or the three of you shall be killed for trespassing.'"

Efraín, looking both dejected and afraid, punctuated the account. "All three whipped us as we retreated. The money is gone. It is irreplaceable. He has the girls, the money, and his mayorales."

About then, a young Indian boy came running from the direction of La Atalaya. "The patrón has told the women providing mita to prepare for a big dinner in the house tomorrow night. A number of hacendados and some of the important *blancos* in the villa of Santa Isabel have been invited."

No one made much eye contact. As for me, I was pissed. The Voice shrieked at me, *It's not your fight. These people don't give a shit about you.* While I processed the situation, the young, hapless husbands-to-be, Marco and Antonio, arrived, determined to "rescue" the girls from the tower that very evening.

Initially, Efraín tried to warn them off, but his grunts weren't eloquent enough to get the job done. Antonio was undeterred. "We know the hacienda. We will borrow skirts and dress as maids. Surprise them and save our wives."

"Those men are students of evil. You are inexperienced in such matters. They will kill you," warned Manuel.

"Are we not *men*—about to marry, don Manuel?"

"Yes, you are men. But you two are gentle. You face animals who love to hurt and kill."

"Yes, don Manuel, but these are our women. *Ours!*"

"Go, then, brothers. Be runa men ... and may God look kindly upon you." Efraín nodded in agreement.

About an hour later, five of the twentyish runa men, including both fiancés, went dressed in borrowed polleras, hoping to bribe one of the serving women into letting them carry a tray up into the tower's large top-story room so they could "surprise" the mayorales. They didn't look much like women to me, even with the fluffy dresses, but they were determined.

It worked, but only in an Ecuadorian sort of way. According to Marco, who returned briefly to the trapiche later that night, one of the younger female servants did accept a bribe. His brother, Antonio, and his cousin, Julio, both made it upstairs with trays, while Marco distracted the tower guard.

But the mayorales upstairs, energized and already in rut from holding down the girls, side by side, while Veintimita alternated his rape between the two, merely decided to have at the "serving girls." When they entered, neither fellow expected their dresses to be suddenly ripped off from behind as they set down the food trays. Antonio saw his bride-to-be spread-eagled next to her sister on the room's huge wooden table and cried out for her.

Thus, he was recognized instantly, even as the dress shredded. The mayorales made do—he was merely sodomized by a giggling Garrote while Baritone held him down.

The next morning, two shepherds would find Antonio in a ravine below the tower sans clothes, an inch of penis, his testicles, and big toes, the corpse naked and almost white. According to accounts that would follow over the next few days among the men in the Los Faiques settlement, they had cut his throat. There were also whispers that someone had defecated on him. Given Ambato, I wasn't shocked like they were—it was El Garrote's calling card.

Cousin Julio would be luckier. They would merely cut off one hand and throw him from the tower, "to live or die as God dictated." God would decide in his favor, in an ambivalent sort of way. He would crawl back to the trapiche at Los Faiques the next day. In shock, he would not be able to tell his full story for several days. But his jumbled, fragmented account was chilling.

Veintimita made both Julio and Feliciana, Antonio's bride-to-be, watch as his mayorales repeatedly sodomized and mutilated poor Antonio. Veintimita acted as "director," scripting for his mayorales and driven to extraordinary lust by the scene as Feliciana knelt and begged for her fiancé's life.

Veintimita, according to the dazed, one-handed Julio, merely laughed and grabbed little Feliciana by the hair and nearly choked her to death while frantically ramming away into her throat as her lover died, the room sprayed with his blood—right up to the rafters. Her sister, Ofélia, still tied to the table, screamed hysterically the whole time.

Shortly after Julio crawled back to us, I sent the sacristan to the Santa Ana clinic in Cuenca with him—the tourniquet he'd applied to his wrist nearly forty-eight hours before had already created a black, smelly stump, crawling with maggots.

Several of us carried Julio up to the Girón/Cuenca highway, the old sacristan crossing himself much too often for comfort. We hid Julio behind a clump of bushes next to the road till one of the bright green mixtos from Machala came down the hill. "Where is my cousin Marco?" he groaned as we laid him out on the mixto's bench—a sixty-sucre fare. No one answered him, which made me curious.

"Well, where *is* Marco?" I asked Manuel as the mixto pulled away with Julio. He looked away, muttering inaudibly. So, I pressed. "Manuel, I took risks, too—where is the other bridegroom?" He answered but would not make eye contact.

"Well, Señor Juan, it seems that when the word of his brother's horrible death reached him, he did not react well. He had failed to reach the tower and realized that he would be viewed as a coward. So, he redeemed himself."

"In what manner, Manuel?"

"He hanged himself from La Atalaya's main gate just as a Land Rover arrived with don Fermín's father and an associate from Cuenca. Dramatic and very inconvenient.

Veintimita is avoiding the tower and sent his two mayorales away before the authorities could arrive. The girls are still locked in the tower room, guarded by two of the young mayorales, but the 'party' for tonight has been 'postponed.' At least he bought time for his bride. Very brave."

I was seething. "Don't make me ask again for current news, Manuel—Veintimita has a great deal of my money...and I have no 'merchandise' to show for it."

"You are right, Señor Juan...I'm sorry. We will let you know if Veintimita schedules another 'party.'"

"Yes—or even goes to the tower for any length of time...I need any information. If I have anything to say about it, the bastard will be tried for murder in a Cuenca court."

"That would only happen if witnesses survived, Señor."

"Do you mean that the girls might be killed?"

"Yes. Now that Antonio's mutilated body has been found, and seen by many, anything could happen. La Atalaya's patrón put Antonio's balls in a bottle of trago—he has several such bottles. This has gone much farther than his usual indulgences, but he is not afraid of the judges. It is the gente whom he most fears...loss of respect."

"And what of the other two young men who went on the raid?"

"They have fled with the arrieros. It is unlikely that they will ever return. Gone to Loja, I imagine."

"And Julio at the clinic in Cuenca?"

"They will kill him, if possible. The mayorales have gone off somewhere. If they find him and make him talk, they will also come for you and Efraín. Perhaps even me."

I nodded and looked him in the eye. "Are you afraid, Manuel?"

"Yes, but I intend to kill the giggler if I have a chance. I bought the frog poison that the arrieros bring from Amazonas Province. Efraín made spikes from an old pitchfork. He has one for you if you want it."

"Covered with *curare* (Quechua, 'poison')?"

"Yes, but the poison is from frog skin—not vines. Very expensive."

"Well, if I get to Garrote first, I'm not saving him for you, Manuel."

"I understand. Efraín feels the same way. I'll leave a spike for you on your bed—be careful of it." We parted at the highway. Manuel went down to the settlement below Los Faiques and I returned to the big house.

I brooded on the balcony in front of my room, dazed by all that had gone on. Rape, sodomy, murder, mutilation... and now I was talking about "frog-poisoned spikes" as if I were in the cast of a 1930s jungle movie about Jívaro headhunters. On the other hand, the Jívaro lived only several hundred miles away. Still, no matter how one cut it, southern Ecuador was surrealistic. Worse yet, the surrealism had already begun to seem normal.

I went downstairs to eat alone, as usual. María, always stoic, was even more distant than customary. The female Indian servants had practiced the survival art of inscrutability for so long that they came off as austere. Impassive to the point of caricature. Truth be told, about then I'd have loved a smile. A nod. Hell, anything...the food wouldn't really go down, so I drank several mugs of tinto and milk. Then smoked my pipe, as I was out of cigarettes.

When I went upstairs to my room, I found a thin length of bamboo lying on the bed. A tongue of flattened iron protruded from one end. I pulled at it gingerly. It proved to be the hand-hammered handle of a grooved, five-inch spike, cut from the straightest part of a pitchfork tine. Two shallow grooves had been incised opposite one another—probably to keep the poison from being rubbed off. The hand-ground tip appeared to be as sharp as a leather needle. This simply had to be a goddamn movie, and I desperately wanted someone to shout, "Cut! It's a wrap," to break the spell.

Later that day I went up to El Cantón and bought cigarettes and a secondhand canvas-sheathed machete, then asked them to sharpen it for me. Noah the Rat was on the verge of peeing himself—I had just given him at least thirty sucres' worth of information, which I intended for him to spread. "The *meeester* bought a machete...it's war."

I also bought a stout mending needle, a small square of canvas, and heavy, waxed thread. Curious minds wanted to know why. "My duffel bag is torn, Noah. Got to fix it. I'm going to Loja with the next mule caravan. I shall record traditional songs in a settlement called Chuquiribamba."

"Oh, very good, *meeester*," grinned Noah the Rat. *Yes, very good, you furtive, smirking prick,* I thought as I stared back.

After dinner, I sewed a canvas sheath into the top of my *right* boot, making a home for the thin, bamboo-covered spike. Since I was a lefty, the mayorales would watch my left hand. At least I hoped so.

Later, Manuel, Efraín, and I held another short council in the trapiche while "repairing" it. We'd already discussed possibilities the night Antonio was murdered in Veintimita's tower. Now it was time to get specific. The plan was simple, perhaps even stupidly so. We were going to rescue the girls ourselves. No more boys and old men were to be sacrificed. In order to pull it off, we needed to lull Veintimita into a false sense of security. I would flee, "terrified," to Loja with a mule train early the next morning, both to establish an alibi and get Veintimita's mayorales to misjudge their advantage—the "underestimated" approach. The mule train's destination really was Chuquiribamba. But mine was just far enough down the trail to stay out of sight.

Tomás Chico's wife, Araceli, would go help her younger sister who lived on La Atalaya with her baby while the sister performed her mita obligations—she, and the girls' grandmother, would be the source of "news." Indian women, unless they were ripe fifteen-year-old virgins, were virtually invisible in southern Ecuador. It could work.

If don Fermín rescheduled the "party" or made an obvious move on the tower, a chaski would bring news to the trapiche at Los Faiques. Then, Manuel would head toward the trailside village of Manú wearing a jet-black poncho and a striped saddle blanket. Manú was only sixteen miles away but, given the terrain, was a rugged five- to six-hour ride.

I'd see Manuel but would not approach him if others were nearby. Manuel was already "scripted"—he would know nothing more than "the *meeester* rose early and went to Loja with the arrieros at dawn—something about songs in a place called Chuquiribamba near Loja. *Meeester* sounded frightened when he told us of his unexpected trip."

At dawn, garbed in felt hat and heavy, striped poncho, I paid the mule skinners to guide me to Chuquiribamba and rode just in front of the *atrasadero*, or "tailman." Forty mules ahead of me, there was only one guy behind to watch me.

I looked back frequently, nervous and in turmoil over a situation I could neither control nor walk away from. Since Eddy had first been molested, one or the other of those two options always worked out. But Ecuador was a different world—its own limbo. Biblical. And you didn't even have to die to get there. As the ill-fitting saddle pounded my ass, I pondered the differences between fear, free will, and plain old screwed.

We descended into the tight, humid valley of the Achucay. The narrow Río Achucay ran nearly as swiftly as the Rircay, but a shallow, treacherous ford yielded a crossing. The arriero in front grabbed my reins, silently leading the way across the glass-slick rocks. After I'd paid up, none of the mule skinners had spoken to me. Few even looked at me.

The first stop, Sebastián de Yuluc, was a settlement, nearly purely Indian, about two hours down the trail. The dark, squat, thatched-roof native houses were scattered along the trail in loose clusters. Dense stands of banana and fields of sugarcane filled in the lower areas. Eucalyptus, corn fields, and small groves of mango dotted the hillsides.

The locals came out in numbers, pawing at me or pointing as I went by. One kid yelled to a group standing on the hill above the trail, "¡Mira al meeester desde Yunguilla! (Check out the mister from Yunguilla!)" Well, at least Veintimita would hear I'd gone.

The caravan stopped there and several machetes and short mattock blades traded hands for cash and bags of coca leaves. I thought about slipping away, but it was far too obvious. So, I pulled off the heavy poncho and rolled it behind the saddle. Too hot.

Twenty minutes later, the veteran mule skinner at the head of the line snapped his chicote and ordered the caravan forward. The big money was another day further on.

About an hour later, I had my chance. We had begun the long climb up the steep hills that crested at about ten thousand feet before descending again into another narrow tongue of the valley of the Achucay near Manú. The trail was shaded from the sun, and I was freezing again. I pulled out of line at about the same time someone shouted to the atrasadero to move forward and assist with an emergency. One of the drover's yucca-fiber load ropes had broken up ahead, merchandise cascading out of his mule's burlap panniers.

I told the atrasadero I needed to stop—the "runs"—and would catch up by evening at the settlement of Moraspamba, if not earlier. Again, he said nothing, nodded, and moved forward, disappearing around a bend ahead. I'd "rented" one of Uribe's older, smaller mules, so the caravan had no ownership in my mount. Dead or alive, they had my fee. Clean profit, if I didn't slow them down.

Another five hours up an even more rugged trail, Moraspamba was the caravan's scheduled overnight stop after "roadside" sales in the villages of Manú and Lluzhapa. The next morning they'd climb to over twelve thousand feet before descending into the narrow lower canyons in Loja.

I pulled my mule uphill to a small meadow and dropped my pants for the benefit of any stragglers, then waited fifteen minutes. It was silent and beautiful; the purple misty haze of the lower Andes was punctuated across the valley below by the gray-greens and golden-straw colors of walled and terraced hillside farms, already a thousand years old.

Sweeping the area with the Nikons, I settled on a grove of trees beneath a rocky crag higher up and about a half mile away. Once there, a small copse under the lip of the hill gave me both protection from the wind and a great view of the trail below.

I made camp there, changing my identity by turning my tan and gray striped poncho inside out to expose a deep blood red. The felt hat went into my duffel and I pulled on a warm, speckled wool native watch cap with traditional ear flaps. The cap disguised my wavy brown, auburn-streaked hair—so unlike the straight jet-black common among these arrieros. From a distance, I was just another itinerant mixed-blood stockman, a *chagra*, on contract rounding up someone's lost sheep or cattle.

At dusk, a young shepherd wearing a dark poncho approached the hill, but seeing the mule and saddle nearby, must have assumed I was one of the arrieros. They were fierce and independent. No one save hacendados screwed with them in rural southern Ecuador. He moved off quietly.

As the last rays of the sun lit up distant snow-covered mountaintops to the north, a lone condor floated across the summit of a mountain to the east. Perfectly silhouetted for one moment by the sun, it was as if I'd been granted a glimpse into Ecuador's past. A past unsullied by the presence of the one species that screws up nearly everything it acquires.

Night fell quickly, bringing a sudden bone-chilling cold with it. The shepherd camped somewhere below. I could hear the faint tones of his panpipes and smell the acrid smoke from his fire, fueled partly by sheep dung. Shivering in the cold, I envied his sheep-shit campfire and wondered what Penrod would be doing in Manhattan. It would be about 9 PM there...

Mr. Yale was probably snugged up in an upscale local watering hole with a classy young "assistant," absorbing a

Tanqueray martini and listening to some decent jazz. In less than an hour, Thelonious Monk would step out onto the stage at Birdland or the Five Spot, his adoring fans totally unaware of condors, indios brutos, and pricks like Veintimita.

The peace and love set who frequented the Village Vanguard, though they thought themselves worldly, couldn't even have imagined places like Yunguilla, Santa Isabel, or Ambato, much less isolated Yuluc. And they certainly wouldn't have been able to process this mountainside where I was now freezing my ass off—or the events that had led to it. Rats the size of small terriers vomiting black goo wouldn't process well, either.

Though I was a wanderer, I liked Manhattan. It wasn't home turf for me, and it was provincial in its own way, but at the moment, I'd have much preferred climbing up the stairs to the "7-11," the legendary upstairs pool hall up on Forty-seventh Street where "Jersey Red," born Jack Breitman, would be screwing his cue together.

I'd played him a while back. One Pocket. That wiry, intense bastard, his red hair in tight natural waves, had gotten down over the balls, fierce as a hawk, and run ten nonstop racks, making absolutely impossible shots. I'd watched, never even getting a shot, then handed him the five hundred bucks I owed—worth every fucking penny just to say I'd played him.

Shooting "Jersey Red" was something you told your grandchildren—if you lived to have any. In contrast, you did not tell grandchildren about mayorales who sodomized young bridegrooms for sport or gang-raped sixteen-year-old twin sisters.

Ecuador, I decided, was right in there with parts of Africa on the human rights issue—in other words, off the scale. Worse, I was afraid of dying in some godforsaken place, like Yunguilla, where even Penrod wouldn't find me, my balls already floating in a jar of trago, the local equivalent of a golf trophy.

It wasn't a good night. My mind kept racing back to the comforts of the States and I was angry. The line that separated me from Garrote was getting fuzzy again. Instead of the lizardlike part of my brain reacting, I needed to get some cortex involved and figure out how to outmaneuver Veintimita—it's hard to outsmart a psycho. But getting those girls away from him might ruin what was left of his weakening hold on reality. Reflecting on the plan Efraín, Manuel, and I had put together in the trapiche, it already seemed too naive to work. And I had no intention of winding up like Antonio.

The next morning, I explored the crag just above me, keeping one eye on the trail below. I found Inca stonework atop the cluster of immense boulders. It had probably been a watchtower over the trail for six hundred years or so.

It dawned on me then that the mule skinners still relied on Inca infrastructure and that the villages they served were nearly all Indian enclaves from Inca times. A study of oral traditions in these settlements really could prove fascinating. I reacted, *I'm losing hold of reality. JA, old boy, you really need to get a grip. You've gotten lost in your own bullshit role.*

I was bored and nervous. The day passed slowly. I wanted Manuel to show up and release me from this lonely exile. The shepherd camped down on the grassy hillside moved on, seeking new grass, and the only folks using the trail below were Indian villagers carrying immense loads of firewood. The second night was both lonelier and colder than the first. In my imagination, I played Jersey Red again—beat his ass this time, then drank icy Ram's Head Ale in celebration.

Cheryl, the petite brunette who wore black patent leather stiletto heels, a little black dress, and one strand of expensive pearls, was a hustler groupie. Rich little Cheryl only fucked winning pool hustlers. After beating Jersey Red, he handed me the ten thousand dollars his stakehorse "Daddy Warbucks" had put up. Cheryl was finally interested. We had steaks at Delmonico's, washed down by dry martinis. Then a room at the Biltmore, where she went down on me. At 4 AM we drifted over to Birdland on Fifty-second Street to listen to Coltrane. Trane's horn was sublime...and seemed far too real for comfort.

As my fantasy passed, I noticed that the sky was clear for a change; I refocused and watched the stars drift across a snow-speckled ridge of mountains to the northeast, trying to identify Veintimita's weak spots. It came to me in a flash late in the night—booze, good booze. A more refined plan formed. A touch hokey, perhaps, but more likely to get us to the girls than the original. And this was Ecuador, where "hokey" seemed to go unnoticed. I slept.

The next day, munching my trail mix and totally frustrated, I began to convince myself that nothing would break right in this situation. That I'd merely sit on this mountain till I starved to death. Impotent. Dumb. And alone.

An hour later fate proved me wrong. A horseman appeared below, moving fast. Black poncho. Striped saddle blanket. Manuel. I rode down the far side of the crag to intercept him. But when he saw me, he turned his horse abruptly. I yelled. He reined in the mare. When I caught up to him he was still uncertain. "You looked like a chagra, Señor Juan."

"As intended. Is there news, Manuel?"

"Yes. But not good. The invitations must have been made from Cuenca—don Fermín's guests began to arrive unexpectedly last night and the party has already begun."

"*¡Pucha carajo!*" I snarled, my own voice sounding totally alien to me. "Have they gone to the tower yet, Manuel?"

"Not yet, but they have been drinking heavily. It will be soon."

Well, I thought to myself, *once Veintimita has partners in crime, he will have gained lots of protection. But it may already be too late to stop that...*

"I will follow you, Manuel, but don't hang back for me. Wait for me at the Pasajé highway. You can take the patrón's mule from there. I'll get a mixto and return to the hacienda separately. If you reach Los Faiques before me, send Efraín immediately to Cuenca for American whiskey. Here are two thousand sucres and a note of instruction. They have what I want at a store next to the Día y Noche. Go."

He grabbed the money, nodded his approval at the strategy, and disappeared at a fast trot. Passing through Sebastián de Yuluc, I caught up with him near the Pasajé highway about four hours later. Mules are surefooted, but not as fast as a horse.

Manuel had already been to Los Faiques, about three miles away, and sent Efraín to Cuenca. Obviously, Uribe had been invited to Veintimita's, since Efraín arrived in the jeep with don Ramón just after dark. Efraín brought four bottles of CC, two of Bacardi demerara-style rum, 180 proof, and a very high-octane bottle of excellent Peruvian pisco.

I wrote a note to Piggy:

*My esteemed don Fermín. I am sorry that I
cannot join your dinner party this evening.
I fell while on a mule trip to Loja and am
recuperating. Please enjoy the enclosed.
At your command, John Alexander, MA.*

I paused a moment, trying not to gag over my bull-shit, then handed the note to Uribe.

Don Ramón was concerned for my fall, but I assured him my back would be better after a day or two of rest and hot compresses. It probably never occurred to him I'd not been invited, or that Veintimita would love to see me dead and mutilated, so he took my note and the booze, impressed with my gift. It would have taken a field hand nearly a year of regular work to purchase it—a waste of money in one sense, but important in another. I needed Veintimita to see me as totally unpredictable...and uncontrollable.

Uribe drove his WWII-vintage jeep over to La Atalaya alone. *Hmm? No driver,* I noted. Efraín stayed below in the office until all was quiet, then we slipped away to a small gathering at Tomás Chico's thatched house.

It surprised me to find Araceli there. She was grim. "They sent all the local serving women away from La Atalaya after preparing enough food for several days—and the two mayorales returned again about an hour ago."

"*¡Carajo!* How will we know what happens next?" I asked her.

"The girls have been kept in the tower's dark lower strong room. If they are moved up to the big top-floor bedroom, there will be lights in the tower. My sister will send a chaski here if that happens."

Our wait might have become both long and tense, but one of the boys outside spotted headlights coming down the hill to Los Faiques just several hours later. Efraín headed back to the big house on a dead run.

Uribe had returned unexpectedly. And it wasn't even midnight. According to Manuel, who followed Efraín, don Ramón came back alone, sullen, and grim faced. About thirty minutes passed before a kid, who could not have been more than twelve, arrived at Tomás's, panting hard and speaking Quechua. Tomás translated, "They are all in the tower. It is brightly lit and the mayorales are guarding the lower stairway. They have shotguns."

Tomás sent three of the young shepherds to check. They returned about 3 AM, confirming the situation. According to the boys, Garrote and Baritone lounged on the tower's outer steps, making loud comments to one another and speculating on when they "would get scraps."

Araceli broke in, "It is useless, then . . . there is a huge bar inside the door, which is iron clad. Protection against raids." Friday night had come and gone, a half dozen of us dozing in Tomás Chico's dank, smelly house, helpless as kittens.

About 8:30 Saturday morning, Uribe's jeep sputtered to life and he headed back to Cuenca alone—another sign that things had turned ugly at Veintimita's. Everyone was tense in the settlement at Los Faiques until word leaked out about noon that Veintimita's mayordomo wanted the women serving mita to return—the party was being extended. More food and cleaning to do. They also ordered more booze.

Araceli was hysterical at the news. She didn't want to return to finish her mita, fearing that many drunken men in rut. But Tomás insisted she go that instant. In contrast,

189

I was elated. I trotted up to the village with Cayé and sent him to Cuenca in a mixto—he carried a note to Livia and Nestor. I needed more whiskey and rum—and as quickly as possible.

Then, we got an unexpected break. The mayorales had taken the girls down to the main house while the Indian women cooked and cleaned the recently vacated tower. Apparently, "the boys" didn't want the locals to see them. But their attempt at secrecy accomplished nothing— accounts of the hacendados sleeping it off in the big house came to us quickly. Meanwhile, the girls were sequestered in a gallery bedroom. The local Indian messengers moved fast. So did we.

CHAPTER SIXTEEN

RESCUE AT
LA ATALAYA TOWER
MARCH 15–22

E fraín and I mounted two of Uribe's best horses, accompanied by three of the teenage boys on mules, and rode to La Atalaya. Dismounting on a trail below, we left the boys with our horses and crawled up the hill.

I followed Efraín along the rear of the big house until we came to the tower from behind. It was no place for a fight—the cliff was only twenty feet from the house's rear wall. But Efraín had chosen this route because the walls were thick, and the small rear windows, almost gun-slits, were about eight feet off the ground. We simply could not be seen unless a guard was posted.

My heart was already pounding like a sledgehammer when we reached the rear corner of the old tower. I was certain one of the mayorales would pop up at any minute.

Efraín and I coordinated—right-handed, he'd leap to the right; me, to the left. We'd charge the mayorales if they still guarded the door. Efraín dropped his fingers, "*Uno, dos, tres—ya!*" We jumped—and scared the living shit out of Araceli and another Indian woman who were at the tower's open door, carrying huge bundles of bedclothes. Araceli regained her composure quickly and motioned us to a door up on the big house gallery. "The girls?" I whispered. She nodded, dropped the bedclothes, and grabbed the other Indian woman. "*La barra,*" she said pointing at the tower door.

Araceli was not stupid. The two of them dragged the huge squared door beam to the cliff and tossed it over, even as Efraín and I crept up to the gallery door. That huge beam sounded like a boxcar careening into the Grand Canyon. Upstairs, Efraín lifted the room's old-fashioned forged-iron lock. It opened.

Efraín eased inside, then reached out, waving me in. El Garrote was passed out on the floor. Nearby, the two naked and bloody girls were tied, butts up, over a huge table.

As we cut them loose, Ofélia moaned, "*No más, Patrón.*" Feliciana was flat-out unconscious. We grabbed blankets to cover them and each slung a girl over our shoulders.

I'd almost made it out with Feliciana when Garrote came to and squeaked loudly. I kicked him hard in the temple and he went limp, but the damage had already been done. A low door in one wall sprung open and Baritone, naked from the waist down, leapt at us, snarling. I yelled "Shit!" in English when Baritone raised the shotgun. Surprised, Baritone froze for a millisecond.

So did I, but Efraín merely grinned and stooped as if in submission. Baritone smiled. *We're fucked,* came the Voice. For once, I was inclined to agree. But, as Baritone put his thumb on the shotgun's hammer, savoring the moment, Efraín took one lightning-fast swipe at him just above the knee.

Baritone glanced down at the pitchfork tine protruding from his inner thigh near the femoral artery, looking amazed, but only managed a wide-eyed gurgle before he went down, gasping. I'd no idea curare worked so fast. On the other hand, the fat prick's twitching body blocked the bedroom door.

Undaunted, Efraín pulled the tine out and we headed through the interior door Baritone had used. It was the hacienda's office. Efraín jerked his head toward the old-fashioned desk as we passed. On top stood the row of Veintimita's trophies—each labeled trago jar contained one pair of testicles. I needed air. But we kept moving as fast as we could.

I staggered a lot with Feliciana, hyperventilating, but Efraín was as strong as a horse. He carried Ofélia as if she weighed forty pounds and also helped me down the stairs. By the time we got to the horses, I stopped to barf.

The boys holding our horses and several mules moved instinctively—like they'd done this before. The two girls went up onto the mules, the two bigger boys behind. The third boy, the girls' youngest brother, it turned out, stayed back with an old mule to block the canyon-side trail that wound back toward Los Faiques. He pulled out his sling, ready to ding any horses that followed.

Efraín and I took turns goosing the mules ahead of us. Thirty minutes later we were on Los Faiques' land again. Feliciana had come to but, disoriented, began to scream. Efraín dismounted and went to her while I watched the trail behind us. Fortunately, she recognized her uncle and shut up. We moved on, talking in low tones and trying to figure out what to do next. The original plan had been to move in at night and take the girls up to the Girón highway. But that wasn't going to work in broad daylight.

With Uribe gone to Cuenca, Tomás Chico's place seemed the best option, so we took the little-used trail that passed along the lower edge of the big house's plazuela, heading down to the settlement below.

As we crossed just below the plazuela, not wanting to be seen, someone yelled at us, and Efraín froze. Something shiny flashed. I looked. Again, a yell. "¡Señor Juan, venga!" It took me a moment to process the flash of chrome from the old green Pontiac parked in one corner of the plazuela. It was Nestor with the booze. I'd forgotten all about it. He yelled again, "Over here, pronto!" I nodded to Efraín, who'd seen, but didn't really "know," Nestor—"He's *confiable*," I whispered.

We got the girls into the back of the Pontiac with their youngest brother, who'd not been pursued. Nestor growled, "I'll take them to Solano. The doctor will come, and Livia will decide what to do next."

"Are you certain, Nestor? There may be trouble."

He patted his waistband. "I hope so. I am ready...and the chance to make decisions again will be good for Livia."

"The Veintimitas will be very angry," I interjected. Nestor grinned. "I mentioned that to my brother, Abelardo, when we went for the liquor. His response was quite gratifying—'Fuck them.'"

At least Nestor was out of the closet as a member of the family, and don Abelardo was finally growing some balls.

"Come to Cuenca with us, Señor Juan. Please, you are not safe here."

I demurred. "I've got business here, Nestor...and," I said, jerking my head, "there is Efraín." Efraín butted in. "Go to Cuenca. There is some protection among the gente. Fermín Veintimita has less power there. Besides, if you go, I don't have to watch over you." I hesitated, so he pushed. "You are hiding in Loja. You were never here, and I have not been at La Atalaya since the sacristan delivered the money. ¡Así es!"

"OK—give me five minutes, Nestor." I grabbed some gear upstairs, then jumped into the Pontiac. Feliciana was hemorrhaging and had gone into shock. Nestor cranked up the old straight eight and sprayed mud through every curve till we reached Cuenca. I got out before we reached the city center, still dressed as a chagra, and headed for Solano.

Two hours later, the entire Gonzáles clan, four packed carloads of them, including Livia, Andy, Abelardo, and his older brother, all went into the city clinic with the girls. That took balls. Big ones...and integrity. Livia stayed with the girls for several days. Feliciana required surgery to repair the damage to her torn anus. Ofélia was in better shape until she learned of her fiancé Marco's death, hanging from La Atalaya's gate.

At that news, pretty little Ofélia's face took on the aspect of a broken porcelain doll. According to Livia, she moaned rhythmically and banged her head against the wall, rocking herself, for two full days. By the morning of the third day she had gone utterly silent. They brought her back to Solano, where Livia put her in an upstairs bedroom.

Even Andy was frightened by Ofélia's blank stare. I suspect she saw herself reflected in Ofélia's dark, unfocused eyes. Just like someone who'd suffered a massive head injury, Ofélia simply did not react to external stimuli. Andy, frantic, began to read about emotionally induced catatonia.

But the most immediate problem was that Ofélia would not eat. After four days at Livia's, they took her back to the clinic, fed her by IV, and put her in the same room with Feliciana. Reunited, she did respond to her twin, but spoke only Quechua. The rest of us simply didn't exist in her private world.

Feliciana, though more gravely injured physically, was doing pretty well, by comparison. She'd seen her fiancé die and was angry. I think that anger saved her. In the end, she directed it outward. Ofélia had merely rolled hers into a roiling ball, which she guarded carefully as if in a dark closet, locking herself away with it for companionship.

The *gente de categoría* (upper class) of Cuenca were tense. People I didn't know came and went from the house on Solano, including a number of very light-skinned, well-dressed matrons. Those matrons usually exited Livia's door, their fleshy mouths drawn into tight little Os, arms crossed, supporting ample bosoms. But few men visited.

I didn't know much, since Livia was pleasant, but only in a distant sort of way. I was simply *there* on the patio, relaxing or smoking as a number of the matrons exited. Several nodded at me, but not one actually spoke. It smelled like a gender war among Cuenca's finest.

Nestor stuck close to Livia—"for her protection," he had said. So I spent a lot of time with Andy. Sometimes two "lessons" a day. If Feliciana was her sister Ofélia's momentary salvation, Andy came to be mine. Eddy even smiled at me once as I gave her a lesson. I loved watching her absorb knowledge, packing that huge head with information.

And her data-retrieval process was impressive. When I asked her a question, she'd close her eyes and frown—then I could actually see her eyeballs moving under her tightly shut lids, back and forth, back and forth—retrieving images of pages once read. When she'd come to the place she wanted, her eyes would pop open and she'd give me the answer.

The downside was her growing fascination with the protective arts. One afternoon I found her out back with a wooden stick, mimicking my daily midmorning practice with the brass-tipped "walking stick." She was at that moment caning the crap out of a bulging burlap sack hanging from a rope.

"Andy!" I'd exclaimed. "Just what are you doing?"

"Practicing. My rod and my staff shall be before me, John Alexander. I must learn to protect myself."

"Andy, that's not healthy. There are adults around you to keep you safe—your mom, Nestor, Abelardo."

"And you, John Alexander. Can you swear that you will always be here to protect me?" Well, hell...I paused on that one just long enough to validate her point. I had no intention of taking her to raise but tried to drop the hint gently.

"Well, Andy...I can't promise to be anywhere *forever*."

"I know. So will you answer a question?"

"Perhaps. What is it?"

"Exactly where are a man's testicles?"

"Huh? Ah...why do you want to know?"

"You are turning red, John Alexander. It is *anatomically* important—not sexually so. I need to know where to kick or thrust the butt of my stick." I think I must have gurgled or something. Whatever it was amused her. "If you can't *tell* me, draw it."

"OK." I drew her a picture on my pocket pad, as modestly as I could, folded it, handed it to her sheepishly, then walked away. As I reached the rear door of the main house, I heard a resounding thwack. *"¡Ya, Fermín! Te quedas gusano emasculado.* (There, Fermín! You are now a ball-less maggot.)"

Andy sounded jubilant and had used the Spanish diminutive to boot. Pure contempt—a soon to be eleven-year-old and already a ball-breaker. Emulating me. I chalked it up to the Ecuador Effect.

CHAPTER SEVENTEEN

FIESTA IN SANTA ISABEL
MARCH 27–30

During my ten days in Cuenca, don Fermín had, according to gossip, become something of a temporary recluse in Yunguilla. His mayorales were nowhere to be seen and his big-shot guests all had sudden "business" taking them away from the region. Duty to "progress" had even required several overseas trips.

One hacendado went to Brazil and two suddenly had business in Ireland. All nonextradition countries, of course.

Someone had again stolen the electric wire at Solano. Andy was concerned about it during one of our lessons.

"John Alexander, if you find wire to buy in Santa Isabel, get some for us to keep in the storeroom. My reading slows down when we use the lanterns. Promise?"

"OK, Andy, but there is no electricity in Santa Isabel."

"Really? Not even streetlights? How do the children study?"

"They don't, Andy. There is no school in the district. The hacendados' families all live in Cuenca. The peasants' kids don't matter."

She scowled. "That's not fair."

While Andy fretted about wire and social equality, I fretted about a sudden knock at the door and the detachment of uniformed cops who were, at any moment, sure to serve the murder warrant on me for Baritone, or Garrote, or both.

The next afternoon I had a pleasant lunch with Livia, but she was clueless about Andy and it was clearly a case of "it's *only* lunch."

"Well, Alex, we haven't seen much of you lately. It's been so hectic here, with the twins."

"It's a tense situation, Livia. I'm preoccupied with legal issues but have made time for Andy."

"So she tells me. Thank you. But she's been very fearful... even when I remind her how safe we are with Nestor here to protect us."

"That's good, Livia. But it's natural for Andy to worry. She tries to protect you, too."

"Oh, Alex, do be serious. Andy isn't thinking of things like that!"

"Perhaps you are right, Livia."

Then she again remarked, "I feel safe with Nestor." It was a complete non sequitur. Oh, well—her hair still smelled like buttercups and fresh straw. The worry lines at the corners of her pretty lips had softened a trifle, and I still wanted to make love to her, preferably right there on the table at Día y Noche, but Andy was right—I just wasn't a forever kind of guy.

Andy also hounded me about lessons in stick fighting. "Mother doesn't understand... *please*," she pleaded. I did finally relent, with misgivings. Like everything else, she absorbed it instantly and practiced with fierce intensity.

Then, on Friday, the twenty-seventh of March, I went back to Santa Isabel—the Fiesta of San Ysidro awaited me. I'd promised a dance to Araceli. I was also deeply curious about the fact that the rumor mill was on overload. Yet no "official" anything was in the wind about don Fermín's little eccentricities—if one can describe gang rape, torture, murder, and sodomy in the same vein as being stupid, drunken, twisted, a bad poker player, and a major loser. Sadly, Ecuador permitted such unusual juxtapositions for those with puesto.

At the hacienda, all was nearly as before. Everyone went about their business. Uribe was in residence—the fiesta, I supposed—so Efraín and Manuel were both busy and studiously distant. Fine by me.

Uribe was different. He asked me directly, "Have you seen Veintimita since the card party?"

"No, don Ramón—not once. I have been in Loja recording songs. Did you wish me to call on him for some reason?"

He stared at me, confused. Fact was I hadn't actually seen Veintimita. But he wasn't buying. "Are you certain? There are rumors."

"Ah. You must be referring to the unfortunate incident in Cuenca at the Día y Noche when one of his mayorales—a big man—bothered a woman I'd taken to dinner. The insolent pig must have had some kind of obsession with her—he followed us one other time, too, and with her little daughter present. Very ugly. The

Gonzáles family's chauffeur gave him a beating the second time. Frankly, the man got off easy. But what has this to do with Señor Veintimita?"

Uribe broke eye contact. Those accustomed to asking questions rarely like to answer them. And so it was with Uribe. He struck me as caught twixt serious inner conflicts. He needed to get along with Veintimita, had huge "close-up ranks—it's in our interest" motives, but actually loathed Piggy. Life is complicated, even for the chosen ones.

He muttered, "Oh, no...just tracking down some silly rumors," and wandered away.

I walked down to Tomás Chico's with my tape recorder. Cover, you know. Araceli was effusive. "My baby is growing and blessed, as she still has her *pulgar* and index finger, so will be able to work someday."

She gave me a hug and modeled her new pollera, twirling like a little girl showing off for mom. Her hair freshly washed and braided, she even smelled OK. Tomás was proud, his chest puffed out.

"You shall have the first dance with her tomorrow night at the fiesta."

"I am honored, Tomás...and she is so beautiful." And at the moment, she was; her strong nose, finely curved lips, and high cheekbones gave her an elegant look that almost overcame the premature wrinkles, furrowed brow, and bad teeth.

Then Tomás pulled me aside and briefed me. "The mayorales are gone, all except one young one and the mayordomo himself, who is running the farm while don Fermín lies around drunk and incoherent. No sign of the big mayoral." *Hell, I guess not,* I smirked to myself, but said nothing.

"And no sign of the giggler, El Garrote." *Well, shit, you can't have everything, can you?* I gloated privately. I didn't know whether or not the toe of my boot had finished him off. Frankly, I hoped so, but the screwy bastard seemed to have more lives than an alley cat.

At least no one had filed murder charges yet against Efraín and me. I'd been waiting for something like that for days. But what had they done with Baritone's body? Surely the curare killed him. He'd collapsed like he'd been hit by a garbage truck.

The thin veneer of tranquility actually unnerved me— I simply did not like Ecuador's endless mysteries. Why were some poor guy's balls floating in a bottle of trago, while the really rotten bastards had so far proven darkly immortal? And if not immortal, why wasn't I already in some windowless stone cell at ten thousand feet above sea level, begging the cholo jailers to ease up on the cattle prod shoved up my ass?

Trouble had become normal, even reassuring, during this Ecuador gig. Peace and tranquility creeped me out and confused my instincts—not to mention the Voice. I needed to finish this assignment and get out before my Dr. Jekyll capacities took over completely.

The fiesta dance took place in a huge, rough-timbered barn near Santa Isabel. Usually used for livestock auctions, it reeked of animals. Earlier in the day, a long procession of men had carried their carved statue of San Ysidro, patron saint of farmers, through the streets of Santa Isabel, then gone to the church. That done, it was party time.

I arrived with Tomás Chico and Araceli. There were already hundreds inside, mostly Indians. The crowd was about 80 percent Indian and 20 percent cholo or poor mestizo. I saw no hacendados—apparently, they partied privately. There were lots of dark purple ponchos, blacks, a variety of reds, and some stripes—typical of the district's mixed-blood mayorales. Most stopped to stare as we entered. It's weird being considered something of a carnival freak—and *meeesters* certainly qualified.

At five foot ten I towered over the crowd, which averaged a spare five feet. I was dressed "European" in a Harris tweed jacket, dark pants, and a cheap panama hat from Machala. The kids gaped.

This being a public event, most tried to speak Spanish. A few of the women, perhaps assuming I didn't understand much of anything, made flamboyant remarks in Spanish about my possible "size." Apparently, some of the Quechua-speaking women did, too—judging from their giggles and the obvious irritation of their nearby men. I'd have been more meaningfully flattered had I any use for my *plátano* other than peeing.

As the locals tired of gaping at me, things settled down, and the pandemonium returned to normal. Several large hearths inside, along with the packed crowd, made the heat and smell hard to deal with. But no one, save me, appeared to notice.

At one hearth, the steaming hot trago was prepared. The combination of brown sugar, boiling water, and cane alcohol was being passed out in an endless stream of large shot glasses. No one washed them once used. My colon constricted involuntarily in anticipation of maladies to come.

But the booze was unavoidable. It tasted like gasoline, flavored with a hint of caramel, and burned like Drano on the way down. It would have sent Penrod straight to intensive care. Me—I was tough, so I managed not to barf up the first esophagus-searing double. After that it got easier.

I danced with Araceli, the crowd leaving quite a circle around us. Tomás told anyone who'd listen, "My woman. Sooo beautiful." She was coy and happy. "Thank you again for saving my huahuita." Lubricated by four or five ounces of 190-proof gasoline, I managed to dance to "Antonio Mocho."

At the second stanza of "Antonio," everyone danced and most broke into Quechua. "*Antonio Mocho machashca llaquipac...*" For folks who rarely talked to strangers and were suspicious of one another, they certainly could stomp their feet and twirl in unison to the distinctive beat. I chalked it up to the truckloads of booze being metabolized around us.

As the booze worked on me, I began to sweat, so I stripped off the Harris tweed and left it, my chicote, and walking stick by the hearth where several of Tomás's extended family were barbecuing rows of fat cuy on sticks.

As I handed Tomás's eldest sister my coat, whip, and stick, she handed me a choice cuy. Ordinarily I didn't willingly eat rodents, but this time it tasted great—rich and smoky.

The cuy gone, I was in a dancing mood, and a number of the *sipa*—the young, single Indian girls—had lined up to dance with *el meeester*, their moms imploring me loudly to accommodate.

They all flirted and asked the very same questions as we danced. "*¿Soltero, meeester?*" "Yep, I'm single." Grins, fluttering eyelashes, then, "*¿Huahuas tiene, meeester?*" "Nope, I have no children." I worked the sipa—"Dance, Señorita?"

About a dozen dances later, I kissed one Indian beauty, who had a smile the size of Rhode Island. The crowd cheered. Penrod and his oh-so-sophisticated current "assistant" would have fainted at the scene. I, on the other hand, shouted, "*¡Trago! ¡Más trago!*"

More glasses of bubbling gasoline were instantly passed to me. *Shit, this stuff is* good, I told myself, *now, if I could just import it to the States on an exclusive basis . . .*

The crowd was jubilant as waves of laughter rolled back and forth from one end of the barn to the other, just like "the wave" at a major league baseball game. Lit up by the booze and still twirling, I didn't even notice when the music stopped.

To my credit, I did notice the look of fear on my young Indian dance partner's face as she backed away from me. Then I focused on the huge empty circle around me. It got very quiet all of a sudden, and my Voice hadn't even warned me. He never seemed to be on duty when I drank.

"Hee, hee, hee, aack. *¡Estás fregado, meeester!*" There stood crazy, gyrating Garrote, machete in one hand, club in another. With him—*No, it can't be,* my brain insisted—was Baritone holding an old hammer shotgun.

Baritone looked weird—one side of his face nearly normal, the other was, well, waxy and sagging like a character straight out of a Dick Tracy comic strip. But I was far too full of trago to be frightened.

I grinned. "You're already dead, you big, ugly son of a bitch." One side of his mouth tried to move, but he couldn't talk. He lurched forward, shakily raising the shotgun with one arm. The waxy side of his body was obviously paralyzed, the bad eye closed—his lumpy, flaccid eyelid quivered, huge and pale, like a freshly opened oyster.

"Pués—of the three of us I'd say that you're more fucked than I am, big man," I taunted again. He twitched and jerked forward again. As the crowd roared in approval at my taunts, I stepped quickly to the side, out of the shotgun's direct line of fire. Like an answered prayer, Baritone fumbled the hammer with his now useless left hand and it didn't go off. Garrote reached to help him.

I refocused while he and Garrote paused, looking confused and checking out the crowd around them, apparently unused to anything but fear and resignation from their intended victims. From behind, Tomás Chico's voice was clear—"Reach back, compadre." I did, and the ironwood butt of the whip was shoved into my open palm.

"¡Ya! ¡Música!" I shouted. The explosive response gave me about one second to move forward—if I wasn't too snockered—and wrap the whip around the shotgun barrel before they managed to cock it. But I never got the chance to play hero. As I prepared to leap forward, another whip flicked out of the circle near Baritone, caught the shotgun, and jerked it away.

Baritone went down groaning, his good arm upraised in supplication. The arm hung there, disembodied for a moment, then disappeared as the crowd closed over him like an angry sea of ants. Garrote, mouth open and teeth bared like a baboon, turned to me screaming in rage. Machete raised, he was already halfway to me. Clumsily, I fumbled the whip and moved back a step. Someone shouted, "Reach back!" and shoved my stick at me. "It's hot," the person said. "Hot" wasn't the right adjective—the brass mountings instantly blistered my hand.

I dipped into a low fencing position, the scalding stick protecting my head and back, then arched up hard, trying to catch Garrote in the forehead. Damn! The stick kept on going. I missed. *You drunken idiot,* I chastised myself and braced for the machete's fatal blow.

But nothing else happened. The music stopped again. Kids gaped, and the crowd roared in approval. I looked up. The fire-heated brass Maltese cross on the head of my stick had gone right into Garrote's open mouth.

I got one whiff of a sickening burned smell as the crowd surged forward and, as with Baritone, consumed him. Those mestizo and cholo guests not wearing ponchos were frantically heading for the exits.

Yet in another minute or two, everything returned to normal. Tomás Chico grabbed me, waving his arms to the fiesta mayorales. "You heard our guest—music, dancing, trago, cuy!"

The crowed cheered. Jubilant. Drunk, I cheered, too. They struck up the song "Leña Verde." "Nice touch," I said to Tomás. He grinned. "Not to worry, Señor Juan—we shall dance all night in peace."

I don't even remember when the dancing ended. I do recall falling a couple of times while negotiating the footpath down to Los Faiques. An odd Sunday if ever there was one. And Sunday's hangover was spectacular. It lasted much longer than Saturday night's trago-induced joie de vivre. My head pounded as I worried about what actually had happened to Baritone and Garrote.

Were they simply whisked away, their butts kicked one more time? Or were they now history, courtesy of an angry mob? And whose whip had flicked out of nowhere to send the shotgun flying? Hangover or not, I needed to find out. As I sobered up, the Voice returned, tormenting me.

About three in the afternoon I struggled down to Tomás Chico's. Every step taken reenergized the nauseating pounding in my skull. In contrast, Tomás was fine. Even ebullient. "Last night was a marvel. Who would have believed those mayorales stupid enough to assault you there among so many they have abused?"

"What happened to them, Tomás?"

"Justice, Señor Juan. Even though your wish was not granted, justice was delivered."

"Wish? *What* wish, Tomás?"

"You requested that they be skinned alive and their hides nailed to La Atalaya's tower door."

"I said *what*?"

"Do you not remember?"

"No," I answered. "So, what *did* happen to them, Tomás?"

"I do not know, Señor Juan—but both were still alive when carried out of the barn."

"Really?"

Araceli broke in, "The skinny one *solo sufrió*... oh... *lliqui similla*."

"Tomás, please translate that."

"Yes, a 'broken mouth.' Both were breathing still. Everyone here in the settlement is definite on that. But after... only those in charge know."

"So, who was 'in charge'?"

"I do not know. But it is usually the men whose family has been wronged."

"Efraín and his clan?" I asked.

"Many could assume this possibility, but one could not say, Señor Juan—between those two mayorales, *many* families were wronged. The wronged might easily number in the hundreds. It might be any of them."

Well, at least I'd gotten the local Indians' company line. I imagined I could hear their testimony. "They were alive when they left, Señor Magistrate. No one knows what happened after, and hundreds could be implicated in a motive for revenge. These two raped, beat, and abused many."

I climbed back up to the big house for coffee to ease the pounding in my skull. Withdrawing to my room with the mug, I drained it, then shuttered the window to darken the room, soaked a rag in water, and lay down, pressing the cool cloth over my eyes.

Sometime after I'd fallen asleep, someone rapped on my door. Efraín wanted to talk. That alone riveted me. "Señor Juan, Veintimita is in an uncontrollable rage. It is said that his mayordomo took him to Cuenca several hours ago to initiate a murder investigation."

"Murder? Tomás Chico insisted that the mayorales were alive when they were carried out last night," I protested, still hopeful.

"They may have been. No one is certain. When the crowd grabbed them, many took the opportunity to deliver their blows. But some of the mestizos who were there, it is said, have offered Veintimita testimony that you murdered Garrote."

That unnerved me. The Voiced weighed in. *Just what did you expect, dumb-ass?* I paused, then asked, "Why would they testify to that if others saw the two alive?"

"Money, favor, debts erased...and because they hate *meeesters* and fear Indians. These local mestizos are talking up the idea of an Indian rebellion against the gente."

"Class and race war, huh?" He nodded. "Anyway, Efraín, thanks for the help with the shotgun—that was you, wasn't it?"

He grinned, enigmatic. "No one really saw who it was, Señor Juan, but you should be very careful. People in Santa Isabel have implicated you."

"Noah among them?" He nodded; I wasn't certain what to do, so I asked, "Should I stay here or go to Cuenca, Efraín?"

"Stay here several days. Be unconcerned. See what happens."

Be unconcerned? As opposed to what? I wondered. Outwardly, Efraín reacted as if it were just another daily problem—something on a scale equal to stripped teeth in his tractor's gearbox. In the States, all this would be ended by, "And that's the way it is...March 30, 1970," as a stone-faced Walter Cronkite signed off the evening news.

CHAPTER EIGHTEEN

DEPOSITION, LOS FAIQUES

APRIL 1

All of a sudden, the gente, spearheaded by Fermín Veintimita, wanted justice. "Law and order" needed to be reestablished in Yunguilla.

Over the next several days a number of conversations began with the phrase, "*se trata de principios* (it's about principles)."

Noah used it when he closed my "account" at El Cantón, his dad nowhere to be seen, and demanded that I settle up. I did—on the spot—requiring him to sign and date my receipt. That made him nervous. His hostility neither offended nor surprised me. He was one of those characters who would do *anything* to gain a seat in the ruling elite's private circles. He meant about as much to me as a piece of toilet paper I'd just wiped with. Less, actually. But he could do damage by spying on me and passing on information.

Nonetheless, I sneered, "Thanks for releasing me from my promise to Los Faiques' patrón, don Ramón, to do business *only* with El Cantón. Much appreciated."

That pissed him off. "Oh, and *meeester*, we *fired* Cayé this morning. He proved to be a thieving Indian after all." I stared hard at Noah, who blinked when I spit on the floor, turned casually, and walked out. In Noah the Rat beat the heart and soul of the wannabe elite in southern Ecuador...principled. Biblical.

It was the same with virtually all of my dealings with "whites" and mestizos in Santa Isabel. On Wednesday, a nervous Efraín woke me early. A magistrate from Cuenca had arrived at Los Faiques, court clerk and typewriter in tow, accompanied by a pistol-toting Ecuadorian army sergeant, no less.

The instant Efraín stepped out, closing the door behind him, the Voice returned. *Run while you can!* I lit a smoke and told him to fuck off.

It was deposition time. Old hat. I'd been down this road a dozen times. Human rights assignments and pissed-off local judiciaries go hand in hand. We went to the table below the gallery. I asked María for tinto and fruit. While the magistrate stood by fretting, and the court clerk looked confused, I ate a leisurely breakfast and didn't even invite them to be seated. Finally, the magistrate, fat, fiftyish, and tiring, asked to sit.

I've won the first round, I gloated. I stood, posing, my hand generously outstretched—"Of course, if you wish. I did not invite you to eat with me because it is not my house. Se trata de principios...you know."

At that, someone hidden around the far corner of the plazuela giggled. "*Meeester*" wasn't sweating the situation—and why should I? Penrod's foundation big shots would simply have phoned golfing buddies at the UN. Even Efraín, still standing at attention nearby, relaxed.

The magistrate got right to it, but I answered in my own way. "Well, we need to back up a bit. Let's start with hostility from two mayorales who allegedly work at La Atalaya. These events all began on a bus when I entered the country several months ago."

I recounted Ambato—the young clerk's eyes bugged out at Garrote defecating on the dying Indian. She stopped typing and looked inquiringly at the magistrate.

"It's part of the record," I insisted. "Type it as stated, please. Good, thank you. Now to the attempt at assaulting Livia Chuca, viuda de Gonzáles, at the Día y Noche in Cuenca...and the second attempt at Puerto Bolívar—all before witnesses."

They didn't like how this was going, but I left out the gang rape and rescue—clear evidence of *intent* to kill Garrote could be attributed to kicking him in the head. That would give them "premeditation." Even without the Voice to reign me in I wasn't that impetuous.

Efraín actually grinned when I got to the fiesta part. "The big one aimed a shotgun at me and said I was 'fregado' in front of three hundred people. Someone jerked it away from him. The other one came after me with a raised machete. I hit him in the mouth with my walking stick. I'm told that the fiesta authorities disarmed them and escorted them out, but you would have to ask others. I went back to dancing. By the way, what charges led to this deposition?"

"Murder, *meeester*," replied the magistrate.

"You mean 'señor,' I believe. And who was murdered?"

The magistrate coughed, looking sheepish. "Well, *Señor*, this is preliminary. The bodies have not yet been found, but they will soon be so." From twenty feet away, Efraín shook his head no almost imperceptibly.

"Well, since someone has involved me, I trust the court will keep me informed."

Feeling like my old, pre-Ecuadorian self for a change, I stood up abruptly, smiled, made eye contact, and said, "I have to get back to work on my research project. Have a good day." Over the next seventy-two hours, a number of the other locals were interviewed briefly. Dozens more asked to be deposed.

By Thursday night, the magistrate and clerk had left Santa Isabel, frustrated. They had no bodies, only about half a dozen scanty cholo or mestizo depositions, and so many juicy Indian ones that he and his clerk did not know what to do.

As the process unfolded, I began to grasp the dimensions of the gente's dilemma. I had stayed at the dance. That was indisputable. I'd been seen by a number of local shepherds falling-down drunk, still accompanied by Araceli and Tomás Chico as I went down the footpath to Los Faiques about 5 AM. The Indians—even a few of the more Indian cholos—backed that story.

In contrast, fewer than a half-dozen wannabe "white" townsmen had accused me of murder in depositions for the magistrate. Even worse for Veintimita's side, Livia, Nestor, and others had been deposed in Cuenca. But it wasn't the weight of the numbers that created the judicial dilemma—it was the absence of bodies, combined with a threat to the *perceived* power of the gente.

Either a lone *meeester* had come to Yunguilla and established nearly instant messiah-like control over hundreds of

Indian serfs—who committed murder and mayhem at his behest—or they had no case.

The deepest problem for the gente and the local hacendados was, absent bodies, to pursue the idea that they'd lost control over "their" own peasants. The elites couldn't afford to have an outsider appear powerful. That was culturally, not to mention sexually, unacceptable.

Ten hacendados standing up in open court claiming that a lone *meeester*—a "sissy little scholar" no less—had wandered into their district and taken control of their "patrimony" simply was not going to happen. They'd become the laughingstock of southern Ecuador. Their precious, macho egos would suffer. Worse yet, the Indians might get ideas.

Thus, a desperate and frustrated Fermín Veintimita emerged from his hole in Yunguilla and thrashed around Cuenca for a few days, whining and trying unsuccessfully to overcome the dilemma.

Then he went to the big port of Guayaquil, returning to La Atalaya through Machala with a new crew of five ominous-looking "mayorales," who all carried pistols along with their whips. Imported muscle. If the courts couldn't give him back his unquestioned power, he'd get it the way he'd always done—old-fashioned brutality.

Efraín and Manuel came upstairs to give me the news. "Two of the new mayorales have already been spotted atop a hill on Los Faiques' land, binoculars trained on the big house, a rifle or shotgun with them," Manuel explained.

"Hired assassins. Professional hunters. They are well fed at La Atalaya. Beef and eggs. Very expensive labor. You must leave, else they will kill you," insisted Efraín.

This did rattle me and, dammit, the Voice piled on, fueling my fear: Given the pressure that UN agencies could put on Ecuador's court system, without bodies the locals couldn't keep me in jail for more than six months or a year. That I could handle. I'd done four months in Guatemala during the '66 assignment and a few ugly weeks in Mexico when I was twenty. But murder in a rural setting? Poof! No more JA—and nothing left behind but one more unsolved, soon forgotten Ecuadorian mystery. So I asked outright, "Any more word on the final whereabouts of Garrote and the other?"

"No," said Manuel. "That will never change, Señor Juan. A mule train leaves from this side of El Tablón tomorrow at dawn. It is going to the village of Trapichillo near the town of Catamayo in Loja. Eight to ten days on the trail each way, it passes through Chuquiribamba and climbs the mountain near there. The round trip takes two to three weeks. The mule train's capitán is a cousin of my wife's. It is safe. *Please* go. These new men of Veintimita's will be gone by the time you return."

Efraín put in his opinion. "Go, and not a word to anyone. Here is your stick. I cleaned and polished it. You may need it." I reached out and took the stick, turning it slowly in my hand. It looked new. Efraín, watching me turn the stick, grinned for once and continued, "I am going to Cuenca for a week or two to oversee manufacture of a new trapiche for don Ramón."

"And your nieces, Efraín?" He stared into the distance as his dark felt hat began to turn in his hands.

"They are safe in a convent up in Imbabura Province. Your friend Señora Gonzáles arranged it. Feliciana is being treated for her *susto* (fright, caused by the casting of spells)."

"And the sacristan?"

"He is with the twins . . . and wishes you well." As Efraín and Manuel walked away, I checked out my stick again for any signs of... "soiling." Nope, spotless. Still, the image of it sticking out of Garrote's open mouth like a giant popsicle made me light-headed. I gulped air to clear my head, but the remembered smell of his scorched flesh washed over me like a foul wave.

The Arriero's Trail to Loja

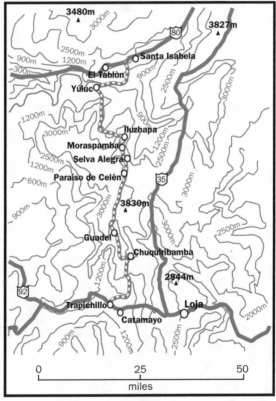

DETAIL

Map by Charlotte Cobb

CHAPTER NINETEEN

LOJA
PROVINCE
APRIL 6–16

At 5 AM the next morning, the mule train's capitán met me on the highway, just beyond Santa Isabel. He emerged at a trot from a dense morning mist, holding the reins of a sturdy cinnamon-colored mule in his off-hand. The mule trailing behind him sported a striped blanket, fancy saddle, and those amazing engraved, brass-toed stirrups that were throwbacks to the colonial period.

"Señor Juan, I am Rafael Trujillo, the capitán." He reached down and handed me the reins. "Here is your mule. You shall be one of my mayorales at the front of the remuda. You will ride with me. Here is your poncho and mayorales hat. Do you have your chicote and a good knife?" I nodded. "Good. Say little until we are well into Loja."

Trujillo cut a striking figure. As straight and square as a railroad tie, he had curly, silvering hair worn long. His knotted hands were the size of dinner plates. A striped poncho, silver-mounted belt, and an ancient gray fedora that tilted to one side added to the effect. Everything about him exuded confidence.

He looked me over, nodded, then wheeled his mule, motioned me to follow, and moved away at a fast trot, never looking back to see if I could stay with him.

Thirty minutes later we were on the trail to Loja. Northern Loja was altogether another world. It might as well have been a separate country. Many of the Saraguros, the local Indians, dressed head-to-toe in black—mourning, it is said, the death of their last Inca ruler, Atahualpa, at the hands of the Spanish. If time had stood still in Ecuador's central sierra, it had never even presumed to march forward in Loja's northern mountains.

The geography was unexpected—*yungas* (subtropical valleys) clung tenaciously to narrow canyon bottoms. In between the valleys, steep hills, seven thousand to nine thousand feet in elevation, were swathed in the highland's normal patchwork of pale green and yellow stone-walled farm plots, which rose up incongruously from the tentative subtropical slivers of humid lowlands. The contrasts were startling.

As we topped the first few "hills," I'd pause to look back, edgy, the Voice yammering at me. *Watch your back— don't trust these characters to do it for you!* Finally, Trujillo commented, "No one is following. The atrasadero knows to signal if anyone is seen." He patted me on the shoulder and smiled. I began to relax.

Rising from the mists above the hills there were distant, purplish outlines of even higher mountains. Three distinct cordilleras angled through Loja like ancient ribs, supporting the lands below: the Andes, the "Cordillera Real" to the Spanish, the lower Cerro de Arcos, and the Cordillera Cordoncillo, which topped out at just over twelve thousand feet southwest of the small city of Saraguro.

For twenty days I rode with Capitán Trujillo up and down every hillside and canyon in central Loja. Hot, then cold. Biting wind, then smothering humidity. Constipated one day from eating bananas purchased for pennies along the trail—the runs the next day from highland water tainted by sheep dung.

Bananas and papayas grew in one narrow canyon, the sweating locals wearing tattered short-sleeved shirts and cheap black-banded panamas from the Cuenca area, then an hour or two later, at nine thousand feet, silent, black-clad Saraguro Indians hoed potatoes with their *lampas* (colonial style hoes/shovels) and herded sheep up on the quilted green and straw-yellow slopes.

This trail was tough work. Of course, had it not been, there'd have been no profit in the mule trains—the only regular connection to the outside world for many of the isolated communities. And northern Loja *was* isolated...

Just after dawn on the second day, we topped an immense hill and emerged above an extensive, grassy tableland. The brilliant, slanting rays of an early-morning sun lit up the fields below us where long rows of shawl-clad Indian women stooped rhythmically, stuffing puffs of yellow into large sacks, then moved forward. Trujillo came to the rear, quickly moving his men on past the scene. I asked him what was up.

"Señor Juan, below us is an hacienda where they grow daisies to use as insecticide. The owners are Swiss, but the managers are local. They treat their Indians badly. There—see the rows of mayorales riding behind the women."

I squinted, pulled out my Nikons, and focused. The mounted mayorales, their striped robes and brass-mounted stirrups glinting in the sun, were rhythmically whipping at the row of women to keep them moving. Stragglers got hit—even if they had babies on their backs.

I passed the binoculars to Trujillo, showing him how to focus them. He shuddered. "The babies...such bastards! Now you know why I want my men over that hill. Half are Indian, but we arrieros are *all* free men. ¡Ya! *Feo.* It's time to go." They moved on quickly in single file.

I hung back to take one last look through my glasses just as the nearest mayoral's whip cracked, leaving a huge spatter of blood where a baby's face had been moments before. Eddy materialized, staring at me with big, teary eyes. I reacted. Before I even realized it, I was down the hill, the cinnamon's nostrils spewing foam.

The mayoral stared in disbelief as I rode him down and drove my bastón's steel spike deep into his cheek-bone, snarling, "Welcome to Judgment Day, you bastard!" I was gone, elated and free again, before he or anyone else could react.

Even better, the mule had displayed the instincts of a war horse. Head down, it had shouldered the mayoral's horse to the ground, grunting in satisfaction before it sped away.

Forty minutes later I caught the rear of the mule train and slowly worked my way forward. Trujillo looked at me suspiciously as I drew even with him. "What happened, Señor?"

"Had the runs, Capitán."

"Are they finished?"

"I think so."

"Good. Stay close to me. Don't stray again." I nodded. He motioned me ahead of him. I knew I'd pissed him off, but I was finally calm inside. I took in a deep breath and relaxed, focusing on the trail.

The old mule trail was wide and worn down three or four feet deep into most of the hillsides. Small patches of unmelted late winter snow clung to sheltered, north-facing notches in the higher peaks. Inca stonework dotted hills overlooking the trail. Ancient tambos.

By the third day I realized that this very trail had once been *the* Inca Empire's equivalent of its own Pan-American Highway—the route through the heart of Loja, which had connected the Incas' northern seat of power, modern Quito, to its first great seat of power, Cuzco, in southern Peru. Each day we rode past scores of stooped, barefooted Indians bearing huge loads, trudging on to the next market town, just as they'd done for at least six hundred years.

No wonder the highland Indians, all the way from southern Colombia south into Peru, spoke basically the same language—Quichua (Quechua in Peru and Bolivia).

Everywhere I went, *huahua* was "baby"; *chagra*, "cowman"; *washka* was "rope"; *huarmi* was "woman"; *Inti*, the sun; and *cuy* was cuy—even to the whites and mestizos, who rarely ate them.

Amazingly, "*meeeester*" was the *only* universally known "Anglo-American" word. So embedded was it that several locals in Santa Isabel had once actually tried to convince me that "*meeester*" was "old castellano," or colonial Spanish.

By the afternoon of the third day, we'd crossed the Río Achucay twice and had sold dozens of forged knife blades and liter tins of Kerex in Manú. We moved on and had begun the long, slow climb up the steep trail to Lluzhapa when I decided to use episodes from this trip in my report to Penrod.

What did it were the Indian women who lined the trail beyond Manú, holding their babies up to us, "Please, *buy* my baby—fifty sucres! No? Twenty. *Please*—I have no food to give my huahuita!"

This episode bothered me deeply. My thoughts again turned to my twin, Eddy, the foster homes, orphanages, and the parents neither of us could actually remember. But the realities of rural northern Loja in 1970 were far worse than anything we'd suffered. *Sold* to a stranger for a pittance...

Here I was, trying to save my own butt in order to write yet another wise-ass report for rich, bored foundation groupies in Manhattan, and avoid the nine-to-five world, when local women were trying to sell their starving babies to strangers—for *one* US dollar. Oddly, these realities calmed me as my own past came into clearer focus.

Quietly, I leaned to Trujillo and asked if I could take notes. "After Lluzhapa and a bit beyond, but not between Selva Alegre and Paraíso de Celén. There is a dirt road there—about a half-day ride where we move along the 'highway' from Saraguro to the Pasajé road—too public. Risky. But you can do as you like once we are able to smoke again past Lluzhapa. That is too far from Yunguilla to be a danger."

"*Gracias. Yo cumplo.* By the way, Capitán—is it common to see the mothers trying to sell their babies?"

"Yes—nearly always. A number of my men were once such infants. At least they were saved. Sometimes we find babies dead along the trail. We bury them when we can."

"Do the mothers simply abandon them?"

"No, Señor Juan—it is tradition that they pray for a miracle before a child is left...they ask the angels to guard them."

"Doesn't sound like it works, does it?" I muttered.

"It is God's decision, Señor Juan."

Lluzhapa, a mountain town—like most settlements with Quechua names—was a slow, slippery, dizzying climb along a high canyon, made miserable by the driving rain. Once there, we gathered in the plazuela of an abandoned hacienda house above the trail. Probably not occupied for a hundred years, descendants of its builders, according to Trujillo, now lived in Saraguro and rented the old house as a hostel to the mule trains during the rainy season.

Mercifully, the rains ceased as we dismounted and tethered the animals. Even better, the big house held the thirty-odd mule skinners easily. I roomed with Trujillo and two other mayorales in what had once been a side parlor. The rest spread their bedrolls out on the rough planks that formed the floor of the huge main room.

The house emanated an odd metallic smell mixed with undertones of mold and ammonia. I simply couldn't place the unusual bitter antiseptic odor.

Trujillo noticed me sniffing and, pointing to the wide floorboards, offered an explanation. "*Quina* planks—from the bark of this tree they once extracted quinine for the *mal aire*. They cut great quantities of it here more than a century ago—even more to the south and east—destroying the forests."

"Really? This far north? I thought all the quinine came from Amazonas Province."

"Yes—it once grew here as well. The debarked trees were then used to build the great house floors. In my great-grandfather's time, he still made money bringing in saw blades and draw knives made in Guayaquil, trading for sacks of quina bark to resell for processing on the coast. It was how my family started in this business. Just two mules and several burros. Tough work in those days."

I rubbed my saddle-numbed butt to regain feeling. "It's still hard, Capitán," I commented.

"Yes. It is work—and the trade is not like it once was, but I now own thirty-four mules and sixty burros. It is quite satisfactory…but I am surprised that you are not more affected by the saddle. You are doing quite well."

I showed him the miracle of pantyhose under my baggy cotton pants. "I cheated," I confided. "In the States, women use these to make their legs and butts more attractive. I use them to prevent chafing. I am sore enough as it is."

He laughed. "They must work well; I was beginning to marvel." Pantyhose, the secret refuge of greenhorns. As night fell, the men in the *sala grande* lit a fire in the old *chimenea*—the afternoon's cold, wind-blown rains had left all our gear sodden and at about seven thousand feet, it was rapidly turning both cold and dark.

The fire didn't help much, but one of the scrawny, hawk-nosed Indian boys who led burros also set the huge tin coffeepot on the fire and began to dry our ponchos, turning them every half hour or so. I shivered, anticipating the coffee and dry poncho. The rest of the house was dank and moldy and pitch-black—the windows' stout, iron-clad shutters were nearly all rusted shut, as they had been for years.

"Where do we pee?" I asked Trujillo before his candle lantern went out.

"Outside is preferable. But the far wall is acceptable." I stepped out quickly while soft light from the main room's fireplace still flickered inside. This old hacienda had never known electricity. Once the fire guttered, utter darkness would prevail.

The night sky was amazing. Clear and about forty degrees Fahrenheit, a sliver of brilliant moon lit up parts of the valley below. A narrow ribbon of rippling silver reflected back from the Río Achucay behind us, to the west. It was probably less than five miles away as the crow flies, yet it had taken us a hard day on the trail's endless switchbacks to reach our stopover.

No wonder time had stood still in parts of the highlands. It might as well have still been 1750 along this trail. Except for an occasional plastic bucket, I'd seen almost nothing of modern manufacture along the way. Even the style of forged axe-heads used by Indian woodcutters was antique.

The arrieros' ponchos, hats, saddles, baggy pants, yucca-fiber ropes, rough-tanned boots, wooly sheepskin chaps, native cotton shirts, braided horsehair belts—even their rawhide chicotes—were all traditional, hand-made items developed centuries before. The arrieros' only "modern" accouterments were old-fashioned sulfured matches and a couple of large blue enameled tinwear coffeepots.

Everything "modern" was carried in the mules and burros' pannier—for sale along the trail—but not actually used by the arrieros themselves. On the first morning, Trujillo had asked me to remove my watch. "Not needed...there will be no one wearing a watch where we are going."

"Do you not carry one, even in your pocket?"

"No, but I have a small compass for when the weather is bad and we can see neither sun nor stars. I also have a glass *ojo*."

"Glass ojo. A glass eye?"

"Yes, for seeing in the distance—nothing like those double glasses of yours, but serviceable." He showed it to me—about a three-power two-segment brass spyglass, it was very well made and at least a century old.

I watched the sky for a few minutes after peeing, then reached for a smoke. The teenage Indian boy posted to watch the livestock grabbed my hand. "¡*No!* The capitán has ordered that no one smoke until we have departed Lluzhapa in the morning. Your safety, meees... meees...uh, *Señor*." Apparently, the *meeester* word was prohibited as well. Trujillo was nothing if not thorough. "Thorough" made sense—being sloppy probably sifted out potential arrieros quickly. Darwinian work in these parts.

Trujillo began to talk to me more after my case of "the runs." At dawn, he confided, "This is my forty-fifth year on the trail, but I don't want my men to know I am so 'old.'" It wouldn't have mattered—the grizzled old trailmaster was revered among his men. They idolized him and many had named sons after him. And why not—as a mestizo who led a band of mixed-race "free men," he'd totally defied the Ecuador Effect.

"And you?" he asked. "Who are you, really?"

"Just an itinerant scholar, Capitán," I said. He laughed.

"Well, then, 'scholar,' ride at the head of the line today. We have more haciendas to pass. I want no 'runs' today!"

"No runs, Capitán. I feel fit."

"Good. We have an understanding."

We left Lluzhapa at midmorning after a breakfast of coffee and quinoa porridge, then a brisk trade in those hand-forged knife blades, sewing needles, and several more axe-heads. As the mule train readied to leave, two helicopters buzzed overhead. One was big and painted a military khaki, but the other was small, new, and had "ESSO" labeled on its door. The mules snorted and some of the burros freaked out, but the arrieros were, nearly to a man, absorbed, gaping upward at the exotic sight.

Trujillo explained to the group, "Ecuadorian Air Force escorting a foreign company's 'machines' to Amazonas Province. They think there is *petróleo* there. The *meeesteres* have been coming to Guayaquil and Machala for a few months now."

"What do you call such an airplane, Capitán?" asked one of the men. Trujillo coughed and leaned to me, sotto voce, "I can't remember the exact word." I leaned to meet him and whispered, "*helicóptero.*"

"Ah, yes," he announced, "helicóptero—that is what they call the flying machines. Our government has had them for a few years down near Huaquillas, to guard the Peruvian frontier, a cousin tells me."

The next two days were consumed by an endless cycle of up and down, hot and cold, wet and dry. We passed yet another group of mayorales herding Indians into a field. Trujillo moved close to me. I grinned, making an obscene local gesture for the runs. He laughed and moved on.

The scrubby area around Moraspamba was the poorest place I'd seen yet. There had been local crop failures and the hunger was desperate. Trujillo gave a sack of cracked wheat to a group of women by the trail, who were wailing for us to take their babies.

I started to give one of the women money, but Trujillo interrupted me. "No good! They will try to walk down to Saraguro—or another big town—to buy grain, and die on the way, their babies still on their backs." So I went to "plan two" and yelled at one of the men that I'd buy a goat to slaughter. He merely shook his head, and looked down.

"The livestock here are long sold or long dead, Patrón. No meat to buy. Not even burros." We moved on. The locals had nothing to trade. No one talked. Our column was quiet, morose.

One of the younger mayorales with me had tears running down his face. Called Cobre Chico (Little Copper) by the others, he was a classic cholo. From his features he was pure Indian, but he was also an accomplished Spanish speaker. Later, when we stopped in the valley beyond Moraspamba to water the animals, I asked him, "Are you OK?" He looked sheepish.

"Yes, Señor. Just reflecting on my own past. I was a *huagcha*, an orphaned child handed to the mestizo arriero everyone called Cobre. He had no sons, so took me, and raised me with his daughters—a good man. I was born somewhere back there across that last mountain. One of those old women along the trail could have been my mother. Others a sister. I pray that it is not so, but the sight of the women—my people—trying to sell their huahuas fills me with sorrow. Forgive my weakness, Señor."

"Nothing to forgive. I never knew my parents, either. It is lonely at times. When I see the hungry children, it touches me."

He stared at me for a moment, mouth slack in surprise. "And you, a *guerrero*? Well, then, perhaps my feelings are not so strange."

"No, not strange, Cobre—but calling me a 'guerrero' *is* strange."

"I saw your bastón go into the mayoral's mouth at the fiesta—so did most of the others. That is why the men call you 'Sinchi.'"

"What does 'sinchi' mean, Cobre?"

"It means 'the strong one,' Señor."

"Strong one?—I was drunk at the fiesta. Had I been sober I'd have shit myself." He laughed, shook his head in disbelief, and spurred his mule forward, downhill toward Selva Alegre—another tongue of tropical forest. The name struck me as ironic—the jungle didn't look all that happy—nor did the village's inhabitants.

Then it was uphill again. A butt-breaking climb up through the clouds, along a rutted dirt track—the highway to Pasajé—and even higher into a cold mist in the gray-green heights at the settlement of Paraíso de Celén. It wasn't a paradise, either, but Trujillo's group sold both machetes and nearly a dozen knife blades.

We stopped for the night. Cold again, and low on food for the mules, several of the men set off down the dirt track, east toward Saraguro. They returned late in the night. To the east there was grain for sale at the village of San Pablo on the León River.

We left at dawn, loaded up on grain, then detoured south into the headwaters of the León. There were no villages for some hours, but local farmers came out to the narrow trail to trade. Lampas, those odd flat-iron blades that looked like a cross between a hoe and a spade, a traditional farming tool, sold well, as did axe-heads.

By midday, we reached a cluster of unpleasantly aromatic, low, thatched houses that announced Llaco. Its black-clad inhabitants sold us two goats for several small boxes of long nails. We camped about a mile upriver and had a goat roast. The meat wasn't done till evening, but it was superb—juicy and tender. The men doing the cooking had added *culantro*, mountain onions, and some garlic to the carcasses before they were put on the spit. A large pot of bean soup laced with *ají*, fiery local chilies, topped off the meal.

After dinner, the men filed past Trujillo with their tin cups to receive a ration of trago from his bottle. They gathered in a tight circle where I passed out smokes and we each tossed back a half ounce of trago. As the men filed away to roll out their bedrolls along the wall of an abandoned Indian house, most stooped to touch the brass head of my bastón before settling in for another cold night.

As the men smoked under their blankets, I pulled Trujillo aside. "What's this business with my stick, Capitán?"

"Power. There are even more haciendas to pass. Your ride into that valley several days ago was foolish. I promised don Manuel, the healer, to protect you. Not easy... and don Fermín Veintimita is your real job. Do not lose sight of it." I started to play stupid, but he patted his cased ojo and asked, "Is it understood?"

"Yes, Capitán, comprendo. I'm quite grateful for your guidance."

"Yes—I am a father to all who never knew one." I looked away as his hand closed gently on my shoulder. I savored the moment. Then he spoke softly.

"You are like Cobre Chico, Sinchi; he, too, is one of 'the chosen.'"

"The chosen? I don't understand."

"We will discuss it over trago on the return trip—if you are still able to ride... it's time to sleep now, Sinchi—the night is short."

The sky was crystal clear—full of stars swirling past the top of the wall behind me. A moon nearing half full lit up yet another ribbon of silver below us as the waters of the León murmured past.

At dawn, the essential rituals were repeated. Pee and roll up the blankets. Feed the livestock while thick, muddy coffee is passed around, gobble hot quinoa, saddle up, and reload the draft animals, then move on.

Single file, we climbed all the way to the windswept *páramo*, the high, treeless grasslands, above the León's headwaters. There we found more remnants of winter's last snowdrifts feeding the creek head. "Far south for snow," declared Trujillo. "It's been an unusual winter."

My maps didn't show this district—big portions of Ecuadorian backcountry had not been subjected to aerial mapping—but between the páramo, the small snowfield, and the buzz I got from a cigarette as we rested the animals, I think we were at about twelve thousand feet in elevation.

By nightfall, we'd been descending a treacherous, uneven track for nearly three hours when the trail suddenly spilled out onto the rocky banks of another rushing creek. There, the ancient trail widened to about fifteen feet—we'd finally rejoined the main backcountry route to Loja and, with it, the upper reaches of the Gualel River. Only two more days to Chuquiribamba. I wondered about the economics of this trip till we arrived in Chuquiribamba's narrow little valley. All the burros and nearly half of the thirty-odd mules were unloaded there. Nails, coils of used wire for a big hacienda's corral, and six ancient treadle sewing machines had been contracted for delivery there.

The local hacendado was anxiously awaiting the wire. He'd saved, according to Trujillo, nearly a thousand sucres on the cost of his wire, but the capitán had earned a "strong profit." Noting the wire, I asked, "Could you find me thirty meters of two-strand electric wire, Capitán?"

"Of course. I'll find some in Machala when we return. Why do you need it?"

"A gift for a friend's house in Cuenca."

He slapped me on the back, laughing, "They say your friend is very beautiful."

Trujillo also made a nice profit on the ancient sewing machines. The Trujillo clan had bought them from a tailor shop in Machala and had them repainted and refurbished. Indian women in Chuquiribamba would use them for handicrafts to sell in Loja's city market. The mule trains survived by servicing communities with no roads and by being "recyclers."

Another long day in the saddle brought us to Trapichillo's dense, oppressive cane fields in the steaming Catamayo valley. Hot, humid, and buggy, it didn't matter. We'd reached the main highway from Machala to Loja. Apart from the helicopters, it had been more than a week since I'd seen a motorized vehicle, much less heard a diesel.

The mule train would return in four days, leaving from the cane press—which wasn't little, in spite of its name. Capitán Trujillo suggested I go on to Loja, the provincial capital. "Enjoy yourself. Relax. They have nice restaurants. A good hotel. Cold beer. Pretty women." The "pretty women" did it. Stick in hand, I grabbed a dilapidated but brightly painted mixto from Catamayo and rode the twenty miles.

Loja, April 17–19

Loja seemed different. Nestled in a bowl of mountains at about sixty-two hundred feet in elevation, a river flowed along each side of the city. It was beautiful. Well-kept colonial houses with red tiled roofs and elegant wooden balconies lined the charming cobbled streets near the old plaza. Nearby, an amazing clock-tower stood over another plaza. Beyond were several more little squares and a number of honest-to-god cafés.

People were friendly and the women *were* pretty. It was a surprisingly sophisticated town. A budding technical university, students, book stalls, clean local buses, good food, and absolutely no goddamn mayorales with chicotes visible anywhere to spoil it.

"Maybe I've been too hard on Ecuador," I told a college girl as we danced a merengue at a pub near the clock-tower. She grinned. "You've been in the sierra too long. You've only seen one aspect of Ecuador. I don't like the highlands, either. Far too conservative. Everyone hates everyone else. Here, it is progressive."

Later that night, I walked her, Susana, along one of the river-walks by the Río Zamora. Under a brilliant, silvery full moon, a surprisingly good string quartet played Bach in a miniature square—students from the local music conservatory. We even had a cappuccino. A cappuccino—not a tinto.

Why folks in Cuenca sneered at Loja had begun to totally escape me. In Azuay, they claimed Loja was primitive. But, based on my trailside interviews, there was no evidence of anything like that more than a few miles south of Lluzhapa.

So, I asked Susana. She giggled. "Not here—in the sierra! There are many tales of the señorial and such things in Azuay and Cañar." Another of Ecuador's mysteries. I didn't say that to her, of course. One can't insult a young lady's hometown and expect to get anywhere with her.

I didn't get laid—Susana was far too nicely raised—but I made a note to talk to Indians in the local handicraft markets and find out if things really were mellower at just two to three thousand feet lower in elevation. They were. Wage labor prevailed. The local wages for Indian labor were very modest, but the traditional mita was a highland phenomenon.

Two nights later, I flagged another rickety mixto back to Trapichillo from Loja. The poor were still desperately poor, even in southern Loja, but the highland's hard edge just wasn't there. It rained each afternoon, but the rain never whispered, "There will be no free will." Instead, the rains ended each day in magnificent rainbows. Lovers even stopped to look at them and snuggle before walking on.

CHAPTER TWENTY

YUNGUILLA REGION

APRIL 24–28

Nearly three weeks on the trail brought a calmer, more thoughtful me back to Yunguilla. My anger had faded into the background. Trujillo's hand on my shoulder, the hard work, open sky, songbirds—even the smell of the saddle's burnished, sweat-soaked leather—had all produced a cleansing effect.

I saw Yunguilla with new eyes. Flowers bloomed everywhere; rich cane fields and the rush of the Rircay each had its own form of beauty. And the immense wall of rock and scrub that rose straight up two thousand feet from the valley's far side was but a timeless backdrop.

Efraín greeted me, Manuel in tow. "You look different, Señor Juan—darker, more like a chagra." Manuel, the shaman, agreed. "You also *seem* different, Señor Juan—*más tranquilo*."

"It's good to see you both...and I do feel good. It was a good trip." I didn't even think to ask about police, politics, power, or Piggy. Since they had nothing to say on those subjects, I headed upstairs to reorganize my gear and review my supplies. I stopped on the gallery to look across the valley...and breathed deeply. Hoping for peace, I inhaled the scents of lime, the trapiche's gear oil and diesel fuel, and the unique woody sweetness of freshly pressed cane.

Just after dawn the next morning, I flagged a bus from the highway above Los Faiques and went to Cuenca. I needed a bath, food, supplies, paper, and both batteries and tapes for my recorder.

It was surrealistic to ride a bus again. It didn't even matter that it was only a repainted school bus that bucked like a bronco and rattled like a Model T. One didn't have to saddle it, brush it, or even whip it or spur it to keep it moving.

The house on Solano was pregnant with surprises. The cook smiled, then gaped at me and disappeared as I entered my quarters. My apartment seemed like a dream world—tile floor, a real bed, electric lights...a *shower*. Just as I prepared to strip and dive in, someone rapped urgently at the door. It was Nestor, shadowed by a timid, distraught Livia hiding behind him.

"Is that you, Señor Juan?" Nestor looked intense, wary. I answered, "Of course it is. I need supplies and a bath...is something wrong?"

Livia reacted. "Oh my God, Alex, we all thought you were...uh, dead...and you look sooo different."

"I'm fine. You look as lovely as ever, Livia—are all of you OK?"

She nodded. "Yes—the authorities have relaxed. Fermín has been wandering the countryside around Santa Isabel looking for you, so we have not been bothered. My God—you *aren't* dead ... and you seem so different. Where *have* you been?"

"I went south for a few weeks. Joined a mule train that trades along the Peruvian frontier. Can you have dinner with me tonight?"

She looked at Nestor, flustered. He looked at her but didn't make eye contact. *I see,* I told myself. "Then how about lunch tomorrow, Livia. Someplace casual?"

"Oh, that would be fine, Alex. We, ah, uh ... "

"Need to talk?" I suggested. She nodded animatedly, while backing away from the door. I pulled it shut gently and headed for the shower. I'd just gotten the boots off and ... whew ... the socks were ripe enough to send an alley cat running for cover. I stood to unbuckle my belt as Andy rocketed through the door. She didn't even knock— and school was still in session.

"Ayeee, John Alexander! I did not believe that you were dead. I told them ... " She grabbed me round the waist, hung on for dear life, and buried her huge head under my shoulder, then rocked back and forth. "I like you, Andy. I missed our lessons, and I didn't mean for you to worry. Truly."

"Oh, John Alexander ... I tried so hard not to miss you, too. Especially when you and Mother ... it was not logical." *Missed me?* The kid missed me? *Gosh, that sounded nice* ... but, embarrassed by the unfamiliarity of her response, I killed the moment.

"Shush, Andy. Our adult issues aren't your problem."

"OK." *OK?* I'd never heard the little genius speak colloquially before. "OK? ... Andy, 'OK' is a breakthrough for you. Now can I quit calling you 'miss'?"

She emitted a squeaky laugh. "Yes, but only because I'm regressing, John Alexander."

"No, Andy—you are finally being a kid. Necessary, before you can actually grow up. Not being logical can be very healthy."

"Oh, you smell. What is that odor?"

"Mule. Mule poop. Ten days without a bath...all mixed in with foot stink."

"You need a shower...and you simply *must* shave. Oooh...you're thinner and the beard makes you look *old*. I like the mustache, though."

"I *know* I need a shower, Andy. Even I can smell myself. That's where I was going when you burst in and regressed."

She laughed. "I'll wait out here. Throw your clothes out—I'll bag them up." I stepped in and tossed out the trail-stiffened duds. "Oh! Gross!" She squeaked again.

She chatted nonstop as I luxuriated in the magical cascade of lukewarm piped water. Once out of the shower, I took a good look in the mirror. Andy was still chattering, but I was thinner, harder, deeply tanned on my exposed parts, and had a ten-day growth of stubble, except for the moustache, which had just over three weeks on it.

I did look different—my face both looked more angular and the eyes a bit softer, less sarcastic. Perhaps I was regressing, too. It's complicated missing out on childhood.

"I need fresh clothes, Andy."

"OK, tell me what to get."

"Let me check the lights first."

"They are functioning today, John Alexander. I checked while you were in the shower."

"Thanks, Andy...blue shirt. Left top drawer. Socks and boxers on the right. Undershirts and handkerchiefs below with the Wranglers. Throw them in while I shave." I left a goatee and the moustache, combing my hair straight back. It was now very wavy from three weeks of rain, sun streaked and longer than usual. I parted it in the middle and emerged. Andy was circumspect. "Hmm."

"Yep, I'm still in partial disguise. Objections?" She shook her head no, while continuing to study me intently. For one moment, I imagined her head swelling again to absorb me like one of her field specimens. But when she spoke again, I realized that she'd merely been absorbed with her thoughts.

"John Alexander, why has don Fermín boasted everywhere that he and his new mayorales killed you?" The tone of her voice implied that she had suffered as a consequence of Fermín's mouth. I smiled at her.

"Don't know, Andy. But we long since decided he was loco. I've only ever seen him once—at a card game, some time ago." She gaped, speechless. Obviously, Fermín Veintimita had been hallucinating publicly again. "Well—not to worry, Andy... want to go shopping with me?"

"Really?"

"Yes—shopping. I need things."

"This will be my first trip to town with you."

"Now, Andy!" I smiled. She moved toward the door.

I bought a classy new Cuenca *superfino*-grade panama hat with wide black band from the Ortega workrooms, then chose a cream-colored linen sport jacket from a pricey little men's shop on Avenida Rocafuerte. I spoke some German to Andy, who laughed. "That's bad!" True, my vocabulary was limited and the accent sucked, but linen and fancy panamas defined the occasional German tourist.

Andy was amused. "I see now—it's 'Herr Alexander.' Am I to spread new rumors that a German is renting from us?"

"If it amuses you, Andy. It could buy peace and quiet here for several days."

"Then you need sunglasses as well—those dark green eyes of yours are your most distinctive feature. When you are angry, they glitter like a cat's."

"They do?"

"Yes, Herr Alexander—they glitter just like a Colombian emerald." Andy picked out pale amber aviator-style glasses in the city market. I checked out the look in the vendor's miniature mirror. The amber tint really did hide my brilliant green irises. I *was* beginning to look different.

Next, a shoe shine...my boots were in terrible shape, so I ate a sandwich with Andy at a café near the cobbler's while they redid my boots in a French burgundy.

She teased me as I lounged in socks at the patio table. "And what is your last name this week, Herr Professor?" Amused, I teased back. "You know very well that my name is Professor Alexander von Humboldt, young lady." She got a major giggle out of the juxtaposition of my last name with the famous nineteenth-century explorer's. He'd even lived in Cuenca briefly.

While we waited for the boots, I gave her a lesson on geography and the birds of Loja—at least those I could identify. She was nuts about the hummingbirds I'd seen on the hillsides along the trail. "You actually saw a green-tailed trainbearer? How long was the tail, John Alexander?"

"Yes, and the tail was this long." My parted index and first fingers gave her about three inches. Her eyes got big. "Green and black. One of the most beautiful hummingbirds

I've ever seen." She leaned back with her sandwich, study-ing me intently for a moment, then closed her eyes and sighed. She was still enjoying her reverie when the boots arrived. I felt a momentary flush of warmth as I tapped her gently on the shoulder.

Once shod, I resupplied for Yunguilla, hailed a cab to take her and the supplies back to Solano, then ate alone in my room. Later, the lights still functioning, I worked long into the night, rerecording from my field notes in Loja. At 4 AM I did a rough outline of my report to Penrod. The magic of electricity was too good to pass up. Then, I slept till ten.

Coffee, sweet rolls, and a letter to Penrod followed. In it was an account of my expenses so far. I was being liberal, just as he'd suggested. Still, he might gag on sev-eral of the more exotic items. "Hospital bill—Cuenca, for informant 'Araceli,' wife of Tomás Chico of Yunguilla—to treat three rat-bitten finger stumps of infant daughter. See attached."

That one should send him straight to the nearest watering hole, hands shaking till his gin and whisper of vermouth arrived...oh, excuse me, "martini." Back at the post office, in fancy panama and linen, I got the "preferred service" reserved for "whites." Very conven-ient—but it didn't exactly endear one to the hordes of "little people."

The cholos and Indians ignored me with the same brooding, intense, and feigned nonchalance that small-town southern blacks had adopted to deal with the local white men who fancied themselves aristocracy. When I'd worked in the South, I discovered that the petite bour-geoisie whites really didn't notice. But I did...and I didn't like the message it sent me: "We may have to tolerate you in this life, but just wait till Judgment Day and your lily-white ass is sizzling in hell..."

At noon I went to meet Livia at a university area café, just off of Avenida 12 de Abril. I'd no clue what the twelfth of April meant in Ecuadorian history, so as I waited for Livia, I made a mental note to ask Andy.

Livia was nearly twenty minutes late and looked flustered. You know, the "I've rehearsed this all night, word-for-word, but it simply must come off as sincere and spontaneous" look. I smiled and stood. No point in explaining how many times I'd already been through this in my twenty-nine years. The first had actually been a foster mother who "simply couldn't keep" Eddy and me. Back to the warehouse at age six. Yeah, I knew the look.

"I feel so, um, ah...confused." The "confused" hadn't been rehearsed. She was ad-libbing. Regaining her composure, she squeezed her eyes shut for a second, stiffened her back, and returned to the script. "Nestor, you see, um...ah."

I couldn't handle it any longer—it was like listening to a stutterer. So I stepped in. JA the Philistine. "Livia...are you trying to say you really care for me but feel safe and comfortable with Nestor?" Her worry lines crinkled and she stared, silent, for a long thirty seconds. Then she shrugged. "Is it *that* obvious, Alex?"

"Yes...but it's also rather natural, Livia."

"I feel like a coward, Alex. The passion for you is real...but, but..."

"Livia. Not long after we met, I thought you might be *the* perfect woman for me. So lovely, warm, and interesting. But I can't be the man you most need. Being around me is an adventure that hasn't proved calming. I cannot live with you here, even if you wished it...so..."

"So, it's all right? I am forgiven?" I nodded. Relieved, the Livia I first met smiled back at me. Sublime. *That* Livia I might have made an exception for, but she came and went too frequently to merit the sacrifice.

"And Andy..." I blurted out.

"I'm surprised you asked, Alex."

"Well, we had an arrangement about her lessons, Livia."

She flipped her hair and tilted her head seductively, giving off the merest hint of buttercups. "Oh, yes. Do continue those when you are around."

"OK, Livia." She smiled, sublime again for one brief moment, reflexively shook her hair again...then poof. Gone again. She abruptly excused herself—to the powder room.

When she returned we ate. Without any hint of emotion, she updated me on some of the intrigues that had occupied Veintimita while I was off skinning mules. Eventually, she even worked up the nerve to ask me the question that had gnawed at her. It came as a non sequitur—in a whisper, no less—but jolted me anyway.

"Alex, did you kill that man, as Fermín and the others insist?" She looked deep into my eyes, subtly bracing herself for the truth, holding her breath. I looked her in the eye.

"I don't think so, Livia. He charged me with a machete and I struck at him with my walking stick. He fell back into the crowd and they got him—he'd raped too many of their daughters...and apparently several sons as well." She shivered. "I'm not even certain that he's dead. I kept thinking that he'd reappear again—giggling. In Yunguilla no one has said what became of him and his partner. I don't think I'll ever know."

She nodded slowly but said nothing. After several more long minutes of silence, I stood up and bid her farewell.

That night, I spoke with Nestor when he stopped at the apartment. "Livia talked to me at lunch. I'll still give Andy her lessons. But I am no longer a...suitor." He shook hands, looking very relieved. "Thank you...thank you. Are you going back to Yunguilla?"

"Yes. Day after tomorrow. Any chance you could give me an early-morning ride out to the Girón highway? I'll hail a mixto from there. More discreet."

"Honored, Señor Juan...and keep the beard and mustache. Distinguished...and very different."

Miraculously, the electricity was still on, so I made the most of it. When Nestor left I went back to work on reports. I'd even saved a label from a bottle of trago I'd purchased at a cheap bodega in Cuenca. The brand was Indio Loco and showed a cross-eyed Indian guy staggering around drunk. And to think some folks in the States were concerned by the boxes of Aunt Jemima pancake mix.

Whatever Ecuador's laws had dictated in 1964's landmark legislation to end outright serfdom on the highland's big estates, it hadn't yet happened on a wide scale. True, the campesinos in southern Azuay *were* being referred to in legal documents as partidarios, instead of *huasipungeros* (Indian serfs), but the euphemisms had no practical meaning in daily life.

I wrote on into the night, slept late again, and gave Andy her lessons the next day. At 5 AM the following dawn I met Nestor a hundred yards from the house, just as the lamplighter climbed his ladder to switch off the electric streetlights thirty yards away.

Nestor drove out of town and left me at the side of the Pasajé highway, my poncho turned backward, like the locals do, its upturned collar protecting my face from the cold morning wind.

Dawn turned to sunrise atop a monster of an ancient cargo truck reeking of moldy canvas and diesel smoke. It farted, groaned, and belched its way up and out of the Cuenca basin.

The páramo above Girón was bleak, in a Scottish highlands sort of way. The biting morning wind came from the west. You could always tell the wind's direction by where the sheep pointed their wooly asses—as if mooning the source of their discomfort.

Then we dropped down into Girón. Rather like a jet's descent pattern at Pittsburgh's airport, it left one just a touch queasy. I'd heard talk about a paved road to Machala, which would skirt Girón following the high, flat páramo above town, but, like real freedom for "partidarios," it wasn't going to happen on my watch.

I unloaded my supplies by the side of the highway near Los Faiques and sent a shepherd's kid to fetch Cayé—that cost me the equivalent of a dime. Ten minutes later, Cayé came puffing up the hill from the valley below the hacienda. The shepherd's boy returned with him to get a piece of the action.

Cayé was amazed. "Mustache, beard. But it *is* you, Patrón."

"Sure it's me, Cayé, I need a hand with the supplies."

Twenty minutes later, supplies stowed and the stray helper tipped, Cayé wanted a word with me. Private. "Veintimita has told many that you were killed on the mountain near Cañaribamba. I did not know if it was so...even Efraín and Manuel have not spoken of you, except to say, 'He left unexpectedly one morning.' When I asked more, they shrugged."

"Well, that's exactly what I did, Cayé. I had personal business elsewhere—*mi huarmichay* (my woman). But no one tried to kill me, or as best I can tell, even tried to follow me. As far as I am concerned, all is normal."

He smiled as I handed him his month's "strong wages." He took the money and started to give me his usual smile, then went all nervous again. Crossing himself, he explained, "But La Atalaya's patrón insists that..." I cut him off.

"Cayé—I was right *here* less than a week ago. I slept in my room here. There *is* no mystery."

"But, Patrón—no one saw you. A stranger passed through about then. But none of us saw *you*." It was my turn to shrug. He left, confused and edgy. *Do I actually seem so different?* I wondered.

I worked at my field notes on the upstairs gallery, tipping María generously to bring up my food and coffee. The air was fresh, the breeze warm, and the sky clearer and brighter than it had been in months. It was almost May and the mild season had come. The cold-driving rains had blown themselves dry, right on schedule.

I saw Tomás Chico, Araceli, and a few others, who, like Cayé, crossed themselves a lot, but others from the settlement mostly stayed away. At a guess, Veintimita's hired guns—who'd hunted me for a full two weeks—had frightened the locals away.

My guess proved wrong. Finally, I asked Tomás Chico what the incessant crossing himself was about. At first he was mute. So I insisted.

"They swore you were dead. In my head I know it is not so—but you look different... and seem different... it is not good to associate with spirit beings, so we cross ourselves."

I tried to reassure him, as I had Cayé, but he was caught squarely between his sense of debt to me and his fear that I really was a garden-variety Bela Lugosi–style spook. *Very odd,* I told myself.

I was still writing at dawn when Señor Uribe's jeep came bouncing down the vehicle trail from the road to Cuenca. He arrived so early that there was no entourage to meet him. I heard the office door open below. I started down to say hello, but Uribe's jeep had already backed out of the plazuela and turned by the time I reached the stairs.

I pushed the shutters closed, went back inside, and slept till nearly noon. After eating rice and locro de papa, I helped Manuel move tack to a nearby storeroom. Uribe wanted to convert the tack room to temporary sleeping quarters. A new baby had arrived and he was going to be spending more time in Cuenca. Since his senior mayordomo, Antonio, was busy managing other family enterprises in the city, the patrón wanted a second mayoral sleeping at the big house.

Efraín, Manuel, and I had just taken a smoke break when the sound of approaching horses drifted down from the hill behind the house. Two of Veintimita's young, rough-looking mayorales reigned in right in front of us and stopped to look down at us as if we were insects. Efraín started toward them as Manuel and I watched, smoking.

The two stared at me. I stared back, finally making one blink. The other took one look at Efraín and spit on the ground. Then they turned their horses hard and galloped off.

I figured those two might return with reinforcements but said nothing. We finished up. Sweat-soaked and stinky, one eye on the trail to La Atalaya, I took a bucket "shower" down below the aqueduct at the far end of the plazuela while María prepared the evening meal of rice, beans, cilantro, and fried green bananas.

I was only a few days away from finishing my basic report and needed but two or three forays down into the settlements below to fill in missing details, so I decided to relax a bit.

That evening, we had an impromptu fiesta. I brought out a pint of rum and Manuel went for his ukulele-like *charango*. Cayé, Tomás Chico, and a couple of carpenters who'd been preparing planks for a new house to be built next to the big one all joined in. They played "Antonio Mocho," my favorite traditional San Juanito–style tune. I'd even learned the Quechua words to it.

Tomás Chico and Cayé were really good on the small *quenas* (flutes), playing both mournful *huayños* and the more frenetic *carnavalitos*.

The traditional Andean music was captivating. Most of the music was dominated by the haunting tones of bamboo flutes, the beat carried by *tonyas*, small traditional hide drums. Manuel's high-pitched charango gave the tunes a lively, tinkly quality that contrasted with the mournful flutes.

The contrasts were so expressive and emotional that I viewed the music as an antidote to the self-repression and emotional censorship that the indigenous campesinos daily imposed upon themselves in order not to ruffle the hacendados' flamboyant sense of entitlement. Those huasipungos—garden plots on which their houses stood—had been granted them at a frightful emotional and physical price since colonial days.

The music, I reasoned, was one compensatory mechanism. Whether that music was first born of driving rains that murmured, "There will be no free will," or from the tears of sorrow that had flowed for more than four hundred years to mourn a people's cultural destruction, I wasn't sure. But, either way, the music had penetrated right into the fibers of my soul, clinging tenaciously to its innermost recesses.

I smoked a cigarette and watched the stars after the musicians drifted away, then slept. Sometime in the night it turned cold. The wind whistled past the gallery posts and floorboards creaked just beyond my door.

My room leaked badly, admitting a widening pool of cold air that swirled across my blankets.

"Strange. It is like winter in Cuenca," said Efraín in the morning. Cold, leaden clouds boiled down the slope from the sierra, enveloping the big house. Then came the rains. Chill, driving sheets of rain poured down, taking exotic blossoms with it and extinguishing delightful splashes of color—washing away the valley's beauty.

Los Faiques,
Wednesday, April 30

And with the rains came Fermín Veintimita. I was standing under the gallery the next morning, swathed in my heavy striped poncho and leaning against a huge support beam when he stumbled out of his Land Rover, the same two surly-looking mayorales with him. The bigger mayoral, his face punctuated by two broken front teeth and a leering grin, carried a double shotgun. I watched him till he relaxed and stepped aside for Veintimita, who moved toward me. In Ecuador, even nature seemed to accommodate powerful hacendados. Almost instantaneously, the rains let up as Veintimita strutted across the sodden plazuela. His piggy little eyes blinking rapidly, he stopped ten paces away, clumsily shifting his weight from one leg to the other. I waited.

Finally he took a deep breath and shouted, "*¡Qué carajo! Estás fregado, meeester.*"

"Did your mayoral, Garrote, get this line from you ...or was it the other way around?" I asked, the tone of my voice so icy and contemptuous that it startled me. The warm, calmer JA who had gotten off a mule from Loja the week before had simply tiptoed away as Veintimita, thirty feet away, raised the antique five-shot Smith and Wesson and leveled it at my head.

The person who stood before Veintimita was JA the eight-year-old orphan who had once regularly taunted foster fathers into beating him so that his weaker twin would be left alone. For a moment, I imagined that I saw little Eddy standing next to me, looking both sad and grateful. Then frightened. *Not to worry, Eddy,* I told myself. *It will be all right. It always is.*

Veintimita interrupted the moment as he thumbed the pistol's hammer back, bobbing and weaving like Muhammad Ali doing the butterfly. The pathetic asshole was drunk. And it was only 8 AM.

Bang! *The prick missed.* I lit a smoke, leaned against the post, and relaxed. I think the slow French inhale undid Piggy as I narrated to myself, *If you are going to die in frigging Ecuador you are not, NOT going to dignify this drunken fool by showing fear.*

Bang! Bang! Bang—a ricocheting *whee*—then Bang! Click. Click. Click. Good Lord. He emptied the whole goddamn thing—and I don't feel anything. *Hey, Eddy, get a load of this badass.* Eddy smiled. I took another deep drag on my cigarette.

Amazing—there wasn't any blood soaking through my poncho and I felt fine. I taunted Veintimita again—Piggy standing there and clutching the pistol in both hands, dry-firing away for dear life. The dense, acrid scent of gunpowder hung in the damp air.

One more luxurious inhale and he screamed incomprehensibly, throwing the pistol at me. It clattered across the brick floor of the downstairs gallery and bounced harmlessly off the wall behind me. Manuel and Efraín, still stiff as statues, stood in the tack room's doorway. Only Cayé had protested, standing near the construction site with Tomás Chico, an impulsive "*¡No!*" escaping his lips when Veintimita first leveled the pistol at me.

Eddy asked, plaintively, *Can we go now, John?* I ignored him, staring at Veintimita, who was foaming and gyrating. Cold and detached, I stared Veintimita down, then nailed what was left of his ego. "*¡Incompetente!*" I snarled. He flinched, not accustomed to being on the receiving end of an unpleasant exchange.

I merely smiled as he stiffened, then flicked my still-lit cigarette at him. As it arced toward him, his eyes nearly bulged out of his head. Sparks flying, the cigarette bounced off his chest. He gasped and jumped like he'd been heart-shot by a .300 H&H magnum, then passed out. His mayorales looked away, disgusted.

As Veintimita's enforcers gathered him up, tossed him into the Rover, and backed away from Los Faiques, I casually climbed the stairs to the gallery above and disappeared into my room. I never even looked back to see if anyone was going to put a rifle slug between my shoulder blades.

But once inside, I shook for about an hour, desperately missing the sense of calm I'd felt upon returning from Loja. Then visions of a jubilant Ed in his newly won green beret distracted me and softened my anxiety.

I missed Ed, already dead for years. Medic. Cambodia. He'd been so proud to become a Ranger. Reading concern in the knit of my brow at his graduation ceremony, he had assured me, "John, I'm *somebody* now. It's finally happened. These guys are like my family. Now I can do things for other people... not just be the one who has to be cared for. Be happy for me, John!"

I smiled without conviction—what do you say to someone who sees himself as a burden, rather than the only person who ever mattered to you?

Seeing me smile, he emitted that sweet, credulous kid grin that always made me want to protect him. "That's more like it, John! Just think—you'll finally be free to do the things you want!" That was the last thing he ever said to me.

My crazy twin had refused to carry a weapon when they drafted him, still sickened by the violence of our chaotic childhood. That didn't change, even when they assigned him to a frontline unit. Poor kid—they simply didn't give medals to conscientious objectors—not even ones who died in a hail of enemy fire while trying to save a mortally wounded comrade. But he had proved he wasn't a coward and had finally gotten the respect he'd always craved. His buddies carried his body all the way back into Vietnam, fourteen miles under fire. At least he'd finally found a family.

I'd been very angry when he died—it had been an expensive way to earn respect. I'd lost the person closest to me and now, here I was, Mr. Ice-water, doing almost exactly the same damn thing in Ecuador—and over a troubled little man no one would even have bothered to piss on in the States.

An urgent banging on my door finally brought me back to Ecuador. "Señor Juan, it's Manuel—are you alive?"

"Yes, Manuel—I'm good." I opened the door. There stood Manuel and Tomás Chico—both freaked out. "Come in. I'm fine…just unnerved a bit."

"Unnerved?" whistled Manuel. "Let's have a look at you." When they found two bullet holes in my poncho and a third in my felt hat, Tomás Chico dropped to his knees and crossed himself…yet again.

CHAPTER TWENTY-ONE

LOS FAIQUES
EARLY MAY

A A few hours after Veintimita swooned and was carried off the field of battle, I became progressively calmer. I quit shaking and the Indians down in the settlements started wandering around the big house's plazuela to get a glimpse of me.

I stepped out and smoked on the balcony but apparently hadn't yet convinced the runa that I was really alive. I reasoned—inaccurately—that since Veintimita had soaked up the alcohol-crazed courage to empty the old five-shot Smith at me, he'd inadvertently confirmed that I wasn't a card-carrying member of the undead.

But the locals, according to Manuel the Shaman, reckoned I'd absorbed a few rounds at close range with no ill effects, reconfirming their suspicions. Manuel suggested a brilliant solution. I agreed, so he fetched the sacristan, who brought holy water and a cross to the plazuela—rebaptizing me in full view.

"This shall purge you of the evil memories of violence and ward off susto from the shooting," the sacristan proclaimed to anyone who could hear. Spooks don't take to holy water and crosses—not in the movies and not in Ecuador.

The subsequent reduction in compulsive genuflecting and parents shielding their kids' eyes to prevent me from casting the *mal de ojo* on them made life seem much more normal. And wherever Veintimita and his mayorales had disappeared to must have been as secluded as a hobbit hole.

The angry rains did not revisit Yunguilla and fresh new flower buds opened within a few days. As I wrote on the balcony, the old crowd began to gather again to witness both the miracles of writing and of life. Several long days later, my report was nearly complete, so I decided to return to Cuenca where I didn't have to invest so much time in watching my back.

Trujillo had delivered the wire I wanted for a gift, so on Thursday, I hailed a mixto and went to Cuenca. When I arrived, Andy met me.

"No light. The wire is gone again, John Alexander."

"No problem, Andy, I brought a house gift. Ask Nestor to install it." She cackled and squeezed my hand. Electric wire—the stuff of dreams. Then I sent her with a list of questions on local history to Professor Saldívar at the University of Cuenca, via Abelardo.

Me, I made myself scarce once the wire was hung, still writing furiously at Solano. On Friday, a radiogram arrived from Penrod. "Expenses significant. Expect SINGULAR report." In Penrodspeak, that meant "eye-popping."

Oh, yeah, Penrod, I laughed to myself, *'singular' is not a problem.*

I gave Andy her lessons and blew off Nestor's concerns that I should not return to Yunguilla. Frankly, after having done a reasonable impression of Humphrey Bogart as don Fermín banged away at me with that old five-shot pistol, no one else seemed to want a piece of me.

I returned to Santa Isabel late on Sunday and couldn't find Cayé, so I went up to the market alone. As usual, there were no eggs to buy that late in the day. On a brighter note, even the mestizos and cholos clustered at their end of the plaza dispensed with the customary shoulder butts and let me pass unmolested. I could smell their fear. So could the dogs. Even the scrawny, ubiquitous *meeester*-hating mongrels didn't fuck with me.

Alone, I walked down to Los Faiques, ate, and began writing again. Around midmorning Monday, I took my writing out to the gallery, drawing the usual crowd of onlookers. About a dozen people watched every pen stroke intently. Writing gave one power. So did melting the bullets in midair, according to a boy of about eleven.

Several of the men reached out unexpectedly and touched me with their crosses. "To gain power," one of them explained. That creeped me out, just as it had on the mule train to Loja, but I nodded and kept on writing. Melting bullets beat being "undead" by a country mile.

At one in the afternoon I went to the table under the gallery to have a bowl of María's tasty culantro-spiced locro. Efraín, Manuel in tow, came over from the office. "Señor Juan, I need..." Palm up, I interrupted him, pulling out the suede tobacco pouch that held my cash. "I have the month's meal money right here, Efraín." Hand extended for the banknote, he looked nonplussed.

"Oh, I forgot about it. It is that I seek your advice...Cayé is missing."

"Hmm...I couldn't find him yesterday, Efraín. Are you certain?"

"Yes, gone." That seemed to empty Efraín's verbal reservoir. As he began fidgeting with the brim of his hat, Manuel butted in.

"He was herding goats for an uncle on the community land up on the mountain. The goats are unattended and he has been gone since Saturday night. A cousin took him food before dark on Saturday."

"Is anyone looking for him?" I asked.

"Two cousins—just boys—but they are on foot. The family has no horses."

"Can we rent several for a day or two? I'll pay a hundred sucres in rent, or reward, if you think that would help."

"It would, Señor Juan. It is not like Cayé. He is so reliable...and you are his patrón." That read, "He is now your responsibility." The burden of puesto. I handed Manuel a one-hundred-sucre note and went back to work. With the hint of a bow, he turned and handed the money to Efraín, the obligatory puesto thing between second mayordomo and the lesser mayoral.

By Tuesday evening, I'd about one hundred pages of notes, handwritten. No ending, yet. But the core of the report was on paper. Given the contents, I'd get it typed in Peru or Colombia. I still had three months of travel money and could continue to interview Indian farmers on the border of either southern Colombia or northern Peru. I planned on departing Ecuador by bus to Quito no later than late May, if possible. It was time to move on.

The trip to Loja had made me realize how badly I needed a change of scenery. I'd even discussed it with Andy during my Cuenca visit, after absorbing Penrod's radiogram. That had been a misstep.

"Oh, John Alexander, can I go with you?"

"I don't think your mother would approve, Andy."

"When are you leaving, John Alexander?"

"Soon, Andy—by the end of the month... OK?"

"Yes, I think you should go. You do not belong here. You are unable to compromise on important social matters. Yet this nation demands precisely that." The tone in her voice was odd—petulance?

"Hmm? Are you irritated with me, Andy?"

"No, John Alexander. Like I said, I want to go with you. I do not wish to compromise either."

"Andy, your mom will have a fit... and I don't know anything about taking care of kids."

"I can take care of myself. I want to go... leave Veintimita behind."

"I know you're worried, Andy, but you can't just abandon your family and go off with me."

"I know. But that is one of the compromises that troubles me."

Whew! That was close, I thought. Me *saddled with a kid... even one I've grown to tolerate.*

"Is that all, Andy?"

"No. My mother's fear of Veintimita has infected me as well. I dream of him coming for me one day. These dreams frighten me. I have them over and over..." She bit her lip, trying not to cry. Recurring dreams were something I understood only too well.

I hugged her for the first time. Being around Andy made me whole—well, more so—and I was starting to like the feeling again. I'd last felt it when I was twenty-one and living in Mexico.

The Rircay Gorge,
Wednesday, May 6

The morning was bright and clear at Los Faiques. Even the layers of billowing cloud that had seemed permanent drifted away, exposing gray-green summits nearby. But Cayé still had not been found.

Manuel saddled a mare for me from Los Faiques' corrals, and I joined the growing hunt.

The lure of a one-hundred-sucre banknote (US$5) had amazing motivational powers. Suddenly, half a dozen men joined the search and shepherds throughout the district were on alert, the scent of a crisp banknote apparently more important than altar boy Cayé himself.

I rode out about 7 AM, Manuel behind me on a large burro. We stopped near the settlement of Calderón where Manuel had a cousin who raised chickens. We breakfasted there. I bought two pricey eggs to top my rice, delighted at the meal and the weather. My zenlike sense of calm was beginning to blossom again.

Manuel and I had decided to descend to the Rircay, then work our way back from its headwaters. That area hadn't been explored and it was near both the communal grazing lands and a tongue of La Atalaya's holdings.

We split up down in the river's jagged canyon. He took the far side of the gorge. His trail was just a treacherous, narrow cut along the mountain. "Not a problem, Señor Juan. The burro and I both know this trail." I nodded and turned the mare uphill toward the easier rim trail. A half hour later, I'd made it to the rim of the Rircay gorge.

I was able to spot Manuel below me on the hillside. Once, he waved his frayed straw sombrero. I waved back then moved on, riding perilously near the canyon rim while trying to get a view of the slopes beneath me. It was dizzying.

Several times I got so close to the edge that I could actually smell the sun-warmed eucalyptus below. Dropping her head and looking down each time I loosened her reins, the mare snorted in fear. I couldn't blame her. As the rim trail climbed, my heart actually raced from those cliff-side views—straight down nearly a thousand feet.

Then the path narrowed to just a two-foot-wide gash gouged out of the canyon's native rock. I was so high up that I could see the twenty-thousand-foot snowcapped peak of Chimborazo glinting in the sun.

Amazed that it could be seen a hundred miles away, I reined in the mare, leaned forward in the saddle, and reached for a smoke.

As I leaned forward, the mare snorted and pulled her ears erect. For a split second, I heard a high-pitched buzzing sound in the canyon. I couldn't place it. I already had the smokes in my hand, ready to pull one out, when I heard a hollow "whunk." The mare stiffened and jumped straight up.

Instinctively, both the mare and I leaned away from the canyon rim. When she came down, she rolled against me, still in the saddle, grinding me into the rock. Warm blood sprayed into the crystalline air, its sick-sweet scent overpowering. My foot came out of the stirrup and I lost the reins as she rose to her front knees.

Unable to find her feet, the mare bounced on me a second time, then rolled the other direction and went over the canyon rim. I'd never heard a horse scream till the moment she floated out into midair.

I think I tried to reach for the smokes, but nothing moved. Across the canyon someone yelled jubilantly, "The horse is down!"

Curious at why my arm hadn't responded to the cigarette mission, I looked down. My poncho was torn, a widening pool of blood staining it. It was mine. My splintered left collarbone had ripped clean through the poncho. Its ragged tip oozed blood and sticky marrow. I fainted.

Later, I awoke, Manuel and Efraín shaking me. I'd been out for more than an hour when they found me sprawled and nicely smashed, one leg hanging over the cliff edge. A shepherd boy on the hill above me, they said, had heard the rifle fire and seen several men on the far ledge. One fired again, to put another round into me after I fainted. It had hit high, spraying me with fragments of needle-sharp rock.

I laughed, mostly to myself, as Manuel recounted this. "You incompetent pricks—didn't anyone ever tell you bastards that those who shoot downhill tend to shoot too high?" I giggled, then fainted again.

They got me propped onto a burro, limp as a rag doll, and had already dragged me partway up the hill when Veintimita and three armed mayorales rode into sight below us.

Manuel and Efraín had been trying to get me onto Los Faiques land when Veintimita's men spotted us, so they had to settle for dumping me onto a plot of wooded communal grazing land where a group of teenage Indian shepherds had gathered to watch the proceedings.

Unfortunately, I was alert and hurting by the time Manuel and Efraín pulled me off the burro and laid me under some dense, shrubby bushes. They intended to stay with me. "No! Get away from here!" I begged, "Go back to Los Faiques and come for me in the morning. If the three of us are killed, or captured together, Veintimita has won. Whichever ones survive will spend their lives in prison!" Manuel nodded. "They are close now..."

I offered each of the Indian boys fifty sucres if I were alive and not in Veintimita's hands when dawn broke. Efraín and Manuel withdrew, leaving the bribed Indian kids to watch over me with nothing but their slings and shepherd sticks for protection.

The shepherd boys hid in the trees and worked their slings furiously when two of the young mayorales cantered up the hill, looking for me. About then, I slipped back into shock. The agonizing deep-bone pain had set in.

According to the kids, they unhorsed one of Veintimita's riders with a well-placed stone and the mayorales went away. Fortunately, it was a pitch-black night— no moon. The boys brought me water in the night and laid a second poncho over me. I started to fantasize again.

I'd taken on Willie Mosconi at Johnston City, Illinois. A race to ten racks of One Pocket. One hundred grand. The whole world was watching. I was about ready to "go over the hill" on him when he looked up at me, larger than life in tie, French cuffs, and that wavy silver hair, then pointed at my stroking shoulder, looking surprised. "It's broken, son! This is no contest."

I looked down. *Damn.* My left collarbone was poking out through my dress shirt. Dark blood spattered my narrow madras tie. I'd had a real chance to take down the king and someone had snapped my goddamn shoulder.

Sexy Cheryl, one hand on her curvy hips, was only ten feet away in pearls and little black dress, watching. She was already hot for me, ready, her scent intoxicating...then, her eyes followed Mosconi's outstretched arm and fixed on my shoulder. She put her hand to her mouth and vanished. "I'm going to get the son of a bitch who did this," I protested as Mosconi walked away.

Sometime in the cold Andean night, I peed myself, but there wasn't much I could do about it. And for about five minutes, the warm pee kept the cold away. Then it cooled. I shivered uncontrollably and drifted into shock again. This time I was on a mule in Loja. At peace...

The Girón Highway, Thursday, May 7

When dawn came, the Indian kids herded the sheep and goats around me—protecting the source of their potential bonus, I assumed. They waited for Manuel and Efraín. An hour later, Manuel arrived alone on a large burro. "Efraín has been detained by family business, Señor Juan. The boys and I will take you up to the Girón road."

"Manuel—I need to pay the boys. Get my tobacco pouch, *cuero marrón*; it's over my kidneys. Fifty sucres apiece, plus a fifty-suc bonus to divide."

Manuel extracted my pouch, nervous, he said, at the idea of either hurting me or handling another man's *bolsa*. "You must, Manuel. I promised these kids and they took one of the mayorales down with their slings." He handed out the money gingerly.

Two of the boys stayed with us while the others moved the herds before Veintimita's men returned with reinforcements.

And Veintimita's men did return—quickly—combing the pastures below us. Persistent bastards! One even had a rifle. Manuel had to take off again, so I was on my own.

The climb to the road above took me the best part of the three hours. Every time I took a step, the protruding collarbone moved, carving away at my chest. I fainted a couple of times, and crawled part of the way, but made it.

My strength gone, the next problem was flagging a mixto. I had unexpected help. Soon after plopping down on the side of the road, the young arriero Cobre, whom I'd talked to on the trail to Loja, rode toward me. At first, I thought he was one of Veintimita's mayorales and tried to crawl under a bush. But he called out, "¡Hola, Sinchi!" He'd been on the lookout for me.

"How did you know of it?" I asked as he propped me up by the side of the road, pulling a long *faja* (woven strap) across the broken shoulder to keep the collarbone from cutting a yet bigger hole in me.

"There are no secrets in Yunguilla. Manuel talked to Trujillo. It is my honor to be here...but you are not in good shape. We must send you to Cuenca soon." Thankfully, the next vehicle to pass was a third-class bus going to Cuenca. Cobre helped me aboard, installing me in the front seat directly behind the driver—too expensive for the campesinos riding it from Pasajé, I assumed.

Cobre tipped his hat as the bus pulled away, a clenched fist raised in defiance. The driver grinned as he leaned back to me, "Rafael Trujillo sends his regards...a cousin. He said you were the only blanco ever to have made the full journey to Loja and back."

"Capitán Trujillo?" I asked through gritted teeth.

"Yes...that Trujillo." He turned back to driving as we headed into the curves. His assistant fiddled with the ubiquitous dashboard radio. "What kind of music do you prefer, *meeester*? Waltzes, cumbias?"

Music...unbelievable! I thought, but I was on autopilot and heard myself answer meekly, "Actually, I like traditional music—pasillos, huayños, San Juanitos... if no one minds." No one did. In fact, at my response, someone actually clapped behind me. The bouncing bus sent waves of agony through me but kept me from fainting... at least, mostly.

Once when I slumped forward, I awoke to find the driver's assistant propping me up in the seat. I groaned from time to time, grossing myself out, but no one else seemed perturbed... the sight of someone injured was just not remarkable in rural Ecuador.

About midday, the bus reached Cuenca and took a short, impromptu detour to deposit me at the door to a private clinic. The driver and assistant helped me out of the bus. I made it inside under my own power and I didn't even get woozy again till they put me on a table, undid the faja that had held me together, and pulled me upright.

My next untidy revelation focused on the fact that they were temporarily out of anesthetic. "An unexpected series of emergencies," the young doctor told me.

Well, at least the Russian novel that passed for Ecuador had a comforting consistency to it... and gave me an excuse to scream as they pulled my upper body back into place.

CHAPTER TWENTY-TWO

THE CLINIC,
CUENCA
MAY 7–10

A part from the initial anesthetic issue, the clinic was decent. I shared a large fourplex room for the first two days. The chicken soup was wonderful, but the conversation on the far side of the room was odd. Several college-age Ecuadorian fellows were babbling in hushed whispers about *las manifestaciones* and what sounded like "Cane Seat, Ohio." Finally, I inquired. The dark-haired fellow, noticing my accent, asked if the "army shot you, too?"

"No, accident."

"You are American?" he asked. It was the first time I'd heard the word "American" in Ecuador. He came over, looked toward the door, and furtively showed me a Quito newspaper displaying a huge photo of the "massacre of Kent State University students on May 5, 1970, by US

National Guard." I goggled. Here I was worrying about human rights in Ecuador, and the States had gone ape-shit in my absence.

So, I had to wait for a nurse's assistant to feed me, my upper body already imprisoned by about twenty pounds of gauze and plaster.

That first evening, when several army guys came in and checked me out, the Voice nearly blew an artery, but a nurse told them I'd fallen from a horse in Santa Isabel. They sneered, spit on the floor, and went away again, muttering something about *meeesters*.

On the second day I was moved to a private room. Don Abelardo and Nestor came to visit and had pulled some strings. Professor Saldívar also showed up briefly, as did several of the American anthropologists doing work in the Cañar district.

John Randall was one of them. He lived in Albuquerque and was a doctoral candidate at the University of New Mexico. He was conducting fieldwork in the village of La Victoria, just south of Cuenca. We compared notes. Victoria, closer to Cuenca, was poor but more *culto*.

"It's because the hacendados' women are closer," I told John. I'd had a clinic-based epiphany of sorts. "In rural Ecuador, uncivilized behavior is directly proportional to the distance of the elite alpha males' wives and daughters...I'll call it Alexander's Rule of Barbarism." Randall smiled, humoring me. Elated, I bid farewell to John—chatting with him had raised my spirits considerably.

Nestor brought Andy to see me that same day, and every day thereafter till I was discharged. She insisted on her lessons, bedside, and petted me endlessly like one would a dog. Frankly, I loved it. But when I asked Andy why

Livia hadn't come to see me, she sounded disgusted. "I don't know, John Alexander—she said it's 'for your own safety,' but I don't believe her…yet, *I* am here." I dropped it.

And I got lots of sleep after don Abelardo decided to post one or another of his burly "gardeners" at my clinic door for several days, lest anyone get more notions.

On the third day, however, I received two fateful visits—Efraín, dark, flat-brimmed hat in hand, decked out as always in suspenders and high-topped rubber boots, came calling. He had news—not one scrap of it uplifting.

"Cayé's body has been found down in the canyon not far from where we found you, Señor Juan. The Indian boy who found him has asked me to claim his reward."

"Oh, no, Efraín! He was such a sweet, decent kid. Just like my brother, Eddy. Cayé always wanted to please." Efraín stared at me, knowing nothing of a brother, but let it pass. I recovered quickly.

"…Did Cayé die accidentally?" I asked, nodding toward the drawer that held my tobacco pouch and the banknotes that remained.

"No. Murdered…in much the same way as was Antonio."

"Veintimita?"

"I think so."

"I'm going to kill him, Efraín—shove my stick up his ass till he chokes on it."

"Good, Señor Juan. I'll help. Oh, I almost forgot— the assassin left a note pinned to Cayé. None of us can read it."

"Put it in my hand—I can't move yet."

It read: "*Meeester. Enjoy yourself—knowing that ALLs neer you is to die this same way.*" Errors or not, the message, written in English, was clear enough. No wonder no

273

one could read it locally. "Yes, Efraín, it's from Veintimita. Have you shown this to Uribe—or others like that?"

"No, Señor Juan. Tomás Chico got it from the Indian boy who found Cayé."

"Well, the maniac intends to go on killing." I translated the message for him. He shook his head. "It seems ungodly... and now the twins, too."

"*What?* Did his men get to the twins up in Imbabura?"

"Not directly. But Ofélia's susto became worse and she hung herself, just as did her true husband, Marco. She told Feliciana that she wanted to be with him. The sacristano brought Ofélia's body home on the train from Quito two days ago and *he* is now missing. That is why I could not help you to the highway."

"Is there no end to this, Efraín?"

"No... Veintimita is possessed of evil. He is a *brujo*. He can be stopped if the hacienda is destroyed. His mayorales will leave if there is no work."

"Efraín—I need to think. Will you still be in Cuenca tomorrow?"

"Yes."

"Good. Can you come back to visit again in the morning—early... before other visitors arrive?" He nodded, again twirling the brim of his hat in his stubby, work-worn fingers.

My rage grew throughout the morning, fueled by memories of my brother. *Why do the bastards always go after the innocents?* I fumed.

Around midafternoon, I was surprised by unexpected visitors—Ramón Uribe, accompanied by a well-dressed guy I'd never seen before and who said nothing.

"Well, *meeester...*" *Meeester?* "...I heard you fell from a bicycle...playing foolish games. I thought you wiser." I didn't yet get what Uribe was trying to tell me.

Perhaps I looked as stupid as I felt. Uribe repeated himself, "You fell from a bicycle, *meeester*." Well, at least Uribe was to the point and made clear where he stood on matters—time to close up ranks with the ruling class. So, I was *not* shot off a horse by Veintimita's private bodyguards. I'd been riding a bicycle—like a foolish kid—and hurt myself.

The guy behind him nodded in agreement while he stared intently at me. He had a distinctive Veintimita-like look about him—the flat eyes, pig face, and some of the emotional emptiness. About fifty and balding, he was imposing in an ominous sort of way. Wearing an expensive silk jacket, open collar, and an elaborate antique crucifix, he blinked *slowly*, like a serpent.

They say some guys just have to lie out on sunny rocks each morning to bring their blood up to operating temperatures. Here was proof. As I watched him I could have sworn a nictitating membrane flicked rapidly across his eyeballs. When he was sure he had my attention, one corner of his mouth turned up momentarily as his eyes did another slow blink. Again, it was followed by the flicking.

That's when I realized who this man was—Veintimita's older brother, Jesús—the one who Efraín told me had fathered the twins.

Finally I responded. "It was your mare I fell from, Señor Uribe—while looking for one of your missing day laborers." My tone was soft, but firm. Uribe shrugged. "You need rest, *meeester*. You are confused."

"You are right, Señor Uribe," I answered softly, "I am quite confused." Uribe relaxed. Serpent man eyed me again, doing one final ten-second blink. No telling how long he'd practiced it. Frankly, it spoke volumes. I averted my eyes. The serpent grinned in triumph and turned away. That's when Uribe slipped. "Let's go, Chuy," the universal Latino nickname for Jesús.

I let them get all the way to the door before I shot the elder Veintimita's ego in the back. "Tell me, Señor Uribe, what kind of man would stand by and let his little brother rape and sodomize his own daughters?" There was a short scuffle at the door, followed by a grunt, but I had already turned my back on them, rolled over in bed, and pulled up the covers.

It was a long, disturbing night and Efraín returned much earlier than I'd expected. He had to wake me. But my mind was clear...I wasn't getting out of Ecuador in one piece if *either* Veintimita brother could prevent it, and it was simply a matter of time till Fermín went for Livia, Andy...or both. The longer I lay there, helpless, the angrier I got.

So Efraín and I made both a detailed plan and a pact—hands on the Bible. War was coming to the Veintimitas' doorstep.

THE ORDER
OF ENGAGEMENT,
CUENCA AND
LA ATALAYA
MAY 11–18

"Efraín—the basic strategy of war is simple. War, well waged, communicates a staged message: 'You are losing'; 'You are helpless'; 'Give up now or you will be erased from the face of the earth'... it's not genteel. But that is why it's called 'war' and not diplomacy.

"The catch, of course, is that the *execution* of war—transforming the message into reality—is never simple. What can go wrong, will go wrong. Thus, every opportunity to wreak havoc must be pursued to the very edge of folly... and every instance where losing becomes likely

277

must be contained." Efraín nodded and grunted, the hat brim turning slowly. I continued.

"Fermín Veintimita habitually uses fear and abuse of power to achieve his ends. So, our first goal is to instill fear in him. Our second—to rob him of power." More animated, Efraín nodded again and leaned forward.

"*¿Hay más, Señor Juan?*"

"Yes—Veintimita resorted to the courts when he lost his mayorales, Garrote and Baritone. Irony or not, that means he actually expected the world to play fair with him. Not that he returns the favor…but *that* stunning imbalance is the primary source of his power. He counts on his opponents to respond in a 'civilized' way. So 'civilized' is out."

At this, Efraín stopped fidgeting with his hat, elated. "Look, Efraín, I can't get out of this bed, but I need you to carry an urgent telegraph to the Western Union affiliate downtown." He nodded. It read: "*Penrod. In hospital. Badly injured. Wire 1,000 DOLLARS. STAT. JA.*"

Efraín took off, looking ten years younger.

He planned to go back to Yunguilla after ordering the telegram and send Manuel to collect the money, if possible. I was a bit stronger by the time Manuel arrived two days later. After sorting our strategy, he left the clinic with six thousand sucres, nearly all of my remaining cash, and a personal message to Capitán Trujillo in El Tablón, down the road from Yunguilla.

Less than a week after the horse had gone out from under me, Veintimita "lost" critical parts of his cane press, his tractor, and the kerosene-driven compressor to the big wooden cooler where he aged his meat after slaughter. A betting man would have wagered that those very items were already being "recycled" by a certain mule train down in Loja.

Veintimita, according to Andy, who'd heard don Abelardo laughing about it on the phone, called every magistrate in Azuay, raging at the lawlessness in Yunguilla. He even made the mistake of again naming me as the most likely suspect. But everyone who counted—that is, the gente—knew I was currently "indisposed" in the clinic.

A day later, Veintimita began to lose sheep by twos and threes. Then his best mare. Several days after the mare disappeared, someone spiked his Rover's gas tank with cane sugar, which turns into something close to molasses when the engine is fired up. Poof! A seized engine.

It was endless—just like the crap an unhinged neighbor pulls over an imagined slight. And, like some neighbors, rather expensive crap at that. Veintimita's mayorales rode all over the place trying to catch the perpetrators.

In less than a week, those mayorales were worn down to nubbins. Me? Well, I was back on Solano, letting Andy bring me soup in exchange for long lessons. Since someone had already stolen my "house gift" wire, the electricity was out again, but I couldn't write anyway. Frustrated by my injuries, the primitive, lizardlike part of my brain was cheered beyond reason when Andy came in one day with Nestor, who was bursting to recount the latest...

"Don Fermín sent his mayorales to summon several magistrates and the local army captain from the highway control station at Abdón Calderón and demand that they 'bring him *every* Indian in the valley of Yunguilla to be tried before a "tribunal" of his mayorales, him serving as judge.'"

I laughed, "Our message is beginning to be received." Nestor continued, "When the magistrates answered that he didn't *own* all those Indians, and had no jurisdiction, don Fermín began to rave, 'I own *every* Indian in

Yunguilla. I am a Veintimita. I have the power of life and death over them. Do as I *order.*' The army captain, himself part Indian, was, people are saying, one gravely offended cholo."

"Oooh. Good!" squealed Andy. "El Gusano is losing it."

"You've been reading your father's psychology books again, haven't you, Andy?"

"Yes, John Alexander—and some of your father's research." *That's more than I've ever done,* I thought to myself. Andy continued, "Veintimita has a classic narcissistic, sociopathic personality disorder. His paranoia is pronounced, and he is susceptible to serious delusions. Clinically very troubling." Nestor laughed. Andy looked perplexed, so I played it straight.

"Well, Andy, is such a personality likely to go into outright delusional hallucinations if further provoked?"

"I'm not certain, John Alexander. I've not read that far. That would require me to review more case histories. Shall I do that?" she asked, fairly salivating at the prospect.

"No, Andy. This man's bad luck is amusing, but of no real consequence to us," I lied. And it didn't really matter. I'd already taken a big chance on this very possibility and placed a rather expensive order with Capitán Trujillo.

Trujillo, as requested, only took a dozen pack mules to Loja—and had only gone as far as Saraguro. He returned fairly quickly with about thirty full outfits of the Saragureños' traditional all-black district dress. Suddenly, everywhere Piggy went near La Atalaya, he saw strange Indians. So did his mayorales.

Every time his mayorales ventured off La Atalaya land, they were accosted by ominous, Saragureño slingers, pelting them with rocks. Swooosh, schwooosh, whirr. *Whoosh.* Smack!

One of Cayé's younger cousins collected a sixty-sucre bonus for unhorsing a mayoral, who fractured an ankle when he hit the deck. The next day, Baritone's replacement, the one who carried the hammer shotgun as his badge of rank, went down like a sacked quarterback. Three of the slingers claimed to have hit him, so they divided the reward. A fifty-sucre bonus went to the kid who had the presence of mind to grab the shotgun and dart off into the trees before the other La Atalaya riders could stop him.

Efraín consulted me about the gun in Cuenca. "Have the shepherd boy return it—right to the big house. But file down the tips of the firing pins slightly—and darken them with candle black before giving it back." Efraín nodded enthusiastically and grinned. He was enjoying himself.

It took only a few days to convince Piggy that the hacendados in northern Loja had lost control of their Indians. Trujillo's men fanned the flame of that rumor among the peasants until it had become gossip all over the valley. True, no one save a select few had actually seen any strange Indians in black.

But such rumors of indigenous uprisings in Ecuador had a long history—a history mixed with several epic incidents of very ugly reality. So, true to human nature, those who most enjoyed passing on the rumor were those who would be least affected by it, if it proved true.

Finally Veintimita lost it. One Sunday in early May, he burst into the constable's office in Santa Isabel, two mayorales in tow. "I am demanding immediate military assistance . . . they have lost control of the Indians in Loja—an army of Indios *salvajes* has come to take Santa Isabel away from us whites!"

Since none of the folks in Santa Isabel had actually seen any strangers, Piggy's tale was allegedly met with an

"Oh, well—he's a Veintimita. We'll have to bring in a dozen soldiers for a couple of days and check this out, but it better be true" sort of response.

At this news, Manuel quietly collected every scrap of the black outfits, paid a final bonus to the slingers, and burned the ponchos after taking them a few miles away into Loja. The army came, poking, prodding, searching old wooden trunks, and occasionally slapping an Indian kid or two around for good measure.

Several of the locals insisted that they'd heard about a vendetta against Veintimita. A few sightings of black ponchos were confirmed among farmers on the mountain across the Rircay, but the army guys, correctly, figured that several of the Indian kids had been raising hell, and couldn't pin it down any further. Most important, no other hacendado had personally seen, heard, or experienced anything out of the ordinary.

When the captain of the unit proposed to "return to barracks," Veintimita went ballistic—demanding that the soldiers find his stolen livestock. This, at least, was tangible.

The inquiry continued. Two days later, Veintimita's "stolen" mare was located in his own brother-in-law's upper corral. The captain's patience was wearing thin. Undaunted, Piggy went on about his stolen equipment. "My trapiche, my tractor, compressor." Then, he made the mistake of throwing open his meat locker door to prove his point.

Whooh! His missing sheep were in there, all right. But the cold room had become rather like a Delmonico's for maggots. According to Araceli, nearly everyone vomited.

The army left and Piggy, in a raving fit of paranoia, withdrew to the big house with his mayorales and a few other toadies. According to local gossip, he just "knew" his own Indians had turned on him. Of the several hundred people who lived on his land, a half dozen may have cooperated—I wasn't really certain. But the rest knew absolutely nothing.

Efraín and I struck, even as a paranoid Fermín Veintimita prepared to impanel his own private "tribunal."

CHAPTER TWENTY-FOUR

LA ATALAYA
MAY 13–19

As the teenage boys Tomás Chico had recruited acted out the last of their "for hire" aggressions against Veintimita, putting the hallucinogenic herb *yahé* in La Atalaya's aqueduct, Efraín and I made final preparations for our strike. That prank left all who drank the water in a dreamlike stupor and the actual psychotics among them seeing even crazier stuff that just wasn't there.

In Cuenca, they had cut off my original cast, replacing it with one covering just the left shoulder, a problem since I was left-handed. So I took long walks to regain strength, but robust upper-body movement was out of the question, given the partial cast.

My own chances of both getting revenge on Veintimita and living to gloat about it were a statistical joke. If I wasn't both careful and lucky, I could wind up just like Veintimita's other victims. Roulette addicts in Vegas had far better odds—but I carefully packed my gear at Solano anyway. One neat pile "to go," the other stuff left in situ as a question mark—a cipher, "Has he really fled the country?" With luck, the abandoned personal effects might buy me another few hours.

Then, there were the gifts. Three envelopes of cash. One for Efraín. Another for Manuel. A third for Tomás Chico. I wrapped half a dozen books in white tissue paper with a note to each recipient: Nestor, don Abelardo, Livia, and Andy. For some reason, I teared up as I wrapped Andy's. I simply wasn't used to saying good-bye to loved ones. No practice. Over the years, all who belonged in that category had either died or left of their own accord.

I took one last look at my father's dissertation—the leather-bound copy of pioneering work in criminal psychology from 1936 that had been sent to the Nobel committee in Stockholm about the time I learned to crawl. It went everywhere with me, encased in its flat leather box. *No,* the Voice said to me, *you aren't going to be coming back from Yunguilla, and you know it, JA.*

It took two belts of pisco to silence the Voice and calm me enough to finish wrapping it. Even so, I shook as I tied the bow. Then, I absorbed three more fingers of the Peruvian brandy—time to write out my last requests, in care of Penrod.

"Penrod, I have exactly $732.61 in a bank in Manhattan. That is to go for flowers each May—Ed's grave at Arlington."

My life insurance policy, bought by parents I only "knew" through photographs, was to pay for my burial, if my body could be found. "At the old church. Rothesay, Isle of Bute, Scotland. Oliver H. Baird and Sons of Phila. will see to the details." *Might as well be buried near my mother and maternal kinsmen, even ones I've never met,* I reasoned.

Done, I stepped outside to smoke. It was late, but cool, quiet, and pleasant. About 5 AM I'd take a mixto to Santa Isabel, sneak onto Los Faiques, and coordinate with Efraín before slipping away again—to hide until we struck. "I've got, at most, twenty-four hours," I sighed. I didn't even realize I'd said it out loud until Andy answered—

"Don't say such things, John Alexander." My heart skipped two full beats, and I damn near had a seizure from the fright she gave me. "Andy? *¡Ayy, carajo!* You scared me to death. Where did you come from?"

"I've been here on the patio for an hour...I'm sorry, but you have behaved oddly for several days...very detached. Are you preparing to do something foolish?" The panic in her voice was thick enough to slice and spread on a sandwich.

"I'm not certain, Andy. But I am quite preoccupied." She sniffled.

"Can I come up, John Alexander?"

"Up? What do you mean?"

"Your lap. I want to be held." Without even thinking, I reached for her. No wiseass comments from me. No psychological diagnosis from her. No clever banter—just a cuddle. She was warm and breathing very rapidly when she first curled up, head under my chin. I stroked the soft inner skin above her wrist rhythmically, just like I did for Eddy when we were kids. Her breathing slowed. She went limp. Eddy smiled at me from somewhere off in the distance and I got that warm "Loja" feeling again.

"I love you, John Alexander," she murmured. I squeezed her tighter. "Even if something happens to you, will you watch over me?"

"OK, Andy."

"Don't say 'OK'—*swear* it to me."

"What if something does happen to me, Andy? How can I swear to that?"

"You can still watch from heaven, if you don't kill anybody."

"Huh? You're the one who first urged me to think of *The Prince*."

"I know. I've been sick inside ever since. I was angry and frightened."

"And now?"

"Not angry enough to want to be like *him...them...* Ecuador. Or for you to be, either."

"I'm already like Ecuador, Andy."

"No, you aren't. I felt a tear. You cried when I got into your lap."

"Well, maybe one tear. But that doesn't make me a saint, Andy."

"You do not have to be a saint, John Alexander. Just not a murderer. I don't require perfection." I didn't know what to say. So said nothing. She relaxed. I listened to her breathe, enjoying the rhythm. A bit later she spoke unexpectedly.

"My head is too big. Did you know that? They all tease me about it in school. Cruel."

"Ignore them, Andy—they have no reason to tease you. They just envy your intelligence." She responded so softly and matter-of-factly that it took me a while to process it.

"See. You lied to make me feel better...I don't mind that. It's kind. But killing someone...don't do that for *me*...promise?"

Without even intending to, I heard myself promising her in a strangely soft and wistful voice.

Dawn came swiftly. I'd gone to bed about 1 AM. Andy followed me into the apartment and slept on one of the big chairs. I was already dressed and ready to go out the door when she awakened. "I want another hug, John Alexander." She reached out for me and pressed her head to my chest again. I pulled her off. My ride was waiting.

Out on the highway, under the light of a three-quarter moon, I chatted with Nestor. "So, this is how it works, eh? I finally get hooked by a *kid*, and she asks me not to kill the son of a bitch who has been raping and mutilating everyone in sight . . . and now I *do* have doubts."

"I agree with her, Juan. If you have a choice, do not kill him. For a man like Veintimita, being alive and powerless is far greater punishment than simply dying." I grunted. He elaborated. "Have you ever killed a man before?" I shrugged and shook my head.

"Good. No need to start now. I'll kill him and his older brother if either come near Livia or Andy. Abelardo and his mayordomos will kill them if they get me first. They swore to it."

"Is that a promise?"

"Yes . . . and where is your bastón?"

"I'm not carrying it—it's in the apartment. Why do you ask?"

"Good. It's your signature. Enough to convict you of anything that might happen."

"You mean, even if someone just saw it?"

"Yes. Enough for any Ecuadorian court—only the rights of the local whites are judged against our national

constitution. Others must accept the mood of the courts."
He paused, thoughtful, then continued...

"Your defiance in the face of disastrous odds is
remarkable, Juan—but cover yourself this time. Mask the
hair, eyes, face—all are distinctive enough to convict you.
Don't be a hero."

"Well, Nestor, I'm more concerned about getting back
alive than a court proceeding...will you be ready to drive
me someplace on short notice if I do get back?"

"Yes—I already gave you my word. Abelardo is leaving
the Pontiac with me at Solano. Day or night. I shall be
waiting." A mixto rolled up the hill from behind us, bound
for the South. "¡Pués, nos vemos, Nestor!"

Poncho, chicote, good boots, and a waving twenty-
sucre note brought the mixto to a stop. "*Kay mixto
Yunguilla manchu, Patrón?* (Going to Yunguilla, boss?)" I
asked in Quechua, my face covered by a wool scarf.

He nodded, jerking his thumb toward the rear. "*¡Atrás!*
(Back with the Indians!)"

It had taken me a long time to figure out that the
combination of simple Quechua and deference worked
as a disguise, even if one was light skinned. No white in
Ecuador would ever give up either their puesto or their
exaggerated cultural identity. One simply could not be
either white or an outlander in poncho and speaking
Quechua. Tomás Chico and Araceli had given me lessons. Priceless.

I'd even gotten ten sucres back in change when I
boarded the truck. They assumed that I already knew the
going rate. It was the cheapest mixto ride I'd gotten yet.

Once under the mixto's canvas tarp, several locals
checked me out. A man near me stared, then grunted,
"*Wiraqucha?* (White guy?)"

"*Manan. Runataq kani* (No. I am part Quechua)," I mumbled. End of conversation. Then silence, dominated by the smell of wet, sweat-soaked wool and the truck's diesel exhaust.

Near Girón, several waterfalls cascaded down the cliffs, sparkling in the early-morning sunlight. The páramo beyond was still clouded over—it would take another several hours of sun to burn off the clouds and expose the green, nearly always lonely and waterlogged, grasslands.

Dotted with small ponds, fat-leaved bushes resembling yucca on steroids, and dense, almost impenetrable clumps of stunted trees, the páramo was its own world—high, cold, windy, wet, and hidden in clouds most of the rainy season. Beautiful in a somber way.

I watched two turkey buzzards drift overhead—good luck omens among the runa. The poncho wearer who had questioned me when I came aboard watched me watching the birds and grinned. "*Chakuy* (Hunting!)."

I ignored him, the scarf still covering my face. Manuel was right—no secrets hereabouts...and the Ecuadorian whites loved to fancy that "their" Indians were both stupid and childlike.

A few minutes later, I banged on the side of the truck to signal a stop on a lonely stretch of road, several miles beyond the army's highway checkpoint at Abdón Calderón. As I struggled with the cast to balance myself and jump down, an arm reached from behind to steady me. When the truck pulled away, someone shouted, "*Allin samiyuq kay* (Good luck!)." I didn't turn but raised my right arm to acknowledge the kindness.

It was an easy downhill walk. Instead of barging right to the big house, I detoured along the hill behind Tomás Chico's place. The uninhabited hillside that rose up to the highway was one of the few "private" routes onto Los Faiques.

I banged softly. *"¡Hola!"*

"Pitaq kanki? (Who is it?)"

"¡Habla Juan, Araceli!"

She opened the squat wooden door, jerking me inside. It always took awhile to adjust to the dark . . . and the smell. "Did anyone see you, Señor Juan?"

"I don't think so. I could see the men down in the cane fields, cutting. Perhaps one of the shepherds?"

"Good. Will you watch the baby? I will let Efraín know you have arrived. There will be a meeting here after the cane cutting is done. Do you need anything from your room?"

"Yes." Amused by the pantyhose, she snickered when I told her. I shrugged. She returned with my supplies about forty minutes later. She fed me rice and potatoes, singing in Quechua to her baby while I ate. I napped while she spun wool, the ancient spindle whorl twirling in harmony to her tune.

At dusk, the men started to drift in. First came Tomás Chico, who ate, then took a nap. An hour later, the twins' aged grandfather, Ezekiel, came with the arriero Cobre in tow. Since Trujillo was off in Loja again, I was surprised to see Cobre. Even later, Manuel and Efraín drifted in.

Efraín looked even more uncomfortable than usual. The dark hat turned rhythmically in his hands.

"Are you ready, Señor Juan? *Hay chuño. Algo de charke.* (We have dried potatoes and a little jerky.)" Then, Manuel butted in.

"We've also got two old mules borrowed from Trujillo. Only you and Efraín will approach the house, but if there is a fight, Cobre will join you."

Cobre grinned. "My machete is sharp. Tonight I am a warrior." My turn to butt in. "No killing unless we, ourselves, are moments from death. Stealth and destruction are the goals." The Bible passed from hand to hand, just as one of the twins' surviving cousins slipped in.

"I am Lorio. I am to hold the horses. Pass me the Bible." Lorio was limping. I didn't like this at all. Still a boy, he couldn't possibly understand the consequences of participating. I protested. "You are too *young*. This is dangerous and you have not yet sworn never to speak of it. Young men brag. They cannot help themselves."

Lorio winced. "Am I not a man?"

"We die, if you aren't *maqt'a* (young man)," I retorted. The tension rose.

Efraín twirled his hat and Araceli took her baby away, covering the child's ears. Lorio, looking sullen, said nothing. I stepped toward him. The kid moved back reflexively and accidentally stomped a baby cuy. It squeaked in agony, jerking—its tiny back broken. Lorio nearly shit himself.

Efraín scowled and started to say something when Manuel intervened.

Pointing to the saddlebag next to Efraín, he said to Lorio, "You are to descend into the canyon below La Atalaya, set off the fireworks in that *alforja* when you hear two rocks fall—about five seconds apart. Then leave. Do not look back. Leave your pony in the lower corral by the river and return to your sheep. You may tell your grandchildren of this *if* the rest of us are already gone. Not before."

The kid whined. "I am a man. Not a boy!" Efraín cut him off, his sinewy arm extended with the saddlebag. "You will be accepted as a man only if you do exactly as asked.

¡No seas huahua! (Don't be a baby!)" Lorio, looking sheepish, reached out and took the bag while Manuel extended the Bible. He put his hand on it and swore, brow still furrowed. *Shit!* I thought to myself. *He's a* kid, *still pissed off that we don't accept him as a "man," just because he's feeling his first testosterone rush. This is trouble.* I was about to butt in again when Manuel spoke...

"Besides, Lorio, if you do speak of it, your sisters will surely suffer the same fate as your twin cousins...and your father will lose his huasipungo. Your balls will be on don Fermín's desk, *and* your family will starve." The kid looked surprised.

"Just what the hell did you think would happen if you screw up?" I snarled.

"Go now," grunted Efraín. "The matches are in the bag—wrapped in burlap." Lorio limped out—all five feet of him—his flat face making his hawk-nose look even more improbable.

Manuel, the shaman, said a prayer beside the smoldering hearth. "Father, help us to end the afflictions that beset our children, yet not ourselves become as the afflicters." I was too pissed off to be swayed by any oblique reference to me.

Five minutes later, Cobre slipped out. "I will have the horses up at the head of the aqueduct." Tomás Chico went with Cobre. He was to watch the trail behind us, armed only with a couple of firecrackers as a signal. I offered Efraín a section of pantyhose to use as a disguise, but he refused it.

A few minutes later, Efraín went. I slipped a piece of pantyhose leg over my head, grotesquely distorting my features. The nylon also darkened my skin and hid my eyes. Until I put on the "disguise," I don't think Araceli grasped the finality of our little venture. She gasped, *"¡Oh, por Diós!"* and crossed herself. I gave her a squeeze and turned to leave. She'd recovered enough to ask one poignant question. "Will we ever see you again?" I shook my head no, and went out the door.

The stars were out. The night was cool and bright. A nearly full moon hung low in the sky. That moon would make the ride easy, but add to other dangers. Cobre was at the aqueduct, as promised. I clasped his arm when we met. He leaned to me. "I have fear, Sinchi...do true warriors fear?"

I answered softly, reassuring myself as much as anyone. "A warrior who is not afraid is already dead, Cobre."

"Thank you, Sinchi. I live."

I turned to Efraín, who was too calm for my taste, and tried again to convince him to disguise himself. "Look at that moon! Bright as day...you have so much to lose," I insisted.

Efraín refused his pantyhose hood a second time, protesting, "I don't want to die dressed as a woman. It will confuse my soul. I have already failed to protect my nieces...so I am ready for a new life."

"If they recognize you, they will hunt you. Even in a place like Loja—or northern Peru. There are Veintimitas in Peru, also."

"Really?"

"Yes, Efraín—the bastards are everywhere." Finally, he pulled the pantyhose over his head.

The horses' hooves carefully padded, a half-hour's slow, stealthy ride took us to the trail near La Atalaya's big house, perched on the edge of a high bedrock promontory. Cobre tethered the horses in a cluster of stunted trees below the trail. I took slow, deep breaths to stay calm, pulled out the Nikons, and glassed the big house. No one about, but kerosene lanterns were still lit in several rooms.

Efraín gathered a cobble in each hand and slithered forward to give Lorio his cue. Several minutes passed before the rocks went crashing over the cliff. Till then, the night had been soft and quiet. My heart hammered and our horses snorted as the rocks ricocheted into the abyss. The fist-sized cobbles sounded like grand pianos as they bounced from one rock outcrop to another, echoing from the far side of the Rircay gorge, then back again.

We waited for the fireworks, but none went off. We had counted on the mayorales to erupt from the big house just after the fireworks began, giving us time to start a fire. Efraín, next to me again, was having a fit. *"¡Qué carajo! ¿Dónde está Lorio?"*

A door slammed. I jerked in response, then pulled the Nikons back onto the house, expecting to see armed men emerge stealthily. Instead, we heard several old-fashioned locks being bolted. A moment later, the lanterns were extinguished. The house was as dark and as silent as a tomb. My pulse slowed and I took a deep breath. We'd be alive for at least a few more minutes. I caressed my own lips, desperate for a smoke. The silence was excruciating, but it gave us time to assess the situation.

"No one is coming out," whispered Efraín, breaking the silence.

"You're right—they are hiding *inside*. We should move now before they become curious and come out."

"Está bien . . . uno, dos, tres." On three, we belly-crawled forward until we were under the nearest corner of the big house's lower gallery, where a cart full of drying corn had been left—part of a new crop for La Atalaya's loft.

I pulled a battered Kerex lantern out of my knapsack and quickly turned it upside down to prime the wick. Efraín struck a match on his trousers and lit it. I reached up and gently tucked the glowing lantern into the piled corn before Efraín patted me on the shoulder. Time to go.

We crawled away from the house like slow-moving sloths—trying to make no noise. Halfway to the nearest clump of bushes I began to breathe normally and congratulate myself. That's when the fireworks went off.

"¡Lorio fregado!" Efraín exclaimed in fright. I nearly had a coronary. My pulse raced from 75 to 150 in five seconds...hard on the pipes.

The doors to the tower flew open and two mayorales carrying rifles bolted toward the rim of the canyon while a third started in our direction. Shit. Time to give up on the slow crawl.

We scrambled to the clump of trees unscathed. It was only another fifty yards to the horses. Then someone shouted, "¡Alto!" We froze till it was obvious that the mayoral coming our direction had been called back to the tower. He slammed the door closed behind him as he went inside. We heard the bar fall. Protecting Piggy, I assumed. It was quiet for a minute.

Then someone shouted, "I see a horse below!" That sent the two remaining mayorales sprinting up the rim of the canyon. The first blush of fire had risen from my lantern like an answered prayer. Then it sputtered and died. "Choclo verde," I whispered. Green corn is hard to ignite. Efraín patted me again in consolation.

We dug deeper into the tree roots, like kids playing hide-and-seek. A night owl's soft, trilling "wrrrooo" came from the trees below. Cobre's "I'm still here and all's well" signal. As the two mayorales opened fire into the canyon below, Efraín answered Cobre with one low whistle. "We wait."

It seemed as if hours passed before the mayorales ran out of ammo and returned to the tower, but it was probably not more than five minutes. When they disappeared inside, Efraín put his mouth to my ear and whispered, "*¡Otra vez!*" I nodded and tensed for round two.

Just as we emerged from the tangle of rocks and roots, the fire unexpectedly whooshed upward at one corner of the gallery. It was suddenly bright as day.

Panting, we scuttled back to our root bed, hunkered down, and turned to admire our handiwork. The fire rose quickly into the second story, then up to one end of the loft. Transfixed, we watched for another several minutes. The whole area was lit up. A firecracker popped faintly about a mile away to the right. That had to be Tomás Chico's signal. Time to go...

Running lopsided from the heavy cast, I tripped and went down hard. Efraín slowed to help me. I was dazed, and my ankle was twisted, so we belly-crawled the rest of the way. Cobre was waiting—"I shall turn left along the rim and make much noise." Brave. Foolhardy...and afraid. But, at the moment, gallant.

Not another word uttered, Efraín helped me onto my big buckskin gelding, nodded once, then wheeled his horse away. Cobre spurred his mule furiously and galloped noisily along the trail in the opposite direction, his antique brass stirrups clanging like cowbells.

CHAPTER TWENTY-FIVE

THE CUENCA
AIRPORT
MAY 20

Riding the mixto to Cuenca, I munched on my share of the charke and chuño, hoping the truck wouldn't break down. Ecuador had a nasty way of sticking it to anyone deluded enough to conjure up the taste of victory. Jubilance would merely backfire on me again if I indulged in it.

So I clung to my mental images of cattle prods and the solemn cadence of an army firing squad, the sergeant shouting out the orders. *"¡Preparen! ¡Apunten! ¡Fuego!"* In that little imaginary scene, Fermín Veintimita shouted at me from the salivating crowd. *"¡Eres jodido,* meeester!*"* That mind-set worked like a charm. I reached Cuenca just before 9 AM.

At Solano, Nestor was waiting. "Your face is scraped up and you are limping. Are you all right? I didn't really think..."

I didn't want him to say it and break the spell, so I interrupted him. "Well, I'm here."

"Are you hurt, Juan?"

"I'm good, Nestor...I fell, twisted an ankle...I've got five minutes to shower, change, and go." I dashed inside, shaved, showered, bandaged the ankle, dandified, and emerged in shades, linen jacket, and panama, my large duffel and a rucksack already at the door. My Harris tweed jacket, a receipt for a bus ticket to Cuzco nestled in its pocket, lay on the bed.

Just as I tried, unsuccessfully, to hoist the bags, Livia burst in, agitated. "Are you leaving, Alex?"

"Livia...where the hell have *you* been all these weeks?"

"I didn't think you would...uh...you know...uh..."

"Survive?"

"Yes...I mean, no...oh, Alex...*are you leaving?*" she repeated.

"Yep. Going right now...adiós, Livia."

"Adiós? *Really*, Alex?" I started to answer, but she surprised me, planting a kiss on my lips, right in front of Nestor. Damn. She still smelled of straw and buttercups. She drew back, look surprised, then frowned. "Alex, what about Anda?"

"Tell her to write me. Lista de Correo, Hermosillo, Sonora, Mexico—in the name J. A. Blanco. Care of Señora Marisol Virreyes." She looked to Nestor for a pen. "Remember it, dammit. *Don't* write it down."

I squeezed her shoulder, picked up the rucksack, and walked past. Nestor had already tossed the big duffel into the Pontiac's backseat. Seated in back, I rolled down the window. "Livia, there are wrapped gifts inside." She nodded, still looking dazed. Nestor at the wheel, we pulled out. "*¿Adónde vamos?*"

"To the airport—take the least obvious route. Fast." The old Pontiac did its part. We stopped several minutes' walk from the airdrome's huge iron gate and Nestor parked discreetly. He carried the big bag till a porter came out, shook my hand, turned, then stopped to look back at me. "Will you ever return?" I shook my head. "My work is done here. See that Andy gets my bastón."

Forty-two endless minutes later, trying to look casual, I climbed up the steel ladder and stepped into the refined old DC-3. I took a forward seat and lit a smoke before we took off.

An elegantly dressed Ecuadorian occupied the seat next to me. "You are European, perhaps?" I nodded in reply.

More curious than culto, he asked my profession. I lied. "Visiting lecturer, University College, London. Colonial New World history. I made a short visit to the university library here."

He nodded, smug. "I hope you have enjoyed your visit to Azuay, Señor. Cuenca is very beautiful. Very culto."

"Yes," I smiled, "very beautiful..."

Finally, the DC-3 hummed down the runway and lifted off. I took a deep breath, exhaled in relief, and leaned to the window to catch one last glimpse of Cuenca. Below me the old green Pontiac glistened in the sun. Nestor waved his panama from the car window. I waved back as the plane circled once to gain altitude before we headed north.

CHAPTER TWENTY-SIX

MEXICO
JULY 1970

Palms swayed. A hot breeze blew out of the Sierra
Madre and branches pregnant with clusters of blood-
red bougainvillea cascaded around me as I read:

My dearest John Alexander,
The present will reach you, I pray, alive and well,
thanks be to God. I miss you so. At times I am des-
perite to have lessons with you again. I received
your gifts—the disertacion and your staff. I have
red the disertacion and one day I shall carry the
staff in formal academic proseciones when I have
earned a professor's chair in Psichologie.

Mother is to marry Nestor in September. Uncle
Abelardo will deliver her to the altar. Mother does

*not know I am writing you. Still she wants to
avoid reality, so I indulge her at Nestor's request.*

*The "V" family pursues investigaciones and
searches to find you. The army came to the apartment here and founded recibts for a bus tickit to
Cuzco. The campesinos in Yunguilla swear that
you are still sighted among them. Even the arrieros
gave testamonie that you ride with them to Loja
now and again. Thus, I am afraid this might never
reach you.*

*I love you and take leave of you with all
respect—wherever you may be.*
Miss Andalucía M. Gonzáles Chuca

*p.d. What does "Likinchu anchayna" mean?
The Indians in Yunguilla call you this.
Please write! Your Andy.*

"What are you reading, *chulo*?" asked Marisol.

"A letter from Ecuador."

"A woman...?" Her tone was edgy.

"Yes—about eleven years old. I gave her English lessons in Ecuador. Brilliant child."

"Lessons for a child...you?"

"Yes, I like kids."

"*¡Mentiras, chulo!*"

"Even for a *vieja* (hooker) you are very cynical, Marisol."

"I'm not cynical—I am a realist, Juan Alejandro. Every
time you lose a fiancée you come back to me, like a fly to
miel, and we spend two weeks in bed."

"Are you complaining?...Anyway, this time I returned
as a dove with a broken wing."

"Yes, I liked you much better before the cast came
off...and when are you going to Tucson again?"

"Tomorrow. I am delivering the final draft of a *tesis* I've been working on. Do you want something?"

"*Of course.* You owe me *two* good pairs of panty-hose...and some Chanel Number 5...and I'm not going to Hermosillo for your *pinche* mail again."

Marisol pouted, trying to sneak a peek over my shoulder, while I penned a response:

> *Dear Andy,*
> *Arrived in Mexico. Am staying with an old friend. I am surrounded by palms,* buganvilla, *and the Sea of Cortez. The sand is soft and white, shells every-where...paradise.*
>
> *I appreciated the newspaper clipping you enclosed. Sounds like it was a big fire. My regards to L., N., and don A. Any news of "the maggot?"*
> *—Me.*
>
> *p.d. Regard your p.d.—"A left-handed some-thing?"...and you don't need to be so formal in the next letter.*

CHAPTER TWENTY-SEVEN

MIDTOWN
MANHATTAN
OCTOBER 1970

"**G**ood Lord, JA—what an extraordinary report. Are you certain of your information, my good fellow? There are serious implications to this report...I mean...good Lord. 'First rights' with the virgins on the haciendas in *this* day and age—that's *explosive.*"

"Quite certain, Penrod, old boy. In fact, epistemologically certain. World Court witness-box certain. In other words, absolomo-fucking-lutely certain."

"Oh, dear...no offense taken, I hope, JA. Certainly. No offense..."

I cut him off. "Penrod. I got shot at, beaten, stomped, starved, shoulders busted, ate crow, rats, and amoebas by the liter, and didn't even get *laid.* What do you mean, 'no offense'?"

"Well, I *do apologize*, JA! Certainly the salary was minimal. But the expenses were..."

I cut him off again. "'Dirt cheap' is the phrase you are looking for, Penrod...and you don't need to bellow at me—my hearing is fine. By the way, tell your friends at the foundation to cut me a bonus check for five thousand dollars. Quickly...or I'll send copies of the report under my own name to both the UN Commission on Human Rights *and* the World Bank Committee on Project Reviews. I'll cut your high-class friends out."

"Oh, JA, do calm down. This is spectacular stuff. The whiskey label alone is priceless testimony. I mean, *really*...Indio Loco in 1970. My God."

"It's not whiskey—it's 'trago,' Penrod; think kerosene. The hacendados who make this crap lace it with formaldehyde to enhance the kick. *Formaldehyde*, Penrod. It gives a whole new meaning to 'fetal alcohol syndrome.' And the cheap cigarettes made for the campesinos are adulterated by straw laced with DDT."

"I read that, JA...do you have proof? Test results?"

"Yes, old boy, tested at Caltech. Results on the way to you any day."

"Well, let me make a phone call, JA. I need fifteen minutes to discuss 'cost' guidelines uptown...I will raise the issue of a bonus."

"Thanks, Penrod."

"Understandable, JA. There is a bottle of lovely brandy in my conference room. Wait there a bit, my good fellow."

Caroline, Penrod's current "assistant-in-a-little-black-dress," poured for me, flirting. "Quite the report, Mr. Alexander. I've never read anything quite like it. So much violence. Rape and..." She was close to panting and I was already indulging myself in another of my private commentaries.

They send these sheltered, upper-class chicks to places like Smith and Vassar. They think that "a walk on the wild side" means missionary-screwing one of the Irish working-class guys drinking Jamieson's in a neighborhood bar in Boston. Then they go marry some fruitcake nicknamed "Binky" or "Bunny" from Yale, who also went to Choate, get laid twice, pop out the boy and girl on schedule, then wind up on the board of the foundation that sends me straight to hell on Ecuatoriana Airlines for five hundred a month. Eventually, they "become involved" by worrying about peasants overseas... never those right here in front of them.

Initially, I thought about snarling at Caroline. But I sipped instead.

"My, you really are the brooding, silent type, Mr. Alexander." I started to answer her, just as Penrod stuck his head in. "Caroline. Ah, I need a word with JA, please." I followed him.

"JA, your bonus check will be cut tomorrow. Forty-five hundred... best I could do." I scowled.

"Really, JA—the bonus is *unprecedented*."

"OK, Penrod. That will work."

"Good. There will be an extra ten thousand after you testify publicly to the UN Commission on Human Rights. OK?"

Ten grand! Holy Moses! Stay calm, I told myself. *Think before you talk, JA.*

"...Only *closed* committee hearings, Penrod. That is *if* there is also immunity from extradition to Ecuador."

Penrod goggled. "What actually happened down there, JA?"

"It got ugly, old boy. No immunity, no testimony...and no open committee. Period."

Penrod tried again. "Public hearings would be more effective, JA." I shook my head no. He stared me down. I didn't blink. It took him a moment to make up his mind. Then, with a shrug, he hollered for Caroline.

"Mr. Alexander needs a grant of immunity from extradition to Ecuador. Call Nicholas Katzenbach. I'll pick up when he's on the line."

Caroline, wide-eyed, blinked at me couple of times, then disappeared. The phone rang. Penrod explained. The former attorney general, known to intimates as "Mr. K," took the gig. Five minutes later, I walked out to the conference room for another sip of brandy. Caroline poured again. "Take me out to dinner, Mr. Alexander? I want to hear all about what did *not* go into your report." Nice legs. "Please, Caroline—my friends call me 'Alex.'" I beamed.

CHAPTER TWENTY-EIGHT

LOCAL POST OFFICE, NEW YORK CITY
NOVEMBER 1970

It was a gorgeous fall day. Leaves turning orange, the sky a crystal blue. I'd just taken the subway downtown from Penrod's office. He'd tried again, unsuccessfully, to get me to agree to open hearings at the UN.

My report had been traveling in some very heady circles and Penrod wanted "maximum exposure." As a consequence of the buzz it had created, I'd gotten some amazing cocktail party invitations. A-List stuff—free booze, free food, free sex.

I even had a "late lunch date" at the Russian Tea Room in two hours. Life was good, and old JA was becoming smug again—so I didn't see it coming when I turned the key on my mailbox and retrieved a letter from Sonora. *Probably Marisol sending on another hopeful perfume request,* I told myself. I pocketed it to read it later.

Lunch was great. The uptown woman's treat...smoked salmon on toast. Big salad. A silky smooth cappuccino and her "private" apartment key for dessert. "Tomorrow afternoon at two, darling. Don't be late!" We parted. I watched her walk away.

I fantasized my way up to the 7-11 and decided to join the crowd of "sweators" ("spectators," to normal folks) who watched the pool games. My ruined stroking shoulder and some truly ugly memories had been the biggest downsides of the Ecuador gig. Money, meals, and room keys were the upsides.

Still, I wish I knew what had happened to Fermín Veintimita. The newspaper article Andy had sent gave no clues, beyond the "extensive fire at the historic Hacienda La Atalaya" and a grainy photo of the ruined tower. But UN hearings were going to raise my exposure. *Well, could be worse,* I told myself and settled onto a bench.

I reached into my jacket pocket for a smoke and came up with the pack of Luckys and the Mexican airmail. Absentmindedly, I tamped the envelope on the bench and tore off the other end. Inside was a note from Marisol— yep, perfume...and "I need fifty dollars, chulo!"

But folded inside her note was a letter from Ecuador in Andy's handwriting.

> *My dearest John Alexander,*
> *Can you come back? Don Fermín has won! You are the only one who can help me now.*
>
> *Nestor is murdered and mother won't talk— not even to me. They would not even permit me at Nestor's funeral. We are living at Uncle's again.*

The dreams have returned. I know HE will come
for me.
I need you to protect me. Help me...please
come soon.
I LOVE you! "Andy" 16/9/1970
p.d. Abelardo's phone is 231–0205 Cuenca...

*September? Holy shit...Nestor dead! Mother of...*I didn't
know I'd said it out loud until one of the stakehorses next
to me asked, "What's that, buddy—you all right?"

I muttered something unintelligible, headed down the
stairs like a scalded cat, and jogged four long blocks to
Penrod's office, hoping he was still in. The outer office was
dark, but I pounded on the glass hallway door anyway. The
door swung open, a disheveled Penrod gaping at me...
"JA, I ah, uh...have a guest inside."

"Doesn't matter, Penrod. I need you to help me phone
Cuenca—*right away.* If the call goes through, you get your
'public' testimony."

"Really?"

"Yep—I don't care who's in there, just help me make a
call...*now.*"

Caroline stepped out, straightening her hose. "JA—is it
about that little girl you were worried about?"

"Yes, I uh..."

"I'll dial for you. Got a number?" I handed her the slip.

Seeing me panic was a new experience for her. We had
a few dates in October. But I had neither the money nor
the power she craved, and I found her simply too "high
maintenance," so we'd finally decided on "cordial."

I'd told her about Andy one night after a forwarded letter came from Ecuador. It had been written in August and
still no one knew what, if anything, had actually happened

to Veintimita. Your typical Ecuadorian mystery. But Uribe's mayordomo, Antonio, at the senior Veintimita's request, had taken over operations at La Atalaya. That was a real break—for La Atalaya's residents.

Caroline reached for the phone and got to work. It took twenty minutes and three tries to get a line into Cuenca. Phone wire, like electric wire, was valuable and therefore among the most regularly stolen commodities in highland Ecuador. In 1970, twenty seconds and one snip from a pair of wire cutters was all it took to isolate an entire district for weeks, the wire already on a mule train to another province.

My heart pounded uncontrollably and I sweat torrents while Caroline snarled at operators on two continents. OK, I was also hyperventilating and got up to pee—twice. Penrod couldn't stand my fidgeting, so he stepped out.

Between snarls, Caroline reached over and patted me. "Well, you'd make a great father, after all—worrying like this...and here I thought you were like a mountain waterfall—turbulent, hypnotic, but ice-cold." It was an odd comparison for a spoiled city girl, and the "father" thing made no sense, but she smiled when she said it, then handed me the phone. "It's ringing, JA. Here. Don't drop it."

The phone buzzed for another long minute before someone actually picked up. *"Diga!"*

"Habla Juan Alejandro desde Nueva York, pidiendo hablar con don Abelardo Gonzáles. (John Alexander speaking from New York, wanting to speak to don Abelardo.)"

"¿Importante es?"

"Crítico!"

"Un momento." Caroline wiped my forehead again. I was still shaking. Then came Abelardo's gravelly voice...

"Thank God it's you. Anda is in a permanent panic and has locked herself away in the upstairs maid's quarters with your bastón. Livia is a nervous wreck. This all has been terrible for them. I didn't think we'd ever hear from you again."

"Andy's letter of September just arrived here this morning."

"Ahh...well, then. That explains it."

"Abelardo, update me. Andy's letter is too panicked to be clear."

"Well, with the Veintimitas it's as ugly as usual. There was a big fire at Atalaya and it is thought Fermín perished. No one really knows. But his older brother, Jesús, went into a rage. Six weeks later, Nestor was found dead in northern Peru, near the village of Namballe."

"Why was Nestor in Peru?"

"In July, Jesús bought a large new holding in northern Peru. Nestor went to find out if he was harboring Fermín there. Right after Nestor's murder, Jesús moved his entire household to Peru...unbelievable! And we can get no magistrate to confront him. Veintimita lawyers from here to Quito have blocked our complaints to start an investigation."

"This is unbelievable. Nestor was a true friend. It must be awful...how is Livia?"

"So-so...she's here with me, but Anda is the *big* problem. Not long after we had the news of Nestor, someone tried to kidnap her at school, but Andy fought off her attacker with your bastón. According to her classmates she broke his arm before he fled. But the other two killed one of my bodyguards. Unfortunately, the attackers escaped, so we could get no useful information.

"That's when Anda locked herself away. I am at my wit's end...she is simply not safe here."

"And Livia?"

"We want to send her away, too. But where?...How?"

"Can you put her on the phone? I'd like to talk to her."

"Just a moment..."

"Hello, Alex."

"Livia..."

"I don't know what to do, Alex."

"What about Popayán?"

"I've thought about it...and the convent might still be safe for me. But I'm afraid for Anda...I mean, I'm afraid of losing her, too. I don't think we should be in the same place. Could you take Andita in New York—for a little while?"

"Livia, I don't know what to do with a kid."

"Alex, please...please!" she sobbed.

"If you get her to Colombia, we'll talk again. I'm not promising more—put Abelardo back on the phone."

"Have you consulted don Benigno Malo, Abelardo?"

"Yes, but he wants to stay at arm's length from any legal proceedings...such a disappointment."

"So, why not ask him for something simpler—like the use of his town car and driver to give Livia and Andy safe passage out of Ecuador and into southern Colombia. He likes the child...he might do that for her. What do you think?"

"That *is* a good suggestion. Should I invite him here, so he can talk to them?"

"Sounds like a plan." Motioning to Caroline for a letterhead, I continued, "Here is how you can reach me quickly after you've spoken to Malo...I'll wait here... Yes—right here!" I hung up the phone, stared at it, and rocked. My eyes watered. Penrod had gone to hide in his inner office—his fear of emotion nearly equal to his toilet phobias—but Caroline surprised me and stayed.

"You look just darling with those tears."

"They aren't tears. I've been working on a cold."

She grinned, warm and natural. "John Alexander—world-class cynic and hard-ass—is like a puppy in the hands of an eleven-year-old girl."

"You mean her *mother*, Caroline."

"But you asked about the child...that's progress."

I'd have been more pissed had she not run her fingers through my hair while she mopped a tear running down my cheek.

"Penrod," she called out. "It's safe to come out now. The two of us are going to wait here till the phone rings. It could be a long time. Are you staying with us? I can order takeout for three..."

Penrod came out, topcoat in hand. "No—I'd better get home. It's late...and I'm sure you have it under control. Make yourselves at home. Long as it takes."

"Thanks, old boy," I heard myself say as the outer door closed and Caroline ordered Indian food. Caroline put on some jazz. Monk—the rare San Francisco sessions. She handed me a brandy, then left me alone till the food came.

I'd collapsed into the big leather chair and thrown my feet up on the coffee table before she stepped in from the conference room. She didn't even dump on me for it. "Dinner's ready. Come on, JA."

She let me eat, watching me intently, but not interrupting me, or my silence. Done, I lit a cigarette and leaned back. "Good food. Thanks...what do I owe you?"

"Nothing, except an answer to a question, JA. No BS—just a straight answer."

"OK, try me."

"Why do you care about them?"

"I don't know, Caroline... but it's become more the kid than the mom."

Caroline leaned to me and whispered, "Do you care enough to give up something for them?"

"Will the open hearings be that much of a deal?" She nodded slowly. "There will be freight to pay, JA."

"I already paid! I thought I'd neutralized Veintimita to keep Livia and Andy safe... failed on that one. I didn't count on the older Veintimita brother taking up the cause."

"So you miscalculated... but what did you already give up, JA?"

"Sex... and a possible relationship."

"Gave up sex? Amazing..."

"Why is that amazing, Caroline? I didn't get any from you, either."

She pursed her lips, then decided to let it go. "Well, when that phone rings, JA, you'll need to know exactly what you are willing to give up *this* time. "If you testify in an open UN committee, it will be spectacular. Tribunals will follow. Lots of publicity. Lots of messy questions about who you really are. The full story—not just the bullshit little anecdotes you laid on me when we went to dinner. Do you understand?"

"Actually, no. That's why I said no to the open committee—I'm used to handing in my own reports, answering a few questions in private, getting my back pay, then enjoying life till the next gig... do you think the phone will actually ring tonight, Caroline?"

"We'll stay till it does." I nodded. High-maintenance Caroline actually had a smart, caring side. She handed me another drink—one finger of brandy—then went to add new 78s to the turntable. I settled in.

At 2:15 AM eastern time, the phone rang. Abelardo, speaking rapidly, sounded upbeat. "Señor Malo left about twenty minutes ago. He'll provide a car, but not till January 4 or 5—just before Day of the Kings. He will be returning to the Quito airport from London on that day...all will seem ordinary. Here—Anda has come out of her room and wants to talk..."

"John Alexander. They killed Nestor. Then they came for me...I want to come to New York to live with you. Mother approves...*please!*"

"Perhaps, Andy—but you must get to Colombia first. Now I need to speak to your uncle again."

"*Please!*" I didn't answer. She sniffled, then let me off the hook. "OK—here's Uncle."

"Look, Abelardo, I can't take Andy—at least for a while. Get her safely to Colombia, then recontact me."

"We'll contact the convent in Colombia. She has a Colombian passport her mother obtained not long after her father died. When should we recontact you?"

"Once they are in Colombia and safe. I have a United Nations hearing coming up after Christmas."

"Do you know the date?"

"I'll ask—wait a second...Caroline, when does Penrod think this hearing will be scheduled?"

"About January 7 or 8. Why?"

"That's about when they'll be traveling to Colombia. Thanks, Caroline." I turned back to Abelardo.

"You can contact me by Western Union through Ms. Caroline Oliphant of Dr. Penrod Thorogood's office here in New York. Let me know when they are safe and out of Ecuador."

I had Thanksgiving dinner with Caroline at her parents' place over in Jersey. It was my first "at home" Thanksgiving since Eddy and I were six. I was very nervous at first, but they were nice folks. Her dad was a professor at Columbia. Her mom was a schoolteacher. No...I wasn't dating Caroline. But she'd quit playing games with me, so we'd become really good friends.

Caroline's old man had even hustled me into applying for grad school—a doctorate in International Studies. We'd see what happened. If I got in, it would come with an assistantship and subsidized housing.

Meanwhile, with foundation money and the promise of the ten-grand bonus, I'd moved downstairs two floors—a big studio with a stone bay-front window on Twenty-second Street, near Eigth. It had a kitchenette and its own bath. Caroline helped me decorate and furnish—everything secondhand, of course. I'd even gotten my books out of storage. The place looked like a scholar's garret.

Everything was falling into place for the UN hearings...but I had ominous visitations from the Voice about Livia and Andy. *They're screwed, but it's not your problem. Look out for numero uno, idiot!*

The decision had been made to sequester them at Malo's house until travel time. Phone and mail contact had ended in mid-November. Security stuff. The resulting void drove me nuts.

Jumpy, I decided to use some of my forty-five-hundred-dollar bonus and spend Christmas in Paris. That proved to be a very good move. While I was gone, someone broke into my old sleeping room two floors up on Twenty-second and strangled the poor bastard who had moved in midmonth. When I returned from Paris just before New Year's, Penrod filled me in.

"Close call, my good man. Thank God you left town! We can't let anything slow down these hearings. You will be staying at a hotel uptown for a few days."

"Jesus, Penrod—screw these hearings. What about the poor jerk who was strangled?" He shrugged. I snarled, "It had better be a very discreet hotel, Penrod." He fled again.

When Penrod was gone, Caroline gave me a big hug and the real skinny. "JA, NYPD thinks it may have been someone associated with an embassy or the UN. An old lady across the street saw a car with diplomatic plates up the block—twice—before the guy living in your old room was killed."

"Really, Caroline? Why would anyone go after *me* at Christmas? What's been going on while I was gone? Nothing has actually happened yet. Couldn't this be a coincidence?"

"JA, don't go stupid on me now. I already explained things to you—this hearing is *public*. It became big news in the international community when your report was leaked the week before Christmas. What were you doing in Paris that you didn't see the news? Your report oozed sex, violence, and serious psychopathology—the French media has been all over it!"

"OK, OK—I was busy. I didn't know."

"Doing what?"

"Do I need to explain the possibilities to you?" She shook her head.

"The guy in your room is *dead*, JA."

"OK, that *could* mean the elites are getting nervous. Pick me a really discreet hotel."

"I already did."

"In that case," I said, "can you get me lists of embassy and UN names—Latinos—Andean countries? Both last names.

Let's see if anything pops up." Penrod was as bad as Andy when it came to furtive listening habits. At this, he stuck his head out of the inner office and nodded at Caroline, who took a shot at him. "Ah, now the blind can see?"

I was already comfortably ensconced in a small, ritzy boutique hotel on Seventy-second Street when Caroline showed up two days later with two huge lists of names— UN and embassies. She hugged me, put a bag of Chinese takeout on the table, and left.

I read. And read...and read. Finally, on pages fifty-four and fifty-five of the agency lists, I hit pay dirt— Veintimitas. A half dozen of them—both by birth and by marriage—were scattered through embassies and UN-related commissions with offices in Manhattan.

The poor murdered jerk in my old room absolutely wasn't a coincidence. Now, to stay healthy till the eighth. *Stay on your toes, JA,* warned the Voice. *The Ecuador Effect is infectious—even here in Manhattan.*

CHAPTER TWENTY-NINE

COMMITTEE PROCEEDINGS, THE UNITED NATIONS, MANHATTAN

JANUARY 1971

The public proceedings were more formal than I imagined and the "commission room" much larger than I expected. There were at least sixty people seated in a gallery behind the secretary general himself and the committee members, all of whom were full ambassadors. I hadn't expected that, or their country cards, water pitchers, headphones, and assistants...the whole megillah.

To the right, a row of pasty-white, dour-faced, black-robed men sat at a separate table. They looked like old-fashioned Quakers, but weren't. I inquired, "Who are the buzzards in black, Penrod?" He whispered that they were a "visiting group of auditors from the World Court in The Hague."

"I'm surprised at all this, Penrod...look at those guys in black staring down the UN ambassadors on the committee..."

"Jurisdictional issues, JA. The World Court received a copy of your report. Obviously, they are interested so, for goodness sake, do be sedate. This is a singular occasion." The secretary's gavel banged before I could give Penrod a wiseass answer to raise his blood pressure.

"Mr. Alexander, may we ask you to summarize your testimony and then take a few questions?"

"Certainly, Mr. Secretary."

"Proceed, Mr. Alexander."

"In late January of 1970, I arrived in Quito, Ecuador, retained by Dr. Penrod Thorogood to represent the interests of a private philanthropic foundation and to determine whether or not the Republic of Ecuador's land reform law of 1964 was in full implementation, as had been represented by that government to the World Bank. That law effectively erased the four-century-old system of 'huasipungos'—temporarily granted house plots to Indians in return for their labor. The house plots of long-term agricultural laborers were to pass to them, their heirs, and assigns in lots of approximately seventeen acres."

"Let me interrupt, sir," one of the ambassadors barked.

"The chair recognizes the honorable ambassador from Belgium."

"Thank you...Mr. Alexander, what, specifically, did your employers ask you to ascertain?"

"Sir, whether or not Ecuador had eradicated the practice of actually buying and selling, with acreage, Indian laborers *and* their families as real estate assets, as it had represented, internationally."

"And?"

"In southern Ecuador, it has *not* ceased, Mr. Ambassador. Please see folio B—titled, 'Dated newspaper clippings of public offerings of land in the provinces of Cañar, Azuay, and northern Loja, Ecuador, 1965–1970.'"

"Give us a moment to flip through these, Mr. Alexander."

"Certainly."

"Oh, dear..."

"The chair recognizes the ambassador from Great Britain. Is your comment for the record, Mr. Ambassador?"

"Yes—but let me complete my response—this is unconscionable. These newspaper pieces are all dated *after* 1964, and..."

"Objection, Mr. Secretary, the ambassador from Colombia objects."

"On what grounds, Mr. Ambassador—these newspaper clippings speak for themselves."

"On the grounds that they are *fabricated*, Mr. Secretary. Ordinary sophistry of yet another passing gringo visitor to the highlands who knows nothing of our culture... a perpetuation of the 'Black Legend' against the Spanish descendants of the conquistadors."

"The ambassador from Ecuador seconds the objection, Mr. Secretary. This testimony must be stricken in its entirety..."

"Do ask to be recognized, Mr. Ambassador—even here in committee. For the record, the secretary so requests... now, we have a second. Shall we call a vote?"

Meanwhile, I was lighting up like a Christmas tree bulb. Nervous, Penrod leaned to me. "It will take a few minutes for them to entertain this objection, JA. Do stay calm. *Please.*"

"But we heard this same Black Legend stuff when we worked the Guatemalan death-squad business."

"You're right, JA. That was an ugly affair."

"OK, Penrod, so who is the character with the pig eyes who keeps whispering to Colombia's ambassador...and what is the Ecuadorian ambassador's full name?"

"Is it important, JA?"

"Oh yeah, Penrod. Could matter a lot."

"Is that what Caroline was working on the other day, JA?"

"Yep—ask her."

"OK. I'll find out, JA." Penrod tiptoed away and consulted with Caroline in the back of the room. She'd made more lists. I took an impromptu smoke break, trying to calm down. Penrod returned six slow puffs later and leaned to me, one eyebrow arched. "The Colombian assistant is Guillermo Zuñiga-Veintimita. The Ecuadorian ambassador is Eusabio Crestón-Veintimita."

"Nice work, Penrod."

"Shhh. They're starting again, JA."

"The objection is not sustained. France, Belgium, and Great Britain vote against the objection. Colombia and Ecuador vote to uphold. Russia and India abstain. Proceed, Mr. Alexander...your summation, please."

"Certainly...I proceeded to southern Ecuador after an incident in the city of Ambato led me to believe that a field base there would be productive."

Pig-Eyes whispered furiously in the Colombian ambassador's ear. He objected again. The secretary both took the objection "under advisement" and answered my silent prayer.

"Describe this incident, Mr. Alexander, in your own words. Let us see if it is pertinent."

"Yes, sir... in Ambato I objected to a man from my bus who defecated on an Indian man who was bleeding to death from a machete wound while lying in the public latrine..." I paused for effect—it was getting very quiet. Penrod looked as if he actually might faint—anything to do with toilets terrified him.

"And..."

"Well, Mr. Secretary, the man was a manager on a hacienda owned by one Fermín Veintimita of Cantón Santa Isabel, Azuay Province, Ecuador. When I protested this individual's behavior, he told me publicly that his 'puesto,' social station, that is, 'permitted it.'"

France popped in this time. "And, just where was this, uh... defec... act, uh, located?"

"In the Indian's face, sir." Several rewarding gasps drifted over from the audience benches.

France waited for the headphone translation. "Excuse me, Mr. Alexander. Clarify, please."

"He evacuated his bowels on the Indian's face, sir." It hadn't really been the French ambassador's question, but I took a forgivable liberty. It worked. The female staffers were going pale. Translators paused, looking at me in shock.

France, now leering at the Ecuadorian ambassador, continued, "And, did you find this hacienda and its owner... what was that name?"

"'Veintimita,' sir. That's V-E-I-N-T-I-M-I-T-A. Yes. I found the place." The Ecuadorian went nuts. "Hearsay! Slander! This has nothing to do with human rights and, if true, everything to do with a disgusting criminal act—that individual's *alleged* employer should not be slandered, Mr. Secretary."

"Well, the ambassador from Ecuador makes a pertinent point, Mr. Alexander. Can you personally testify to any incidents involving human rights of those on the haciendas?"

"Yes, sir. In late April of the year 1970 . . . let's see, folio C, entitled, 'The kidnap, rape, and sodomy of the twin Chaski sisters.'" As intended, that title pulled folks right to the edge of their seats.

"This past April, Fermín Veintimita, employer of the man who defecated on the Indian in Ambato, claimed his right of *señoría*, or feudal rights, sometimes referred to as 'señorial,' over the Chaski sisters—twin sixteen-year-olds born to an Indian woman on his hacienda. The señorial, in this case, meant 'first rights' of intercourse with the girls prior to their marriage to the Lloque brothers, Marco and Antonio . . ."

"Mr. Alexander," the secretary cut in, "is this hearsay?"

"No, sir. Veintimita publicly demanded ten thousand sucres to forego his sexual rights—more than six years' wages for a field hand, like the girls' father. I personally paid half of that sum on the foundation's behalf. Family members of the twins and a widow in Cuenca paid the rest—in order to release the girls whom he then held in the stone tower of his hacienda."

"I object! Stop this testimony!" shrieked the Ecuadorian ambassador. But I was on a roll, and I turned to let him have it before the secretary could reestablish control. Too late.

"Mr. Alexander, members of the committee, we will take an hour's adjournment to review files. These proceedings reopen at 3 PM."

I paced and rehearsed during the break. Penrod dithered. "Don't be rude, JA, it will only dilute your impact." I nodded. The gavel came down and the Ecuadorian ambassador repeated his protest. I was ice-cold.

"I'm not at all surprised that you object, Mr. Ambassador—the Veintimitas of Cuenca are members of your own wife's family...but I will shorten my verbal testimony, given the documentation that the committee already has before it—including a death threat written in Veintimita's own hand that was recovered from the mutilated body of an Indian boy who did chores for me. See folio D." It got quiet.

"Mr. Secretary, the events that followed were ugly: the payment before witnesses was accepted, yet the girls were not released. Rather, the price of their virginity was doubled...and before it could be paid, Veintimita invited a number of local hacendados to share in their rape. Afterward, several fled the country to Ireland. Another to Brazil. The girls' husbands-to-be, Marco and Antonio Lloque, attempted to save the girls in the tower. Antonio was caught and sodomized in the presence of his wife-to-be, his throat slit. His castrated body was later found in a ravine near the Veintimitas' hacienda..."

I paused to look around. The row of buzzards in black were salivating. And the press table had begun to fill up. *Not bad.* "Do continue, Mr. Alexander."

"When I left Ecuador, the poor fellow's testicles were floating in a labeled jar that Veintimita kept with others like it, in his hacienda office." I paused again while someone grabbed the Ecuadorian ambassador, who had started toward me, fists balled. Two uniformed bailiffs of some sort held him back. He foamed at the mouth, spitting as he screamed...

"You are a *nobody*! An ignorant *meeester*! How DARE you make such accusations..."

Caroline grabbed me from behind during the pause. "JA—read this *now*!" I looked down. It was a telegram from A. Gonzáles, Cuenca:

Livia murdered in Pasto, Colombia. Anda missing. Phone. A.

I stared in disbelief. A wave of nausea swirled in my gut, then rose over me like an immense whitecap hanging over a fragile spit of sand. Finally, it crashed down with a roar, sucking sand, water, and me out into the sea.

I wasn't even aware that Caroline and Penrod had asked for a continuance until morning. Caroline explained in the taxi as we headed uptown to my hotel.

"JA—you scared us to death. You were pale as a ghost. Do you need to go to a hospital?"

"No, just shock, I think."

"Shall I stay with you awhile?"

"I need to call Cuenca. Could you help me with that?" Ten minutes later I had Abelardo on the phone. "Malo's car must have been followed to Pasto yesterday. They were in the bus station. Someone stepped out of the crowd as they boarded the bus; Livia's throat was slashed and Anda taken before Malo's men could react."

"Any trace of Andy?"

"No, Señor Alexander. As usual, the witnesses are afraid to talk. No trace of anyone..."

I hung up the phone and fell onto the bed. Caroline closed the door, gently reminding me that the taxi would pick me up at eight thirty sharp.

Later, nursing a half liter of Maker's Mark, I lay on the bed in my elegant hotel room and wondered what the hell I was going to do next. Return to Ecuador and I was a dead man...stay in Manhattan after testifying—same outcome. Either way, my life was going to change...big time.

Then I got to thinking about Livia...the orphaned college girl from Colombia had been consumed by Ecuador after all. It was a stormy winter night. My one floor-to-ceiling window rattled in the wind...why Livia? Why? Why?

But, in my heart, I knew the answer. She'd defied Ecuador and its ruling elite. Refused a Veintimita. Then flirted with an untamed *meeester*. Finally, settled for Nestor, a man beneath her puesto—the ultimate Ecuadorian sin.

Livia's essence seemed to fill the room with her distinctive scent of flowers and straw. The window rattled again. Her face materialized. She looked right at me, tears in her eyes.

"Please, Alex...Anda needs you. She chose *you*! If you can't do it for me, do it for yourself. Save her. *Cheat them*...and have your little family. You can't change Ecuador, but you can break the cycle for my Andita..."

The window rattled once more and she was gone, leaving behind her ephemeral scent of buttercups, the magical signature of her soul...I cried for her and Andy, just like I'd once cried for Eddy. Then I cried for me—the fire *had* helped some, I lied to myself. In fact, I'd always known that others would be punished to compensate—the Ecuador Effect was remorseless, unremitting, merciless. "There will be no free will."

Morning spared me more nightmares. It was a cold, gray day and the rain had already turned to sleet when the taxi pulled up. I drank a coffee as the gavel fell.

The Ecuadorian ambassador went first. I didn't even look up till something different in the tone of his voice caught my attention. Jubilance? When I glanced up, he grinned, triumphant.

"Mr. Alexander," warned the secretary general, "do keep you testimony to pertinent, firsthand knowledge." I nodded and began.

"I am John Alexander, and I am mortified at your reaction, Mr. Ambassador. The worst of this situation was that those two girls had been fathered by Fermín Veintimita's older brother, Jesús, who had demanded the señorial of their Indian mother nearly seventeen years before. The girls raped and sodomized by Fermín Veintimita were his own *nieces*."

The French ambassador gasped, even as Ecuador sneered. I pressed—"This testimony *is* pertinent. Incest as a property right *is* about human rights, Mr. Secretary. The right to take a child's virginity merely because she was born on property one has inherited means highland Ecuador is still in the sixteenth century—not the twentieth."

I stood abruptly and looked into the faces of those gathered. Most could not make eye contact. Several of the women sniffled. Even the Colombian ambassador, looking disgusted, had waved his whispering advisor away. I turned to the secretary's podium...

The Ecuadorian ambassador snarled, "You have no right to slander a civilized country as you have...on hearsay...it is a matter of *honor*. Your testimony is of no consequence. *You* are of no consequence."

Eddy materialized and smiled at me. "It's OK to be angry, John."

"Thanks, Eddy," I said out loud. The Ecuadorian ambassador gaped. I smiled at my brother and stepped forward, but Eddy wasn't through.

"Save her, John! Save her." I nodded at Eddy and took a deep breath...

"Mr. Ambassador. I have no more time for you. Yesterday, even as I was giving testimony here, one or another of your in-laws likely initiated the murder of the woman who paid part of the Chaski sisters' unsuccessful sex ransom, and also kidnapped her eleven-year-old daughter. I know that my testimony here may change nothing in Ecuador, but don't insult all of us born and raised in civilized nations by fretting over Ecuador's 'honor.' With regard to treatment of its indigenous peoples, it has none."

He reacted. "You insolent..." The gavel came down. I put in my parting shot. "Tell your family I'm coming to get the child. And it will be hacendados' rules!"

Penrod gaped. I leaned over and whispered, "Better get these World Court indictments quickly, old boy...the life expectancy of certain suspects is declining rapidly." He went pale.

I turned and walked out. Reporters mobbed me on the way. I waved them off. "No interviews...I've got a kid to find before the bastards kill her, too."

CHAPTER THIRTY

NAMBALLE DISTRICT, PERU

APRIL 1971

The lush valley below glistened in the late afternoon sun as we looked down on the sign naming the Veintimitas' Hacienda El Refugio. "Jesús Veintimita's private joke," teased Cobre as he adjusted the sights on the old 7 mm Mauser I'd bought him.

I checked the range to the far ridge with the reticles of my binoculars and carefully lowered the bipod to steady my heavy-barreled Ruger No. 1.

Cobre Chico had met me at the Guayaquil airport in Ecuador and signed on for a shot at glory...and six hundred dollars, in cash. Initially, he'd laughed at my single-shot Ruger. But, firing from long range, we'd finally driven the Veintimita brothers out of their plantation house nearly a week before, then picked off their hired may-orales one by one. The big .338 Winchester spoke for itself.

Now the Veintimitas were trapped on a rocky ridge below us. We still weren't certain how many of them were left. We figured at least one mayoral was guarding Andy somewhere.

"Sinchi—do you see the girl?" whispered Cobre.

"No, but there is movement. Here—take the binocu-lars and put up your hat. I'll use the scope."

"Sinchi—I've got don Fermín in view again!"

"Is he still limping?"

"Yes. Just like before. Maybe more." I'd first spotted him with the binoculars three days before. He'd been hob-bling along a trail, Andy in front of him.

"What's he doing, Cobre?"

"Getting ready to shoot at us again," snickered Cobre.

Fermín still couldn't shoot worth a damn, but Jesús was good . . . in fact, he was very good. He'd just put a third hole in Cobre's hat.

"Sinchi—the muzzle dust came up just to the right of the jagged boulder. Right in the notch at the base."

"Good man! Here's my hat. Move it slowly to your right."

I caught the next puff of dust in the scope, held my breath, and squeezed slowly. The Ruger echoed across the gorge like a thunderclap. Its huge slug chewed rock as it sailed angrily into the notch across the valley. An immense cloud of dust bil-lowed out and hung in the air. The firing stopped.

We gave it five minutes, then waved hats. Nothing. Another five minutes and we took turns standing. Still nothing. Time to check their hideaway.

We crept into the tiny bowl where the Veintimitas had made their stand. Tin cans, rifle casings, toilet paper, cigarette butts, and two empty liter bottles of pisco were scattered about haphazardly. I worked along one edge of the bowl, while Cobre crept along the other. It was silent except for the occasional brassy sound of a used rifle casing underfoot.

When I reached the big boulder, Cobre raised his hand twenty yards away—pointing urgently toward the notch. I slung the Ruger over my shoulder and pulled out a short-barreled Smith .44 Special. It took another ten minutes to inch our way to the shallow dugout under the boulder. I held my breath and finally heard the slow, raspy breathing that had caught Cobre's attention.

I waited, then threw a rifle brass into the dugout as Cobre covered the hole. Nothing. So I went in muzzle first, Cobre behind me. There lay Jesús Veintimita, his eyelids fluttering in anger. "I'm paralyzed. Kill me!"

Cobre raised the Mauser. I stopped him. "It is for God to determine, Veintimita... now tell me where the girl is or I will drag you out into the sun and cut off your eyelids." He sneered.

"Where's the girl?" I repeated.

"Fuck you in the ass, *meeester*." Cobre drew his knife and bent over to cut off his lids, but Eddy reappeared, shaking his head no. I stopped Cobre.

Disappointed, Cobre spit in his face. "It's Indian spit, hacendado... to disgrace you when you meet your own kind in hell."

I leaned to Jesús, smiled, and ripped the antique crucifix from around his neck. Again, his eyelids flickered in rage...

"Fuck you, *meeester*," he rasped. We left him face up out in the sun, blinking at a distant speck in the heavens. "You won't get there," commented Cobre, looking up. "When the spirits come for you, they will turn you over for your descent into hell."

Thirty minutes later we found Fermín Veintimita sprawled on a grassy hillside nearly a thousand feet below his brother. Dead. The side of his head was bashed in, and his antique pistol, the one he'd used to try and shoot me back at Los Faiques, lay empty a few feet away. Cobre tore the crucifix from his neck, holding it up to admire... "May I have this one, Sinchi?" I nodded.

The only tracks leading away from Fermín were an adult's, punctuated every few feet by the faint, dusty imprint of a walking stick's sharp tip. We followed the tracks and occasional blood spatters for about two hundred yards to the narrow head of a goatherd's trail down into the valley. He'd stumbled there, dropping my brass-tipped bastón as he slid down the steep slope on his ass, leaving fragments of his work pants and one run-over boot heel wedged under a sharp, jutting rock in the trail.

"Shall we hunt him, Sinchi?"

"No—he's not going to talk. Look at the blood and hair on my stick."

"He killed his patrón?"

"Yes, Cobre...and I don't give a shit about some mestizo mayoral. We've got to find the girl!" We backtracked to Fermín's body, working a widening circle.

Finally, we found a grassy spot at the edge of the bowl where the mayoral had stood with Andy, then headed toward Fermín. From the look of her tracks she'd taken off on a dead run. We followed the small prints a few yards as dusk set in.

"Anyone with her, Cobre?"

"No, Sinchi. She moved fast. I thought they'd tie her."

"Me, too. Why would they let her run away?"

Another look around Fermín's body solved the mystery. A short curl of frayed rope lay hidden near a bush. Andy had apparently slipped out of her yucca-fiber bindings when her captor charged Veintimita.

Cobre pieced it together. "The patrón tried to kill the girl and emptied his pistol but hit his own man. Look at the blood spatters near his tracks as he went for Veintimita. Then he left her and fled down the goat trail."

"She's alone then." Cobre nodded in answer. "Any blood spatters, Cobre?" He shook his head.

"Thank God," I murmured. As the sun dipped below the coastal range, Cobre followed Andy's track on all fours.

"She ran toward the next ridge, Sinchi. Shall we follow?"

"No, it's too late. If we chase her in the dark, she'll continue to run and fall over a cliff."

"Are you certain, Sinchi? There will be a quarter moon tonight."

"At first light, Cobre. She's alive and she's finally free."

Her tracks already fading in the heavy morning mist, we found her shortly after dawn. She was fast asleep, curled up in a ball under a bush in the cloud forest that carpeted the lower slopes.

I put my finger to my lips. Cobre nodded. We eased down three yards from her, sat, and let her sleep. No sign of the Voice or Eddy anywhere; I was on my own. Hypnotized by the rhythm of her breathing, I closed my eyes and drifted off.

Later, Cobre struck a match. I opened my eyes with a start to see Andy leaning over me.

"Please don't be a dream," she murmured, eyes wide. Her fingertips touched my face.

"I'm real, Andy. It's time to go . . ."

Finis